OPALS & A NIMBUS UNILLUSTRATED PB

UNILLUSTRATED EDITION

A NIMBUS
BOOK ONE

NANDER

EDITED BY
SAMANTHA STEWERT

EDITED BY
CRAB EDITING

To my husband, David. You are my angel, my Fabian, and my reason for living. You are everything wonderful in the world.

"I who am chasing you am not your enemy. Nymph, wait! This is the way a sheep runs from the wolf, a deer from the mountain lion, […] but it is love that is driving me to follow you! Pity me!"

— OVID'S METAMORPHOSES

Note from the Author

Thank you so much for picking up my book. Before you dive in, we should touch base on a few light things and some very heavy things.

Let's start with the light. Over a year in the making, Opals & a Nimbus started as therapy that no one was ever supposed to read. It was a tribute to what I loved most and found challenge or growth in. I compiled my love of meteorology, my career as a nurse, my favorite books and childhood shows, and my second career as a union organizer into a magical fantasy story complete with an absurd amount of spice. Many of the characters are inspired by, and often even named after, real people I love very much in my life. Some scenes were inspired by poems or short stories I wrote when I was 12. With the right community behind me, I was inspired to take that crazy first draft and fine-tune it into a story palatable enough for you, the reader. At the same time, I also wrote a tandem cookbook that you can pair with this novel. The Opals & A Nimbus Official Cookbook has recipes for almost anything the characters eat. Additionally, it has alternate POV excerpts and behind-the-scenes information.

Now for the heavy. This book contains topics that may be troubling to some readers. You're encouraged to read the trigger warnings. Please understand that although I have done my absolute best to cover all bases with the warnings, it may, unfortunately, be an incomplete list—your mental health matters. If you are under the care of a mental health provider that you don't feel is the best fit, know that it is not unheard of, so keep trying until you find one that works. But you should never stop medication without the supervision of a qualified provider.

Although the characters in this book are often very welcoming of death, that is not a normal thought process. So, while it may seem romanticized if you're having feelings of suicide or ambivalent thoughts about living, you must talk to a qualified provider about that as soon as possible.

Lastly, some themes in this book cater to a subset of BDSM kinks that can be seen as violent, disturbing, or perhaps interesting to those unfamiliar with them. The dynamics in this book were not crafted to represent a normal and healthy relationship in the BDSM community. Consent is *always* required, and it is important to learn about the nuances of consensual non-consent before exploring it with others. Some sexual acts in this book are dangerous, and you're advised not to attempt recreating them.

For Non-Spicy Readers, you can skip the spicy scenes by looking for the door symbols. When the open door symbol appears, it indicates a spicy scene is starting. When the closed door symbol appears, it indicates the spicy scene has ended. Please note that even skipping the marked scenes is not foolproof, and there will be sexual situations or discussions.

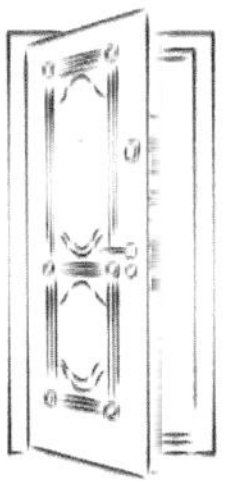

Spicy scene begins

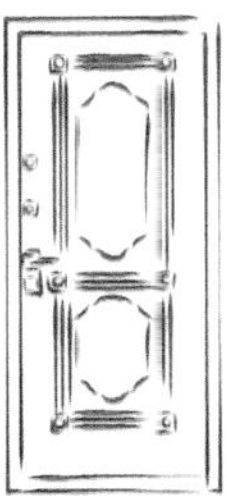

Spicy scene ends

TRIGGER WARNINGS
INCLUDE, BUT ARE NOT LIMITED TO

XI

- Explicit Sexual Scenes
- Aggressive Sexual Situations
- Dubious Consent
- Choking, breath play
- BDSM themes akin to CNC or other
- Stalking
- Breaking and entering
- Poisoning
- Non-consensual detainment
- Motor vehicle accidents
- Death and grieving
- Gore & violence, including but not limited to war, defenestration, decapitation, evisceration, mass casualty, graphic wounds, and stabbing.
- Vomiting
- Natural disasters/Severe weather, including tornados
- Ghosts
- Sapphic scenes, Nonbinary/trans representation
- Squirting
- Homophobia/transphobia
- Microaggressions
- Anti-union campaigns
- Mental illness
- Medical malpractice
- Healthcare worker-related work trauma
- Pizza in the break room

PROLOGUE

Three staff members sat at the nursing station to chart their care tasks for the eighty residents on their wing of *Mayflower Nursing Home & Rehab*. Stacy and Karey, the only two Nursing Assistants on B-wing, groaned with exhaustion from attempting to feed, bathe, and calm their forty patients each. Dignity was apparently something *Mayflower* couldn't afford, even after being bought out by a major health system, *Amett Health*. Janet Francis, a seasoned Vocational Nurse who was responsible for medicating those eighty residents within a two-hour window, grumbled to herself about how she was "Too old for this shit," and the Nurse Manager could "shove the medication cart up her ass." Apparently, the buy-out did not afford them safe staffing either. They were just as short-staffed as they had ever been.

An alarm startled the three women, and instinctually, they jumped from their seats and ran to the room. The sound was unmistakably a bed alarm, a device that rang when a patient got out of bed. The last thing Janet needed was a resident with a broken hip at 21:00. The three providers shuffled to Room 1, where Maria Hernandez, who appeared to be asleep, was…walking?

"Ms. Hernandez? Are you awake, dear? Let's get you back in bed," Janet said. No response. *Mayflower* had invested in bed alarms that auto-silenced when the patient returned to the center of the pad. Janet and Stacy guided the elderly woman back to bed and silenced the alarm. But they were soon startled by another alarm sounding in the hall.

"I got it," Karey called and waved off the two women before leaving. Karey trotted briskly to the room next door where the new alarm had sounded, but before she could reach the entrance, yet another bed alarm pierced the air. Janet and Stacy, having just settled Ms. Hernandez back in her bed, ran out into the hall as a fourth alarm sounded. The trio exchanged confused expressions as room-by-room bed alarms sounded.

"What the hell is going on?" Janet huffed, exasperated. The three providers split up. But in no time at all, the problem became unmanageable. Almost every remotely mobile patient on B-wing wandered down the hall. Their eyes were wide in a fixed, glossy stare.

"Call A-wing and C-wing. We need help here, *STAT*. Shit, call the rehab building. Get anyone here," Janet bellowed to Stacy over the high-pitched sirens. Janet's forehead dampened under her short-cropped, salt and pepper curls. Her back in tatters after years of lifting patients without proper equipment, she could only hobble so fast. Her mind, however, was sharp as ever. She quickly called for Karey to prioritize the wanderers by fall history. They both clambered to the sides of patients known to have the weakest gaits. Although, as she looked around, Janet noted that they seemed to be oddly steady.

"Janet, no one is answering!" Stacy exclaimed, sprinting back.

They could hardly hear each other over the more than seventy-bed alarms ringing throughout the hall.

Now, a new sound erupted. It was a noise like flimsy metal banging. Following the sound, Janet, Stacy, and Karey watched in grim realization. The residents were gathered at the exit to the large garden courtyard. The locked double doors were bowing under the pressure of their persistent pushing. The doors of the ramshackle facility were as rickety as they came. It was only a matter of time before they gave way. With a loud clack, the doors did just that. The residents filed onto the courtyard garden. Following behind them in disbelief, the three providers reached the exit. They stared in wonder.

The courtyard was flanked on all sides by the three wings of the facility and one grand four-story building. The full moon hung perfectly centered over the enclosed courtyard. Eerie shadows were cast onto the residents' faces. The moon darkened their eye sockets into hollow graves and illuminated their thin white hair like spirits clinging to their skulls. Stacy spotted movement across the large yard of grass and now trampled flower beds.

"Janet, look," Stacy said, pointing at the courtyard exits for A-wing. The doors were wide open. Its residents marched out into the same single-file line of wanderers. They all trailed from the edges of the yard toward its center in a wide spiraling path. The A-wing nurse followed behind the last of her residents. She was slack-jawed as her gaze caught Janet's. They watched each other idly for a moment.

Janet turned her gaze to the C-wing exit on the right side of the courtyard. Just the same, the doors were open. C-wing residents merged into the spiraling parade of zombies. The C-wing staff watched, horrified at their patients' strange behavior.

Janet noted that no patients erupted from the rehabilitation center. The windows of the grand building were all dark—closed off for emergency repairs. It was empty, leaving the sparse staff between the three wings to their own devices. They were alone.

A hundred and fifty patients had walked into the spiral formation. At last, there was a breakaway. Now, in unison, the residents halted. It was as if a conveyor belt of the undead was jammed. The onslaught of bed alarms blared from each wing's doorway into the outdoor space. Simultaneously, the zombies each relaxed a wrinkled hand, releasing a single, kiwi-sized, blue stone. The stones dropped to the ground with a dull thud. Then, without any intervention, the residents retreated to their rooms as if every single one of them unanimously decided to simply lay back down.

Heart pounding, Janet pressed her sweaty, aching back against the hall of B-wing just inside the doorway. The residents shuffled past her, their glazed eyes missing her completely. With each alarm that surrendered under the weight of a resident returning to bed, the silence grew louder. It was both relieving and frightening to the three. When the last of the residents cleared the hall, the women stood still in utter quiet for only a moment. Then, Janet took charge.

"Stacy, page Doctor Greggs for an emergency call back on the status of all patients. Then, I want you to start vital signs in Room 80, working down to 41. Alert me with anything critical. Then get me the number of O'doherty Sameal from the clinical research binder," Janet stated flatly and calmly to a very stunned Stacy. "And then make us a strong pot of coffee."

Janet set off to assess all eighty patients, starting with Room 1. She hooked Karey's arm in with her own to pull her from the stupor in which she was trapped. When done, she would review the charts, looking for anything that the affected residents had in common that could have altered their behavior. This was going to be the strangest report she had ever given a doctor, and for the first time in many years, Janet was not quite sure what to recommend as an intervention.

"What should I do?" Karey asked, still shaking as Janet led her forward.

"Come with me. Start vitals in Room 1, working up to 40. Work ahead if you have to. Call me with any critical results."

"God, this night couldn't get any worse."

Janet shifted narrow eyes at Karey with a twisted expression, as if she had just cursed them all. "Don't ever say that on my shift. For God's sake, girl." Janet wasn't usually harsh on the new ones, nor was she a particularly superstitious nurse, but tonight she was on edge.

In Room 1 Maria Hernandez, like all the other residents, had returned to her bed. Janet placed her stethoscope against Maria's chest. She lay still in bed, staring straight up at the ceiling, but when her eyelids did finally shut, they moved rapidly as she dreamed vividly.

High up in the night sky, just above *Mayflower*, a male figure sat perched in a slouch on a dense cloud of his own making. The light of the full moon and the mist that danced just inches above his taupe skin gave his bare torso an ethereal glow under a diamond-like shimmer. He grimaced looking down at the elaborate labyrinth of small blue stones in the courtyard. His muscled shoulder flexed as he lifted one hand, and with a sweep of his wrist, he produced a cold, dry wind. It spiraled around him viciously, tossing about the messy locks of his undercut from their charcoal roots to pure white ends. Closing his eyelids over black tourmaline irises, he released the frigid gust into the night sky where it grew. He raised a thick charcoal brow and glanced at the cloud beneath him, which also grew larger.

After sucking in a sharp breath, he jumped from the perch and plummeted toward earth. The fabric of his dark jeans flapped furiously in the crisp air that rushed past them. The salt of the sea breeze danced in his throat. He relaxed into the plunge and lazily observed the approaching earth. The air became warm and thick with humidity.

Then his body dissipated into a mist that circulated like dust pulled up by a wind. The man had vanished, the space he held a second before now limpid and barren. Above his void, the sky slowly churned, working to build twisting chaos in his wake.

I

DAPHNE: IT'S A FULL MOON

I loved a good Negroni. I liked to savor it. And Mindy, the gorgeous brunette bartender at Mac's, was a master at her craft. I loved this place for many reasons, and Mindy was just one of them. In this open-air rooftop bar on the outskirts of downtown Miami, Mindy looked absolutely moon-kissed tonight. Her warm, light brown skin shimmered at the cheekbone from her gold dust highlighter and nude makeup. Her stiletto nails, decorated in a perfect French manicure, sparkled with citrus droplets as she rubbed a lemon around the rim of a glass. The breeze was warm and ran through her silky black hair. I could almost see the scent of her shampoo carrying in the breeze. The electric violinist played covers of today's hits. It truly was a vibe.

Mac's was one of the few bars that catered to a mature crowd. Young adults, who were newly sufficient in their careers, came to blow off steam. O'doherty and I stopped visiting the bars in the city proper a few years ago as we grew tired of the typical rowdy patrons, overpoured drinks, sticky bar tops, and too-loud music. At one point, that was our hunting ground. I'd always been a workaholic, but I frequented those places to pick up a capable guy to have fun with for a night.

As my late 20s came, I wanted better quality of many things. Not just food, bedsheets, and cars, but booty calls, too. The guys in those bars were pretty typical. You see them from across the room, and they give you a sly smile. They'd either bite or lick their lips, then give you a quick once-over with their eyes. It was flattery followed by an empty promise to rock your world.

O'doherty lost interest for the same reasons I had, but what's more, she'd always been more interested in finding a boyfriend rather than a one-night stand. She could quickly tell if the guy hitting on her was a fuckboy or not. Even so, her relationships usually didn't last long. She'd give them a chance if they seemed promising. But she'd also cut them loose for simple reasons, once even using "caveman feet" as the reason she couldn't continue seeing someone.

I never cared for anyone she dated anyway. O'doherty was special, and I always expected her to find someone who was just as intelligent and ambitious as she was. She had a presence about her, but no one worth a shit ever picked up on it.

The quickly dissolving luster of the inner city was a reason for us being friends with benefits. Occasionally, we would hook up with each other rather than settle for whatever underwhelming specimen of a man the night dragged in. For a few years now, we've maintained a perfect balance between incredible fucking and an otherwise normal friendship.

Anyway, since then, we branched out farther from the busy city and eventually found Mac's. And there we were, unwinding from a hard work week. The rooftop overlooked a well-financed business district with a nice view of the glowing neon lights of Miami a few miles away.

The warm night air tickled my skin, and goosebumps almost stubbled my freshly shaved legs. Both the skilled notes of the electric violin and bass from his other equipment thrummed through my body. Alcohol laced my blood, dulling my senses. I could smell the remnants of salt from a distant sea breeze mixing with the smell of the scratch kitchen. Mindy was like a ballerina. She made a true show of making every drink. A fouetté to pluck a garnish, a battement when serving the drink. I didn't realize how distracted I was until abrupt commentary jolted me out of it.

"When are you going to proposition her for a threesome?" O'doherty asked in a too-loud voice.

My eyes went wide, darting at her.

"You wanna take that down a notch?" I hissed.

I found her grinning, tongue peeking through her straight teeth, and adorable, upturned nose crinkled. O'doherty's tawny skin was dewy. Her well-defined, raven-black curls spiraled down her back.

"Oh, stop, no one is going to hear! Besides, your stare is more conspicuous than anything."

I hadn't realized I was staring. I was sure Mindy was used to the attention. Still, I never wanted to make her uncomfortable. I smiled at her, shaking my head. An arm came into view on my right, holding a plate of shrimp toast.

"For you, Ms. Daphne. The usual," the man holding the dish said in a deep and buttery voice. The nurse in me wondered what his vocal cords looked like compared to the average person.

"Thank you, Jay," I said. Jay grinned wide as he glided to offer O'doherty her food.

"Of course, of course, of course. And for you, Ms. Ah'Dartay, your favorite, made special," he said, placing the steaming dish of wild boar stuffed peppers down in front of her. O'doherty would never correct him on his mispronunciation of her name, *Oh-Dah-oar-Tee*. Partly, this was because she preferred it to the nickname I had given her since childhood—Odie. His mispronunciation was one of the few she didn't mind. His voice alone earned her forgiveness.

"Oh! Jay, this smells incredible!"

Jay smiled down and cupped our shoulders with each hand.

"Mhm, mhm, mhm," he hummed knowingly. It was unlikely there had ever been a complaint about the food there. "Is there anything else you need? Another drink?"

"Oh no, thank you. This is perfect. I have to work early," I said, disappointed.

"Unfortunately, the same is true for me," O'doherty sighed, sipping her diet Moscow mule. Jay nodded before walking away.

"Tomorrow is your last shift, right?" O'doherty asked. I nodded at her widely, my mouth too full to give a verbal answer. "Okay, so? How did it go? Did you get everything you need?" She probed, taking a bite out of her food and rolling her tuscany brown eyes back at how delicious it was.

"Ha, yeah!" I said. I put my fork down, excited to tell her. My hands flailed as I spoke. "That hospital is a shit hole. The nurses are pissed. *Everyone* is pissed, really. They haven't gotten raises in three years. Their insurance is garbage and takes chunks out of their paychecks. They're doing the work of two, pay for parking, and get this!"

O'doherty nodded, picking at her food but eating up the gossip. "The Director of Nursing just got a half-a-million dollar pay raise and a million-dollar bonus."

"Ugh! I swear. You know they monopolized the entire East Coast," she scowled.

It's true. *Amett Health Systems* was one of the nation's largest healthcare organizations. Not only did they buy up hundreds of local hospitals, but they bought nursing homes and rehabs too. They partnered with a major pharmaceutical company, *Parson & Dodds,* to 'make access to healthcare more affordable.' *Amett* also dumped billions into mental health facilities owned by *Heartly,* another system that was marking its territory on the nation's map.

I couldn't be butthurt about *that.* I owed my mental stability to *Heartly* and my psychiatrist there, Dr. Benton Bailey. Where my gratitude ran dry was that *Amett Health Systems* paid *all* of their top executives multi-million-dollar salaries. Meanwhile, their lowest-paid employees had to work multiple jobs, driving for Uber and whatnot, just to make ends meet. They missed family events and hardly got a day off, for God's sake.

Anyway. A little over four months back, I was in North Miami, near *Amett Health*'s main hospital. I was eating at a bagel shop when I overheard two nurses ranting about the shit work conditions.

"A patient is going to die again, and guess who's going to jail? Us! Did you see what they did to that nurse in Tennessee? Ya. It's open season on all nurses, and you think Lyndie Pratt is going to stick her neck out for us? Ha! No."

"That'll be the day. Please. The only time Lyndie ever touched a patient was when she shook their hand for a photo op after they survived a mass shooting. She had a business degree before her nursing degree, and doesn't that show!" her companion snapped.

The rant went on for the entire meal, an exchange of alternating islander accents, not uncommon in Miami. I could hardly focus, hearing their stories. I knew their frustration all too well.

I had been a nurse for eight years but left staff nursing after only four. Hospitals were run like businesses with little concern for mortality or anyone's damn safety. After being assaulted by patients and retaliated against by management, I left. I did go back as a travel nurse occasionally, working as a temp through an agency. The thing was, I didn't do it for the same reasons most nurses did. When I did it, it was because I was working undercover as a salt. *Salting* is a union-organizing tactic. Basically, a union paid someone—yours truly—to apply for a job at a company and, once employed, begin union-organizing efforts under the radar. I loved it, and I was one of the best around.

In other words, the second those nurses at the bagel shop laid out every disgraceful thing happening at *Amett Health — Northern Miami Hospital,* I was hell-bent on infiltrating the company under the guise of a travel nurse and helping them organize a union.

So how did I do it? Well, most union efforts in a hospital start in either the ICU or ED. Luckily, my experience got me placement into almost *any* unit at *Northern.* This assignment was for ICU, but if other units were short, I'd get sent to them. This worked out beautifully. Networking with as many nurses as possible during the eighteen-week period was exactly what I needed to do. I asked to be on night shift for the first nine weeks of my contract and the next nine weeks on days. This was *not* a normal request, but the hospital's facilitator didn't even notice. I always worked overtime and made a bunch of friends on both shifts. I got a pulse on what mattered to them and what they were angry about.

"So, has the hospital changed a lot since you started?" I once asked one of the nurses while we waited for our turn to pull medications from the Pyxis medication machine. She huffed and looked up from her phone, then glanced around to make sure no manager was in earshot.

"I've been here for twelve years, and it has *never* been this bad. They changed management, you know? Now, we have a bunch of master's degrees with no clinical experience telling us how to do our job. It's dangerous."

"That's an understatement," the other nurse had said as she banged her palm on the bottom of the medication drawer. Finally, she was able to pop open its lid. "Ancient-ass equipment, too."

"Shh, shh, shh," the first nurse warned as the clicking of heels sounded around the corner. Lyndie Pratt, the DON, looked up from her phone.

"Good morning, dearies," she had said before trotting off with swaying hips. She stopped short. "Daphne, one of your whiteboards hasn't been updated, by the way. I know you're temporary, but—"

"Just waiting to pull my meds, and I'm all over it!"

Lyndie tucked her lips in a smile and hummed, clearly put off by my cutting her short. "Thank you."

Not a moment after the sound of her heels disappeared had both nurses mocked Lyndie's smug face, exaggerating the words *"Dearies."* The nurse pulling medications had slammed the drawer shut and turned on her heels. "It's all yours, girlfriend."

"You know the thing that bothers me most," the first nurse had said as she scanned her thumbprint to access the machine. I tilted my head in curiosity. "I can't keep my patients safe, and they pressure you to chart like you can. Did I pass my medications and do my assessments on time? *No.* But they basically tell you to change the time on stuff so they don't get dinged. It's not right."

"That's illegal. If you get caught falsifying your charting…"

"I know, but if we stand up to them, we are targeted, fired, and blacklisted. I choose my battles. You know they roomed NICU babies in a spare storage closet upstairs, too, right? They're all stable 'growers and feeders,' but still…" She turned with her medications in hand and sighed heavily before walking off, calling over her shoulder,

"Any drawer below the fourth will stick, by the way. Just give it a nice wack."

My mouth hung open as I scanned my thumb into the machine. Like fricking clockwork, a code blue alert rang for one of my patients. "*Shit.*"

The more I had asked around, the worse the stories got. I floated from ICU to PCU, and that's where the most disturbing stories were heard.

"A few months ago, they pulled the sitter for a psych patient to save money. Someone left their purse on the bed. That patient got a lighter out of it and tried to burn off their restraints. But they set the sheets, and themselves, on fire! We were all so busy no one even knew until we started smelling their burning skin," one nurse shook her head in disgust while badging out of the computer.

"That's just the tip of the iceberg. We can't keep staff, so we have nurses fresh out of school being trained by nurses who graduated six months ago. It's the blind leading the blind. And then admin will butter them up, tell them they're 'doing so good' they can come off of orientation early. Just last week, one of them pulled a central line from a groin and didn't think to hold pressure, so the patient started bleeding out. Luckily, the tech went in for vitals and saw his pressure tanking. Huge hematoma, the size of a damn melon! But 'what could *the nurse* have done differently?'" she said angrily with air quotes. She wiped sweat from her brow and cracked her back. "Staff us safely and pay us better so people stay! *That's* what could be done differently."

"What have you guys done before to try and change things?" I had asked.

"Oh, we've had meetings and even emailed the CEO. We basically just get gaslit and told they're doing their best, and no one is applying. *Lies,* of course. When I asked why we haven't gotten a raise, they said we 'shouldn't be doing it for the money.'"

"Empathy manipulation..."

"Mmhmm." The nurses shuffled off to answer call bells.

I glanced around the empty nursing station and grabbed the staffing binder. My heart raced as I snapped pictures of the staffing list for the unit, just as I had with any other I floated to. The lists would be useful if they decided to organize a union and needed a roster to cross-reference. I slapped the binder shut and pushed it into the cubby.

"Can I help you with something?" I turned to see the nursing house supervisor looking at me with furrowed brows.

"I was looking for the scheduling binder. Have you seen it? Someone needs me to swap shifts with them on days," I bluffed.

She crossed the space and plucked a much fatter binder from a few slots to the left of the other. "Here you go, honey. But make sure you two approve it with a manager. If no one shows up for the shift, you both get the write-up," she said with raised brows and an extended index finger.

"For sure. Thanks."

The salt mission was going almost too perfectly. Especially considering management didn't have a clue what was going on right under their noses. It was one of the worst assignments I had ever been on, and the next shift was going to be my last.

I realized I had been blabbering for too long again.

"Anyways! Nurses love a good party, so for my going away celebration, I've got the most trusted and loved nurses from several units coming," I finished. "What about you? I didn't know you had work early."

"Ohhh," she said, hinting that there was a fun reason. "I

received an interesting call from a facility an hour ago. *Mayflower*. You know the nursing home? Apparently, that new dementia medication we are researching in clinical trials has a pretty problematic side effect."

"Yeah?" I asked curiously as she sipped her drink.

"*Yes*. About a month after therapy begins, the patients experience *sleepwalking*. All of them *at the same time,* unfortunately. It is a significant complication given how those nursing homes are so poorly understaffed. I mean, *hundreds* of residents were affected."

My eyes went wide with cautious humor. My spine straightened as I held my breath. I tucked my lips together to suck in a smile. The thought of countless bed alarms dinging while hundreds of residents roamed the halls, just a few nurse aides and nurses panicking to herd them back to their rooms? It's too crazy not to elicit some humor. Still, I tried to stifle my reaction out of respect for the patients and pity for the staff. It would make a good story one day.

"Is everyone safe?" I asked slowly, my expression yielding only to speak the words before I finally started in on my own food again.

"Yes. Surprisingly, I'm hearing there have not been any injuries. I'm going to assess the patients and interview the staff early before they leave in the morning. Apparently, a lot of them got outside, too."

"So, what are you going to do, Odie?" I asked, finally allowing myself to chuckle. "Do you think the doctor will discontinue the medication trial? They can't just have 100 plus elderly folks roaming the halls and chillin' in the streets every night."

"I don't know, Daphne. And honestly…" O'doherty sighed and pointed up at the bright disc in the sky, "it's a full moon. We all know how *that* can mysteriously alter someone's brain chemistry. Maybe it was sundowning. Maybe it was a fluke. I'll have more information tomorrow."

"That is one *hell* of a fluke," I barked out before sipping my Negroni.

O'doherty had left bedside nursing when I did, and for the same reasons. After that, she started working as a Clinical Research Coordinator. She studied the efficacy of new medications in patients. Conveniently, she was employed by *Amett Health*'s clinical research department at their sister university. She had access to any of their facilities that were running medication trials that she was on. The medication she was studying, Meriflec, was a product of none other than *Parson & Dodds*.

They claimed it worked as a supplement medication to the treatment regimen for Dementia, Parkinson's Disease, and the like. Sure. According to Odie, *Mayflower Nursing and Rehab* had seen a reduction in symptoms with no definitive side effects since the study started a couple of weeks prior. That was, until tonight.

"Well, it's late and we both have a big day ahead. I don't think either of us should try to pick anyone up, so why don't we just head to my place?" I asked with a suggestive smile.

O'doherty smirked at the gesture. "Okay, but is it a firm no on inviting Mindy?" she poked. I hushed her before letting out a nervous laugh. We packed up our food and left a large tip for Jay and Mindy as we passed the bar on the way to the elevator.

Jay called the valet for us as soon as the tab was paid, so we didn't wait very long. A prideful smile creased my face as the valet driver pulled up my black BMW M3. Its metallic midnight blue double race stripe was offset to the driver's side and shimmered in the firelight of the heat lamps out front. Wide front fenders complimented the fearsome low rumble of its engine. The bluish glow of LED headlights cast long shadows of the valet's legs across the pavers as he crossed its path to hand me the keys.

I wasted no time opening the passenger door for O'doherty and let her in. I discreetly glanced at the carbon fiber splitter on the front of the car for damage as I crossed to the driver's side. After a deep squat into my white leather seat, I found O'doherty's hand laying palm-up to grab a chunk of my ass. She squeezed firmly, and I jolted.

"Ahh! Not when I'm driving," I squeal, smacking her arm. I pressed down the clutch and guided it to first gear. With laughter and a lead foot, we drove into the night under the clear, moonlit Miami sky.

2

O'DOHERTY: AFTER SUCH PASSIONS

MY HAND WAS PROPPED OUT OF THE PASSENGER WINDOW, RIDING THE gusts of warm night air as we ripped down the road. Up and down my hand swooped and whooshed in serpentine. A chilled drizzle stung my hand. I looked up at the sky to see the stacks of clouds rolling in over the full moon.

"Where did that come from?" I asked no one in particular.

"Right? Is it just me, or have the weather reports been really off the mark lately?" Daphne suggested. As Floridians we were used to poking fun at the mess of ever-changing spaghetti models created by TV meteorologists during hurricane season. Lately though? They really seemed to be miscalculating basic forecasts.

What was predicted as clear skies and warm weather for the next week was clearly panning out differently. By the time we pulled into Daphne's driveway, the weather abruptly shifted. The sky was smeared with gray clouds, backlit with thin streaks of moonlight. The icy droplets were fatter now. I had long since rolled up my window, now warming my damp hand between my thighs.

Thankfully, Daphne's garage had a remote-controlled door at her duplex. She would never leave her precious car exposed to the elements if it could be avoided. She fell in love with the car far before she found out it was a stick shift, a feature she liked to joke was 'basically an anti-theft device nowadays'.

She lived on the left side of the structure—a small, two-bedroom, two-bath bachelorette pad that she shared only with her dog. Polpette, or *meatball* in Italian, was a fat little lump of a brindle English bulldog mix that earned every bit of her name. Daphne acquired the companion four years ago when she evidently just hopped in her car. Daphne put a few flyers out in an attempt to find the owner, but no one claimed her. So, she gladly took her in and often referred to her as her first-born baby. As soon as we entered the house, Polpette's snorting and wheezing pants picked up at a rapid speed.

"Hi, Polly!" Daphne shrieked in excitement. Polpette couldn't simply wag her stubby tail; she wagged her entire bottom half. She made stunted hops off her two front paws. "Come on, baby. You have to go potty before the storm gets bad! Come on."

Polpette's paws could hardly manage to change direction as they slid on the large white tile of the kitchen. After slipping under the weight of her chubby body, her paws finally found purchase. She wasted no time veering left and chasing Daphne out of the kitchen archway. She hopped into the foyer that opened into the small living room. Daphne and Polpette raced to the back sliding glass door that opened into a fenced backyard.

I dropped my purse on the coffee table. Polpette's protest at the rain made us both laugh. Finally, the meatball trotted begrudgingly into the damp yard, taking shelter under an enormous California Bay Laurel tree. It had to be ancient, with its massive trunk and thick limbs that twisted and parted. It was a grand sight of winding bark that would be perfect for climbing if we were kids again.

I looked around, taking note of the minimalist design. Daphne's space was…utilitarian, leaning toward functionality rather than style. Unlike my inclination toward a warm and inviting ambiance with vibrant colors and eclectic décor, the pale walls and gray furnishings lent a cold aesthetic. The cool white bulbs gave off the same sterile feeling that was all too similar to that of a medical facility.

Her duplex featured a layout with substantial walls. Each room was appointed for private use. The left wall extended the entire length of the home and was interrupted only by two entryways. One entryway led to a short hall across from the kitchen entrance, providing access to the guest bed and bath. The second entryway led to her bedroom and ensuite at the rear. On the opposing side of the lengthy wall, the kitchen was enclosed, positioned between the garage and living room. Only a pass-through cutout connected it to the latter. Glancing at the modest counter within that opening, my eyes caught sight of a prescription bottle.

"Oh shoot," I said.

"What's up?" Daphne asked, taking a break from praising Polpette for completing the simple task of peeing in the rain.

"Ah…" I hesitated, not wanting to burden her. Her eyes widened expectantly. "I left my medication at home."

Daphne snorted and waved me off. "Is that all? Just grab one of mine. Get one out for me while you're at it," she instructed light-heartedly.

She leaned out of the doorway, whistling for Polpette to get back inside. The wind was picking up and lightning flashed from all directions. Polpette did not protest one bit and trotted in, wet and unamused. I grabbed a towel and threw it to Daphne, who promptly used it to swaddle the meatball like a newborn baby. She then proceeded to coo at her.

I shook my head at the ridiculous coddling while shaking out two tablets of Zerpotine. The medication was not the most popular of the antidepressants on the market. Dr. Bailey, however, raved about the medication. Daphne and I both saw Dr. Bailey. I started seeing him as a preteen when a tidal wave of hormones stirred up a storm of emotions. So, when Daphne started having similar behavior issues, my godmother, Selene, recommended him to her parents.

I walked toward her room, pulling the hem of my dress upward. My mass of curls caught in the garment, bowing it like a sail catching a wind. Daphne, now crouched to finish drying the disgruntled fur baby, glanced up at me. Her eyes were round and wide, with a thin, rusty red ring around the pupil that popped from the emerald green in the rest of her irises. The green complimented her long, wavy chestnut hair and lightly tanned skin. She had features nearly balanced to perfection. That is, aside from a longer nose. It gave her a sophisticated look that clashed with her crass vernacular.

I finish pulling my dress over my head. My curls cascaded down the length of my back. I dropped it to the floor and held a tablet out for her.

"Here you go," I said, trying to rouse some attention. She took the tablet on her tongue. It would never *not* gross me out how Daphne could dry-swallow a pill. I cringed.

She continued drying Polpetta and checking her phone for work emails. I headed to her bathroom to scoop water from the sink and take my own. I sighed audibly on the way, now annoyed that she suggested we mess around tonight but gave more attention to everyone and everything else but me.

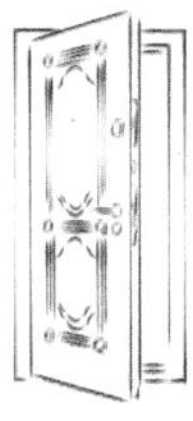

I was already undressed, now scrolling social media, waiting for her. I sighed heavily again. Then Daphne's silhouette filled the doorway. The light of the living room was at her back, obscuring her features in the shadows of the bedroom. She pulled her top over her head. Before the last of her hair could escape the modest garb, I caught the detail of her breast in the back glow. They had a bottom-heavy fullness with pink peaks that angled upward. She shimmied out of her shorts and shut the door.

"I'm coming, I'm coming. You're so impatient," she laughed, crawling up the bed. With a giggle, she lowered her full lips to mine and used her tongue to scoop my top lip before biting down on it softly. All of my annoyance disappeared, replaced with warmth and anticipation. She sucked my lip into her mouth and laid her warm, naked body against mine. "Mmm," she simpered.

My fingers traced down gently to her nipple. I propped it between my two first fingers and squeezed, gently pinching them. She smiled and leaned down again to kiss me. I hummed into the contact. Her soft touch was an intoxicating contrast to the abrasive eagerness of every man I had been with. It always made me want her more than just physically. She wasted no time now, moving her hand down between my legs, finding me soaked. My breathing picked up. My face heated.

"Oh fuck…" she whispered. She lowered her lips to my breasts. Her thumb dipped into my moisture, dragging it up. Then her tongue swirled in circles around my nipples as she swirled her thumb around my clit. The tickle of her tongue made my center warm. My legs spread easily, eager for more. She moved to my other breast and moaned as my nipple hardened in her mouth. The vibrations against my peaks made my toes curl.

Her thumb pushed below my clit. It traveled across my sensitive lips before pressing on the tight opening between my cheeks. I gasped at the threat, unsure if I was prepared for the intrusion. She pushed gently to barely stretch it open. My cheeks flushed. She lowered her face toward my pussy, and her nipple plucked from between my fingers. With her free hand, she barely rubbed my clit and placed light kisses on my thigh. I couldn't take the edging.

"Daph," I groaned. She licked the sensitive skin where my thigh met my lips. I bucked my hips in response. Suddenly, her tongue dragged up my warmth, past my entrance. She sucked my clit into her mouth. I drew a deep breath and flinched as the sensitive flesh was taken in. Her warm tongue massaged it slowly. I sank into the plea-sure, relaxing my body. Then she slid three fingers in swiftly. The blunt entry caught me off guard, and I gasped with surprise. "Yes," I moaned.

She worked wide plunges of her fingers into me at a measured pace, over and over. My body rocked with every friction-born push and pull. I pressed my legs open as far as I could. My breathy moans kept pace with her forceful pleasure. I was losing what control I had, gripping her silky, brown hair in my fist. I looked down past my hard-ened nipples as they bounced. I met her gaze, panting faster. She could see how close I was and knew exactly how to push me over the edge.

Still sucking, the tip of her tongue became firm. Gently, she flicked the underside of my sensitive clit. Her fingers tucked upward inside me. They massaged the most sensitive part of my center. Her fingertips awakened a collection of nerves, and she released a pool of arousal from me. The wetness leaked from me, and my body yielded to her beckoning. Ultimate pleasure barreled forward. I let out a heady moan and unraveled.

"Yes!" I yelled. The orgasm crashed through me. It stole my breath. The wetness that evacuated my center glazed Daphne's chin. As the orgasm began to fade, the tingles of pleasure still lingered on my thighs, lips, and clit. She softened her licks. Her thrusts became slower and more gentle. Relieved moans escaped me as the last of my pleasure evaporated into the scent of sex in the air.

Slowly, she withdrew her fingers, and she kissed my lips. My heart raced as I tried to come down. My legs were sore from the force of the spread. It was painful to even try closing them. She was incredible. I didn't know that I'd ever have another lover who knew how to make me cum so easily.

I bit my lips as she straddled me, stalking up my body toward my face. I deepened the bite on my lip to hold back words that were too heavy. Her knees reached either side of my face. Her narrow waist crowned thick thighs, the bare flesh between them rounded.

My lips parted, and her center lowered to my mouth. As she spread her thick lips farther, my mouth sank deeper. She leaned over, grabbing the headboard for support, and began rocking her hips. My tongue traced along her center. I captured her clit in my mouth. As I sucked it gently, she grinded hard and slow. I reached up to massage her breast. I pinched her peak. She moaned low. With my free hand, I pressed my two middle fingers into her warmth. "That's it, Odie," she praised. I worked them in and out, letting her set the pace with the rocking of her hips. She rode my fingers as they pressed gently inside of her.

Her wetness soaked my chin. I wanted to taste more of her. Curling my fingers forward inside her, I massaged the same spot she had. "Oh fuck," she said, her hips picking up speed. My fingers massaged her harder and faster. She threw her head back, moaning loudly. Her rocking slowed, and the headboard groaned, and she came in my mouth. As she worked through the last of her pleasure, she slowly settled her weight on my face. I waited, hungry for air, as her moans softened.

"Oh fuck," she said in a quiet breathy voice.

Finally, she lifted her hips, and I filled my hungry lungs with cold air. She looked down at me, smiling, her breasts still heaving with every breath.

"Are you okay? Was I too rough?" she asked.

"Amazing," was all I could manage as I regained my breath.

She smiled and swung her leg off of me. "We are too good at this, Odie. Lord help the men who marry us."

It amazed me how casual she could be after such passions. She had seamlessly redirected the mood, and I was painfully reminded that she didn't want what I did from this. I smiled, looking up at her, and smacked her ass.

"Let's get cleaned up and get some sleep," I said, matching her casual finesse. There wasn't a hint of longing on my face. Like a switch flipped, we were just two friends again.

3

O'DOHERTY: LIKE A LABYRINTH

A HIGH-PITCHED RINGING RAPPED ON MY EARDRUMS, AND I PRIED MY eyes wide from a deep sleep. I scrambled to find my phone while Daphne grumbled next to me.

"What time is it? Jeeeesuhs!" She groaned into the darkness. My hand slapped the nightstand blindly, finally landing a finger on the edge of my phone. I answered.

"Hello?" My voice rasped too quietly to be heard. I stole a swig of water from Daphne's nightstand. I could bet on her always having fresh water next to the bed. I swallowed and tried again. "Hello?"

"Hi, is this O'doherty Sameal, the nurse coordinating clinical research for Meriflec at *Mayflower*?" the woman inquired, her voice trembling.

"Yes, this is she."

"This is Janet Francis, one of the night nurses at *Mayflower*. We spoke last night about the sleepwalking incident."

"Yes. I recall that. Is everything alright?" I tried my best not to sound too groggy, although I was sure the breaking in my voice would be expected this late. *Or is it early?*

"There was a storm last night. Half the building was destroyed in a tornado. There have been multiple casualties, including many patients in your trial." The woman sounded shaken yet able to articulate herself reasonably well. I was suddenly very awake. "The storm hit around 3:00 AM, and with the staff on hand, our response was limited to only a few patients at a time. We don't have a number yet on mortality or a complete list of names. The residents are currently being transported to *Amett Health Northern Miami Hospital* for treatment and are in questionable condition. We are relying on local emergency response to help us get everyone triaged and move out. You may not be able to do your evaluations this morning, but if you're still free, we could sure use—"

"Of course, I'll be there as soon as possible." I ended the call, taking a moment to process. I wasn't sure when I sat up, but I was clutching the comforter over my bare chest, legs hanging over the side of the bed.

"What's up?" Daphne was propped up on her elbows, still laying naked on her belly. Her messy locks glowed softly in the light of my phone. I looked down at it. It was a quarter after four in the morning.

"Daphne, you have to get to work as soon as possible." I paused. She gave me a moment to articulate myself better. Coming to her knees, she crawled through plush sheets over to me in long, swaying strides. I felt the warmth of her chest press on my shoulder blade. "*Mayflower* was hit by a tornado. Patients are being transported to *Northern Miami*. They don't have a number, which means…"

"Okay," she stated plainly. There was no room for trepidation in healthcare. You had to become grounded rather quickly and focus on the priorities. Daphne selected a pair of emerald-green scrubs from the closet and passed them to me. She chose a similar style set in a classic shade of navy blue for herself.

"I thought you had to wear royal blue at this facility?"

"It's my last day, I don't give a shit. What are they gonna do, send me home during a mass casualty for dress code?" She smirked with sarcasm, pulling the top over the spilling cups of her bra. Judging by her hamper, the real reason was that she went out with me instead of laundering her uniform. "I'll drop you off at *Mayflower* on the way… or do you wanna swing by your place to get your car first?"

"Drop me off. I can ride with an ambulance to the hospital when I'm finished."

Daphne called Polpette. The lazy meatball pretended to sleep, but a groan and narrow glance gave her away. "Polpette! Move your giant ass!" Daphne prodded the blob with her foot. With a grumble and a slow stretch, Polpette achingly pushed her body from her bed. She yawned deep and wide. A shake of her head sent ripples through her loose, furry skin, and she trotted at glacial speed toward the sliding glass door, where Daphne ushered her out with urgency. "Come on, come on! Go potty. Shit! It's freaking cold out!" She shivered.

Cold? I wondered on my way to the kitchen. It was early summer.

Polpette returned promptly after a short pee on the massive tree and trotted over to the couch. She was clearly over the inconvenient weather lately. Daphne locked the back door and snatched a dark blue throw blanket from the couch, draping it over her shoulders.

"I filled her bowls already. Let's go," I said calmly, cradling two protein shakes for the road. I sipped the low-calorie one to swallow the morning dose and left a tablet on the counter for Daph. We didn't bother to pack food for lunch. Even on a good day, we didn't often get a lunch break, let alone during a mass casualty event.

We hurried into Daphne's car, the roar of the engine rumbling through my core. Daphne shivered as if the plush throw she draped around herself was useless. I adjusted the heat. Daphne's phone dinged as a message preview appeared on the screen. Maria, the Nursing House Supervisor at *Northern Miami Hospital* was asking for anyone who wasn't already scheduled to come in immediately if they could. I responded for Daphne as she drove.

I'm on my way now.

I then texted Ms. Rivera, the older woman who lived on the other side of the duplex and often joked that she'd one day steal Polpette for good.

I'll be working long hours today. Please check on Polly if you can. Key is in the usual place! Chocolate a L' Orange Cheesecake in fridge :)"

FORTY MINUTES LATER, WE ARRIVED AT *MAYFLOWER*—OR WHAT WAS left of it. The drive normally would not have taken that long, but the roads were hazardous with debris, and the sun had not yet risen. Everyone on the roadway drove as if they were navigating a minefield. We cupped our mouths at the sight of *Mayflower* in ruins.

Fire trucks opened spotlights, flooding the piles with pale light at harsh angles. Ambulances came and went as patients were taken to the hospital. The structure had been reduced to boulders of cinder block and mortar on one side. On the other side was a busted skeleton of roofless walls. I opened the car door, wasting no time, but Daphne's grip caught my arm.

"Good luck," she said, offering me a sharpie.

"You too," I replied. I grabbed and pocketed the marker. "Thank you."

I walked toward the rubble-shrouded building that sunk into the indigo cast of predawn.

BY SUNRISE WE HAD ROWS OF PATIENTS LINED UP AND TRIAGED. Firefighters carried them out, laying them in a clearing by the ambulances. The other nurses and I took their vitals and collected personal information, which we recorded on their chests with Sharpie markers.

Victims who could walk or had minor injuries were tagged green in triage, signifying *low priority*. Victims with serious injuries that weren't an immediate threat to their lives were marked yellow—or *delay transport/treatment*. Victims with abnormal or compromised breathing, altered mental status, or those showing reduced blood perfusion got tagged red—*immediate care needed*. And finally, those who weren't breathing, could not be aroused or had severe injuries they were unlikely to survive got tagged black—*expectant*. The black tag was a death notice, and pain management was the only merciful option when resources were this scarce.

Our one stroke of luck was that April, a wound care nurse, was scheduled to make rounds at *Mayflower* this morning to reassess some pressure wounds. When she got the same call I had this morning, she didn't hesitate to come as soon as she could.

Janet, the nurse who'd called, made sure to give the firefighters directions to the supply rooms in hopes they weren't part of the building that was ripped away. The nursing assistants with her, Karey and Stacy, did their best to follow her lead calmly.

The team from A-wing joined the efforts. Much like the B-wing crew, A-wing had one nurse and two CNAs, all faring well in the storm. I had seen them together before while evaluating my patients in the medication trial. The only thing different from their flow this morning was the absence of playful banter.

The C-wing staff were not so fortunate. The older nurse had suffered lacerations to the head and had a splinted wrist, yet she refused to leave for medical care. There was only one CNA scheduled with her that night, and he had been sent to the hospital urgently. April and I worked alongside the nurse, checking periodically that her mental status was unchanged. She brushed off the extra attention.

Between the three groups, only fifteen patients had family members caring for them in any way the nurses could allow them to. "Don't remove the bloody gauze," I instructed a man. He held his father's frail arm, blood soaking through the gauze he pressed to it and staining his gloved fingers. "Just add more over it and keep the pressure firm. Elevate it over the level of the heart." It was a stroke of luck that they all seemed to be relatively collected. Perhaps it was shock, but it was useful all the same.

The roofless building was missing chunks of walls, with C-wing suffering the most damage. Among the rubble were bedpans, warped walkers, and other random medical equipment. Every so often, I'd find blue stones with white shimmering flecks. They were smooth and oblong and about the size of a kiwi. When the sun hit the horizon, the condensation on the stone captured its early rays. The stone lit up. It was like tiny prisms exploding with colorful shards of light. I could have sworn the flecks started to move, but looking more closely, I saw it was the reflection of the clouds floating through the sky.

I spotted an odd speck on a smaller cloud and leaned in close. "What the..." I murmured under my breath. I turned my eyes quickly to the sky to see the cloud and what I swore was something looking down from it. I blinked hard twice, my eyes still itchy from lack of sleep. When I refocused, the strange speck was gone, the low cloud dissipating like stretched cotton. I didn't take the time to decide if my tired eyes were playing tricks on me. There was still much work to be done. I pocketed the strange stone and tended to my patients.

The cries of agony from the black-tagged patients faded to an eerie silence, and the last of the red-tagged patients were loaded into the ambulance. Finally, an hour early, the day shift staff arrived. The murmur of shift-change report started to hum in the open wreckage while they tended to the yellow-tagged patients.

"I'M GETTING OUT OF HERE, KID. I APPRECIATE YOUR HELP," JANET said, pocketing her badge. She was done with a longer-than-usual report.

"Hey, Janet, do you have a moment?" I stumbled carefully after her. She turned her heavy body and nodded.

"The patients—you said they were sleepwalking. Is there any chance you found similarities in their charts?"

"The only similarity they had was Meriflec. But there were eighteen patients total in the facility who were prescribed that medication and weren't affected as… strangely." She narrowed her eyes and tilted her head with a brief shake. "Those patients are similar too; in that we usually have trouble medicating them. We have to crush the medication and mix it in applesauce, you know? More often than not, they either don't finish the applesauce or just refuse to eat it all together."

"They were affected strangely, you say. How do you mean?" I pressed, curiosity on my face.

"Well, those eighteen patients just sat at the edge of the bed." She shrugged.

"And the rest?" I tilted my chin.

She pressed her lips together. "They stood up and walked single file to the courtyard. Then in a circle-like formation. They stopped, dropped rocks, and then just went to bed. All at the same time. Like they were linked in the mind." She gave an animated yet authentic shiver.

"Rocks?" I challenged, with a crinkle in my nose.

"Rocks. And when they went back to bed the rocks were still laying there in a…" she shook her head and motioned her arms in confused waves, "a pattern. Like a *labyrinth*. It's gone now; the storm made a mess of it."

"Where did they get the rocks?"

Maybe it wasn't *Meriflec,* I pondered. Maybe these rocks had something to do with it.

"Honey, I don't know. I barely have time to pee most shifts. All I can tell you is it was the *weirdest* thing I have *ever* seen in my career —in my life! Their vital signs were stable; they had no memory of it, and before I could put a thing about it in their charts, a storm rolled through. Damn near right on top of us!"

I pulled the stone from my pocket and presented it to Janet. "Is this one of them?"

"Eh heh!" she blurted sharply in an unamused laugh and then threw her hands up in refusal, stepping back. That would be one of them, and if I were you, I'd get rid of it!" Janet walked past me toward a car waiting for her. "My ride's here. Call me with anything else, preferably after 3:00 PM. I'm beat."

. . .

I TURNED AROUND, SQUINTING AGAINST THE SUN, AND WALKED toward the six patients left there who were in the Meriflec trial. None of them had any recollection of the sleepwalking incident. None of them were good historians. None of them could remember where the stones came from. But luckily the last patient I spoke with, Mariella Vasquez, had company.

Mariella's grandson, Fabian, was one of the few family members of the residents who spent most of his free time at the bedside. I'd always miss him on my rounds and started to wonder if Mariella was imagining this grandson she spoke of. She would often describe him as "such a handsome, smart boy, and single too!"

She wasn't wrong. He was a doll. He had smooth, tanned, olive skin, dark blonde hair with loose curls styled in a pompadour cut, and amber eyes with round, wire-frame glasses. A large, bright smile drew my attention. He wasn't much taller than me and had a sturdiness to him. Fabian wasn't some gym rat with rippling muscles, but he took good care of himself and seemed naturally solid. But the thing that stood out most about Fabian was his radiant positivity. His presence surrounded everything like a fire burning with life. His kind laugh gave you a feeling of safety. He looked to be a really happy guy.

Janet had called the families after the sleepwalking incident to see if any of them were available to stay with their family members in case of another sleepwalking event. Fabian, as always, came as soon as he could. Now, he was crouched by Mariella, helping her drink from a bottle of water. Mariella was tagged green in triage—"minor." According to Mariella, this was thanks to her grandson, who heard the storm as it formed. He was able to lift her from her bed and carry her to the center of the larger building before the roof came off. He shielded her body with his own, undoubtedly taking the hit of debris.

"The rocks came from the pharmaceutical representatives," he offered after hearing my questions go unanswered. I turned my attention to him and squinted as questions bubbled in my mind. "At the start of the medication trial, the representatives came by to educate all of the patients and their families on the medication. They left a packet of papers and offered the rocks as paperweights."

"You are *sure*?" I asked, confused. It didn't entirely make sense.

"Yeah, I was there. Nana doesn't have the best memory, so I usually come here to receive the education on new treatments for her," he said, nodding. He turned around to grab the educational packet from his pack, and I noticed a large blood stain on the back of his shirt where the material tore away.

"You're hurt!" I scorned him. "Why didn't you say anything?"

"Oh no, no… It's fine. You guys are busy… It doesn't hurt that bad," he answered, stumbling over the words. He would clearly be tagged green, but the day shift was here now, and many patients had either died or left for the hospital. I had plenty of time.

"I'll take a look now," I corrected sternly, "let's see it."

Sheepishly, he swayed and sighed, obviously not wanting to be fussed over when others were in worse shape.

"Fabian! Take that filthy shirt off right now and let the nurse take a look!" Mariella barked.

"Okay! Okay." He surrendered hastily to appease his grandmother. And then he began peeling his shirt over his head. *My God.* His body was magnificent. I was distracted by the thin trail of short hairs dropping to the edge of his low-hanging waistband and didn't realize his head was stuck in the collar until he started to stumble. "Oo, oo, oo."

I closed the distance between us, quickly steadying him with my hand on his side. With my other hand, I pulled his collar forward where it was snagged on his chin. The heat of his perfect body under my hand made me blush. The flush over my cheeks seemed perfectly natural paired with the laughter that escaped me. His glasses were getting pulled off now, too. I pinched them at the bridge of the wire-frames while he finished disrobing clumsily.

"You are a mess," I said, shaking my head. I gingerly replaced his glasses back on his face.

"Thanks." He smiled with pressed lips just before turning around to let me examine his back. My smile disappeared immediately. I sucked in a quiet breath that straightened my back. It was worse than I thought.

"You will need stitches at minimum..." I said, inspecting the wound and signaling him to turn his back to the sun for better light. "And it probably wouldn't hurt to get antibiotics and a tetanus shot. I need to clean this, okay?"

"Ah huh," he replied. Two gashes marred his back. The first gash measured approximately four inches long and two inches wide with jagged edges. The thin layer of slick yellow fat beneath his skin poked out just as jaggedly. Coagulated blood pooled in the middle of the wound like dark cherry jam. The second gash was similar but measured approximately twelve inches, and its jagged edges caused flaps of skin to flop over outward, spreading the gash about five inches at its widest. Even more of the fat's boba-like texture could be seen. Thick, curdled blood hid the muscle beneath. Dark blood stained every bit of skin below it, a mixture of crusted, dry sanguine and slippery, oozing clots. I retrieved a bottle of sterile saline, which we were lucky to recover from a supply room earlier at April's demand.

"This may be uncomfortable. I'll get you some pain medication first," I said, turning.

"No," he said quickly. "No, no. I'm fine without it. Leave it for the others."

"Your wounds are serious. I can at least get you—"

"It's fine, please. Go ahead and clean it." I shook my head regretfully while I poured sterile saline over the wound, rinsing any dirt and debris from it. He hissed and oohed and ahhed. I dabbed it with wet gauze, and he flinched. "Sorry," he said. I shook my head again.

"We can take a break and I can go get some medication. Really, it is not a problem."

"No, no. That's all right. I can't take care of Nana here if I'm all woozy, can I?" He winked at Mariella who looked at him with sadness for his suffering. I shook my head as I worked, wishing he would let me give him some comfort. He was trying very hard not to show it, but the way his entire body trembled and sweat beaded on his brow, I could tell it was bad. He breathed through it.

"You're doing great." I used wet gauze to gently pat parts of the wound, cleaning it a little more. I took care not to disturb the clotting that slowed his bleeding. It took a long while to clean carefully, and we sat in silence while he breathed purposefully in meditation. Only Mariella's prayers for him could be heard as she traced rosary beads through her fingers. The texture of the trapezius muscle could be spotted through the larger wound, but it was still shining thick with blood and facia.

"I don't see any more debris. It can't stay open like this though. I'm going to apply a dressing and you'll need to get this closed up as soon as possible so it doesn't get infected," I explained, dampening gauze.

"The hospitals are going to be slammed," he said with uncertainty.

"We can try an urgent care center. They usually do stitches; it's cheaper, and the wait times are less." I said, hoping there wasn't an exception for massive gashes. "I'll give them a call."

I laid moist gauze over the wounds and covered them with a large ABD pad. The wounds required nearly a half a roll of tape, which was a sparse commodity by now. I stepped away to call the local urgent care and explain the situation. I scanned the sky, looking for the strange speck, as I waited on hold. I couldn't help feeling as if it… whatever *it* was, was watching me. I found nothing out of the ordinary. Finally, the receptionist picked up again, pulling my attention from the sky.

"Thank you for holding. I spoke to our Nurse Practitioner and he can handle the wounds."

"And antibiotics and a tetanus shot?"

"Yes, of course."

"Great. Thank you so much. I'll let him know."

I hung up the phone and scanned the sky one more time before turning back to them.

"They can get you in now. I suggest you go sooner than later. That is very high risk for infection." Fabian stood up, slapping his thighs, and extended a hand to Mariella.

"Okay. Well, Nana, it looks like you're coming with me for now. Can't really let you sleep in a parking lot, now can I?" he joked.

"I wouldn't advise driving. You've lost a lot of blood and haven't slept much at all. That's not safe," I pressed.

"Really, I'm fine. I can't thank you enough," he said, guiding Mariella to a stand and making sure she was steady.

I nodded, "Well, good luck. It was nice meeting you. And I'll see you soon, Ms. Vasquez." I turned to walk away, hoping to catch a ride with an ambulance to the hospital. As I carefully stepped over rubble, I heard the hurried whispers of Mariella coming from behind me, and then a slap. "Go, go, go!" I heard her say in hushed tones before Fabian called out after me.

"Ah hey, nurse?"

I paused and turned, looking at the shirtless man in front of me. The harsh angle of the rising sun bounced off the wire frames of his glasses and contrasted with every subtle dip and bulge of his body.

"Hey, if you want to grab some food tonight, maybe," he shook his head, "when things die down, of course. Maybe I, Ah…could give you a call?" He swallowed hard.

My brows flinched in surprise. Over his shoulder I could see the kyphosed back of his grandmother leaning closer for a listen. I had never gone for guys like him before—the hot nerd type—but maybe that's why others have never been viable. Fabian was… precious and sweet… and a little clumsy. And if Daphne met someone that struck her as special, she would not hesitate, so why should I? It all made sense, but for some reason I felt nervous at the thought of telling her. It was a silly fear, I decided.

"That would be really nice. Yes. I would love to." I smiled genuinely back at him. "I think after today I might need to unwind."

His cheeks flushed, and his smile crooked to the side as he pulled out his phone. "I'm so sorry. I can't believe I haven't asked you this yet. What's your name?" he asked.

"O'doherty."

"Well, it's so nice to meet you, O'doherty." My name on his lips caused a flutter in my throat. We traded numbers and I continued my quest for an ambulance heading to the hospital. From the gleeful squeals of Mariella, I guessed she saw my answer written on Fabian's face. A smile met my eyes, and I climbed into an ambulance ready to pull out. I watched the sky the entire ride, rolling the stone in my pocket.

4

DAPHNE: THE CLOUD WAITED FOR HIM

FOUR EMPTY BODY BAGS WEIGH ABOUT SIX POUNDS. *WHY DO THEY feel so much heavier?* They asked me to work in the Emergency Department, and I hurried down to receive patients. At 16:00, on my way to replenish our stock of postmortem supplies in the ER, my body was starting to ache.

Amett Health recently bought out *Mayflower*, but they had not merged their electronic charting system yet. Without charts from nursing homes or any documentation, we had to assume that every patient was a *Full Code. That* meant if they died, we would have to do CPR with the works. Few things are more depressing than the crunching of a ninety-year-old rib cage under your hands. You could feel the bone cracking beneath their thin, damp skin. CPR was not what Hollywood advertised. There was no dignity or cleanliness or gentleness. It is wet, naked, sweaty, loud, and aggressive, in *none* of the good ways. It's not the way a great-grandparent should go, and surviving it can often be painful and short-lived. Today was a prime example.

The twister didn't last long, nor did it travel very far, but *Mayflower* was not the only place to get hit. The disaster area was pretty well populated, with condos and apartments full of people who had little or no warning. They'd been coming in all day, some getting CPR as they came through the doors. One even groaned about it being a force of evil.

Even though our shift was about to end, not one staff member had eaten, drank, or documented. ER was *holding*, which meant the inpatient units had no empty beds available, causing a backflow of patients. They filled every room and lined the halls, yet the hospital refused to divert to other facilities. I wasn't surprised. This type of shit was why I was there in the first place.

O'doherty came in around 07:00 to see what she could find in any test results of patients who had been in the Meriflec trial. We were both too busy to chat about anything she might have discovered, but judging from the things I saw—and her flat expression—I didn't think she found much. I admired her studious nature. She was always the better student—top of our class. Odie was as smart as she was beautiful but carried herself as a modest professional around others. She stood from the computer, grabbed her bag, and started toward the door.

"Hey," I called. "You good?" I wondered if she hadn't seen that I was back from central supply. It was strange for her to not say goodbye.

"Yeah, I just, I have to get going," she said. Her tone told me she was leaving something out.

"Yeah? You have plans tonight? Remember, I'm having the going away party across the street after work if you want to stop by for a drink," I offered.

Carlotta, an ER nurse invited to the gathering, overheard me as she passed and hollered "aye ohhh," with a fist in the air.

"I… yeah, I do. I have plans, I mean. I have a… date, actually." She corked a smile and raised her brows. My eyes widened, and my head cocked. I had clearly missed something. When had she met someone, and who was it that was making her so weird?

"Oh! Well, I can't wait to hear all about it. Have fun." I smiled. She waved, biting her lip and turning her eyes to the floor as she walked out. Something felt very off about all of that.

Clicking heels caught my attention, and I looked up to see the ridiculous sight of the Director of Nursing, Lyndie Pratt, in scrubs and red-bottom heels. Staff hurrying by gave her a once-over and faked smiles.

"Excuse me, everyone! I know you are all so busy and doing *amazing* work during this difficult time," she announced in her peppy voice. No one wanted to stop, but they did. The hope that she would spout her bull-shit quickly was palpable in the room. "I want to thank you guys for your hard work and dedication. We have catered a late lunch for you, so I hope you take a moment for yourself to grab some pizza from the breakroom."

I rolled my eyes hard. As if any of us would have time to eat that stale cheese pizza before the end of the shift. I took a moment to sip my water. The cold drink soothed my dry, itchy throat.

"Ah, and let us all remember that food and drink stay in the break-room. Thank you, guys!" she finished with a squint and pursed smile.

I continued sipping, my eyes not breaking from Lyndie. Everyone else promptly hurried to tend to their patients. It was the first drink I had today, and the icy hydration was worth the defiance. She closed the distance between us and tapped on the lip of my tumbler while I still took a long sip from the straw.

"You have to take that in the breakroom," Lyndie pressed with a tight smile.

I took a moment to sip again and swallowed loudly. Then I smiled back and walked into the breakroom. As much as I would've loved to tell her to piss off just then, it would probably do more harm than—

"And, Daphne, the next time you come out of dress code, we'll have to send you home. You understand, right?" she added, propping the break room door open behind me.

Does she really want to pull a power trip right now? Today of all days?

My anger was just below my skin. Her pinched face, blonde blowout, and smug tone had been up my ass since the day I started here. Her pale blue eyes were like knives in my back, a back sweaty and sore from the all-day fight with death.

"Actually, today is my last day. My contract is up at 7:00 PM," I said, putting my tumbler on the table. I turned back around and pushed the door wider, making my way through the crowded threshold. The smell of overapplied, expensive perfume steamed off her as she watched me closely, her entire body imposing. For a moment, the rage got the best of me. "But I guess if I come back, I'll try heels with my scrubs," I said before breaking free from the doorway.

Damn it. Why can't I just bite my tongue?

I walked toward the nursing station, smirking and grabbing my report sheet before turning for the medication room.

"Daphne, can I have a word with you in my office?" she called to me from the doorway, her jaw jetting to the side.

"Lyndie, I've hardly had a chance to chart. I've got three medications set to run dry any second now. A talk would not be safe or smart."

"Dawn can help with that. Can't you, Dawn?" She turned her gaze to the tall, tattooed nurse who had just sat down to chart. Dawn stiffened, clenched her teeth, and turned with a forced smile. She waited to speak until the delirious patient in a nearby hall bed stopped screaming about an "evil sky man" who "made the storm to kill us all."

"Actually, no, I can't. I just sat down and—"

"It will just be a moment, thanks!" Lyndie interrupted. She walked closer.

"I'm off at 7:15, Lyndie. That'll be a better time for all of us." I turned to walk away. I wasn't letting her strong arm either of us or letting my patients go without proper monitoring. Lyndie stepped in front of me. The noisy area seemed to quiet just a bit, and suddenly, providers were busy looking at their papers a bit closer.

"Well, I'm off in *twenty* minutes, so—" Lyndie started before I cut her off with a sarcastic laugh that filled the space. Patients cried in agony around my cackle.

"Of course you are! Of course, you're leaving your staff at 4:30 during a mass casualty. My apologies. Here I thought you were wearing scrubs for an actual reason," I snapped. I was done. The day had taken its toll, and the last thing I needed was the condescending tone of some priss who couldn't prime a line of tube feed if her life depended on it. I knew I needed to reel it back, but the dam had burst, and the flood was unstoppable.

"Give your patients to Dawn, Carlotta, Rashi, and Samuel. They will split your team. Finish your charting. Then clock out. Your contract is up *now*." Lyndie tightened her lips and shook her head. "I am just so disappointed in your lack of professionalism. This does not align with our values."

Lyndie was gone before I could even process what happened. *This is a joke, right?* I turned to Dawn, who was pursing her lips.

"I'm not leavin' 'til my charting is done. Don't worry," I said, patting the counter and turning to continue my tasks.

The delirious patient grabbed my arm tightly as I passed and pulled me to her. Her beady black eyes fixed on me. "The storm maker will come back. He will kill us all," she warned, her wrinkled lips shaking just as much as her voice.

I managed to get my arm out of her clutches. "No one is going to hurt you here. Not on my watch," I winked. Then I went to find her nurse and suggested a little Haldol for the poor thing to help her calm down.

I bought time and made sure my patients were set by 18:00. Then, I was grabbing my scrub jacket and pens from my locker and clocking out of *Amett Health Northern Miami Hospital* for the last time. I took a moment and texted some of the nurses the piping hot tea. I smiled while walking out of that miserable hell. In organizing, many problems could be harvested for momentum. This harvest would be plentiful.

BY THE TIME I MADE THE TREK TO MY CAR ON THE FAR SIDE OF THE lot by the intersection, my head was starting to clear. I grabbed my computer bag and walked the rest of the way to the restaurant. It was just a few blocks away and across that intersection. Besides, the weather was nice. The warm breeze and low sun were peaceful. I admired the merchandise in the large store windows on the way there: crystal figurines in one window and fine jewelry in another. I never wore jewelry, but sometimes I imagined that I could be as fashionable and delicate as Odie. Maybe then I could pull off some of those unique pieces.

There was something easing about the sound of my feet hitting the sidewalk. Occasionally, the rolling of sparkling blue stones that I kicked would add to it. Finally, I picked one up and studied it for a moment. I hadn't seen anything like the small kiwi-sized oval. I pocketed it for good luck.

When I reached the restaurant, I had time to get settled and start planning. By 19:30 nurses started showing up. All of them looked at me with intense curiosity, stemming from the text I had sent after leaving work.

> Lyndie Pratt just sent me home early. ER was drowning and I had to split my team up between the others. Then she went home for the day! I'll tell you more later.

The text hadn't gotten an immediate response. Everyone was too busy to check their personal phones. But at shift change, the pinging seemed to never end.

> "?!?!"
>
> "whaaat?"
>
> "She did not!"

These were just a few of many reactions. They were not going to miss out on the details. Lyndie had burned all of them at one point and badly. But all of the pent-up anger would do them no good if it wasn't a *productive* conversation about what was possible. Possibly the most important thing I learned while on my assignment was who the most beloved and helpful nurses were on each floor, the ones other nurses would follow into battle—*the leaders*. I kept them close.

About twenty nurses sat at the table. The fiercest of them all, Jesula, was a day-shift nurse from the ICU who often picked up night shifts. Jesula and I hit it off the most out of all of the leaders I had ID'd. We'd pair up as buddies almost every shift we worked together. We never let each other's patients be dirty, or their medications run dry. And I went out for drinks with her the most out of all the leaders I met.

"Oftentimes, you'll find yourself trying to bridge the gap between what you know is *right* and what you're *capable* of doing in these work conditions. If you put your patient's well-being first, you will limit the moral injury from that," Jesula would say to the many new graduates she trained. They looked at her like she was nursing scripture incarnate. They hurried along after her like baby ducks. Of everyone sitting at that table, Jesula was a *must* to have on board.

Anyway, I started the conversation by butchering the story of what happened with Lyndie. Dawn chimed in eagerly to ask, "How are you going to leave out the part where Lyndie was wearing Louis Vuittons with scrubs?" Laughter erupted. By the time the story was through, they were sharing their stories about how Lyndie and other executives had screwed them or talked down to them.

"We told Lyndie we were drowning on the Med Surg unit, and all she said was, 'It's a good thing you can swim.' What does that even mean?" a nurse named Dean said.

"Can I have one day off without being asked to be a team player and pickup? That's really all I ask. Well, that and for them to stop giving me so many patients. I mean, on the mother/baby unit, one extra patient is really two! It's insane," said a nurse named Valentina. The complaints rolled in. There was plenty of shared anger, but it was time to start talking about a solution and give them the hope they needed.

"Well, have all of you considered quitting?" I asked, rolling the lucky blue stone in my fingers. A hush fell over the group.

"They've monopolized most of Florida. That's not really an option, unless we all move," Dawn said.

"Well, then it seems like you only have two choices. Continue letting them gamble with your patients' safety until you get fired or quit…" I shrugged and then leaned in. "Or you guys stand together and build the power you need to meet them as equals and make real change happen." Mischievous smiles started to appear as the group looked at each other, none of them really sure what I meant.

"How would something like that go?" Jesula asked in a Haitian accent, folding her hands and listening carefully. Jesula had a presence that harnessed respect. Everyone at the table glanced from her to me, co-signing the question. I carefully listed a series of steps and milestones: gauging interest, getting complete and accurate lists, getting formal commitments through union cards, and then going public and having an election. *Ánimo.*

"We technically need about thirty-three percent to sign the cards for an election to be possible, but we definitely wouldn't move forward unless we had more than double that number. As for the election, if fifty percent plus one person vote *yes* in the election, you win the right to begin bargaining your first contract as an official union," I finished.

They started talking about how to start gathering support and lists. I supplemented the conversation with my observations about the staff including who trusts whom and who was too close with management to trust. As expected, there were concerns raised that were perfectly reasonable.

"What happens if we are caught? Can't they fire us?" Dean asked.

"That's a very legitimate concern," I affirmed. "Organizing with your coworkers is a protected activity. The question is, are you going to stand with each other right now…or stand on the sidelines?"

A planter outside of the restaurant toppled over and banged against the glass. The entire restaurant seemed to gasp at once and fall silent before the murmurs picked up again. *This goddamn weather…* I thought, clutching the stone. I glanced back at them, waiting for an answer.

"I'm in," Dawn declared. "I'm sick of them gambling with my patients' lives."

"Me too," Valentina offered harshly. "Our moms and babies deserve better than this. If we don't do something, someone's going to get seriously hurt!"

"Count me in," Myra smiled. "If the only thing that comes of it is Lyndie sweating, it's worth every second!" she added with a growl. One by one, the other leaders committed, and the other staff followed —all but one very fierce woman.

I turned my head to Jesula. She was a midsized Haitian woman with long box braids, impeccably smooth skin of dark umber, and sparkling eyes of rich swirling browns that looked like polished burlwood. If she endorsed this effort, everyone else would surely get behind it. If she didn't…the last few months of salting would have been for nothing.

She was the sole provider for her home—she had four kids and six grandchildren. Her husband had diabetes and high blood pressure, and he relied on her insurance for life-saving medications. If she managed to stay with *Amett* for a few more years, she'd see a pretty sweet retirement. Like so many workers there, this could feel too risky for her.

I studied her and noticed a sideways smile appear on her coral-painted lips. I rubbed my fingertip around the rim of my glass. "What will it be, Jesula? Fight back or let them drive you out?" I asked, with not a hint of fear showing. Truthfully, sweat ran down my back and was pooling between my ass cheeks. Everyone was quiet.

"I say," she started, "it's high time Lyndie learned who she's messing with!"

Cheers erupted, and goosebumps popped up on the entire surface of my body. "Let's do this!" she cheered.

I ordered a round of mimosas to celebrate and helped them make a plan for how to start networking and getting lists. By 21:15 they all had a purpose and were empowered, but a storm was brewing and we were all eager to outrun it.

I tucked my credit card and ID into the check holder and gave it to the waiter. Then I returned my wallet to my purse that hung from the back of the chair. When I lifted my gaze back to the table, I felt someone staring. It was Jesula.

"Now. Are you going to explain to me how you know so much about all this?" she inquired below the ruckus, in a tone meant for our ears only. She arched a brow, sipped her cocktail, and smacked her lips, "Or are you going to insult my intelligence?"

I sat back and sighed. "I saw you in a bagel shop a few months ago. I heard you, your passion," I started. "It reminded me why I left my bedside job and why I do what I do. So… I'm a nurse, but taking care of patients is not my main gig. My main gig is taking care of the workers."

Jesula sat back in her chair and smiled at me, but it didn't meet her eyes. "And you truly believe we can do this?"

The check returned. I added a generous tip and signed it while Jesula waited for my answer. "I do. But it doesn't matter what I believe." I patted the check holder on the table and tucked my card and ID in my pocket. "What matters is that none of you lose sight of what matters to you most."

Jesula nodded in what I hoped was an offer of understanding. "I don't like secrets," she said, getting up from the table. By then most of the nurses had already been on their way out, hurrying to their cars in the wind. Jesula and Dean were the last to walk out of the door. I grabbed my computer bag and took a deep breath when I rose to my feet. I shrugged into the sleeves of my scrub jacket, feeling a chill.

The walk to my car was short but hurried. It was dark, the wind had picked up, and the dark sky was a fog of rumbling clouds. I was thankful for the scrub jacket. I pulled out my phone. There were no messages since this morning aside from the nurses'. *Odie must be having fun,* I thought. I slid it open.

Hey, how's your date going?

When I got to my car, I tugged the handle, but it wouldn't open. I tried again, moving my hips closer so the key fob in my pocket could get a better signal. Only, my key fob wasn't in my pocket, was it? It was in my purse, which I then realized was still on the back of the chair at the restaurant.

"Fuck…" I groaned. It was a long damn day, and all I wanted was to be home. I left my hand on the handle, closed my eyes, and lifted my face to the sky. I took a deep breath and felt the small droplets of rain on my face. It felt pretty nice. I stayed a moment, getting lost in meditation as I listened to the rain hit the pavement at increasing speed. I started to sway in the wind and reminded myself that I need to open my eyes soon and get moving if I want to save my computer from the rain.

Just one more minute…

The cool rain rolled down my cheeks, washing away a layer of grief from work and anxiety from the meeting. I let out a breath. Then a blinding pain seared my brow. I pulled myself out of the trance, bending over to guard my face from another assault. "FUCK!"

When I pulled my hand away from my head, blood ran through my fingers. Harder pelts could be heard striking the pavement. With a quick look I realized it was marble-sized hail.

"Fuuuuck!" I worked into a sprint. Covering my head with my computer bag, I crossed the street. I ran faster, trying to dodge the hail. In the distance I could see the waiter was already outside. He was trying to spot me before I got too far without my purse. I tried to wave him down.

"Hi! Hey!" I called, running past the shops toward him. He jogged over, passed me my purse, and then rushed back for shelter. He looked at me as if expecting me to follow. "Thanks!" I hollered. I turned the other way, hoping my car wasn't getting dinged up.

I made it just past the first block before hearing the sound of a freight train. Looking to my right I could see the dark shadow of a funnel cloud. It was forming just a couple blocks away, illuminated by lightning and sparks from power lines. I saw it touch down and head in my direction. Dread filled my gut.

I look toward the restaurant and then back toward my car. They were about the same distance. Neither were likely to do well in a tornado. I backtracked and darted around the corner of the jewelry store. I ran fast down the alley toward a wooded area. There was an irrigation canal behind those woods. I knew it would be the lowest ground I could find. The question was, could I make it there? I had to try.

The sound of my feet crashing against wet pavement shifted to the crunching of leaves. The deeper I ran, the darker it was. No light from street lamps or store signs could reach that far back. I struggled to navigate in the darkness. I pulled out my phone to use its light. It only helped me see a few feet ahead. Occasionally lightning cracked overhead letting me see a little farther in front of me.

The rain poured relentlessly. The hail grew larger and more frequent. My computer bag shielded my head, yet I still cringed as hail pelted my body. The train-like sound only got louder. Blood dripping from my brow blurred my vision, tinting it red. With every flash of lightning, the blood gave a dreadful red tinge to the dark woods. The trees behind me groaned as they bent until they were ripped from their roots or snapped at their trunks. I cried out, running deeper and faster. Branches and debris stung my skin in the whirling wet wind. Red flashes of tree limbs zipped past my face. My soaked scrubs clung to my frame. Finally, a clearing came into view. The canal was close.

But a branch caught my shin. I toppled over just inches from the canal's drop-off. My body hit the wet ground with a hard smack. Then my bag and purse flew forward. They bounced and tumbled down the steep canal, landing at the waterline. The light of my phone behind me caught my attention. I lunged for it, but something else caught my eye. My jaw dropped at the sight.

Under a bolt of lightning that stabbed the sky, the world lit up for a long moment. The roaring twister was closing in just a football field's length away. It was a terrifying machine of nightmares coiling around itself. But just a few yards ahead of me was a man. He just stood there, his hands up. It was like he expected to wrestle the storm.

"Get down!" I screamed. But my voice was lost in the ripping wind. I pushed against the wind to get to him. The strobing lightning guided me. Rain cleaned the blood from my vision just enough to see him better. I would pull his crazy ass down to the safety of the canal. I grabbed his arm and pulled. "Hey!"

The man startled, pushing me down. He raised an open palm and stopped to meet my eyes. Laying at his feet I looked up at him. My eyes squinted against the sting of pine needles, and rain. But he stared at me unflinchingly. He looked shocked that I was there. He was thin, tall, and pale. He had dark, medium-length hair. But his eyes were what stunned me. His irises were a shimmering opalescent. It was as if the gem itself were pushed into his damn sockets. Every flash of lightning made them shimmer in pale pastels. His shirtless body was wet. A slow, weightless barrier surrounded his skin a few inches. It was like an aura of mist.

I drew a sharp breath and backed up on my arms, kicking against the ground. My heart pounded at the inhuman sight. His mouth moved to yell but I could hear nothing over the chaos. Then he pointed behind me. The rain slapped my face. My wet hair tossed in the wind as I slid farther back. Still unable to pull my eyes from him, I gripped the earth beneath me for grounding. He screamed again into the vacuum. His body then turned toward a gray mass growing in front of him. It was a small storm cloud… Hovering just feet above the ground, the cloud waited for him. He jumped on the cloud, and it lifted him higher and closer to the storm. He lifted his arms again in a strange fighting stance, palms open and forward.

I flipped to my knees. Scrambling to crawl away, I shivered violently. I was hallucinating, and I couldn't waste any more time. I made it to my feet, still crouched and panting. The edge of the canal looked like a rough descent. Gripping a thick root, I started to lower myself into it. Then my head was hit by something large and hard. The root ripped out of my palm, skinning it raw. My vision strobed as I fell forward. I tumbled down the steep, muddy drop-off and landed at the waterline with a splash. Laying on my back, I groaned and looked to the sky. As my vision faded to dark, I could only see a brief glimpse of the man surfing atop a cloud high above me, using an unseen force to send ripples into the storm.

5

O'DOHERTY: OVER THE LACE

My hearty laughter definitely had people staring. Fabian covered his face, all of it flushed a deep red, and he laughed between words.

"And that little medication mix up was when I realized that I wasn't best suited to care for Nana alone."

"Well, you did your best and that's what matters," I said with cheeks aching from a constant smile. He was funny and so sweet. There was no reason why we shouldn't have had an instant rapport. It was certainly not that I didn't have an affinity for him. There was just something blocking it, I guess. *Someone.*

Very punctually, he had picked me up with flowers in hand. He opened every door and pulled out my seat at the restaurant—all the things a gentleman would do to court you. He inquired about my life and listened intently. He told me about his life too.

"I'm a computer programmer," he said.

"Oh! Good with computers. That is a super valuable skill these days. But do you know how to tap into my payroll and get me a raise?" I joked.

"I may or may not have a talent for hacking."

I tilted my head and raised my brows. "Oh? Okay!"

"I may or may not have gotten into a little trouble as a teenager with it too, so… I don't do anything crazy anymore," he said, moving his hands.

"Why not? You have to have a little fun, right?"

"Well, at my age fun means buying a really good vacuum, designing video games, and cooking great food."

"What, no wild late nights and partying these days?" I laughed, swirling my drink.

He paused for a moment and shook his head slowly. "Nahhh. I only ever drink on special occasions, and even then it's not much."

"Well then, to Nana, who finally got her way," I raised my wine glass in a toast. He gently clicked his glass against mine. Mariella had apparently been telling him all about me just as frequently as she would tell me about him. Despite almost dying this morning, she was absolutely elated that the universe finally crossed our paths. She had been trying to play matchmaker with us for months upon months. So much so that she called an old friend whose son owned the restaurant and got us an impossible reservation at the last minute.

"Oh, she hasn't stopped talking about it," he said, reaching under his glasses to rub his eyes. "She speaks very highly of you, by the way."

I hummed with a smile. "She's very kind. So, what now? It will be a while before *Mayflower* is rebuilt," I asked.

"Oh, I have a home health company coming by. *Mayflower* was great, and I've learned a lot from them about helping her. But I think it's better this way," he said. He truly cared. It shouldn't surprise me to meet someone who didn't discard their loved ones, never to give them a second thought. But that's the hapless world we live in. Fabian had an uncommon compassion and consideration.

"Awe, that's sweet. I'm sure she appreciates it."

"What else am I supposed to do?" he asked, laughing.

"And how about your back? How is it?" I asked. He had cringed a few times throughout the night and guarded his movements, but hadn't so much as complained.

"All patched up." He nodded, and I studied him harder, calling his bluff. "It's pretty tender," he admitted with a chuckle. "How about you? Did you find anything out about the patients?"

"No! Nothing. The only things that they have in common are rocks and Meriflec. I wish I would have come sooner," I signed.

"You wish you could have been there for the storm?"

"No…" I smiled. "Janet said the patients made some kind of *labyrinth* with the rocks. That would have been interesting to see. I can't be certain it would have answered my questions, but…"

"Well, why didn't you just ask?" he said nonchalantly, bending to the side with a semblance of pain to retrieve his phone from his back pocket. He pulled up a photo and offered me the phone. I hesitated in disbelief that he actually had a picture. I accepted the phone, doubting such fortune, and studied the photo. It was dark, but a clear pattern was discernible. "I took it as soon as I got there," he said. "It was 100% creepier in real life."

"What *is* this?" Shivers crawled down my spine. The photograph was confounding. The stones created a detailed pattern of winding pathways within a circle, with a single starburst in the center like a spinning star. If it was a maze or labyrinth or some other symbol, I didn't know.

"I'm not sure," Fabian shrugged. "I haven't had a chance to look into it yet, but I have plans to dig. There's something very creepy about it for sure."

I eyed him curiously, "You don't strike me as superstitious."

"Oh, I'm not! But this is no coincidence or a prank. Nana would have told me if she was in on it."

"Do you mind sending me a copy?" I asked.

"Not at all. Please do," he insisted and shared the photo to my phone.

THE CONVERSATION CARRIED EFFORTLESSLY ON THE DRIVE BACK TO my place. It wasn't until he got out to open my door that I heard silence for the first time tonight. But as he crossed the front of the car, something caught my eye back by the neighbor's house. My hair stood up on the back of my neck at what I thought was an unfamiliar face staring me down. I sat up straight to get a better look. But it disappeared into the shadows before I could make it out. I steadied my heart. Yet still, I had the profound feeling of being watched as we walked to the door, the wind nearly flinging up my skirt. I clung to Fabian's arm as I scanned the area again, finding nothing. His presence made me feel safe.

"Thank you for dinner. I had so much fun," I said. He took a deep inhale and nodded nervously, inching in. For a moment I felt terrible. He'd done nothing wrong at all, yet here I was hesitating. I couldn't shake the nagging feelings I had for Daphne—feelings I knew very well she didn't have for me. He deserved better. *I deserve better too*, I thought.

"I'd like to see you again soon," he said. I smiled up at him and he leaned in, resting a hand on my waist. My stomach tightened. I was suddenly very aware of my breathing. In love with Daphne or not,

Fabian did something to me that my body couldn't help but react to. I drew myself closer to him and met his lips. They were soft and, warm and caring. The surface of his tongue slipped between my lips on the second kiss, and heat washed over me. The third kiss was longer, and I traced my tongue across his bottom lip. My heart thumped hard against my ribs. When he pulled away, I realized my hands were on his chest. I noticed how warm and sturdy he felt.

I wasn't ready for him to leave. Not when his touch warmed me so easily. I had no reservations about him, no nagging feeling that something was amiss. My body urged me to keep him close.

"Do you want to come in?" I whispered. He worried his brows, nodding slowly.

A moment later, I was in his arms, pressed against the wall of the foyer, my legs around him. He kissed me deeper but still softly. His tongue swept into my mouth and my body lit up. Heavy breathing and short moans escaped us as we clambered into the kitchen. He placed me on the low breakfast bar. One hand braced my lower back. The other softly intertwined in my hair.

He pulled off his jacket and threw it on the counter with a clunk. A blue stone rolled out of the pocket across the granite countertop. It stopped near the stone I had placed there earlier.

"You got a souvenir too, huh?" I joked as he nipped at my neck. He laughed behind my ear and nodded. Then he dragged his tongue down my neck to my collarbone. I almost melted.

His arm swept me toward the edge of the counter. Then he grinded himself between my legs. I could feel his hard length pushing against my thigh through his pants. My hand reached down to explore the bulge. I traced a notable length before grabbing the entire shaft. The girth of it made me shrink in excitement. He scoffed at the ease of his arousal under my touch. I pulled up his shirt and he broke the kiss, sucking at my bottom lip before removing the garment.

He laid me down gently and pulled my silky coral top up below my breasts. He slowly kissed down the center of my abdomen. Finally, his lips met the seam of my charcoal skirt. My center heated as he massaged my inner thigh, working closer to my panties. His hands stopped at the hem of my skirt.

"Is this okay?" he asked, looking up at me.

"Yeah," I breathed, eager for the heat of his tongue. He worked my skirt over my wide hips. I opened my legs farther for him. With trembling lips he paused at the sight of my black lace panties.

"Ugh, that's beautiful," he whispered, leaning down and kissing over them. I could feel the heat of his breath through the thin material. The wet warmth between my legs started to build. "Tell me if you want to slow down, okay?" He offered before kissing over my panties again. This time his lips applied warm pressure to my clit over the lace. Then his warm tongue traced over the lace, dampening it and teasing me. I reached down and mussed his soft hair. In voiceless consent, I pulled his head toward me gently.

He moved a finger under my panties to pull them to the side. My heart leaped into my throat. The moment was invaded by a blaring alert. We both jolted.

"Ahh! sorry. Just a second." He pulled his phone out, promptly silencing the severe weather warning. He threw it on the counter. The rain pattered against the window. The flashes of distant lightning illuminated the room through the cracked blinds. It calmed me. He wasted no time dipping his face back down. Inching my panties to the side, he slowly kissed wherever skin became exposed. He traced his tongue up the side of my lip. I gave a breathy moan. Again, we were startled, now by the full-volume ringtone of his phone.

"Ugh. Why now?" He scrubbed his face.

"Maybe you should take that. It could be an emergency," I offered, with the hope he would turn it off and continue. He studied his phone. To my delight, he silenced the call again and propped my knee on his shoulder, kissing my inner thighs generously, working his way back to my panties. His hot breath barely reached my panties before his text tone pinged multiple times. He paused, resting his forehead on my lower belly. He grunted in frustration and kissed my panties again. "I'm so sorry." Another kiss. "I am *so* sorry." The phone rang again. He stood to answer it.

I bit my lip and sat up, pulling at the bottom of my skirt and smoothing it. "It's fine."

"Hello? What's up?" Fabian said into his phone, almost harshly. I could hear a voice speaking loudly but could not make out the words. Fabian's eyes squinted and his face scrunched. "Ahh. Okay. It's Okay. Calm down; I'll be there soon." He was helping me up and off the counter before the call was finished.

"What happened?" I asked.

"That was my sister. Nana had an episode. She's going to the hospital. They think she had a stroke."

"I'm so sorry. I hope she's okay." I straightened my skirt. He adjusted himself in his pants and threw his shirt back.

"I'm making this up to you, okay?" he said, cupping my face gently and giving me a quick kiss. He shimmied into his jacket. "I'll make you breakfast or… or dinner?"

"Just take care of Nana first. When she's settled, give me a call and let me know she's okay. We'll go from there." I smiled. We walked to the door and he kissed my hand. The streetlamps shining through the yellow, pink, and red stained glass of my door left a whimsical pattern on his face. He placed another apologetic kiss on my hand as he pulled himself toward the door.

"I'll see you soon," he said before ducking into the rain.

"Tell Nana I'll be by to see her tomorrow!" I called after him.

As soon as the door clicked shut, I leaned against its stained glass and smiled wide. I pushed myself off the door to get my medication from the kitchen. When I sipped my water to wash down the Zerpotine, the two blue stones caught my eye. I pushed them closer together with my nail and smirked at the possibility of having something real for once. I skipped through the open space between my kitchen and living room, finally stopping in my bedroom to peel off my clothes and take a cold shower.

6

DAPHNE: BUT I WAS FLOATING

COLD WATER WAS DRIPPING, ECHOING LOUDLY AND POOLING UNDER me. I forced my eyes open, and above me I saw… *metal?* Yes. Ribbed metal surrounded me. It was dark and cold and wet. I worked my weight onto my elbows, and I took note of the frigid puddle under me. My head spun for a moment as I lifted it, but the weight of my saturated hair grounded me. Cold as fuck, I shivered and took in my surroundings. *Where am I?*

It was dark. At my feet, the cold metal cylinder was open like a balcony to a dirt and gravel earth lit by the moonlight. The sound of lapping water could be heard nearby. My breath was a faint fog. The soaked scrub jacket clung to my body and gave me no warmth. I squeezed out my hair with numb fingers and moved myself to the opening, keeping my gaze on the ground to gauge the drop-off.

Only a couple of yards. I can make it.

With a push and a leap, my feet found the damp dirt, sending a sharp sting up my shins. My knees buckled, and my hands broke the forward fall. Under the weight of my body, water seeped up from the dirt and around my fingers, chilling them more. Dirt stuck to the cuffs of my scrub jack and made its way under my nails. Pushing up to a stand made the world spin for a moment. My legs trembled like a newborn fawn. I threw out my arms and steadied myself.

But nothing could have steadied my heart from what was in front of me. Tremors shot through my entire body. They were not just from the cold reaching my bones but from the eight-foot dams on either side of me. Tree limbs, branches, and rock were cemented with a thin layer of ice on both sides. They held a backflow of stormwater in the irrigation canal. My feet moved quickly as I turned to the steep wall, looking for any path out. As if carved out on purpose, a narrow stairway of ice and earth climbed up the wall of the canal to the right of the irrigation drain I had been lying in. Each step was made of pine needles and dirt frozen solid. To the side of it, a fallen tree—trimmed to its short limbs—acted as a railing. I swallowed hard.

I wasted no time to stare in awe. It didn't matter who crafted the stairway. The icy dams were creaking like an old ship. I gripped the tree railing for stability. Then I climbed the steps, thankful for the bark embedded on their surface. I would definitely slip without their traction. The groaning of the dams seemed to grow louder with every chest-rattling thump of my heart, and I hurried up the makeshift stairway.

As soon as I was at the top, the sound of breaking wood and rushing water crashed behind me. I gasped, spinning to see the dams breaking under the weight of water. The water churned and splashed from either side. Violently, it surged and collided around the freed wood. The stairway melted into the chaos below. I stepped back frantically, only to fall on my ass.

It wasn't until then that I could feel a change in the atmosphere around me. I felt as though I had stepped from a forcefield back into the exposed world. The bright moonlight above the rough waters dimmed, and suddenly, things were less mystical and utterly normal. This did nothing to calm my pounding heart or trembling body. In fact, the frightening feeling only amplified when, in my periphery, I caught the sight of my belongings stacked neatly a few yards away under a broken tree.

I stood on my feet and took in my surroundings. Memories of a man with opal eyes crashed over me in waves. *Is he here? Is he real?* It was too dark to be certain. I didn't see anyone here. Despite feeling the pressing of eyes on me, I was almost certain I was alone. I wiped my nose on my sleeve and scooped up my belongings.

Dread scraped down my back as the sound of sticks snapped in the darkness. I charged forward. Again, the snapping of sticks came from another direction. Alone in the woods with a creep was not where I wanted to be. Rescued or not, he could have easily carried me back to a public area. Instead, he hid my half-live body in an irrigation drain in the back of the woods.

I figured this would be an uncomfortable hike full of sharp, splintered earth. But to my surprise, I had a clear path ahead. It was like the twister left the footprint of a giant between the canal and the street. The only exception was about seven meters of bent trees at either end. I ran for it.

When I finally reached the street, the sight was devastating. The buildings were all but toppled, windows shattered. My eyes blurred in and out as I somehow made it back to my car. It was just a block to the main road that led to the intersection where I parked. It was incredible to see the drastic difference from one side of the road to the other. On one side was ruin that worsened the farther back it went. On the other side, it was untouched, and there in the hospital's parking lot, parked at the corner, was my M3 in almost perfect condition.

. . .

I CLIMBED IN MY CAR AND IMMEDIATELY CHECKED MY MIRRORS TO look for any cloud-riding weirdos, and I sighed in relief when I saw none. I looked at the hospital ahead. Clearly, I had suffered head injuries and had been hallucinating. It would be in my best interest to check myself in and get looked at. But the flashing lights of ambulances told me they were overwhelmed by the second local tragedy in days.

What was even more concerning was the idea of Lyndie Pratt getting wind that I was a patient and catching me in a vulnerable state. Who knew what she might suggest to the staff when catching news of my hallucinations.

Anyway. It was the middle of the night. I was tired. I was no longer bleeding. Even though I suspected it was due to shock, I didn't feel pain either. *I'm fine.*

But with the chattering of my teeth, the concern for hypothermia came to the forefront of my mind. I stripped down to nothing, leaving my sopping wet clothes on the fiberless mat of my passenger side floor. "Thank God for illegal window tint," I muttered under my breath.

I grabbed the fleece blanket that I used on the way to work and wrapped it around my naked body at the shoulder. When I started my car, I immediately adjusted the heat settings, opening the blanket in front of the hot vents while looking around for anyone who might have seen me undress. *When the fuck did Miami get this cold?*

The shivering started to steady as the heat blew into the blanket from the air vents and kissed my bare skin, but I still craved a hot coffee to warm my bones. The time was 03:30. The unscathed coffee shop down the street was open, and nothing could stop me from a steaming cup of their dark roast. *Come hell or... Twister.*

I lowered the fleece throw, tucking it under my armpits and wearing it like a towel. Then, I compressed the clutch to move into first gear. A quick glance at my shifter caused me to recoil with a gasp, and I stalled the car out in a jolting clunk of angry gears. My wrist was draped with something incredible. I was wearing a bracelet that I had never seen before. I studied the beautiful piece closely in disbelief.

What the f...

The bracelet had flat, oblong links of shiny white gold, boasting elaborate tendrils in their hollow center. Cradled in the tendrils were sparkling round cuts of the most vibrant and flawlessly clear amethysts I had ever seen. Between each link were oval-shaped obsidian beads. Carved into the obsidian stone were matching tendrils filled with white gold. It was breathtaking. I flipped my palm upward to find the round magnetic clasp also crafted of white gold. One side of the clasp was engraved with an infinity symbol. I turned it to study the other side and drew breath to find it paved with tiny yet perfect rose quartz.

Great, I have a stalker now.

I wedged my thumbnail between the magnets to release the band. This gift was too extravagant to be given by a stranger without equally intense expectations.

The magnetic clasp separated and fell to my lap, but before it could land, excruciating pain hit me at all angles. My head split in anguish. My brow stung where the hail first struck me. Every inch of my body that had been hit now throbbed and stung. Every space in between was stiff and achy. I felt intense hunger, fatigue, and dizziness. My panic amplified. I groaned and panted and hissed. My hands shook, not from cold but from pain.

I retrieved the bracelet. Trembling, I refastened the piece, and like magic, my ailments nearly disappeared. I shook my head, trying to make sense of it. I took measured breaths to calm myself.

One thing at a time. Coffee. Home. Sleep.

THE COFFEE WAS NEARLY GONE BY THE TIME I PULLED INTO MY driveway. My power must have been out because the garage door wouldn't open. I pushed open the front door, and Polpetta greeted me anxiously in the dark. I heard some of my clothes fall out of my hand, but between the awkward hold of my fleece blanket and Polpetta urging me to go potty, I didn't bother picking them up. We hurried to the back of the house, where she waited for her chance to potty under her favorite tree.

The tree was a beastly thing that clawed roots deep into the earth. I draped my soaked scrubs over a low branch to dry and hurried inside to escape the cold. I left the door open for Polpetta to roam as long as she wanted while I headed for a much-needed shower. I silently hoped the hot water tank had a reserve of warmth. And thank the water heater Gods, it did. I let out a long sigh as the water warmed my skin.

After a too-short shower, I dried off in the bathroom, trying to peer into the mirror through the darkness. I used the towel to squeeze out my hair. I couldn't see much, but in the shadows, I could tell welts had formed from being hit with hail. But still, they didn't hurt.

I threw on a loose and cozy waffle pajama set and sat at the side of my bed, studying the bracelet in the light from my window. Was I imagining the pain? Should I try to remove it again? Even if it was a gift from a wack job, it was incredibly unique and gorgeous. I didn't entirely wish to be rid of it. *Am I crazy?* What was real and what wasn't?

My mind was spinning with everything I had seen. I didn't have the mental battery to challenge myself again. Not tonight. *One thing at a time. Sleep.* Yet the coffee left me wired, a poor choice for 4:00 AM. I noticed the cup of water on my nightstand and grabbed it. A cold sip of fresh ice water poured down my throat and—*Ice water? What the fuck...* I hadn't gotten ice water. As quickly as panic grew in me, it disappeared and was replaced by absolute euphoria unlike anything I had ever experienced. I laid back and felt as though my body was lifted on a breeze and weightlessly floating.

But I *was* floating, hovering above my bed five feet in the air as the tickle of wind wrapped around me, grazing every inch of my body to lift it. It tussled my hair dry, and with a strong puff, it fluffed the mattress below me. And slowly I sank as if gravity was no demanding thing, rocking down closer to my bed. The covers still hovered over me as they followed me downward, fluffing and straightening under their own gust. I was as weightless as a feather, unafraid, accepting, and connected to everything around me. My fears about the man in the woods were too distant to remember; the only regard for him now was a note of his robust features.

The memory of him drew my hands between my thighs. My sinking halted, and I stayed laying on nothing but air, still feet above my bed. It was like floating in space. The covers hovering above me stalled and then folded toward the foot. *Did these sheets come alive with magic?* I laughed out loud at the silly thought. The giggle echoed in my ears.

I felt electrically charged on every part of my body, like zaps of neon light buzzing on the surface of my skin as my fingers worked circles around my clit. My bottoms tugged low, even without hands to pull them, and I took a deep, calm breath. The only sensation was a dense breeze on my hips and calves as my bottoms reached my ankles.

My head fell to the side in pleasure from my fingers sliding on my most sensitive part, but the wind shackled my wrists and pressed them over my head. I should have been scared, but I could only bite my lip at the invisible aggression. Through lazy eyelids, my vision was blurred, but I could see the form of a man outside my window. Again, no fear. There was only an inviting bliss cradling my body, and I smiled as I dug my teeth further into my lip. This illusion outside my window was an intoxicating replica of the man in the woods. So much so that I noted the colorful sparkle of his eyes through the darkness between us.

A cold wind danced up my loose top and turned icy as it skated over my nipples. I moaned with a half giggle that echoed almost endlessly. Warm liquid expanded in my core, between my legs, stretching me wider and thrusting itself deeper. It pumped inside me the way I imagined he would. It felt as though the warmth of a man was endlessly emptying into me and moving over every inch between my legs in densely contained splashes. Waves crashed up against my clit, over and over again.

The pleasure made my eyes roll shut, but they inched open again to see the blurry silhouette of the man. He leaned against my window with one hand, the other hand gripping himself below his undone belt and firmly massaging his length. The light was too dim for me to appreciate his pleasuring in full, but I sent a challenging stare into his sparkling eyes. I could see the neon electricity that hummed and crackled in the space between us.

Another breeze up my shirt felt like ice being rubbed over my peaks. The crashing waves of warm liquid poured into me harder. Every part of me was entirely too sensitive to bear it. It pushed me gently over the edge. My release was a slow ecstasy. Through my drug-induced euphoria, my moans sounded like music echoing in the air. The sounds were dueted by a growl of a man matching my climax with his. The sounds intermingled with phantom tunes that played in my ears now. He was still there, the illusion, watching me... Waiting for me. I could feel him in my being as if connected by the pull of a magnet.

Lost in the music of moans and the warm, sizzling pleasure on my skin, my body sank again into the plush of the mattress. I lay limply, staring at my magnificent illusion of the man with a heaving chest, tucking himself back into his jeans. He disappeared from outside my window, and a moment later, he stood at my bedside, a sparkling mist swirling around him.

Slowly, the rush of warm water retreated from my center and evaporated into a steamy mist that lifted from me. A moan escaped me at the strange feeling of withdrawal. My nipples warmed, and the wet spots on my bedding and clothes dried.

The covers floated down, unfolding, and lay snuggly on top of me. The warmth of the covers and the safety of his watch were the last comforts I needed to fall into a deep sleep. The last I saw of this illusion was him kneeling near my bed.

7

O'DOHERTY: DARLING RITUALS

I WOKE UP WITH A LONG STRETCH AND FELT REFRESHED. HASTILY, I scrambled for my phone to see if Fabian called. My phone was still lying on the kitchen counter. I jogged from my room in my underwear to grab it. Unlike Daphne's closed-off duplex, I preferred an open concept that seamlessly integrated rooms. I loved a lot of natural light and warm, rich colors. From the living room, you could see past the kitchen counter to an adorable dinette in the back. There, the table was tucked in a nook with three windows.

I scooped up my phone and sat at the dinette with a cup of orange juice. I had a missed message from Daphne. My heart skipped a few beats, nervous to tell her about my date. But then a smile creased my cheeks when my eyes fell on a missed call from Fabian.

My fingers typed feverishly, responding to him. He answered immediately.

> She's doing better but is weak. They're
> keeping her here for observation.

I am so sorry to hear that. We can do a rain check on dinner.

Oh, no way! Nana already insisted I come see you. She doesn't like to be fussed over, trust me. She'll kill me if I don't.

Are you sure?

I'm very sure. I'm on my way to pick up some steaks.

Oh steaks? I love steak.

Good I'll get you a nice cut and I'll make some homemade macaroni and cheese and some prosciutto wrapped asparagus. How's that sound? 😎

That sounds amazing. I can make dessert then.

How about that? I'll get those sugar free jellos

Too late. I'm already making you apple pie. You cook next time. 🥧

He mentioned he liked to cook, but I never expected anything so extravagant. I called Daphne next, shamefully debating if I should hang up before she had a chance to answer. But I waited, pacing through the kitchen to the living room. The line rang and rang…and rang until it went to voicemail. *That's odd. She's always up this early.*

I put my phone down on the counter and thumbed the two blue stones. In my periphery, I noticed a glimmer coming from the foyer floor. I pushed off the counter to take a closer look. Water had gotten in from the storm last night.

This weather…

I skated a towel along the floor with my foot quickly. There was no time to waste on pondering the weather. I wanted to stop by the regional office for pharmaceutical representatives to see what I could find out about these rocks and where they came from. Although unlikely, perhaps their supplier had contamination that led to the peculiar behavior. Afterward, I would go to the hospital to assess the trial patients and see if they could recall anything remarkable about the rocks or their strange symptoms.

The drive to the regional office was more prolonged than expected. Traffic was gridlocked. Those native to the area knew to leave early because Miami is exactly one hour away from Miami. I watched a long trail of taillights glow red on the highway against the dark and dusty lavender sky. The morning radio show would usually perk me up. Today, however, their segment on the recent storm damage had me unsettled.

The National Weather Service issued a statement this morning. The recent thunderstorms and tornadoes developed unexpectedly and too quickly to issue a warning to the community. The tornadoes have been relatively weak, short-lived, and haven't traveled very far. Chief Meteorologist Mikayla Nook stated this morning that they are working on an advanced detection system and will continue to give the community the best early detection and warning systems they have available. It is strongly advised to avoid or evacuate areas with unexpectedly poor weather and hail. Take shelter in the center of a structure or reach the lowest ground.

Occasionally, commercials for *Amett Health* would chime in, discussing their disaster relief programs for communities affected by the recent tornadoes. Despite the narrator's calming voice and the upbeat background music, the commercials sounded disingenuous to me, like a smart business opportunity. I hadn't missed that nearly all of the communities affected were wealthy areas that were in close proximity to *Amett Health* facilities. They undoubtedly wanted to capitalize off of their tragedy by offering mental health services through their partners, *Heartly*.

After last night's storm— I scoffed and flipped the radio. The reports were repetitive, so I turned on an upbeat playlist from my phone.

WHEN I ARRIVED AT THE OFFICE, IT LOOKED VERY ORDINARY. THE beige two-story building was built sometime in the eighties, I guessed based off of the large, jaggedly rounded rock face trim and steep sloping brown metal roof. It was maintained well, and the vibrant Hibiscus flowers offered gorgeous pops of pinkish-red color.

I walked through the glass double doors to find a pleasantly updated interior lobby. In the center was a curved receptionist desk, flanked posteriorly by two halls. The desk was manned by a slim, young blonde woman with bright pink lipstick and a tight, low bun. She greeted me with a smile, and I returned the gesture as I took long strides toward her.

"Hi, I'm O'doherty, the research specialist for Meriflec. I was wondering who I could talk to about the Meriflec trial at *Mayflower*?" I asked pleasantly.

"Oh. Uhh. Let me see if I can find that out for you," she said while thumbing through her directory. "Are there any particular questions you have?"

"Yes. Thank you. I would like to know about the sourcing of their promotional material."

"Mmhm. Okay, just a moment." She smiled and dialed a number from her desk phone. It was noticeably deserted in the lounge aside from us. There was complete silence apart from her dialing and the diffuser sending a wonderful lavender mist into the air. She spoke into the receiver and told the person about my inquiry.

"Yes, she's here now…. Okay. I'll let her know," she said cheerfully before docking the receiver. "Ms. Alex Graves will be right with you. Have a seat." Her slim hand motioned to the lobby with far too many chairs. I sat in the closest one and waited patiently as the receptionist typed away and thumbed through folders.

Clicking heels echoed with increasing volume as they approached from the hall to the right. Moments later, a slight, older woman with thin lips and gray hair done up in a French roll greeted me with her arm outstretched. I grasped her cold, wrinkled hand for a shake.

"Hello, Ms.…?"

"Sameal. O'doherty Sameal. I'm a nurse with the clinical research—"

"Yes, yes. Gisele told me. I have only a few minutes. We can speak in my office," she cut in and relinquished my hand swiftly. The harshness of her demeanor didn't go unnoticed. I felt a familiar flutter in my gut that usually arose when interacting with confident yet short-tempered people. It was the same feeling that caused me to humble myself and behave overly amiable. I shoved the feeling down and lifted my chin, remembering I was there in a professional capacity with an obligation to my patients.

I followed her down the hall to the right, past several empty offices and a stairwell. A wall plaque by the stairs indicated the second-story suites were vacant. Her office at the end of the hall was somehow both drab and streamlined. I settled in the chair across her desk and pushed myself to start the conversation in a confident tone.

"I'd like to know where your company sourced this item," I stated, retrieving the stone from my pocket, with a napkin as a barrier, and placing it on her desk. Her nostrils flared slightly at the sight, and I noticed a stillness flash upon her face. *What was that emotion?* A bored irritation was now in its place.

"A rock? You came to talk about rocks, Ms. Sameal?" she said, scratching the side of her mouth with an almond-shaped nail before folding her hands on her desk. If I hadn't imagined her initial reaction, she was nearly convincing me I had.

"It's my understanding your pharmaceutical reps left these with the residents after completing patient education on Meriflec. Every patient who received one exhibited a strange behavior, and it's my job to rule out external causes so as to not assume it is a side effect of the medication itself," I pressed.

"And you think these rocks are brainwashing them?" she retorted impatiently with wide eyes and a mocking shake of her chin that shook her wrinkled jowls.

"The rocks could have been contaminated by a substance that can alter one's neurological function. I need to investigate that," I answered calmly. The conflict drew a knot in my throat. I strained to stop from swallowing it, determined not to show any sign of weakness.

"Ms. Sameal, perhaps you have time to chase nonsensical theories. However, I do not," she pushed, emphasizing the *t*. She was very clearly about to dismiss me.

"It's strange for a pharmaceutical representative to educate a patient. Usually that's the nurse's job. The reps educate the physicians and occasionally hold in-services for the staff. But you guys? You made a whole packet for hundreds of patients, complete with a rather stunning paperweight, and hand-delivered it yourselves," I challenged with furrowed brows. My stomach was in knots from the boldness of my accusation. I could feel my vision tunneling from the nerves. But I had to make some implication to draw out any answer. The change in her breathing pattern and pursing of her lips told me it worked. *What is she hiding?*

"Staffing isn't so great at that facility, is it? We offered to educate the patients instead of expecting the staff to. We are *invested* in the *success* of this *trial*," she retorted, her almond-shaped nail tapping the desk with each word. "If I could give you some advice, kiddo, stick to your scope," she popped the *p*. "*You* are not a mineralogist or a neurologist *OR* a parasomnia specialist for *that* matter. I have a meeting. See yourself out." She emphasized the *t*.

I grabbed the rock with the tissue barrier, wrapped it once, and pocketed it, keeping eye contact with her purely to maintain my confident façade. "Thank you for your time," I said softly to show no bother, and moved unhurried to the door.

As soon as I closed her office door, I let out a breath and swallowed hard. My heart was racing from the rage of her belittling words and crassness.

"What a *witch,*" I huffed under my breath. My nerves calmed more the further I walked from her domineering presence. But I stopped cold in my tracks when I reached the airy lobby, and a realization came over me.

Parasomnia specialist? I recalled.

I hadn't elaborated on exactly *what* the patient's strange behavior was, yet somehow she knew they were sleepwalking. *How would she know?* It isn't typical for reps or their management to be notified of an incident, and surely no one would dare bother *her* with unconfirmed reports of a faulty product. So how did she know about the sleepwalking?

"Ma'am? Are you okay?" Gisele asked in a sweet voice.

"Yes. Thank you. I have a long drive ahead. May I use your restroom?"

"Sure, it's down this hall." She pointed to the other side of her desk. The hall to the left of her led me to several doors. I passed a dark, empty conference room with a glass window on the door, a broom closet, and two restrooms. Finally, I reached the last door. There, at the end of the hall, was a supply room. I tested the handle and found it unlocked.

Perfect.

I checked the hall behind me for movement. It was a pointless caution. Most representatives worked from their cars, traveling to different facilities. They only checked into the offices for supplies, meetings, and HR issues. Gisela and Alex were surely the only two people here this early. Regardless, I hurried through the threshold and flipped a switch before closing the door quietly. Flickering fluorescent light cast a yellow hue on metal shelves. Flesh-toned filing cabinets lined the walls of the stuffy room. I studied the various cardboard boxes that were shelved haphazardly. Finally, I came upon an open box at the bottom. Inside the box were several of the blue stones. Some were cracked, and some were whole. These stones were all lackluster compared to the ones Fabian and I found at *Mayflower*.

I pulled the box forward and tried to identify any markings that would indicate the supplier's name. I had no such luck. Then, after closing the flaps with a huff, I smiled at the sight of a shipping label on the flap.

"Darling Rituals," I read aloud, squinting my eyes. I pulled out my phone. With shaking hands, I captured a photo of the label. I tried to ensure the address and name were legible. But the lighting was too dark, my hands too shaky. I couldn't linger any longer. I was losing my nerve. I ripped off the labeled cardboard flap and shoved the box back in place. I pocketed the flap in a large side pocket of my scrub pants.

Then I leaned an ear against the cold door. Silence told me no one was around. Quietly, I opened the door and slipped out. I walked down the hall, smoothing out my scrubs and white coat. But I felt as though the walls had eyes. Just as I passed the conference room door, I swore a white-haired man had materialized behind its window. I drew breath and turned to face him. No one was there.

Why am I so paranoid lately?

As soon as my car door shut, I let out a huff. I took out the cardboard flap with the shipping label and typed the address into my phone's navigation app. The location was a few hours away, and I still had to visit my patients in the hospital. I certainly would *not* be missing dinner with Fabian, either. It would, unfortunately, have to wait.

I fastened my seatbelt and started the car. My eyes were meant to focus on the rearview mirror as I pulled out of the parking spot, but a form behind the glass doors of the building caught my attention. It was hard to tell through the darkly tinted glass, which now reflected the first rays of the morning sun, but the form appeared to be that of a young man. He had white hair with charcoal roots and was staring at me intensely with black eyes. I froze, looking back at him. And then he simply walked away.

8

DAPHNE: A CLOUD RIDING CREEPER

I woke up with drool soaking my cheek. I had slept harder than a patient on Propofol. Why else was I on *this* side of the bed? From the angle and intensity of the light through my window I could tell it was late in the day. I drew a deep breath through my nose, squinted through heavy lids, and lifted myself on an elbow in silent search for my phone. The sluggish patting of my hands over the covers was no use. I tried to piece together where I left it last night.

Last night.

I sat up fast at the memory of what happened. It was sobering. The light flooding my face from the window adjusted my eyes quickly and painfully. Was it a memory or was that head injury worse than I thought? I hurried to look for clues of what was reality and dream.

The glass of ice water.

On my nightstand, the glass still sat filled with water. Next to it was my phone, plugged into the spare charger. *The power's back on.*

The water mixed without a hint of sediment as I swirled the bottom of the glass. There was no odor either. I grabbed it and headed for my door, eyeing Polpetta on the way out.

"Polly, come, it's time to go potty," I called from my door jam. It occurred to me that Polpette was inside. I looked out of my door jam at the back door. It was closed—locked even.

The lock clicked as I pushed it free. A whoosh of the slider opening was followed by the sounds of evening traffic and kids still playing in the street. I was met by a wall of humidity when I stepped out cautiously, Polpetta sprinting past my heels to mark the twisted bark of a large tree. I walked to the left, toward my bedroom window. The rain had washed away any chance of seeing footprints or evidence of a man's release.

With a fling of my arm, the water splashed into the grass. I got my scrubs from the low-hanging branch and brought them across the space into the garage where the washer and dryer were. I stopped only to drop the glass in the sink before starting the small load of laundry and heading to the bathroom to assess my wounds.

The reflection in the bathroom mirror took me by surprise. My brow was bruised and cut but clean and not too swollen. I flinched as I prodded it with my fingertip, more out of anticipation than actual pain. The pain was surprisingly not that bad, yet the shock and adrenaline letdown was long gone. For the day after, it actually looked days ahead in its healing. It was an eyesore all the same. The same could be said for the scattering of scrapes and welts that marked my body. The back of my head, however, had a large knot from the blow that knocked me into the canal. Visions of the opal-eyed man yelling at me in the storm just before the fall flashed before my eyes as I traced the lump with my fingers.

The stunning bracelet that was still on my wrist came to mind, and I looked at it as my hand fell from my head. So far I had no reason to believe that the strange things that happened were anything more than the result of head trauma. Now that I was clear-headed and well-rested, testing the effects of removing the bracelet again would give me some insight.

My fingers trembled as I wedged my thumbnail between the magnets of the white gold and jewel-encrusted clasp. I wasn't sure I wanted to know what would happen when the piece was removed. After a moment of hesitation, I laughed off such a silly fear and pushed my nail in to separate the clasp.

The bracelet landed in the sink with delicate clinks, but my heave of agony was louder. The pain was nauseating and threw me off balance. Hunger burned in my stomach. My skin stung and throbbed. My head was in a vise. My shaking hand found the jeweled links. I refastened it as quickly as my unsteady fingers would allow me to. As soon as the magnets connected the pain was dulled to almost nothing. I panted and gasped for a moment before letting out a sob. I covered my mouth as I fell against the wall behind me.

Was he real? Did he rescue me? Did he break into my home and drug me? Did he touch me? Did he... ride a storm cloud and... give me an enchanted bracelet?

A laugh escaped my tear-soaked face at how freaking ridiculous it all sounded.

What the hell am I saying?

But last night he was as real as the walls around me. I was wearing a bracelet that took away my pain. My stomach churned. I fell to my knees in front of the toilet, and bile spilled out.

"This can't be real," I groaned into the bowl with a nasally voice, and the words echoed back from the vomit-stained water. I spat foul-tasting saliva into the bowl and wiped my mouth. "Get it together, Daph." Polpette sat next to me, crying and nudging my elbow up with her nose. She demanded cuddles, and I wrapped my arm around her, pulling her close.

"Did you see anyone last night, Polly?" I asked through glassy eyes and congested sinuses. She sniffed me and lowered her head on my lap. The reality of my state was sobering. I was never the person who sat defeated on her bathroom floor, crying and scared. Who was to say bits of reality and dreams weren't jumbled together? All I could do then was pick myself up and face this head on.

I pulled myself from the floor and cleaned myself up. I chose a long-sleeve shirt and jeans to cover my welts and went to the kitchen to get food. I made a toasted tuna fish sandwich with Swiss cheese and opened an extra can for Polly. Then I found my place at my high-top two seater in the corner of my kitchen by the window.

I took my time eating the meal. It wasn't until I dropped the dish in the sink that the empty countertop of the kitchen's cutaway caught my attention. My medication had always been there since the day I moved in, but it wasn't. Then I realized I hadn't taken my medication the night before or the morning before that… or at least I couldn't remember taking it. I sucked the stray mess of tuna mix off my thumb and took a quick look around the kitchen.

It couldn't have gone far…

I washed my hands, flicked the water off into the sink, and started the search for the bottle. I searched for nearly an hour and could find not one stray pill. The medication was nowhere, not the trash, the freezer, nor the dustiest space under my bed.

"Odie…" I sighed. She had forgotten her meds the other night when she slept over. She must have taken them by mistake.

That has to be it, I thought. I startled at a loud noise, my heart pumping. *It's just the washer.* I walked into the garage to the screeching buzzer and pulled the scrubs from the washer's barrel. When I opened the dryer door to move them in, I froze.

The plush blanket I had wrapped myself in last night, along with my panties and bra I had dropped on the floor, was in the dryer. I reached in and shuttered at the faint warmth that was still on its plush folds. It smelled freshly washed and had the distinct scent of dryer sheets. I slept all night and day. One thing I was sure of was that at no point today was I in a state fit to do a load of laundry. Whoever did this left before I woke up. *Did they take my medication with them?*

The thought pissed me off. However, that was neither here nor there. Today would be night two without my medication, and compliance has always been stressed. It was too late to call Dr. Bailey's office for a refill. I decided to visit O'doherty and see if she had swiped mine or if I could snag a few of hers to hold me over. I grabbed my purse and phone, locked up, and headed over.

The drive wasn't too far, and if it weren't for traffic, I'd have arrived sooner. The sight of an unfamiliar Durango in her driveway grabbed my attention as I made my way to the front door and knocked. The door was framed in a reddish-stained rosewood. It had a large mosaic of pink and red flowers in the stained glass. Chatter quieted from inside, and soon O'doherty swung open the door. Her happy face shifted into worry.

"Daph, what happened?" she fussed, giving me a once-over. Her reaction confirmed that she was not the person who washed my laundry. She fussed over me, moving her hands over my arms and taking me in. I walked past her and dropped my keys on her foyer table. "Are you okay?"

"Yeah, I got caught in a storm last night. Got hit with some hail and shit. I'm fine." I brushed off the concern and made my way to the living room. To my surprise, some cute guy with wire frame glasses was standing behind the kitchen counter packing up leftovers. He gave me a curious look as I entered.

"This is Fabian. I met him at *Mayflower* during the aftermath of the storm," O'doherty offered, walking in from behind me. She cradled her elbows in her arms and was tense. She looked like she was doing the walk of shame, for God's sake. As if we didn't dish about our sexcapades regularly. "Fabian, this is my best friend, Daphne."

Fabian wiped his hands on his apron, came from behind the counter with a genuine smile, and extended a hand. "Oh, it's so good to meet you," he said.

I shook his hand, not entirely in the mood for peopling, but tried to be cordial since I was clearly crashing their date. "Yeah. Nice to meet you too." I turned my eyes to Odie. "I'm so sorry. I didn't realize you had company. I should've called," I said apologetically.

"Oh, no, no! Are you kidding?" she stammered far too enthusiastically.

I pushed some hair behind my ear, ready to excuse myself, but the bracelet caught her eye. She grabbed my wrist and studied it.

"Oh, Daph! This is gorgeous. I've never seen anything like it. Where did you get this?" O'doherty fawned.

"Ah…" I stumbled over my words. I thought better than to trauma dump the strange details on her, especially in front of someone I didn't know. "A man gave it to me."

"A man?"

"Yeah. He actually helped me during the storm." I nodded, pointing to my bruised and scabbed brow. "He got me to safety and then gave me the bracelet… I think. It's kind of a blur," I said with fake confusion. It was then I realized *all* of the details were strange.

"So a kind stranger just gave you a one-of-a-kind piece of expensive jewelry after heroically rescuing you from a storm? And that is that? Are you *seeing* him again?" She prodded with a strange energy. The question brought a tremble to my lip that she couldn't help but notice. "Daph? Is everything alright?"

"Yeah. I'm fine. Listen, can I talk to you for a second," I asked, pointing to the foyer.

"Yeah." She nodded quietly in concern before glancing back at Fabian and gesturing shyly to the foyer. I led her behind the cover of the foyer wall and leaned in close.

"Hey, the other night did you accidentally take my bottle of Zerpotine with you?" I asked quietly.

"No. I left it right on the counter of the kitchen nook where it always is."

"You're sure?"

"Yes, I'm certain. Why? Can you not find it?"

"No. I turned the place upside down. It's just… gone."

"Where do you think it is?" She asked.

"Ahhh," I stumbled over my words again.

A cloud-riding creeper broke into my house and stole them before drugging me into a horny slumber.

"I'm not sure. But Dr. Bailey's office was closed by the time I realized it, and I don't think I took it last night."

"Oh! Okay. Don't worry about it. You can take some of mine until you get a refill. No problem," she assured. Her hand lifted to my brow to study the nasty injury. It's a shame she left bedside nursing; she was a very nurturing provider. "Shoot, Daph. Are you sure you're alright?"

I smiled convincingly. It was not the time, and I wasn't sure what to make of any of it anyway. "I'm fine. Promise."

But I was not fine. I was scared and confused. I didn't want to be alone or fall asleep when a stranger knew how to get into my house and take advantage of me in a vulnerable state. How could someone be so kind as to save me, ease my pain, and take care of my home but be so fucked up that they steal my antidepressants, drug me, and jerk off to my drug-induced lust. Was this all to scare me? Would he come back?

O'doherty dropped five tablets into a sandwich bag and passed them to me.

"Thanks," I said with a smile. "I'm gonna get out of here and leave you guys to it."

"Are you sure? I made plenty. You look like you could use a hot meal," Fabian offered sincerely, in what I can only describe as a voice of radiant positivity.

"Yeah, why don't you hang out for a little bit?" O'doherty agreed. I wanted to say yes, and I shouldn't have been alone. But I wouldn't ruin what looked to be a really fun night, especially not for some insane phantom.

"Oh! No, guys. I just ate, and honestly, I think I should get some more rest. You guys enjoy." I started to back away, turning for the door, O'die not far behind. "Fabian, it was great to meet you. I hope we can get to know each other soon," I said, waving.

"Oh, you too! Plan on it!" He smiled wide and started packing the food again.

I opened the door and turned to Odie.

"I want to know *everything*," I whispered loudly with a sultry grin. She laughed nervously and hushed me, passing my keys into my hands. The door shut behind me, and suddenly my smile didn't feel as fake as it did a moment before. She seemed happy. And despite the storm of emotions inside of me, I loved this for her. I drove home ready to drink a nice glass of wine and rig every entrance. I wouldn't be caught off guard again.

$$9$$

O'DOHERTY: A CHILLED EMPTINESS

NERVES BOUNCED IN MY STOMACH LIKE A TRAMPOLINE. THERE WAS no reason for that interaction to be so uncomfortable, evidenced by the fact that Daphne was clearly with someone else earlier. I had been holding my guard up this whole time with Fabian, and for what? If she were at all bothered by his presence, she would have stayed to interfere. *It's time to move on.*

Neither of us were sure where to pick up the conversation. The elephant in the room, I decided, was a good place to start.

"Zerpotine," I smiled and raddled the bottle in my hand. "It's an antidepressant. We both take the same dose." The stigma of mental health disorders was unfortunately alive and well. I was not quite sure how this would change his view of me. Would he think I was a mess? Would he think I had too much baggage or deem me too difficult to love? I swallowed, waiting for a reply that I would undoubtedly read too far into.

"Well, that's very convenient for you both," he smirked, offering a leftover piece of prosciutto. I accepted and delighted in its savory flavor. He didn't even flinch at the mention of antidepressants. A wave of relief settled into my bones, and I finally felt relaxed enough to admire him again.

Still, the nagging thought that rattled in my brain was how *off* Daphne behaved. Was it Fabian, or did something happen? I had not missed the quick tremble of her lip at the mention of seeing this mystery man again. Did something happen to him? I knew I needed to spend time with her tomorrow after work. I would bring her dinner and get caught up on the two new men in our lives.

I shook her from my thoughts, something I promised myself I'd be more intentional about when with him. No sooner was I laughing at his adorable attempts to impress me by flipping food like a hibachi chef.

We couldn't possibly dig into the pie. I had already eaten enough and worried I wouldn't fit into my scrubs tomorrow or, god forbid, he saw me naked after eating. The sweet smell of the apple filling permeated the house, and I decided the smell was dessert enough. Fabian had put on some soft music in the living room and took my waist for a dance. I bit my lip and glided into his warm arms. The smell of his cologne was an enticing blend of bergamot, tangerines, and rosemary that drew me closer to him. I had to admit, it had never been this easy with anyone. Comfort consumed me as I listened to his heart through his chest. *I like this guy. This is how I should be treated by someone who cares.*

I twirled under his arm and came back to him, clamping my arm around his back. His flinch indicated that I hit a wound.

"I'm so sorry. Are you alright?"

"Fine." He smiled without missing a beat.

"You know I have some leftover pain medication from my

wisdom teeth extraction. It's the good stuff. You do not have to suffer," I offered.

"Mmm," he pressed his lips together in a fake ponder. His honey eyes lowered to me, and he wrinkled his nose. "I don't do narcotics."

I giggled and decided to tease. "What's wrong? Are you afraid you're going to get loopy, and I'll take advantage of you?"

"If that were the case, I'd take them all day," he laughed, raising his brows to match the flirtatious energy. We swayed, and I could tell he wasn't finished explaining, so I paused and gave him an attentive look. "I'm seven years sober. I had a problem, and I hurt a lot of people." His tone was suddenly low, and a familiar anxiety filled his demeanor. He must have worried I would judge him for it. Nothing could be farther from the truth. He had a natural radiance and purity that was unassailable. "I stole a lot of Nana's jewelry and sold it. Dropped out of college and lost a scholarship." He nodded widely. "I was lucky to get help so fast and get it under control before I threw my whole life away. But I'd rather have my back sliced open a hundred more times before I ever chance it again."

"I apologize. I didn't know," I offered.

"Don't be. I finished my degree, and I've spent more time than Nana can tolerate trying to make it up to her," he laughed. "I'm very lucky to have such a good support system. It's not always the case."

"That actually explains a lot: how dedicated you are to Nana and how often your sister calls to check in."

"Nana raised us for most of our lives. She deserves no less. And my sister is just nosey, to be honest."

I huffed out a laugh. "So what are you planning on doing for the pain? There must be something."

"Actually, there's this lady who does holistic healing with crystals and herbs and stuff. I'm going to see her tomorrow. Maybe there's something to it. Realign my *chakras,"* he danced with the words as they left his mouth. His expression stilled for a moment, and he swept a strand of curls from my face.

"What?" I said nervously, not used to being looked at so intently.

"You look beautiful. That's all."

My heart danced, and I bit my lips. I'd be lying if I said I didn't absolutely adore him, and I wanted to make sure he knew it. The urge to press my lips to his superseded anything else. It was as if his radiant soul would leave some residue on my battered heart and heal it. He leaned into the kiss and ran his fingers through my hair. Every part of my body was humming with excitement. His tongue slipped into my mouth. The swaying of our dance only sank us deeper into each other. My finger explored just below his belly button. The pace of our kiss picked up.

He pulled back his lips but stayed close, looking at me intensely.

"Hey…I really like you," he said quietly. "If you want to take it slow, I'm not going anywhere." His next kiss pulled at my bottom lip, and he paused again to give me a chance to process the thought. Of course he would say that; he was perfect. I didn't know why but going slow brought comfort to me. I craved him; I wanted him, but there was something more there. If we dove all the way in and we did not work out, I think he would shatter any hope I had of having some-thing normal with anyone.

That's what this odd feeling is... It's normalcy.

"I would like that," I whispered. A sideways smile and the tight-ening of his arm around my waist made me feel safe. His lips returned to mine warmly. Our rocking dance was guided by his hips against mine. My fingers betrayed me. They returned to the sensitive place above his belt buckle. I made a teasing motion of nudging the pin of his buckle forward.

"I thought you said slow," he whispered into a kiss with a light laugh. His honey and amber eyes sparkled.

"I do want to go *slow*…but you've worked me up quite a bit with that tongue," I playfully whispered between our teeth.

He nodded with a lazy smile. Fingers through my hair, he walked me backward toward the counter. "Alright then, I'll start and you can set the pace," he said between kisses. The cold counter made contact with my back. His deep stare closed with his lips on mine.

His hand traveled low, massaging my thigh under my skirt and making its way up to the hem of my panties.

"Is this okay?" he asked in a muffled volume before moving them farther.

"Yeah," I said with a shaky voice. His warm touch slipped under my panties. He dipped his fingers between my lips. I inhaled to calm myself and looked up at him with wide eyes. The wetness was significant, and he let out a low groan between us.

"Oh…" he whispered, closing his eyes and dropping his forehead to mine. He consumed my space. His fingers found my clit, and he rubbed it in gentle circles, staring at me with hot intensity.

"You like that?" He licked his lips nervously. "Do you want me to stay here?" I bit my lip with indecision. I loved the way his fingers massaged my sensitive spot, but I shook my head narrowly. I needed his hands all over me.

"I want you to show me what you would do to me," I managed to admit, tracing my finger over the zipper of his jeans. The words didn't sound like my own. I was out of my head with anticipation. His brows worried. His breathing picked up. A flush flooded his face as if he had run a mile. His free arm crossed my body. Grabbing my arm, he guided me to turn around. He reached around me. Slowly he tucked his hands inside my panties again to rub circles against my clit. He pressed himself against me. I could feel his hard length against the back of my hip.

"Bend over for me?" he asked with a warm breath in my ear. The struggle to restrain his excitement was clear in his voice. I simpered.

I bent to rest my body on the chilled granite. His hand reached past me and grabbed something beyond my head. It was a cucumber he had washed earlier for a salad we decided not to make. He brought it into my view, then took it behind me. His fingers still working circles, I felt the cool cucumber rub up the inside of my thigh from behind. My brain failed to decide what to think of it. The higher its chilly end traced, the more my brain misfired. His fingers paused their circular strokes to pull my panties to the side. He wedged them on a knuckle and continued their massage.

Then he nudged the thick end of the cucumber at my heated entrance. I took a deep breath that challenged my breast against the granite.

"Do you want me to show you with *this*?" he asked plainly. I couldn't believe the boldness of the question—that *he*...

"Yes," I breathed out without hesitation. How often would I get fucked with a cucumber? I wanted him to make me cum. The strange improvisation made me curious.

Yes.

He leaned into me with more weight, letting out a deep breath. Again, I could feel his hardened shaft press into the back of my hip from behind his jeans.

"First, you'd feel me push into you," he said while pushing the blunt end just into my entrance. I gasped. The chilled, rounded end was difficult to ignore against my heat. He twisted it in tiny pumps to soak the tip.

"And then you'd feel me sink myself deep inside of you," he said as he worked it in with small twisting plunges. It slowly reached its full depth as he pushed it into me. The thick fruit filled me with an unmistakable chill. His circling fingers stayed true. He bent over, and his body pressed down on mine, pushing me harder into the counter. He gave me another thrust of the fruit, still slow but with more force at its depth.

"I'd pin you down and enjoy feeling you stretch around me." He gave another thrust. His hips moved in unison, grinding his length against me. He picked up the pace. My center relaxed, inviting him to take his pleasure. My wetness lapped as he continued to fuck me with the thick fruit. I whined quietly with each thrust.

"I'd fuck you slowly and struggle not to fill you with cum when you make those sweet little noises." My moaning turned to a gravely groan. My legs inched open further. Eagerly, I lifted my heels. The thought of him releasing inside of me without control made my heart race. My breath fogged the granite. He bit into my shoulder gently and groaned. I felt my release approaching. He circled my clit faster. I released my lip from a bite and let out a heady moan.

"I'd make you say my name when you cum around my cock." His words were drawing me out of myself. The girth and coolness of the cucumber was overwhelming. The gentle, steady rubbing of my soaked clit was making my knees weaker. I parted them farther in eager submission. He was rubbing his bulge against my hip and ass with each thrust. I moaned again at the thought of him taking his pleasure from me, the thought of him filling my pussy with his hot cum. The thrusts quickened, his hips with them.

"I'd fuck my cum into you so deep, you'd feel it warming your belly," he said in a pained voice. His hot lips brushed my back. My body rocked from the force of his fucking. The thought of his warm cum dripping down my thigh sent me over the edge. My moans turned long and whining and loud. He growled, pressing his lips into my back and fucking me harder.

"Say my name, baby. Say it," he demanded. He fucked the cucumber into me harder and faster as I came. His every thrust now fought my contracting center. I pressed my face into the counter and clawed at the hard stone. I came undone.

"Fabian!" I yelped in a cracked voice. "Fabian! Fabian!" I couldn't stop calling for him. His name was my surrender. He kept strong, consistent thrusts through my helpless state of ecstasy. My face contorted as if sour citrus stung my taste buds. The orgasm took my body prisoner. "Fabian! Fabian!"

"Oh fuck, baby. Oh shit," he grunted through clenched teeth. My bare ass felt the soaking of his jeans around his length. His primal groans caressed my ear as he finished me off with measured thrusts.

"Ahhh," he called out. Then, kissing my shoulder, he rested all of his weight on me, clearly taken by his own release. I lay there breathless. The rise and fall of our chests battled for space. I whimpered his name just twice more between tired pants before reverting to barely audible breaths of satisfied rest.

"Are you okay?" He checked with another kiss on my shoulder blade.

"Yeah," I said in the voice of a woman with not a thought in her mind. My mouth twitched for a smile but failed to hold it as relaxation still pulled at me. I was more calm than I had been in a long while.

"I'm going to take this out now, nice and slow," he warned as I felt the thick cucumber become more absent, leaving a chilled emptiness I'd never forget. "But if it was me inside of you, I wouldn't take myself out. I'd sleep between your lips, soaking myself in your cum."

I let out a breath of satisfaction as the last of the cucumber was pulled from me with a noticeable resistance that pulled at my lips. The pooling of fog on the counter with this breath was much wider and lingered longer. He gently moved my panties back into place and scooped an arm under me to pull me upright and against him. I breathed deeply to ward off the tunneling of lightheadedness. Then he pressed a warm kiss into my neck.

I was recovering from the bliss, sinking my back into his chest. Engulfed in his arms, he traced wet, pruned fingertips on my side. Then a crunching sound cut through the air. I opened my eyes and looked at him in shock at what I saw. He had taken a bite out of the cucumber and was chewing behind a smile.

My shocked laughter filled the room. He smiled back at me, still chomping. "This is the most delicious cucumber I've ever eaten," he managed with a full mouth.

Laughter carried for a long moment, and he pulled me back into a dance. Swaying, we held each other in silence for a while before he whispered in my ear. "When's your bedtime, Dotey?"

Dote-ee. I love it. I squirmed internally.

"Oh, early." I sighed at the stark reality ahead of me. "I have to get up and check out the crystal place that sold the blue stones to the pharmaceutical company."

"Well, you kick me out whenever," he said, kissing my temple. "I'll keep you up all night if you don't."

"You can stay the night if you want. It's late," I said, peeling my face from his chest and looking at him gently, "I would have to wash your pants though."

He choked on a laugh. "Ha! You noticed that, huh? Yeah. I'll give my sister a call and see if she is okay to stay with Nana at the hospital for the night."

I smiled, looking up at him.

"Hey, do you think you could take one of those blue rocks to that healer person you're going to? See if she can perhaps… detect anything *weird* about it. Maybe she can tell us what it even is?" I asked, wiggling my fingers with "*weird*."

"Sure, I could do that."

We cleaned up and slept next to each other for the first time. He lay on his stomach to keep pressure off his wounds. Shamelessly, he wore my tight, pink pajama pants with tiny mustaches printed on them. They actually complemented his tanned, olive skin. I lay on my side admiring his face and the way the top of his ear had a weird little fold to it. It was the first time I had seen him without glasses. He was angelic, and I waited a long moment before I turned out the lights.

That was slow enough.

IO

O'DOHERTY: THE SEASON OF GIFTING

THE MORNING TRAFFIC WAS INSUFFERABLE YET AGAIN. IT WAS AS dull as always, and my bottom started to go numb. A muted gray-blue filled the sky, and beads of rain collected on the windshield of my hybrid before the rubber wipers loudly skidded across to clean them away. The GPS read that I had 20 minutes until I'd arrive, but the way this morning was going, I was sure it would take longer. From the moment of my waking, it was as if the universe was trying to stop me from going to the crystal store in the neighboring town of Homestead.

The day started incredibly. Fabian had woken me up with nuzzled kisses on my neck moments before my alarm sounded. His hands trailed up my shirt and stopped just under my breast. I could feel the length of him warmly pressed against my leg from beneath the pink mustache pajama pants. My hands worked through his dark blond curls, and I pulled his face up for a proper kiss.

"I have to go to work."

"Pick this up later tonight then?" he asked, kissing my collarbone.

"I actually need to see Daphne tonight," I said hesitantly. I realized then just how long I had gone without thinking about her or feeling riddled with guilt. "Something seemed really off with her last night."

"Yeah, she did look a bit rough. Okay. Well, just let me know. Hey, do you like eggs benedict?" he asked, jumping out of bed. When he stretched, I couldn't help but notice his broad, toned shoulders. He had the faint outline of a four-pack, and there was no hiding that bulge in his pants. *This man is delicious.* "Honey? Eggs benny?"

"Oh! Yes. Thank you."

Fabian whipped up the incredible breakfast while I showered and did my lengthy hair and skin routine. I scarfed it down, wishing I had more time to enjoy it. That's where the morning took a turn.

It was on the way out that Fabian noticed my tire was slashed. "Anyone suspicious hanging around?" he asked while changing the tire. Possibilities of who the vandal could have been escaped me. I kept to myself and rarely rocked the boat, if ever; no, rocking the boat was Daphne's specialty. So who could I possibly have crossed to warrant such an act?

"Probably some teenagers out to impress their friends," I told Fabian in an attempt to calm him.

"You know, my friend has a home security business. I can have him put cameras up. I don't like this," he said as he finished and wiped his brow.

"I'll keep that in mind, but I'm sure it's nothing, really. Jerk kids," I said before kissing him.

"Okay. Well, be safe. Call me if anything is wrong, okay?" he said, wiping the grime from the tire change on his freshly washed jeans.

Almost immediately after that, there was the tree incident. The turning lane for the on-ramp I had to take to get to the crystal shop was backed up. A tree somehow had made its way onto the ramp. Any detour would cost me time I simply did not have. I pondered going to the shop another day or not at all. What would I find at a family-owned crystal shop in the middle of nowhere? I was better off taking a note from Alex Graves's snarky remarks and pursuing a mineralogist. But something was nagging at me that I couldn't put my finger on, so I waited. In a little over 30 minutes, the road was cleared.

Now, a storm was stirring up ahead. As was the trend lately, this storm was completely random and unexpected. The morning radio show warned people to take precautions and avoid any areas with unpredictable weather. I was not amongst those heeding the warning as I drove into a wall of rain that grew denser and more sideways the further I went.

According to my GPS, my exit came up on the right and I made my way to the off ramp. It was something I'd surely miss if I were left to decipher the signs through the thick veil of rain in the gloomy pre-dawn light. The morning radio show was going in and out, and my GPS decided to freeze.

Luckily I had already memorized the route from here and wasn't too far away. It was just a matter of *seeing* where I was going. I could see well enough to take a left onto the road from the off ramp but that was it. I had to pull my car to the shoulder until the conditions were less precarious.

I sat back in my seat, car in park on a grassy shoulder. As my hazard lights blinked, I hoped the sound of heavy rain would not make me have to pee. I was unfamiliar with the area and had no idea where the nearest facilities were.

Bored, I reached into my pocket and studied the stone that always seemed to be cold to the touch. The longer I stared at it, the odder it felt. In this light, with condensation collecting around it, the white specs seemed to float again. It was hypnotizing. I gazed at it dreamily, the world around me slipping away. The blue stone with floating flecks was the only thing I could see. It looked as though it was vibrating slowly, even though my fingers no longer registered that I was touching it.

The crash of hail on my windshield snapped me from the trance. Another bang sounded on the roof before I could fully process a crack spidering across my windshield. I tucked the stone in my pocket and sat up straight. There was nothing to be done but watch and listen as my car was battered. I didn't know where to go for shelter. Another crash came against the windshield, and I yelped. A second crack splintered out.

A rumbling noise surrounded me. My heart rate surged as adrenaline flooded my veins. My car lifted from the ground and I screamed. My only instinct was to duck away from the glass and cover the back of my head and neck.

I could feel my car moving like a rollercoaster. Up it tilted, then to the side. Then it did a 180-degree spin that bucked me like I was riding a mechanical bull. I hollered in fear. My crouched body slammed into the dash and then into the passenger seat. I could feel my car lurching forward. It dropped as if thrown from the grip of a pitcher. With a jerk and bounce—neither one ferocious enough to match the crescendo of events—my car was now grounded. The rumbling sound became distant and the rain much lighter.

My head rose slowly from below the dash to meet the sight ahead. If some magical force was not trying to send me a sign before, it *was* now. My car was perfectly centered in the paved on-ramp to the highway, facing the direction from which I came.

The problem was I was a realist. I didn't believe in magic and all of those fantastical tales. I was not injured, my car was still in fine working condition, and I was only a few miles away from my destination. I shook off the alarm and reminded myself that some days are just full of surprises. All of these things were merely coincidences. Still, I couldn't help but tremble.

The tires crunched on wet pavement as the car reversed. The storm had moved ahead and seemed to be weakening. My GPS was no longer frozen, and the radio cut back on. The bloodcurdling sound of the emergency alert system assaulted my ears as it screeched out tornado warnings from my phone and car stereo. I slapped the radio off and silenced the phone's alert with a curse.

"A little late for that," I snapped at my phone before throwing it in the passenger seat.

I drove cautiously and was glad for it. By the time I reached the outskirts of the small town where the shop was located, a tornado had torn it to shreds. As I walked toward the wreckage, the flashing lights of emergency vehicles caused goosebumps to crawl up my arms. I got out of my car and scanned the ruined area. There, in a pile of bricks, was a wooden door sign with sunflowers painted on it. It read, "Darling Rituals." The owner was being loaded on a stretcher with a c-collar fastened around her neck and an oxygen mask strapped to her face. She looked moments away from losing consciousness, a result, no doubt, of the bleeding head wound the old biddy had suffered.

The smooth rock tumbled between my fingers in my pocket as I turned around to return to my car. There was nothing left to find here. The shop owner would probably be taken to the small 84 bed hospital in town—a hospital I would not have privileges to visit professionally.

Then I slowed my pace as I felt, yet again, eyes boring into me. There was an intrusive presence tugging at my instincts. My gaze flipped up and over my shoulders to catch whoever it was. There were plenty of first responders bustling about, but no one in particular was taking any apparent interest in me at first glance.

There! Behind the ambulance that the shop owner was loaded into, a familiar form of a young, white-haired man caught my eye. His skin was taupe, and his top-heavy lips a pouty mauve. My blood ran cold as I locked eyes with him, noting their unusual darkness. Mindlessly, I walked toward him at a brisk pace, pushing away any hesitation. There wasn't much hesitation, actually. I was surprised to find an unusual intrepidity taking over as I charged toward the stalker effortlessly. He walked behind the ambulance, which, immediately thereafter, pulled away with lights and sirens blazing. The piece of road the ambulance left behind was empty; there was no sign of the man.

I curled my lip at the vanishing act.

What the... I spun around, looking for any sign of him. He was gone.

MY CAR STARTED WITHOUT HESITATION, AND I HAD NO FURTHER obstacles on my way to the hospital. In fact, my luck had turned, much like my car in the storm. I arrived there just before the staff started the shift-change report. I sat at a computer in the intensive care unit, where several of my patients were still hospitalized. I researched their charts to make sure all protocols were being followed. I combed through their lab work, vital signs, imaging results, and physical assessments for anything similar, yet off.

The shift-change report began and two nurses sat at the computer next to me to discuss the first patient one of them would hand off to the other. The night shift nurse shared the basics.

"Room 19. The patient's name is Colee Calusa; she's a 78 year old female with no known allergies, full code, and standard precautions.

Past medical history of A-fib, gout, hyperlipidemia, and GERD," the night nurse stated robotically. Before moving on to the head-to-toe assessment of the patient, she explained the history of the current illness and hospitalization. This caught my ear.

"She presented to the hospital about an hour ago with a head injury to the occipital region sustained during a tornado that tore down her store. She owns a crystal and healing shop in Homestead, but their hospitals are overwhelmed, so they brought her here. She's had a CT of the head and neck pending results, so she's on bed rest with a c-collar."

I kept my eyes on a long paragraph displayed on my screen and pretended to read it as I eavesdropped. *What are the chances?* She continued, now going through her assessment, and I listened for the one thing I needed to hear.

"She has an 18 gauge IV in the right AC and a 20 gauge in the right forearm. Normal saline running KVO. She's drowsy and oriented to self but not time or place. Fall risk. On bed rest but ambulatory at baseline. Pupils are round, equal, and reactive to light."

That's all I needed to know. She was awake, perhaps not with the best recollection and definitely with a concussion, but I could see what she remembered about the stones. Nothing was adding up about them, and I was going to find out what it was.

I glanced over at her room, which was darkened. I could slip in for a moment to ask about the rock and be out in no time. I only had a few minutes before the nurses would finish their report, so I had to act quickly.

I made it to the doorway, confirmed the nurses were still distracted, and disappeared into the shadows of her room. The room was dim apart from the bluish-pink glow coming through the window. Palm trees in the darkness outside swayed against the pink and lavender sky. I found Colee Calusa resting in her bed, sleeping, and pulled up a folded wooden chair to her bedside. Her long, frizzy gray hair complemented her light yellow-brown skin.

"Mrs. Calusa?" My question woke her with a startle. "I am so sorry to wake you. My name is O'doherty. I was wondering if I could ask you a few questions."

"Colee Calusa, February 20th, 19—"

"Oh no, that's okay. Not those questions." I laughed. She clearly had the hospital's routine questions down pat already.

"Oh?" She shifted her body momentarily as if about to sit up but remembered she was supposed to lay flat. Her hooded eyes above round cheekbones shifted to me.

"I understand you were at your store this morning before the storm hit."

"That's right. What *used to be* my store. I came in early to start inventory," she offered.

"Darling Rituals, is it?"

"That's right," her fingernail scratched at the sheets. "That *was* it. Before it was *taken* from me."

I retrieved the blue stone from my pocket and held it in the pink glow of the sunrise through the window.

"Is this one of your products, Mrs. Calusa?"

Her eyes lifted to meet the rock, and her gaze turned gaunt. "What do you want?" she demanded, now looking down her aquiline nose.

"I was wondering if you could tell me more about it—what it is, where it came from? If there's anything, uhhh…"

"I don't know anything about it! Get out!" The visceral reaction took me back. My hand snapped down. I glanced at the door and back. "You heard me! Take that damned rock and stay away from me!"

"Mrs. Calusa, I'm sorry if I've offended you. I... I..."

"Excuse me, can I help you?" The two nurses stood in the doorway expectantly.

"I... I thought she was someone else." I forced an embarrassed laugh and tucked my hair behind my ear.

"You can't be in here. You need to leave," the other nurse said.

"Oh... of course," I stood up and started for the door, gesturing back at Mrs. Calusa apologetically. Her face trembled, and her cataracted eyes were distant.

"I'll be back in to go over your plan of care soon, Mrs. Calusa," the day shift nurse spoke through the threshold as I walked away from the room. They stayed at the doorway to finish their shift report like bouncers at a club. The stone in my pocket rolled between my fidgeting fingers. I came to a doorway a few rooms down, the room of a trial patient. Before entering the room, my eyes offered a humorous look to the nurses. I pointed at the doorway before me as if to say, *"Ahh, this is the one!"* They didn't seem amused despite the nod they gave in reply.

I walked into the room of my patient, who was intubated and not in any shape to be interviewed. She, like so many others from *Mayflower*, was now awaiting hospice and orders for withdrawal of care. In other words, the family was planning to allow natural death. Allowing someone a peaceful and dignified transition from life was one of the most beautiful gifts you could give to a loved one. It's also one of the hardest gifts to give. And for so many residents of *Mayflower*, it was the season of gifting.

I pressed my stethoscope to her chest and listened to the thumping of her heart, the world around her a muffled mess of unrecognizable sounds. I moved it to another area to better listen to the other valves of her heart. This time, the muffled mess of sounds in the background was louder and more alarming. Running nurses outside of the room stole my attention, and the bell of the stethoscope peeled from her sticky skin, amplifying the sounds. It was unmistakably a code blue alarm. Someone was dying. My skin prickled with a sick suspicion.

From the door of my patient's room, I could see the nurses pushing the code cart into the room of Colee Calusa. "Oh," my voice shook out. I hurried over and I watched from outside of room 19. For 46 minutes the nurses took turns compressing her chest. They gave every necessary medication. I watched as respiratory therapists gave breaths through a bag valve mask. They worked the code with text-book perfection. I stood stunned at the next pulse check. There was no pulse; the practically flat, jittery line of asystole sliced through the monitor. Sadie, the nurse practitioner leading the code, called it off.

"That's it, guys. We're not getting this one back. Let's get her cleaned up," Sadie directed regretfully. "Has anyone reached her family?"

"Yes, the daughter. Demi Calusa. She's on her way…" The chatter faded to background noise as my mind spiraled.

They couldn't save her. For reasons unknown as of yet, Colee Calusa—who was perfectly alive moments ago—was dead.

I was becoming increasingly convinced that nothing about the series of events happening was a coincidence.

II

DAPHNE: UP VERY FUCKING HIGH

It amazed me that my laptop wasn't in worse shape after taking a wet tumble a few nights ago. A few loose keys rock under the command of my fingers as I complete emails and update my spreadsheets for the follow-up with the nurses. Follow-up had to be tight, and organizing every piece of information was imperative.

I had no time to dwell on things that may not come to pass. I had taken what measures I could last night. Empty soda cans were strung together with shoestrings, and I placed them on door handles and window locks as a makeshift alarm. In a few weeks a proper security system would be installed. For now I'd sleep with a knife under my pillow and keep pepper spray on me at all times.

I scheduled a follow-up with the nurses for the next day. Then, I made an appointment with my mentor in the union. He'd already urged me to use my clearance at *Amett* to get any additional lists of employees I could, but I was certain I had done my best already. Lastly, I called Dr. Bailey's office and asked to come by for a refill tomorrow. I had enough left from Odie, but there was no need to delay.

Today, I was stopping by the hospital's administration building to return my badge before Lyndie Pratt blew her gasket. I purposely waited until after 17:00 to leave for the offices. I knew how early she liked to go home, and I had no desire to run into her. All I had to do was leave the badge in a box outside of the HR office—in and out!

I GOT TO THE ADMINISTRATIVE OFFICES JUST AFTER 18:30. AT THE door, I saw the baby-faced security guard who had started just before I did. I was flirtatious with him during the contract for sport. I coyly explained my business, and after a giggle and light touch of his arm, he gladly let me in.

No one would be in their office this late, so I walked carefreely through the dim hall of the fourth floor. To the left, the black box mounted on the wall outside of the HR office came into view. My badge slipped easily through the slotted top and clinked when it reached the bottom. That was it— so informal and quick; my time working there was over.

Light reached out of a cracked door to an office a few rooms down. *Who could possibly be here this late?* Curiosity and boredom steered my legs toward the door.

"Lyndie Pratt, DON," the wall plaque read. There was no way Lyndie was still there; I was almost certain of it. My eyes peeped through the opening to find a vacant office. I looked around me. There was no sign of movement. My mentor's words crept into my mind: *Get as many lists as you can.* The temptation to slip into her office and snag the entire list of staff names creeped into my mind. A complete and accurate list of employees eligible for an election would

move us months ahead of the game and spare the nurses from many ebbs in the campaign.

It was probably against some law, but I sure as fuck wasn't going to miss this opportunity. I slipped in and rushed behind the desk. I felt no shame or guilt for the invasion. This was war. I wasn't the best salt around because I played fairly.

The office was standard in decor but larger than I expected. It even had a small closet and large inlaid bookshelves decorated with rhinestone-encrusted picture frames. A water cooler sat next to a tall, leafy live plant. Her desk was a sophisticated rosewood with not a scratch on it. A large window looked out to the palm trees and sparkling neon skyscrapers downtown. To my surprise, her desktop was unlocked, the screen bright, and programs already logged in to.

"Ha!" I laughed. "Oh, this is freaking beautiful." I bit my lip as I went to work. Lyndie was not lazy or messy or careless. Open programs meant she was still here and not likely far, so I had to be quick.

```
>select: "contains"
RN/LPN/CNA/RT/ST/PT/OT/Tech(s)/Radiology/Nutri-
tional Services/ Environmental
Services/Transport
>deselect: "contains" Manager/supervisor/charge
>function: print
>function: email > |
```

I entered the address of a burner email not associated with my identity and hit send. Hot pages were already flying swiftly from the expensive laserjet printer. Hard copies wouldn't hurt to have on hand just in case the list didn't pull through uncoded via email. There were twelve more pages to go, but the sound of a door opening in the distance caused a moment of panic.

"Fuck," I whispered under my breath.

The sound of heels echoing down the hall told me who was coming. *Six more pages.* I worried that the printer wasn't quick enough. I wasn't leaving without the lists. The tapping of heels was nearly at the door. I exited the program. I bent down to swipe the stack of warm pages that had finally finished printing. I folded them and tucked the stack in the back of my pants, under my shirt. There was no time to move now. The clicking was as close as the hall could take them. I prepared to improvise. *This should be fun.*

A slender hand pushed the door open by the wood with a paper towel still in her grip. Lyndie's gaze was fixed on her phone. Her free hand dialed a number. My lips parted to speak before she saw me. I could bluff this. Confidence was innocence. But the words could not escape me. A large hand cupped my mouth, and another constricted my throat.

The world felt wet and my skin evaporated into a cold mist, then my muscles, then my bones. My entire existence was dissolved one instant—the next, it rematerialized, like ice that thawed to flesh. When my bones, muscles, skin, and soul were reunited, I was in a dark place. Nothing was visible. I was still tightly imprisoned by the clutches of an unknown assailant. His grip on my throat was too tight. No air could move in or out of my lungs. I could make no sound. Panic took over me as I struggled to breathe. The strength of his grip was unrelenting and painful. His body was pressed against my back intimately, breath hot on my earlobe.

"I'm going to let you go, and you're going to stay absolutely quiet. Do you understand?" the voice said in a muffled volume. His voice was an almost unearthly baritone—his pitch low enough to sound just short of demonic. He took all the time in the world to enunciate each goddamn syllable as if I wasn't starving for air.

I struggled and clawed at his arm. Finally, I nodded furiously in a promise to stay quiet. When he released my throat, I expected to take loud gasps for air. But the hand that still cupped my mouth and nose was somehow able to send pure oxygen down my windpipe and into my chest. Cool, dry oxygen rushed into my airway with uncomfortable pressure. The pressure burned my throat, and I clawed at his arm again in a plea to be less aggressive. The air pressure reduced, and I sighed in relief, sinking down.

"Quiet," he hissed against my ear. Now he wrapped his arms tightly around me, pinning my arms at my side and pressing my back into him harder. He smelled like burning wood and leather. Under those notes, I could smell a bit of cognac and sandalwood. *At least I'm not being attacked by someone who smells like shit. A win is a win.*

I felt him lean sideways, taking my body with him. Lyndie's voice came from the other side of the flimsy door. Suddenly, I could smell her strong perfume on a garment nearby. It was clear now that we were hidden in her office closet.

I was already pissed off, but to know I couldn't call for help without raising some very concerning questions made my jaw tighten painfully. Begrudgingly, I stayed quiet. I wasn't sure how we got there, but I knew I wasn't imagining the pain he left around my neck. That shit was sore as hell, and I wanted to elbow this fuck in the dick for it.

Anyways. Lyndie was on the phone with someone. It sounded more business than personal.

"The plan worked out beautifully. The residents successfully carried out the ritual. The barriers are now significantly weakened in six regions across the east coast of North America," she reported.

"The locations that didn't succeed were noted to have faulty stones, or perhaps they didn't charge well." A pause in her conversation made me curious what the response to *that* was.

"No, I don't think it had anything to do with that. Our physician has never failed with it before." Another pause was followed by a short giggle. "Yes, we've already processed our insurance policies, so that's worked out very well, and I do thank you again for his attention to the communities selected. The payouts will be well worth this partnership in itself."

I couldn't make sense of what I was hearing. A low, baritone growl in my ear told me that my assailant knew something of it. He tightened his grip around me. I tried to throw my shoulder into him as if to say, *"Fuck off."* He was too strong, and it barely made the giant fucker move.

"Well, I'd be happy to discuss phase two with you soon. It's been a pleasure working with His Highness."

Highness?

The sound of a phone hitting the table told me the phone call had ended. Now, I had more questions than answers. But those questions disappeared as I felt my skin grow cold and wet before evaporating into a cool mist again; then, my muscles and my bones and my soul followed. Reforming from ice to flesh somewhere with a damn good view of the sky, my body was whole again. I was still pressed against him, his hand cupping my mouth.

I faced the low sun, its light bouncing off the ocean in a white stripe. The sky was orange and pink with stretches of thin blue clouds. It looked like a mural painted by Lisa Frank. The ocean was calm, and… Panic flooded my body. I was never a fan of heights, and we were up very fucking high. Beneath my feet was nothing more than a small floating storm cloud. Below it were miles and miles of nothingness that made the buildings and palm trees look like little more than specks.

The storm cloud grew in length. It was a dusky lavender on the dark side, but it picked up orange light where the setting sun hit it. He let me go. I couldn't move, afraid my feet would find a faulty spot, and I'd fall to my death. I started breathing faster, not only from the thinner air but from the fear that shook me to my core.

The cloud was wider now, with rounded stacks of different heights surrounding us on most sides. There was a strange solid floor at my feet that felt like it was shifting, even though I knew it wasn't. I felt the urge to shift my weight at the pseudo-movement beneath me.

He walked past me, turned around, and sat on a dark cloud puff that grew under him as he dropped, like a low stool of dusky cotton. He rested his elbows on his knees and let his long arms hang down as he studied me with opal eyes in what looked like disappointment. I looked back at him speechless. I didn't know what for, but I waited. Our hair continuously tossed around in the wind as we stared at each other.

"You're very weak," he stated matter-of-factly, his voice still unreal.

"*What?*" I breathed out, confused. He choked me out and teleported me onto a cloud, and *that's* all this guy had to say to me?

"You should sit down."

Sitting would have been great if my body would let me move at all. Instead, I took in the sight of him. He could pass as human if it weren't for his eyes and the aura of mist dancing inches above his pale skin.

"What are you?" I said through bruised vocal cords.

"A caeluman," he answered as if it was basic knowledge. "Like you."

"*What...*" My head was throbbing slightly, and nausea had started to set in. He stood up and closed the distance between us, allowing me to memorize his face. He was tall and thin yet very toned, with broad shoulders and long arms. His wavy, medium-length hair was black until the sunlight revealed navy blue wherever it hit directly. His face was oblong, with low brows, a long midface, and a strong nose. A sharply angled jaw connected with his rounded chin just below full lips. And of course, his eyes. His narrow eyes were piercing with opalescent irises. The sun caught every fleck of shimmering pale pastels.

"There's a war coming. Your friend down there is working with a King in the European Caelo-Kingdom."

"Lyndie is *not* my friend. And she's a frigid bitch, but she's not capable of..." I scoffed and pressed my fingers into my temples. I felt fatigued; my head now throbbed harder, and a sour taste crept at the sides of my tongue. Chills ran over me. Saliva pooled, and I could feel vomit threatening to come up. He grabbed my wrist, studying the bracelet on it.

"Why are you sick?" he asked flatly.

Good question. That bracelet held back most of my ailments. I fell to my hands and knees at the side of the cloud to release the vomit from my mouth. As I looked down at the distant earth, shivering from the cold and gasping for air between heaves, I realized why I was feeling so ill.

"Altitude sickness..." I spit chunky acid and gasped before I continued. "Most likely. Quick assent. My body isn't used to the pressure and thin air," I rattled off between deep breaths. I wiped my nose on my sleeve and hoped he would take us to the ground. Instead, he knelt down, cupped a hand over my lips, and conjured water to wash away the leftover vomit from my mouth. The taste of fresh mint and lemongrass laced my lips and tongue. Then he sent pure oxygen into my lungs again, this time very gently. The cloud started to descend slowly, sending a flip through my already sour stomach, like the one I got when an elevator suddenly started to drop. I lost my sense of balance and swayed over the edge. Gasping, I shot back, gripping him at the sleeves of his biceps.

"You'll have to stop taking those pills. They're poison," he said plainly, an order more than a suggestion. My eyes shot to him in anger. I shoved his hand from my mouth.

"You! You broke into my house!" I started in an angry shout. "You stole my medication? You…" My heart sank and twisted in my stomach. "You drugged me," I jabbed in a breathy tone, falling back on my hands and backing away from him. Any space I earned vanished as the cloud under me rolled, bringing my body back to him.

The sky was now a deeper hot pink and dusty navy as the sun set lower. My body unwillingly moved toward him with nauseating motion until he was closer than before. His hand again cupped my trembling mouth, this time leaving a space. I accepted the air out of necessity, my head freshly throbbing from the force of my yelling.

"You were injured. It was a healing elixir," he spoke with disregard for the terror bursting out of me.

"No, you drugged me and…" My voice broke as a tear fell from my eye and nearly froze in the frigid air "…you did *something* to me." I wasn't quite sure what it was he had done that morning or if I was remembering it correctly at all, but the power he displayed now confirmed he was capable of it. He had done something with water and air to arouse me or push me toward climax at minimum. Shame hung over me, knowing the memory wasn't an unpleasant one, but I felt violated nonetheless. I despised him for taking advantage of me.

He showed only a moment of reflection before addressing the charge emotionlessly. "I didn't know how weak they made you—"

"*What* are you talking about?" I cringed, shrinking back from him. "Who made me *weak*? What the fuck does that even mean?"

"You're caeluman, like me. Your parents hid you with humans to protect you. But he found you, and he found a way to keep you weak."

"Who?" I whispered, unsure if I wanted to hear his answer.

"Ouran. He's a tyrant—a conqueror." I stared at him blankly. None of that sank in.

"Get me down from here," I said sternly. My strength was coming back the closer we approached the earth, which unfortunately was still far beneath us. I would show fear for not a second longer, nor would I continue to entertain his bullshit story. "Get me down and leave me the fuck alone."

"I can't do that, Daphne," he said, unaffected by my blunt demands.

"Why not?"

"I'll show you. Come with me to Loanan." He lowered his hand. The sun was sinking over his shoulder, only making the glow of his eyes more godlike. The low drum of his voice echoed through his throat heavily. The wind tousled his black-blue hair, and I could smell the smokey scent of him again. That study-hungry part of my brain couldn't help the intrigue, and I cursed myself for being drawn to the enigma. A pang of panic drew me back to myself.

"No," I said softly. "This isn't real. I have a job… People are depending on me. How do I get down? Get me—"

"More people are depending on you to come home to Loanan."

"I can't…" I shook my head. "Give me my medicine. Let me down. Please."

"You can't take that medicine," he pushed back, enunciating the words even more carefully than usual. "They are poisoning you."

"I'll just get a refill," I spat with a twitch at my lip.

"It's convenient that they give you unlimited refills anytime you need," he offered, in what I assume was his attempt at sarcasm. I paused at the thought. It *was* unique as medication refills go. "I can make you come. You can't exactly get out of this situation."

My heart raced. I could feel warm liquid dripping from my nose. He pulled a cloth from his pocket and dabbed the warmth. Blood stained it. The nosebleed was likely from the cold, dry air he forcefully pushed through my face. I grabbed the cloth and pressed it there, turning my head from his reach in anger.

"But I'm not. I'm giving you the choice." Calm came over me for the first time since appearing on this God-forsaken cloud. His hand lifted my chin, and he examined my neck.

"I didn't know you were this weak." He looked at me with distant eyes. Then he cupped his hands together, and a cloud-shaped charm of obsidian grew in his palms. He clipped it onto the bracelet. My throat soothed. My temples stopped aching. Freezing snot and blood still dripped from my nose and I sniffled, dabbing it away with shaking hands.

"Come with me. Just for a week. Then you can decide what's real."

"I have to go home," I pressed softly, a rogue tear escaping from my eye.

He pulled me forward by the hand, helping me up, and cupped my shoulders. The strange sensation of evaporating enveloped me again. Then our bodies reformed outside of the administration building, in a dim alley between buildings. The sun was nearly set, and the shadows of the tall buildings hugged us. His hands still cupped my shoulders, and I hesitated to push myself from his grip until I felt grounded.

"Press the paved end of the bracelet's clasp with your thumb when you have an answer for me," he said flatly, wiping the tear from my cheek. I pulled back from the affection, sickened by him.

"I gave you an answer." I shook my head and finally pulled from his grip.

"One week is all I ask. It's a matter of life and death."

I narrowed my eyes at him, retreating into myself. As I walked away, I was unable to take my eyes off of him for a few paces before turning for my car. When I reached it, I looked back for him once more, but he was gone.

12

O'DOHERTY: STAY AWAY

I ARRIVED AT DAPHNE'S PLACE HOURS AGO AND WAS DISTURBED walking through the door to find empty soda cans hanging by shoe strings on the doors and windows. I propped one in my hand and furrowed my brows before dropping it.

"Okaaaay…"

Her place was kind of a mess. I put the food in the oven to stay warm, feeling guilty that I had already picked at it. Then I took Polpetta for a walk since Daphne wasn't home yet. We had made dinner plans earlier tonight, but for some reason, she was not answering her phone. She was unusually late, and I was starting to worry.

When I first got there, I curled up on the couch and texted Fabian a teasing photo of my lace panties that barely covered my backside.

!!!!!!! Well, thank God I'm not still at the healer. She might've seen my raging boner.

How did it go with the healer anyway?

Well, it started late. As soon as she saw the blue stone she told me to take it out of her shop and then spent 20 minutes smudging away the negative energy from it.

Did she say anything about it?

Just that it's cursed and dangerous and to take it far away from anyone I care about.

Before he left, she had insisted on upselling him smudge sticks for his home. He bought one for each of us to appease the troubled woman. We laughed about it, but he was truly feeling better, so I was thankful for whatever gift she had.

I told him about the frightening morning and the sad events at the hospital during shift change. I left out the part of the disappearing man, not wanting him to think I was crazy or worry about my tire. Then I broke the news that we lost four more patients today from complications after the storm. I had lost count of how many patients had passed away since then.

Poor Nana. A lot of them were her friends. I don't think I have the heart to tell her.

How about I just don't tell you and then you're not actually keeping anything from her?

He offered to stay overnight if I needed company. I certainly wouldn't mind waking up next to him again—so long as Nana wasn't getting lonely, that is.

Nana would shove me out of the house with her own two hands if she had the strength.

He asked when he should come, so I checked the time and realized it was already pretty late. It was past dark, and I hadn't heard a word from her.

> Actually… Daphne isn't back yet and I'm a bit worried. Let me get back to you.

Her phone went straight to voicemail. My texts were sent but not read. I tried several more times but to no avail. Her parents answered on the third ring. When they told me she hadn't stopped by and asked why, I simply said that Daphne was "just running a little late."

"No biggy! See you guys soon."

I opened her laptop to see if I could find any clues about what she might have stopped to do after turning in her badge. Her work spreadsheet was last updated about five hours ago. I hesitated, but my worry gnawed at me, and I decided to dig a little deeper. I checked her search history and furrowed my brows at the strange commands.

"Legends of men who ride on clouds," I read aloud with a twisted face. I clicked on it and shook my head at the results. Daphne did not watch cartoons, and although she had always been a very spiritual person who led with her heart, she was still fairly practical. This did not make sense for her. The search command below it was another head-scratcher.

`Obsidian and amethyst for healing.`

In all the years we knew each other, Western Medicine had been our norm and rarely failed us. What could possibly spark an interest in such a scarcely researched or documented healing practice? Then again, it seemed to be working for Fabian, so maybe it was gaining popularity. The third search command was the only one that seemed normal for Daphne, yet was more concerning than the others.

vivid hallucinations after a head injury.

She told me she was caught in a storm and must have downplayed how badly she was hurt. No wonder she seemed so off. My heart sank with guilt, knowing I left her to process the traumatic event alone while I was messing around. I should have insisted she stay. I should have—

The garage door opened, and the low rumble of her engine shook the air. I snapped her computer shut. Polpetta leaped from the couch and sprinted into the kitchen, barking and howling. I followed her in anticipation.

I waited in the threshold of the kitchen until Daphne walked in through the garage entrance. A chill pricked down my body at the sight of her. Her eyes met mine. I could tell by the leaking mascara that she had been crying. Her hair was frizzy and knotted. The stain of blood under her nose and shirt drew a gasp from me. The fresh red mark around her neck nearly made my knees buckle. Guilt consumed me. Once again, I was so caught up in my infatuation that I hadn't even realized my best friend was in danger.

"Daph…" I could hardly breathe out her name, and my hand flew up to my mouth. She ran her hands through her hair and came to hug me apologetically.

"I'm so sorry. I didn't realize how late it was," she said in a forced calm voice. The odd casualness in her tone clashed harshly with her physical presentation.

"Daph, what happened?" I sobbed, "You're bleeding. You've been crying. And—"

One hand lifted to wave me off and the other to lift a cloth to her nose. She shook her head. A soft smile failed to reach her eyes, and she sniffled.

"It's nothing. I got sick, and the pressure of vomiting must have irritated my nose," she said in a broken voice, never quite looking at me. As she dabbed the blood away, a black charm dangled from her bracelet. That charm wasn't there the night before. I'd studied it closely enough to know. I reached out my hand and propped the charm on my fingertips to bring it to the light. Black obsidian carved smoothly into the shape of a fluffy cloud was secured to the bracelet with an s-shaped tendril of white gold. The tendril was encrusted at its two curved ends with large amethysts.

"You saw him again, then?"

Her face was strange. She seemed nervous yet smiled when she nodded.

"Should I worry about this man, Daph? You look like you've been through hell." I tried to match her smile with feigned humor in my words, but my smile sputtered out as nerves tugged at me.

"No. I just got sick. It's fine," she said, clearly unaware that her marked neck was calling her bluff. "Did you eat yet? I'm starving." She moved quickly to set down her belongings as she changed the subject.

"It's in the oven. I'll heat it up," I said, uncomfortable with the lie hanging between us. I heated up the oven while Daphne scratched at Polpetta and headed into her room to get cleaned up. I followed her slowly, waiting to confront her.

And I did, in silence. She stood topless in her bathroom, looking at herself in the mirror as I came to the threshold behind her. Tears fell from my eyes at the welts and bruises marking her arms and back, notably older than the red splotches that warmed her neck.

"Odie, this isn't what it looks like," she said, turning to me.

"Then what is it, Daph? Why does it look like someone tried to garrotte you?"

"*Garrotte* me?"

"What's with the soda cans? Why do you seem so skittish?" I interrogated her through tears. She embraced me for a moment before pulling away and making eye contact.

"I was caught in a storm the other night and was hit by hail and debris. I was sick today. There have been break-ins nearby. And I'm just a little worn down. But everything is fine," she insisted, holding my shoulders and looking deep into my eyes.

"And this man? Who is he? What's his name?" I challenged, not at all satisfied with her answers. My heart sank at the blank stare on her face. Did she not even know his name? The man who had now showered her with expensive gifts twice hadn't introduced himself once? She busted out in a laugh, and I didn't know if I should be worried or relieved.

"I don't know. He saved me twice, and I have no idea who he is." Her laughter was louder now and becoming contagious. I cracked a smile.

"*Twice?* Daph, what aren't you telling me?" I said, leaning against the door jam and looking at her sideways.

"I… I got mugged today. He stopped them, and, umm.." she paused, shaking her head and looking at her bracelet. "He gave me a good luck charm."

"You got mugged?" Why hadn't she led with that? "And he saved you but then left without giving you his name or trading numbers?" I swayed my head on my neck with the words.

"He was in a hurry. Had a concerning…phone call to address." She laughed and shrugged her shoulders. "I don't think I'll be seeing him again anyways. He's going far away. So, let's get to the real tea. *Who* was that hottie cutting up at your house?"

My mind wasn't at all at ease, but I could tell she didn't want to talk about this anymore, and prying would make her shut down. She'd never let a man put their hands on her and still stick around. I rolled my eyes with a laugh and turned to check on the food.

We talked over stuffed clams, farfalle salad, and white wine. I ate entirely too much, getting lost in conversation. She updated me on work and what the nurses wanted to do. Everything seemed normal for a short time, but something in her was distant still.

She swiftly turned the topic and pressed about how my night went. Usually, we'd dish out the juicy details of our sex life, but I held back this time. I really liked Fabian, and more importantly, I respected him. I resorted to saying, "We agreed to go slow," but that I could "tell he was a very generous lover."

"*How* generous, Odie? Have you seen his pepperoni yet?" She leaned forward, chewing her food theatrically with a smile. But sharing such personal things about him would be a betrayal.

"I'm very confident it won't be an issue." I dabbed my lips, not giving an inch more. I changed the topic to one meant to segue into my concerns about her search history without admitting I'd snooped on her laptop. "He saw a healer today and asked about these stones I found at *Mayflower*." I pulled out the stone and set it on the table. "She said it's cursed!"

Daphne's eyes focused on it, and she picked it up with narrow brows. "That's so strange. I found the same ones on my way to the restaurant the other night before the storm. I have one here some-where." Her voice trailed off at the end. She looked around for a moment and then bit her nails in a slump. "I must have misplaced it. I haven't seen it since before the storm." Her voice trailed off again. She was being very…off.

"You've been misplacing a lot of things lately, huh," I joked.

"This isn't like you. Maybe you should get your head scanned," I suggested. I hoped she would say something to calm my worries. Instead, she looked as though she had just realized something, never making eye contact, and walked over to her purse to dig through it.

"Daph?" I asked, following her with the two empty plates. I set them in the sink. "You okay?"

"Ah. Yeah. Just a second. Be right back." She hurried into her room. The small counter that looked out to her living room was empty. The medication I had given to her—where was it? I followed her into her room where she sifted through the pockets of her clothes from today, turning them out empty.

"That fucking son of a bitch," she murmured under her breath.

"Who?" I asked, startling her with my quiet approach.

"No one. It's nothing."

"Daph, where is the medication I gave you?"

She shook her head and tightened the ends of her mouth with a defeated tuck of her lips. "I don't know. But I'm going to see Dr. Bailey tomorrow, so don't worry. I'll pay you back."

"Daph, I'm worried about *you,* not about getting my pills back. You're the most organized person I know, and you haven't been yourself."

"Odie…" she sighed, brushing my worries off for what felt like the hundredth time tonight. Was I exaggerating? Was I overthinking all of these strange things?

"Daph, maybe I should stay with you until you see Dr. Bailey? He can write you an order for a CT? You might have a concussion."

"I said I'm fine, Odie," she snapped, standing up. She moved into the living room. I followed her, refusing to be ignored. I knew something was wrong.

"Are you hallucinating, Daph?" Silence hung in the air for a long moment, and I knew I messed up.

"Why would you ask that?" she turned and asked with a cocked head. My eyes moved to the computer before I could think better of it. Her brows shot up. "You looked through my computer, Odie? Really?"

"You were late. You weren't answering my phone calls or texts. I was worried!" I replied with urgency.

"I said everything was fine! I can't believe you would do that and try to dance around it all night, trying to get answers from me!" She grabbed the laptop and carried it to the guestroom. "Why does everyone think they can just fuck with my shit? I'm so sick of it!" she barked while locking the guest room door. I met her in the foyer as she came out of the hall.

"I'm going to get out of here," I said. I already had my purse in hand and dug through it for my pill bottle. Luckily, I brought it with me, not knowing how late I'd be here. I left a tablet on her counter and headed to the door. She chewed her cheek, twisting her toe into the tile.

"I'm sorry, Daph. I'm just worried about you," I said before opening the door, soda cans clanging together under the knob. I wasn't exactly sure that I was sorry, though. Something was clearly wrong, but maybe I needed to let it pass. She had the right to be angry at me for violating her privacy, but there'd never been such a wall between us before. Was I overstepping, or was she in danger? I couldn't sort out my feelings, but that didn't matter just then because something on my car came into view.

A pale scrap of paper flapped in the breeze against my cracked windshield, trapped under a wiper blade. I looked around for any sign of who might have left it there. The street was deserted and quiet in the humid night, aside from the chirping of crickets and croaking of toads. I shivered.

I inched toward my car and grabbed the paper. The second I unfolded the note, my bones went cold with fear and rage. The two words were written with expert calligraphy on torn white paper with wide purple ruling.

Stay Away.

I3

DAPHNE: PERFECTLY HAUNTING

THE NURSES WERE FIRED UP AND FOLLOWING THROUGH WITH THEIR missions. We'd met at a restaurant a few hours prior, to follow up on progress. Covered in a long-sleeved shirt and casual scarf to hide my marks, I coordinated the meeting with ease. I hadn't shared with them that I had the entire list already. It would come in handy when we got closer to getting authorization cards and voting. But for now, it was important that they were doing this work for themselves and taking responsibility. It was important for them to understand the process and build relationships with each other too. They were doing all of that wonderfully and already starting to bond. As far as organizing went, it was too good to be true.

"This is great work, guys! All of you got a list of employees from your units. How did you get them so fast?" I asked while they entered their new data into the online spreadsheet I organized for them.

"The scheduling program, Kronos," Carlotta replied with a sly grin.

"Great! We'll use these lists to do name-by-names. Whoever is done first, let me know, and I'll walk you through it."

"I'm about done," Dean said. I pulled up a seat next to him.

"Awesome. Let's go down the list of names. You'll add notes about them in this column, and we'll score them 0-3 here." I pointed to the screen, the bracelet hanging from my wrist distracting me for a moment. "We want to note things like, are they well liked and well respected by their coworkers, and if so, why. And what matters to them at work?"

We worked through every column, making notes and figuring out what kind of manpower we had.

"Great. And here. Who are they friends with? Who would they pull into the supply room to cry to? This is how we grow our network." When all was done, we had the usual mimosa over lighter conversation, and eventually everyone started their goodbyes. I stayed behind to wrap up a summary of progress to discuss with my mentor. Jesula was once again the last to leave, along with Dawn. Jesula looked me over and spoke as bluntly as she always had.

"What's going on, my dear? Something's off with you," she asked. I thought I had hidden my fluster pretty well, but I guess some people had a keener sense for matters of the spirit. Dawn waited for my response too, her chin resting on her fist.

"Oh, nothing you need to worry about. It's a whole lot of nothing," I waved them off, the clink of my charm bracelet calling my bluff.

"I told you I don't like secrets, so if there is something going on—out with it, girl."

I couldn't afford to have two strong leaders lose trust in me, and I was truly a shit liar. Odie figuring me out was a testament to that. But how would I explain *this* without sounding crazy?

"I don't know that you guys would believe me if I told you."

"Try me," Jesula said, leaning back and crossing her arms. I didn't have the mental battery to construct a lie that could get past *this* woman, so I continued carefully with my words, trying to be as honest as I could.

"Okay," I started, closing my laptop and folding my hands on the table. "I think Lyndie Pratt is involved in something pretty terrible. I overheard a phone conversation, and it was…concerning. But I just don't know how it's possible." I tucked my lips, unsure of how to skirt around the crazy details.

"What is it you think she's involved in?" Dawn asked with a seriousness that made me let out a laugh and cock my head.

"I think she has something to do with the storms. Collecting insurance on the *Mayflower* disaster and wealthy patients in the area affected by it. It sounded planned. I can't explain how that's possible, but that's the only explanation for what I heard on her phone call." I shrugged, ready to be called crazy.

"And?" Jesula pressed sternly. This woman could see right through me. I felt exposed. I squinted, uncomfortable with sharing much more. But I decided that if they thought it was nuts, I'd just laugh it off with them. I needed their trust. Here went nothing.

"You know the fairytales we hear as kids? Magic—mermaids—all of that nonsense that we *know* isn't real?"

"Well, I'll stop you right there, my dear, because mermaids *are* real," Jesula retorted confidently. "I've seen them myself plenty when I was younger, back in Haiti. I knew one well, as a matter of fact."

Any other day I would have nodded out of respect but refused to actually believe it. I had never met someone who actually believed mermaids were real, and I'd have been shocked that someone as no-nonsense as Jesula would swear to such a thing. But yesterday I stood on a cloud with a man who could breathe into me with his hands and had eyes like shimmering opal. I looked at her for a moment and considered that maybe I could tell her more than I thought.

"And magic? Is that something you've seen too?"

"Yes!"

"I grew up around paganism and am Wiccan myself. Magic, I'd say, is something people from all over the world practice in different ways, usually when they have a strong connection to spiritualism and nature," Dawn offered. "Would you think I was crazy if I told you I did witchcraft?"

These women were more open-minded than I gave them credit for. More so, it sounded as though I was preaching to the choir. I offered a line of trust, biting on my nails for comfort.

"I met a man. He's not like anyone I've ever met. He can do… things. It's strange, and I'm not sure I can bring myself to even say it. But he thinks Lyndie's working with powerful people, and there may be a storm coming," I said uncomfortably. "He's not… I mean, according to him, he isn't… *human*."

"So, you have a witness to this phone call, I take it?" Dawn asked. I was shocked for a moment that *this* was her only concern about what I just said.

"It's not that simple. None of it is simple." I scratched at the table aimlessly and then looked up at Jesula. "You knew a mermaid, you say?"

"That's right." She nodded. She didn't at all look surprised or bothered by what I said either.

"How do you know if they're good or bad? These *other beings*. How do you know which ones are good and which are evil?"

Jesula leaned in and gave me a soft look of someone well practiced in patience. "A good rule of thumb is that if you are categorizing someone as good or bad based on a group they belong to, *you* are the one in the wrong. We are all our *own* people; some are good, and some are bad. Sometimes you have to take a leap of faith and figure it out the hard way."

The three of us sat in silence for a moment. I felt foolish for needing advice on something as simple as prejudice. I was also thankful for the advice; when she validated what I said by simply advising how to approach it, she gave me the first sense of calm I had felt around the thought of him. She made his existence less shocking or unbelievable. This man was just a being, and I wouldn't learn what he truly cared about unless I was willing to start some type of rapport. That would start with not being terrified that he existed. He wanted something from me. The ball was in *my* court.

Jesula stood up to leave, Dawn following behind her. Her warm hand patted my back supportively before she left the restaurant, and in that moment I was reminded why she was so treasured on the unit. She was impervious to bullshit, wiser than the average person, and confident in who she was. She had a fearlessness about her, and she inspired such trust.

"Thank you," I mouthed.

After they left, I slid open my phone screen and saw a message from Odie.

> I'm sorry. I hope you're okay.

I wasn't ready to tell Odie. I knew her well enough to *know* she'd freak out. But her fears weren't unwarranted. He had kind of tried to… '*garrotte*' me or whatever. I responded.

> I'm sorry too. I'm fine. We'll talk later. Xo

I pocketed the phone and planned to talk to her soon. I packed up my computer, made sure I had *all* of my belongings this time, and made my way out. I had an appointment with Dr. Bailey and needed to make sure I got my medication, *and* that I hid it well.

I SAT IN MY M3, PARKED IN THE LOT OF THE *HEARTLY MENTAL HEALTH* clinic in North Miami with fifteen minutes to spare. There was always something calming about sitting in silence in my quiet car. I basked in the heat. My eyes drifted to the sky a number of times on the way there, but I had to keep my eyes on the road. Even though I couldn't see him, I could almost feel him stalking me from above. I needed to prepare for our next talk.

Now parked, I reclined my seat, opened the sunroof, and indulged in the shapes of the clouds and the gorgeous blue that they floated in. I wondered which, if any, were his. I bet his was the cloud shaped like a giant dick.

Jesula's words gave me clarity though. I was ready for our next encounter. There were few things that I knew about him, so I took time to recall what they were and piece it together.

First, I knew he was caeluman. From what I'd researched, the word was rooted in Latin. Much like the word "human" originated from the Latin term *humus*—meaning ground—caeluman had the Latin word root *caelum*—meaning sky. He had some control over the weather and its elements and could create stunning jewels with healing properties. I wondered if all caeluman could do that. I wondered what else he could do.

I also knew that he firmly believed there was a war coming with a rival kingdom above the European continent led by the Conqueror

Ouran. *Loanan must be a kingdom here in North America.* If Lyndie was working with the rival kingdom for her own financial gain, what was it she had agreed to help them with? What business could a conqueror of the skies want with powerless humans?

Lastly, I knew that he believed I am a caeluman too. He claimed I was hidden with humans by my birth parents. Hair stood up on the back of my neck at the late realization. How could he know I wasn't raised by my birth parents? He suggested that Ouran's people had found me and used my medication to keep me weak. This made the least sense of it all. Why would Ouran want me weak, and if I was a threat, why not just kill me?

Nothing about the things I knew fit into place. Most bothersome right now was that if any of this was true, then I was sitting in the parking lot of a man who'd been betraying my trust since I was a kid. With two minutes left until I'd walk into a potential viper's nest, I had some decisions to make. Fully aware of how insane all of this sounded, I decided to proceed with caution as I gathered my belongings to go in. I tucked my bracelet in the long sleeve of my shirt, adjusted my sheer silk scarf, and made my way into the building.

His office was softly lit with natural light that soaked into the lucy-blue wall paint. He decorated it in excess with model sailboats and nautical souvenirs. One souvenir that I had seen countless times now caught my curiosity: a wooden figurehead for the bow of an old ship was carved into a mermaid and mounted on his wall.

Dr. Bailey was a hefty man with wavy brown hair, peppered with gray on the sides. He had square-framed glasses and pinched facial features that were swallowed up in plump cheeks. He always dressed in breezy business casual—a button-up top with no tie that was never tucked into his tan dress pants.

He had been promoted to Regional Director when *Amett Health* started its partnership with *Heartly* and began the post-storm relief programs. Luckily for Odie and I, we were one of the few patients he didn't have to transfer to his partners. *Heartly's* deal with *Amett Health* and *Parson & Dodds* elevated the once small local company of *Heartly* into a multi-million-dollar national organization within a short time.

He guided me to the bolstered chaise lounge. It would have seemed pretty cliche for a psychiatrist if it weren't for how well the distressed-brown leather couch complimented the aesthetic of his office.

"So, Daph," he clapped his hands on his knees as he sat across from me in a matching armchair. "How did you, of all people, lose your medication?" he asked with a jolly humor not meant to shame.

"I'm not sure. I think I may just be stressed from work. I'm taking on a huge campaign." I shrugged with a smile. It wasn't a lie. This was a huge facility that served the community I lived in. If this went wrong and I ever needed medical treatment, I wasn't sure how I'd feel about facing the staff. Organizing would be hard for everyone involved, and failure could have real consequences for them. Even if they resented me, I knew they'd never cause harm, but it'd be an uncomfortable interaction nonetheless. What if management had a say in my care while I was vulnerable? If I ever wanted to return to bedside nursing, how far would I need to travel? The thoughts gave me a pinch of anxiety.

"You've talked about these campaigns before with excitement. What's different this time?"

"There's a lot at stake for the staff and for me."

"This is important to you," he said. It was more of a statement than a question.

"Of course. It's always important. These are people who give everything to their patients and to the hospital. It's time they have a voice, a say in how things are done and how they're compensated. They deserve this."

"And if they fail, how would that make you feel?" The question was strange because the answer was so obvious.

"Pretty shitty. Heartbroken like I did more harm than good."

"So, their failure is yours?"

"In a way, yes. My job is to set them up for success. I'm supposed to empower them with the tools they need to win."

"And you're doing that?"

"Yes. I'm giving a hundred percent."

"It sounds like you're holding onto things that are out of your control. You're no superhuman, you know."

I paused and then let out a short laugh. *Strange choice of words for someone who may be complicit in poisoning me.*

"One thing is for sure, Daphne. You're no good to—"

"To anyone else unless I'm okay. I know," I finished his sentence for him, nodding. I'd heard this mantra countless times.

"So, how can we ensure you don't misplace your medication again?" he asked, cutting to the point.

"I was actually wondering if I could try coming off of it. I felt fine the days I didn't take it or was late." I shrugged.

He leaned back in his chair and took a deep breath that raised his large belly. Lifting his brows, he replied, "Daphne, coming off of this medication can have some real serious side effects. On the days you didn't take it, did you experience any paranoia, mood swings, hallucinations, nausea, and vomiting, or missing periods of time?"

I thought for a moment about the last forty-eight hours.

"Nope, nothing out of the ordinary," I said casually.

"Well, that's good to hear, but what about that... ahh..." He motioned a finger at his brow, undoubtedly referencing my almost healed cut.

"Oh, no," I waved him off. "I got hit with hail. It's nothing."

"Well, I'm concerned about your misplacing medications. You may not realize the missing time, but it sounds like it's affected you more than you think. I don't advise going off of it. So, I'm going to refill your Zerpotine, and in the meantime, I think we should revisit the relaxation techniques again." He gestured to the chaise, and I lay on it, a silent agreement that I was far from relaxed.

This conversation didn't go as I had planned, and my mind was swimming with suspicion. The one chance I took at challenging him about the medication was shot down. What was worse was I felt less certain about what was reality and what was in my head. *I'm no super-human.*

I hadn't even realized the white noise or the humming of his tuning forks until he started guiding me through the session. Dr. Bailey started by having me focus on the ceiling tile just above me that was slightly different from the others. It had more texture and was a brighter white. Once my eyes locked on it, he guided me to imagine the most peaceful place I could think of. He asked me where I was and how I would describe it. My answer was always the same.

"The sky. On a cloud. The air is crisp and cool and tastes like salt water. It's quiet, and I'm weightless." My vision had long since tunneled to the bright ceiling tile, and the divots of texture seemed to form into the curves of a cloud. The couch was no longer a stiff anchor but a cool, breathable cloud that carried my weight and my burdens. He instructed me on tightening and relaxing my muscles one by one, from head to toe. Soon, the feeling of tension slipped away— slipped away into the cloud around me, and then rained down to earth where I couldn't get wet. The storm couldn't touch me from here. The white noise and tuning forks swallowed the sound of his voice until all I could hear was the humming breeze around me.

I knew this place well and loved it here. It was the place I went to during every session. This time, the space felt even more real because I had been here in real life just the day before. And just like the day before, I was now here with the man who had given me breath from his hands. His face hovered above mine as I lay on the plush cumulus cloud, his body close to me as he propped himself up on one forearm. I looked into his eyes, the only sense of caring on an otherwise emotionless face. His hands hovered over my lips, and I swore I could feel his warmth. Everything felt so real. His lips parted to speak to me in his otherworldly baritone.

"*Wake up, Daphne,*" his voice echoed.

I drew a deep breath of cool, pure oxygen from his warm palm. I suddenly became grounded on the chaise, aware of the session still going on, although not entirely removed from the tantric state. It wasn't until Dr. Bailey continued his strange narrative that I snapped completely out of it and looked at him as if woken from a nightmare.

He was startled.

"What did you say?" I asked, confused and alarmed. But like a dream forgotten moments after waking, the memory of what he said was fading. *The storm? ...Man?* The rest of it was gone. I clung to what fragments of words I could remember and recited them in my head so I didn't forget them.

"Daphne, you're more anxious than usual. Perhaps you should try some additional medications," he said, putting down his tuning fork and reaching for a prescription pad.

"No," I responded, sitting up and coming back to reality. The room was dimmer than before. It was raining now, and the large window was taking a beating from the wind-whipped palm fronds outside. The howling wind sounded like a voice warning me to leave. "I'm feeling much better, thank you."

I stood up and grabbed my stuff off the couch. His eyes narrowed, and he hesitated to stand. "I sent your refill to the pharmacy down the hall. They have standing orders to refill it early if needed. Don't hesitate to call."

"Thank you, Dr. Bailey," I said with a tight smile, unable to meet his eyes. He followed me to the door and held his stance at the doorway as I walked down the hall.

"Daphne," he said, the authority in his voice stopping my feet in their tracks. "Be careful out there. These storms are dangerous." He tapped his brow, and I nodded before turning for the pharmacy.

The pharmacist had my medication ready when I got to the window. It was the only pharmacy in the area that carried a supply consistently. I asked for a spare medicine bottle and she gave me one without question. It was only when I dumped the pills from their bottle and into the new one and then tucked them in my underwear that a look of confusion came over her face. I filled the original bottle with Tic Tacs, dropped it in the paper bag that the medication came in, and asked her to re-staple it. She gave a few blinks before doing it, clearly caught off guard.

As she stapled the bag, I caught the cold stare of a pharmacy tech with crystal blue eyes standing some ways behind her. I kept my eyes locked on his. He disappeared behind a shelf as the pharmacist handed me the re-stapled bag. I shook off his uncomfortable gawking.

I wasn't sure who was right or wrong, but neither the caeluman nor Dr. Bailey would have authority over if I took my medication or not. That decision would be my own.

I carried the paper bag of candy pills in hand, hardly trying to hide it as I shielded my body from the rain. By the time I got in my car, I was drenched. I brushed the wet hair from my forehead and removed my scarf, throwing it in the back seat. The slap of wet fabric sounded closer than I expected, and I turned around to see what it hit.

"Hello, Daphne," the caeluman said casually. I yelped and nearly jumped out of my seat, then breathed to calm myself.

"What are you doing here?" I asked. This was not the line of questioning I had planned, a common theme today.

"You place too much trust in him. He's making you weak."

I took a moment to collect myself. I was going to take control of this conversation. There would be no more stumbling over my words or looking like a deer in headlights.

"At least come sit in the front seat like a normal person."

The rain was a wall around us, a welcome shield from anyone who might have seen his misty teleportation into my front seat. I turned on my car, ready to act as casually as I could while talking to a damn sky fae.

"What's your name, anyway?" I asked plainly while my hands stayed busy working the controls like a pilot readying for lift-off. The sudden blow of heat from the air vents alarmed him, and he narrowed his brows. I noted the reaction and assumed he'd never been in a car. I couldn't have planned this better. My car was fast, responsive, and loud. If I wanted to turn the power structure in my favor, this would definitely be the way. I looked at him expectantly, brows raised.

"Pol Phoebus," he said. He grabbed at the door when I not-so-gracelessly reversed out of the parking spot. I tried to stifle my smirk as I made full use of first gear, picking up speed with unnecessary quickness. The highway was close by, and we made our way to an on ramp in no time. I shifted through gears, causing purposeful jerks as I weaved in and out of traffic.

"If you're going to stalk me, there'll be rules from now on," I said in a very unamused tone. His only response was to look at me expressionlessly. "For starters," I grabbed the brown bag containing my candy pills. "No more messing with my medication."

"No. It's poison," he snapped back through a stiff jaw.

"You told me that, and I'm considering it. But forcing my hand will only push me away. It's my decision *if* and *when* I stop taking it. Period." He continued to stare, and I wondered what thoughts were behind his opal eyes.

"Any other rules?"

"Yes! As a matter of fact. No more breaking into my house," I exclaimed, rolling my neck as I looked at him. His eyes darted between me and the road. I looked back to the road out of responsibility, not at all worried about appeasing him.

"And you won't be medicating me again unless I give my expressed, *informed* consent," I added flatly. The subject made me uncomfortable as I remembered the intimate moment. Heat pooled on my cheeks, but I pushed it away. Still, the memory of him pulling his pleasure from himself at my window made my back straighten. I could tell by the slight turning of his face that he felt *something* about it too. I recovered first.

"Can you do that, Pol?"

He took his time to answer, calculating his thoughts. "Yes. So, you're coming with me to Loanan now?"

"No."

"No?"

"In the short time I've known you, you've given me more reason to question your intentions than reason to trust you. I need answers," I said, looking at him for a short moment before returning my attention to the road. He was agreeable so far. It was a good time to level with him. "...and time to process this," I added more gently.

"If you stop this monstrosity, I'll tell you anything you want to know."

My face twisted in offense. Surely, he wasn't talking about the most gorgeous, modern muscle car still being made in a manual stick shift? *I might do donuts just out of spite.* But it would be in the best interest of building a relationship to let up. I took the approaching exit and pulled into the parking spot of an ice cream shop, all while sucking my teeth.

"You can't expect me to drop everything in my life to run off with a stranger without any way to come and go. I need time, Pol. I need to *know* you." I spoke calmly.

"I can show you how to come and go yourself. You wouldn't rely on me. Everything you want to know is in Loanan." His eyes met the bruise on my neck. This morning it was purple. By now it had faded to a splotchy blue-yellow. It was healing quickly, and my welts were nearly gone too. He raised his hand to my neck, and I backed away with an offended grimace. I hoped my scowl hid how flush his touch made me.

"Let me give you more reason to trust me," he said, drawing me in. I leaned forward, slightly lifting my chin, our faces closer. I steadied my breathing and studied his face. I noticed what little eye contact he'd make. He had a unique, poetic beauty to him. I might have even liked it if he hadn't been such a Goddamn asshole right off the bat. His face was perfectly haunting, and my cheeks heated again as his long fingers wrapped around my neck. I swallowed hard. I had stuck my neck into a lion's mouth. My nostrils flared at the looming threat. I stared at him with angry suspicion.

I felt contact much harder than flesh grazing my neck. His hand pulled away slowly, his fingertips meeting his thumb. The dropping of white gold and obsidian tapped my collarbones and chest. The necklace, a twin of my bracelet, hung from my neck. A pendant of raw amethyst geode the size of a small oyster weighted the chain to a point over my covered cleavage. I propped the stone on my fingers and studied it in awe. Then I looked up to find his eyes no farther away than before. He was looking down at either the pendant or the way my wet shirt clung to my tightened breasts.

This guy clearly doesn't understand personal space. It's a good thing he smells good.

"Do you like it?"

"It's beautiful," I said with a pause. "Why are you giving me these?"

"They'll heal you faster, reduce your pain, and protect your energy."

"But why? *Why* are you healing me?" I asked while lifting my chin. It only drew our mouths nearer, an unintended closeness that I wouldn't back down from. I would show no fear. He didn't budge either and glanced at my lips.

"To protect you. I need you. *Alive.*"

I pulled back from him and sunk into my seat, humored by his gall. Every answer he gave me left me with more questions.

"I'll come to your tree every night when the sun is three fingers to the horizon and make sure you are safe. You can ask me anything and...*know* me. And then you're coming with me to Loanan."

"So, you're just going to hang out under my tree all night until I cave, Pol?"

He didn't answer right away, so we sat in silence. He reached a finger under my sleeve and drew out the bracelet. My chest fluttered at the feeling of his skin touching mine as he rotated the piece until finding the clasp. My heart was pounding, but I wouldn't turn my eyes to his face. "Push your thumb over—"

"I know how to reach you."

I pulled my arm away and shifted the car back into reverse, then released the emergency brake. He took that for what it was: the conversation was over.

"I'll see you tonight," he said, and then misted from my passenger seat.

I huffed out a heavy breath and tilted my head up. Every interaction with him cost more energy than I had to spend.

14

O'DOHERTY – MY SAFE PLACE

AFTER A BIT OF RADIO-SILENCE, DAPHNE AND I RECONCILED OUR grievances. Now, a month later, our friendship was still adrift. She kept her distance. When I did see her, she seemed off, but I wouldn't pry again. I did, however, complement the stunning necklace she'd acquired, purposely remarking how well it matched the bracelet that man had given her—the same man she insisted she 'wouldn't be seeing again.'

"Pol. His name is Pol," she finally told me, grabbing the amethyst and tracing her thumb over its sharp points. She wouldn't say much else about the man, although I had my suspicions.

In the month since our fight, she hadn't invited me over and seemed lost in her mind when I did see her. If it were anyone else, I'd be very disturbed by the fact that almost every time she saw him she was both injured and then gifted a gorgeous piece of jewelry. Or that she seemed secluded from friends; or that she had a new solemnity in her mood. These were all signs of abuse.

But the necklace, from what I could tell, didn't come with any new bruises or wounds; although she did dress conservatively, so they could have been hidden. Her work *was* stressful and time-consuming, yet that had never affected her like this before. I couldn't tell what I was overthinking and what I wasn't. *If I could meet him, it would give me perspective.*

I tried to cajole her into bringing this *Pol* to my Godmother's BBQ today. According to Daphne, he lived far away, and she rarely saw him. At least our parents would get to meet Fabian. It wasn't often I brought someone home to meet my family, but he was the most incredible person I had ever met. The space from Daphne only nourished my relationship with him.

He woke me up in the mornings, usually by kissing me from my ear lobe to the crook of my neck. I simpered when I awoke.

"Morning, honey," he'd say, tucking his hand into my panties and moving his lips to my chest. He slowly worked his hand down further, and my hands would eventually do the same to him. I would never get enough of how he touched me or the noises he made when I touched him. We took our time to learn each other well. It was effortless to enjoy him.

"You nervous?" he asked, pulling me from my daydream. "You look deep in thought." His hand rested on my thigh as he drove.

"No, I was just thinking about this morning," I said, biting my lip with a smile.

"I do make some damn good pancakes," he replied with a shrug, knowing full well I wasn't talking about *that*. He wasn't wrong though. He made the pancakes from scratch and added this Mediterranean extract to the batter. It gave the pancakes the subtle flavor of biscottis that made me want to dunk a piece in my coffee.

He brought a side of Watergate salad for the BBQ, insisting it would impress Selene. It looked absolutely revolting, but when I stole a spoonful, I was surprised to find that it was an amazingly refreshing dessert. No one in their right mind would want to try the green mystery dish; the name alone would deter them enough. But I wanted them to try it and love it like I did, to adore him the way I did. He was so proud of the dish, and I was so proud of him.

We pulled into the driveway and Fabian admired the black M3 parked in the driveway.

"Damn!"

"That's Daphne's baby," I said, opening the car door. She hadn't spent time with him since they'd first met. I couldn't help but wonder if it had anything to do with our blooming relationship. I wondered if she was resentful that I was no longer available to be intimate with. The possibility made me angry. She had no right to be mad at *me*, of all people. She had ample opportunity for us to be more before Fabian was in the picture.

A wall of cool air and potpourri was a welcome change from the humidity outdoors. We let ourselves into the large, cozy home, and my eyes met my godmother's as we turned the corner from the foyer.

"Oh, sweetie! You look nice," she said in her faint British accent. She hugged me, squeezing the fat on my arms, and then inspected my curls. "I'm so glad to see you're managing your hair."

I cringed internally. Selene was a tall, thin white woman with a silky, straight bob of silver hanging just past her shoulders and impossibly blue eyes. Growing up, she had no idea how to manage my mixed hair and never took the time to learn. Instead, she insisted on keeping it short when I was younger. I'd been mastering it beautifully myself, with the guidance of internet influencers, for over a decade now. Yet here she was parroting the same backhanded compliment.

"Selene, this is Fabian," I beamed, my body framing him to the left.

"It's nice to meet you," Fabian said, reaching out his free hand for a shake and smiling big.

"Oh, you too. You can call me Selene," she said with contained enthusiasm. "And what's this?" She reached out her thin, perfectly manicured fingers to cup the bowl.

"Oh, I made a Watergate salad. It's a dessert."

"Ohhh okay. That's so sweet." She looked at it with disingenuous surprise. If she was disgusted by the look of it, I couldn't blame her, but the least she could do was fake it. "I'll put that right over here next to the cranberry brie tarts. Everyone is out back."

The pool deck overlooked the Biscayne Bay. As reluctant as I was to revisit the hot, humid air, the view was welcoming and nostalgic. For all of the difficulties that came with being raised by Selene, my reprieve was the Bay. Selene had never done harm to me, but her cold, reserved nature and overbearing insistence on perfection was stressful. What warmth and peace the home lacked inside, despite its cozy appearance, the pool deck had made up for. I'd study here, relax here, and sometimes sneak out just to watch the water lap at the flood wall as it shimmered in the moonlight.

Selene always made sure I had the best things, and every opportunity to succeed. But money and status couldn't buy a mother's affection. I'd sit on the flood wall with my feet kicking back and forth over the edge and imagine what my life would be like with my real parents instead. Would it be this hard to earn their approval? Would I be good enough for them?

My parents died when I was a baby. I don't really remember them. Selene was my Godmother and took me in. In doing so, she relocated us to America, away from any real family I'd ever know, away from my roots. When she moved us here, she quickly befriended an older Italian couple who also had an adopted daughter the same age. Daphne and I had been best friends ever since.

"Ciao, Bella!" Giuseppe hollered in his raspy voice. He waddled over to me with outstretched arms of tanned olive skin and age spots. Carmella was just behind him, a petite, slender woman with a helmet of black permed hair and shimmering flamingo pink lipstick. Daphne's parents loved loudly, and I indulged in their fuss.

"Hi!" I shrieked with delight.

"Oh, who is this-ah handsome young man? Look at that face!" Carmella said in a thick Italian accent. She placed her hands on Fabian's cheeks as if holding a precious gem up to the light.

"I'm Fabian. It's nice to meet you," he said, smiling, though his cheeks were being smooshed together.

"Oh, you sweet boy," she said, patting his cheek. They shuffled back to the table with hands waving at us to sit. "You're hungry, yes? I make-ah you a plate! You're *too* ah-*skinny*." I knew if Selene heard that remark she would let out a "hmph," always one to comment on how heavy I was getting and how I'd better watch my shape. Carmella pinched my arm and scurried to the kitchen.

"Hey, Daphne, how have you been? I haven't seen you in a while," Fabian said, addressing her with a kind energy.

"Oh, great, thanks. Just very busy with work. It's a big project," she replied, fiddling with the sharp edges of her geode pendant as if testing her skin's resilience. Her smile lacked energy lately, and she seemed withdrawn. A sensation of bitterness ignited in my gut at the coldness she'd shown him, but I let it go.

"That's some car you got out there!" he added jovially. Giuseppe threw his hands in the air and let out a noise of inspired opinion.

"Aye, it is beautiful, yes. But it sucks up-ah the gas! *Why* do you want to pour so much money into this?" He gesticulated at his daughter with thumb pressed to fingertips. Daphne let a laugh through her nose and shook her head. "Maybe the storms will scoop it away-ah. What will you buy next?" Daphne's face looked long and ponderous at the question.

The storms had been bad this past month and hit close to home for all of us. Just a few days prior, a tree had nearly crashed through her parents' roof as they slept. It was purely an act of God that the tree, which you could tell had snapped toward their bedroom, was blown off to the side and fell in a twist, missing them completely.

"You know, I was researching these storms. The mainstream media isn't covering it, but the storms are happening all over the east coast of America," Fabian offered.

"How long ago did that start?" Daphne finally chimed in. The pendant had stilled in her fingers.

"Around the same time they started here. In fact, the night of the *Mayflower* storm, thirty other nursing homes in the country were taken out by tornadoes! It's almost too much to be a coincidence," he beamed with a humored suspicion. Daphne responded with a look of muted distaste, nodded, and turned her eyes to the water. She stopped fumbling with the pendant and tucked it inside her shirt, then crossed her arms. *What is her problem with him?*

Carmella plopped two plates stacked with manicotti in front of Fabian and me, her chunky gold-plated ring clinking on the tabletop. "Nursing homes? Well, it looks like we *are-ah* safer at home after all," she said. "*Eat-ah. Eat!*"

Selene had come out behind her and sat in a chair next to Daphne, three bowls of Greek salad in her hands. She put one down in front of me.

"Start with the salad, dear." I blinked twice and shoved it away, taking a defiant forkful of manicotti instead. She shook her head and put the other bowl in front of Daphne, who didn't seem to notice. "Earth to Daphne," Selene said, snapping her fingers in front of Daphne. Daphne looked back, smiling at the salad thankfully. As soon as Selene turned her attention to Fabian and me, Daphne slipped Polpetta some black olives from the salad. "Well then, can your research tell us when these storms will stop? My tennis club is terrified to meet up. I'm rather bored."

"The storms have only gotten stronger and more frequent from what I can tell. And the rocks Doetey found? They were found wherever the storms were!"

Selene looked at him doubtfully. "Surely you don't believe there's some hocus pocus going on here? That's ridiculous. They're just rocks," she said before biting into her salad. Fabian looked unbothered by the dismissal, but the qualm of bitterness revived in my gut.

"Well, I think there may be something to it!" I said confidently. Selene fixed her eyes on me, raised her brows, and paused her chewing. She looked both curious and displeased. "I sent one of them to a mineralogist just a few weeks ago. There are plenty of things that can have an effect on someone's neurological status, or…"

"…Or the weather? Ha! O'doherty, don't be silly."

I was used to her speaking to me this way. But now that Fabian had shown me support and affection unlike I had ever experienced, it bothered me more. No one had ever made me feel so important. It infuriated me that she treated Fabian that way too. What added to my bitterness was that Daphne, who would normally buffer the hits and side with me, was just sitting there picking at her food. Would either of them show him some damn courtesy?

"Refill, anyone?" I said, pushing my chair out.

"I have to go, actually," Daphne said, standing with me. "Odie,

I'm sorry to ask at the last minute, but could you watch Polly for me? I have to travel for work. It just came up."

"Sure. Of course. How long will you be gone?" I said as if saying 'yes' to her was programmed in me, as if I wasn't stewing a moment before.

"About a week. A week and a half tops. But I have to pack. Can you take her home with you? I have food for her in the car; I'll leave it here."

"Okay. Yeah." I shrugged as Fabian picked up the furry blob.

"Oh, what a good girl! Good girl! You ready for endless belly rubs and *bacon*?" he promised her. Polpetta's tail could have sent her flying through the yard the way it wagged so fast. She let out a small bark at him and then sniffed his face.

"Where are you going?" Selene asked with her cool blue eyes squinting up at Daphne.

"Ah, Massachusetts. There's a great class about organizing being taught by Marshall Ganz at Harvard. He's kind of a big deal. The union is offering to pay for it, so I'm going to check it out."

"I thought you already took that online?" I wondered out loud.

"It's… different. That was a public narrative thing." She picked up her purse, kissed her parents, and then scratched at Polpetta, who was still happily wrapped in Fabian's arms. "She's already forgotten about me," she joked meekly as Polpetta continued to sniff and nuzzle Fabian. I wondered if the comment had another purpose, and it only fueled my bitterness. But then she was walking across the yard to the gate, waving the last of her goodbyes. I thought better of going after her and spoiling my mood. I would need my patience in strong reserve to get through a meal with Selene.

Giuseppe and Carmela kept the company warm and inviting.

Conversation carried easier through the meal with them to lead it, their raspy voices and heady cackles loud.

"I will go get the dessert-ah. I heard you made a strange bowl of green pudding," Carmella said. I smiled tightly at Fabian, cringing inside.

Giuseppe's face twisted at the sight of it. Then he looked at Fabian with the most genuine excitement he could manage.

"Oh, looks-ah good," he lied.

"Trust me. It is good!" I insisted. He nodded politely.

Selene put up a soft hand to decline the dessert. I took her bowl from Carmella and set it down in front of Selene. "Try it." I was firmer than usual with her today, determined not to let her insult Fabian. She morphed her face into an awkward smile as she moved her eyes to Fabian. She pulled a small spoonful to her mouth, the first to try it. Everyone's eyes were on her.

"Oh! That is delightful, actually," she said.

"I'm so glad you like it!" he said cheerfully. I smiled at him proudly.

I followed Selene into the kitchen to put up some dishes and talk alone. I didn't know why her approval still meant so much at my age, yet here I was.

"So what do you think of him?"

She shrugged. I shrugged back.

"That's it? You have nothing to say about him?"

"O'doherty, I've known him for little more than a couple of hours. What could I have to say about him?"

"That he's *nice*... He's smart and successful and treats me well. That he's cute. That he...he cooks well. *Anything*?"

She seemed put out. "Yes, he seems very sweet."

"It figures. You're impossible to impress. He could be the perfect person, and you wouldn't give him a second thought." I dried my hands. She was taken back by the change in my behavior today.

"Oh, stop it. He's very nice. I just don't want you getting your heart so set on someone and then it doesn't work out! Then what?"

"Why wouldn't it work out?" I let out an angry laugh.

"I didn't say that. I said it may not, so why fuss so soon?"

"Nice, Selene," I said, dropping the washcloth on the counter and walking outside. "Come on, Polly, let's go!" I called. We said our goodbyes to Carmella and Giuseppe, who were sad to see us leave so quickly. I didn't want to be here anymore though. Fabian was my safe place. He didn't deserve to deal with Selene and he made me realize I didn't either. Not even the soft lapping of water on the Biscayne Bay could keep me there.

15

DAPHNE: JUST ABOVE THE CLOUD LINE

THE SUN WAS GETTING LOW. HE'D BE HERE SOON. I'D MADE SOME phone calls and started packing a duffel bag for the trip. My mentor agreed to take the reins for the time I was away, but I wasn't worried. Jesula had been taking charge. She was a natural. If it wasn't for her, I didn't know if I'd feel comfortable pulling away from work, but I had to. This shit hit too close to home.

I'd be back before she and the other nurses were ready to launch union authorization cards. We only needed a *minimum* of 33% of nurses to sign them, ideally double that. Using the lists the nurses put together—and all of the lists I lifted—it wouldn't be hard. My mentor guessed we had about a month to go. The nurses were almost done reaching out to their coworkers. The more people they spoke to, the more people were ready to back the cause.

I had grown close with the original nurse group. I would consider them friends if I didn't have to distance myself professionally. Jesula was an exception. She was the only one who knew I was going on a trip with Pol.

"I should be back in a week, week and a half tops. If I'm not…" I didn't know what to say. I didn't even like this man very much, let alone trust him.

"Be careful," was all she said.

My laptop and planner sat on my bed next to my backpack. I wasn't sure what I should bring with me. Would this stuff even work there? Was I going off the grid? I decided to wait to pack them until Pol came. He was here every night, as promised, when the sun was three fingers above the horizon, except for the other night when I sent him into a storm.

THE FIRST NIGHT HE CAME, I SAW HIM THROUGH THE BLINDS, SITTING on a low branch of the laurel tree. It was late, and I didn't appreciate the hovering. *Creep.* I flipped him off and shut the blinds that night and every night after for a week. I could tell it had pissed him off, and I wondered when he was going to lose patience and take away my choice. *I could make you come.* Polpetta wouldn't come to bed, keeping her nose pressed against the glass of the slider and watching him until he left. He was always gone by morning.

By the second week, Jesula gave me a stern talking to. It was nothing I didn't already know; I wasn't getting anywhere by shutting him out. Even if he was being rude and trying to put pressure on me, I couldn't ignore him forever. So I walked outside, sat on the bending curve of the tree trunk, and asked what he did out there all night.

"Protective enchantments, sleep, and wait." It was this type of small talk that went on for the next six nights. I learned little things about him—his favorite color was gray, he preferred poultry, was the eldest child of two, and he played the lyre. I shared that my favorite color was lavender, I preferred seafood, I was an only child from what

I knew, and I never learned an instrument well but really loved to paddle board. He never had pets, but Polly was growing on him. I told him about Odie and the stupid things we did as kids, like picking out shapes in the clouds. He thought that was strange. He even told me a little about his magic.

"Why is your cloud always so...stormy?"

"Riding clouds have different formations. The most common is cumulus. I prefer the nimbus. It's faster and more comfortable to me. Everyone is different," he said, moving from his cloud to a low branch.

I ran my hand through the gray rolling puff. It *felt* wet and warm, but my hand didn't get wet at all. It flickered with phantom lightning, and I jerked my hand back. I gave him side-eye.

"It's temperamental," he said flatly, though I thought he was humoring himself.

I would give him an hour of my time before turning in. He'd always end the night telling me to go with him.

By the third week, I had gotten more comfortable with him. But most of my questions were met with him repeating the same goddamn thing. "Come to Loanan. There's plenty of answers there."

"What *will* you tell me then?" I asked, frustrated.

"There are barriers that should be in place to keep the weather naturally occurring. With the barriers in place, no one but high caeluman in a given kingdom should be able to change the weather in their districts of your realm. And they only do that with approval from their councils. Ouran found a way to tear down the strongest anchor points of our barriers. Since then, the rest have been weakening. Ouran's men launch more storm attacks on the humans in districts both under Loanan and across the east coast. It threatens the oldest treaties we have with humans."

"How did he weaken the barriers though?"

"Come to Loanan, I'll explain it there."

I rolled my eyes. He jumped off the tree limb and closed the distance, staring down at me intensely.

"Don't make me force you."

I pushed myself off the tree and walked inside, hiding the flush of my cheeks. As I closed my blinds, I kept my middle finger in view until the curtains were completely shut.

The rest of the week I bitched about Lyndie Pratt and listened as he told me how he fights the storms to weaken and contain them.

"That's what I was doing the night we met. I was fighting the storm to break it up."

"Care to explain why you shoved my body in a drainage pipe? And I swear on all that is holy if you tell me the answers are in Loanan, I'm gonna…"

"I was hiding you. The storm wasn't natural. Whoever made it was close. I went to hunt them. I hid you to keep you safe."

A silence hung between us for a moment. "Thanks…" I managed, suddenly finding the dirt interesting. "So you're the reason for the freezing weather then, or is that your friends? You know it isn't good for the iguanas here; they fall out of the trees." He looked at me with opal eyes and raised a hand. Snow flurries fell from above me. I stood quickly and laughed, looking up at the flurries as they powdered my hair and face.

"It's a spell. Cold air on the ground makes it harder for a tornado to form, not impossible, but hard enough."

I turned a palm toward the sky to catch them. The snow stopped midair and bunched together into a snowball. Before my eyes, the ball transformed into one large crystallized snowflake, big enough to fit into the palm of my hand. Its spikes had gorgeous swirls, and it shimmered in the moonlight. I reached for it and drew it close to my eyes to look closer.

"How did you do that?"

"Come to Loanan. I'll show you."

Suddenly the snowflake evaporated from my fingers. I narrowed my eyes. "It's past my bedtime." Our hour slipped away from us faster each night.

As this, the fourth week, came to us, I could tell his patience was thinning. The storms were getting worse—bigger, stronger, and more frequent. They were always short-lived and never traveled far, thanks mostly to Pol and his army. A few days ago he came when the sun was two fingers from the horizon. *He's late.* He looked like *he* had woken up in an irrigation drain himself. His normal aura-like mist was clearly weak. He sat on the thick tree limb like a wet cat and was clenching his jaw before I could even say hi.

"Fighting another storm? Must have been a rough one. You look like hell, Pol." I silently guessed it was the work of Ouran's son, Prince Nahveel. Pol had seen him trying to brew a storm recently. He jumped down from the branch.

"We are running out of time, Daphne. I know you're still medicated; you're as weak as the day I met you. Get your stuff. We're leaving," he said flatly. My temper boiled. What right did he have to question my medical choices? What the hell did he even know about my medication anyway? And I was sure as hell not being told where to go and when.

"I don't owe you anything, you get that, right?" I snapped before turning around and walking back toward the slider.

"Daphne!" He called after me.

The moment I crossed the threshold my phone screeched out an alarm. A tornado warning was in place for the area my parents lived.

Take shelter now… My heart sank. I turned to see Pol already at the open slider.

"Pol…" the air went out of my lungs. My heart twisted. "Please, my parents." My hands trembled over my mouth.

"You stop taking the pills tonight, and you'll come with me to Loanan."

"Pol! You can't be serious! They'll die," I yelled through a hoarse scream, tears threatening to fall. I charged at him and banged my fists on his chest. His weak mist kicked up around my punching. He didn't flinch. I bunched his damp shirt in my fists, giving it an angry tug. "Pol!" I begged in angry desperation.

His lip twitched. He grabbed my hands and shoved them away. Then he turned and jumped on the nimbus forming behind him.

"Stay here. I'll be back as soon as I can," was all he said before crouching and leaning into the storm cloud. He went ripping through the sky up and to the east, like a surfer riding the swell of a title wave.

He made it to them with only moments to spare. The tornado was a massive F4 that dug up foundations and leveled block structures. The strong winds broke a nearby tree. It would have crushed my parents' skulls in their sleep. But Pol caught it on a gust of his wind. He threw it to the side.

Pol pushed his way into the storm's wall. His aura was weakened from his earlier fight. He was struck by splintered wood and shattered glass. Tree limbs knocked the wind out of him. Still, he pushed through to the storm's center. He could hardly recover there. With little strength left, he countered the rotation. A thunderous holler rumbled from his chest as he made the wind stop. He locked a rush of dry, frigid air around its foot. The storm paused, and the projectiles within it did too. They floated for a second like gravity was gone. Then they fell to the ground, on and around him.

When the last of the debris hit the dirt, he cast cold air around the entire area to dampen storm potential. Tired, he limped to my parents' house on foot. He lay in their yard for a moment to rest before pulling himself up to their window. He saw them still fast asleep, hearing aids on the charger and oblivious to their cheated doom.

He fell onto his cloud; a thin cirrus was all he could manage. He pulled it to the sky and came back to me. When his cirrus made landfall by the tree, it was barely a fog. His mist aura was hardly even there anymore.

"Pol," I yelled, running to him. He lay in my grass, goosebumps pinching his battered skin. My knees crashed against the cold earth next to him. "Are they…" My breath caught in my throat.

"They're fine."

I let out a sob and cried into my hands, rocking myself. Tears blurred my vision and burned my sclerae, but I focused my attention on his exhausted body.

"Come on. Let's get you inside and clean you up." Polpetta whimpered and nudged him with her nose. He was a beast of a man. He was as heavy as a steel coffin and had hardly the strength to shuffle inside by himself. His skin was like wet ice. I wrapped the blue throw over him and led him into the guest bathroom.

He sat on the closed toilet while I drew him a warm bath, adding Epsom salt infused with peppermint and eucalyptus. I had a large claw tub that took a while to fill but would fit his giant body.

I draped my necklace of obsidian and amethyst around his neck. He let out a shuddering sigh of relief and then drew a sharp breath. I wedged my nail to the clamp of my bracelet, but he stopped me with his icy hands.

"The necklace is working just fine. Thank you," he said, standing and peeling off his shirt.

Glass shards and splinters stuck out of his left side, dark blood trickling from their punctures. I grabbed my tweezers from the cabinet and heard wet clothes hit the floor behind me. I looked into the mirror as I closed it and saw his bare ass. He was a pasty man, thin-framed and long but toned. The crimson blood against his ivory skin held my attention. It mocked me for being such a bitch earlier as it trailed past his bruises.

"I'll get some ice packs," I said, pulling my eyes from him.

"I can make my own ice bandages," he replied over the sound of water waking around his seat.

"You shouldn't use your power in this condition. I'll get it." I grabbed his clothes off the ground and took them to the wash. A brown leather pouch and belt, I decided, were best removed from the garments first. I left them in the guestroom. Then I mixed alcohol and water in some sandwich bags and laid them in the freezer to use as malleable ice packs later. For the time being, he'd have to settle for the hard ice packs I used for my lunch box.

By the time I returned to the bathroom, the blood-stained water covered his groin. I grabbed the tweezers and a bowl and kneeled near the tub.

"I'm going to get the splinters and glass out," I warned before starting. He never flinched. The glass clinked in a bowl as I dropped them in. The cloth soaked red as I applied pressure to each wound, cleansing them and adding liquid bandages where I could and others where needed. He was an easy patient.

"Thank you," I finally said.

"You could have saved them yourself if you would have come with me."

"Pol…"

"I know. You don't owe me anything," he said, raising a dripping hand from the water to shut me up. "This won't stop anytime soon. They're not safe here. At least get them out."

But my parents had refused to leave for Italy weeks ago. They were happy with their lives well lived and fearless of death. They weren't safe here though, not yet. "I'll stop the medication, starting now. And if you give me a few days to sort out my work, you have my word." He turned to look at me.

"You'll come to Loanan?"

"Yes. I will. I just need a couple days for wor—"

"Okay." He leaned back into the tub, letting the warm, red water lap at his back. Some of the bandages became soaked and lifted. I sucked my teeth and reached in to check the wounds.

"You're healing already…" I said, pulling my hand from the water and looking up at him with furrowed brows. His mouth didn't flinch, but I could feel how happy he was with me.

His energy changed—the tension between us let up for the first time. I was relieved, actually. In an instant, things felt easier. I studied his face, wondering how he could show no emotion but still get his mood across to me.

I helped him dry off and finished bandaging the deeper wounds that weren't closing as quickly, trying not to look down. I won't lie, I was curious if he had a magic dick or something. Finally, he wrapped the towel around his waist.

"You're staying in the guest room," I said. He turned around, standing close and staring down at me. I couldn't help but swallow hard and back away, but I stayed firm, leading him to the guest room. "You'll have to sleep…naked. I don't have anything that will fit you."

I turned to grab him some food, shrinking away from the crowded doorway and swelling with heat as I felt his stare on me again. I walked through the hall and heard his towel fall to the floor. The bed groaned as he got into it.

I came back with hot zuppa toscana, only to find him holding the brown pouch. That was when he told me it contained the same stuff he'd used on me, a healing elixir called Eveom, and he mixed a pinch into the soup. My face burned for a moment, but I sat on the side of the bed anyway. I was going to make sure he ate every bite.

The sheets lay dangerously low, and I tried not to look down again. He told me what had happened with my parents, and I laughed for a moment, knowing they had slept through the entire thing.

"Did you have enough?" I asked, noticing his bowl was empty.

"Yes, thank you."

"Don't mention it," I said, getting up and taking the dish. "I made bagels. They're on the counter. If you wake up first, help yourself." I called for Polly at the doorway, but she apparently would rather sleep with a stranger. *Traitor.*

"Thank you again, Pol," I said before closing the door.

As always, he was gone by the time I woke up. He put my necklace back on me while I slept. I cringed, hoping I didn't look like a hot mess while he was in there—not that I cared what he thought of me. I grabbed a bagel and noticed one was missing from the bag. A smirk crossed my cheek.

Still, I felt nervous about what I had promised. But no one I loved was safe and if I could have some control over that, I was going to take it. And anyway… Now, I truly *did* owe him.

"ARE YOU READY?" I LOOKED AT THE DOORWAY OF MY ROOM. POL was looking better.

"Yeah. Do you guys have Wi-Fi there?" I said, pointing to my laptop.

"I can't tell if you're joking."

"Forget it." I decided I'd have plenty to do in a hidden sky kingdom anyway. He made his way to me and prodded through my bag. I smacked his hand away when he saw my black thong.

"I suggest a jacket," he said.

He led me outside and held out a hand to help me on his storm cloud. I hesitated and looked over to him.

"How often do these things give out?"

"My clouds don't give out, princess."

I huffed a small laugh. "But if it does, and I fall?"

"I won't let anything happen to you." He offered his hand again. "Trust me."

The cloud rumbled with low thunder and rolled at the edges. I had demanded that he not mist me again. The abrupt change in altitude made me sick just thinking about it. But the strange feeling of standing on a cloud was no comfort either. I was reminded of the unsteady feeling it gave me to stand on it. It was like coming off of an escalator when you feel like the ground is still moving even though it's still. Only this feeling wasn't fleeting. It was constant. He jumped up behind me, his mouth not far from my ear.

"On your knees."

My breath hitched. I fell to my knees.

"Slow, please," I said as he crouched behind me and leaned in. His chest rested on my back, hands bracing my hips firmly against him.

"I'll go as slow as you do on the highway. How does that sound?"

Fuck. I squinted. The nimbus jetted up, and I let out a scream that started near the earth and ended high in the sky.

We stopped farther up than I ever wanted to be. Rows of neighborhoods and shopping centers and streets below us looked so tiny from here. Lakes and ponds and trees lay farther off under the glow of the setting sun. The darkened coastline and city lay in front of us. Small patches of Miami and the surrounding cities were flattened by storms. It was gorgeous enough to calm me, and I caught my breath and let out a laugh.

Turning the cloud, he pointed upward over the dark Atlantic Ocean. "It's there. Between the stratosphere and troposphere, there is a gateway to the Regnum Caelorum." I shivered into my jacket, realizing it was no match for the cold this far up.

He grabbed my wrist and propped the bracelet on his fingertips. He created a marble of stunning amber and encased it in a ring of white gold with swirling rays projecting like fire. *A charm of the sun,* I realized. He fastened it to the bracelet with a white gold tendril shaped into an S. The link had polished gems of amber at either curving end. Warmth pulsed in my bones.

He wrapped an arm around me, reached for my chest, and propped the amethyst geode in his fingers. Much like the charm he created for my bracelet, the geode shifted with his magic. Short amber spikes grew between the purple, the shape of a sun forming in the center of the peace. Warmth kissed my skin. I felt like I was laying in the sand on Miami Beach in the high sun, coated in coconut tanning oils and fighting off sleep.

My body relaxed into his chest, forgetting the terrifying journey and icy air. Besides, if the cloud *did* give out, I wanted to be within his reach. I let myself lean into him. I didn't worry if it was welcome. I could sense he was comfortable. I thought I even caught him smelling my hair.

He cupped my mouth, giving me air. The cloud slowly rose and spun, turning our view again toward the setting sun over land. A gust of wind shifted over my shoulder and brushed my cheek. A large bird had flown past; its black feathers with an oily purple tint, long, narrow wings, and deeply forked tail were dark and distinct against the setting sun. A round, red swell on its chest looked like the sun too. It was beautiful.

The skyline of Maimi cast shadows into the ocean and through low hanging clouds. The orange glow of the sun burned brightly behind them.

"It won't be long," he shared.

"What are we waiting for?" I wondered out loud. Was his magic stronger in moonlight, the same way he described stones sometimes charged?

"The sunset," he answered. He looked down at me, noting the curiosity in my lowered brows. "It's a better view just above the cloud line. It's beautiful below it too. I watch every night that I can."

I let out a laugh and turned to him fully. "You've been rushing me to come to Loanan for over a month, and you're stopping to see the sunset?"

"I haven't seen the sunset in a month, so yes. I'm stopping."

I snickered at how bothered he was by a silly broken routine.

"Shhh," he commanded. The sun made his opal eyes shimmer blue, then pink, then lavender, then green, picking up flecks of new colors wherever the light hit. I found it hard to take my eyes off of them but didn't want to gawk. I turned to see the setting sun shimmying into the horizon, sinking back into him again and smelling his smokey scent. He wrapped an arm around my waist, warming me further as we watched the sunset. It wasn't often that I sat to enjoy beauty, and I promised to be kinder to myself in the future. Then I caught myself mindlessly grazing my thumb over his fingers.

The light burned orange as it sunk into the darkness. Long shadows blanketed the land. The sun shrank smaller, and soon the bead of brilliant orange disappeared, and the earth fell dark. The sky above us was left an ombré palette of dusky purple to deep blue. Stars and planets appeared, shimmering like diamonds thrown across a dark suede blanket. And the moon was now large and bright. We slowly floated up to the barrier at the highest point of the troposphere. He reached out a hand above us and ripples in the air grew like a pebble thrown in water.

"Ad caelum, mi domus," he spoke in his haunting baritone, causing the ripples to glow in the moonlight. He tightened his arm around my waist, pulling me against him harder as his nimbus pushed us through the portal.

I felt nothing but soft, light air as the world around us changed. A new layer of earth was revealed. A ground of firm white clouds and azolla was impregnated with a civilization unlike any I had ever seen —all under the same sparkling ombré sky.

16

DAPHNE—CAN YOU FEEL IT?

THE RIPPLES DISAPPEARED, AND HE LET ME GO. I WENT TO GRAB HIS arm and steady myself in the unfamiliar space, but he had already walked ahead. I was left to gawk at the world around me. An entire kingdom surrounded us outside of the large courtyard we stood in.

I looked ahead toward the end of the courtyard. As night fell, a gorgeous palace stood tall, formed from a massive cumulonimbus cloud. It was like I was looking up at the sky to search for familiar shapes in the clouds and found one shaped like a Victorian palace on a grand hill. Its smooth, clouded walls were a ghostly gray-white that stood out in the creeping darkness.

My feet were planted, jaw slack, and Pol turned around to grab my arm and pull me forward. His aura of mist was gone. We walked uphill along a slick, black road approaching the tall walls that surrounded the palace. The night darkened as we got closer. It was light enough under the moon that I could see cloud stacks in the shapes of buildings that made up the city around it, but it wasn't bright enough to see their details.

"I'll show you to your quarters," he said, walking toward a tall iron gate guarded on each side by two very average looking men—not what I would've pictured for heaven's gates. "You'll have a chance to get settled and cleaned up before dinner. Then, I will give you a tour of the palace before we go to bed."

I looked down at my wide-cut jeans and black, long-sleeve top. I was dressed casually, not realizing I'd be a guest in such a fancy place.

"Why are we at a castle, Pol? What is this place?" I whispered as we came to the gate. The guards bowed, and the black iron gate to the palace groaned as they opened, allowing me to take in the full majesty of the structure behind it.

"It's home. Loanan Palace," he said, leading me up a great stairway. The steps looked like polished stone, but the insides moved. The way gray and white clouds inside them mixed together looked like veins in a marble slab. The stairs rose from a field of purple water hyacinths that floated in a ghostly white fog. Another guard opened the tall, black doors to the palace with a wide swing that I thought should have caused the hinges to groan.

"It's beautiful," I breathed, looking up at the ceiling of clouds lighting the room in strikes of cool white. It was like lightning trapped in time. The floors were charcoal gray stone, like any I would see back home. But the walls were ethereal. Like the stairs, they were white-gray. The clouds inside of them were clinging to an invisible barrier molded into the shape of cinder blocks. The same for pillars and frames. It gave the room the appearance it was moving, though I felt more steady on this charcoal stone than I had since leaving my home.

The foyer was a room in itself, with halls on either side skirting the front wall. Art unlike anything I had ever seen hung in large, cloudy frames. Inside one frame, lightning struck without a sound. In another, a comet fell with a long, fiery tail. In another, the moon moved through phases, and in another, the sun set on the horizon and rose again. Two stairways ahead, one a mirror of the other, curved up on either side of the room, and behind them, twin stairways led down. A deep, wide hall lay behind them.

"I'm glad you like it," he said, heading to one of the downward sets of stairs. "This way." I followed him down the curved staircase along the left wall, lugging my bag with me. I half expected him to walk me down into a dungeon, as the cloud-gilded walls grew a deeper shade of gray with the descent.

"Allow me," a voice said from behind. A young man in a charcoal suit offered to take my bag. "I wasn't aware you'd be returning today, Your Highness. You've been gone for so long. I'll be sure to have your rooms in order," he said to Pol nervously. *Your Highness? He skated past some details, didn't he?*

"Thank you," I offered, handing him the duffel bag. His eye caught my jeweled necklace, and a flash of surprise shifted his face for a moment. He looked at Pol, bowed, and scurried off. Pol waited for me to catch up to him, and he continued by my side but much slower. We were both very tired. We stopped at the bottom of the stairs, though I didn't think you could really call anything a "ground floor" this far up.

"Your room is adjacent to mine. If you need anything, don't hesitate to knock," he said, walking me toward the back of the palace. We were walking down a wide corridor lined with dark-stained double doors. The lightning-lit ceiling was dimmer here, still silent, yet it seemed stormier and more volatile than in the entry hall. The bolts here sliced through clouds of a much darker gray than the upper levels. Despite the dimness, I could see the unmistakable ridges of wooden floors contrasting with the light from a large inlaid window at the end of the hall. I saw the deep ash blue of the sparsely decorated walls.

We stopped at the last two sets of double doors, one to the left and one to the right. "I have something for you," Pol said, turning to his doors on the left. I waited, leaning on the door frame, and took in the large room.

I saw a lit fireplace with a thick mantle of dark-stained wood straight ahead. To its left, a dark, solid-wood bed was made with a gray goose-down comforter. In front of the fireplace was a bolstered leather chair in a charcoal color. Underneath it was a vintage rug with purples and golds and grays. On top of the mantle, there was a dark-stained wooden lyre made in the shape of a crescent moon, and strung with seventeen silver-colored strings. The walls were ceiling to floor with bookshelves.

A draft caught me off guard. I leaned in and looked around the door to find a missing wall to the right. There, in his room, an entire wall was open to the world. Clouds and oceans and city lights twinkled like tiny specks below on the strip of Florida's southeastern tip. I inched farther into the room, eager to get a closer look without being rude.

"Is that real?" I asked.

"Yes. That's Miami there." He forgot to point again. He was holding a box that he got from one of the shelves and handed it to me.

"You'll want to be presentable in the common areas. You can wear this tomorrow night if you'd like. There will be a welcoming dinner so you can get acquainted with the court. No one will be walking around this late though. Once you're settled in tonight, let me know and I'll walk you up."

I nodded and took one more look at the phantom wall before

crossing the hall and opening my door. My room was an exact mirror of his, but with a feather-filled duvet of dusty lavender; my leather chair was deep purple; the vintage throw rug below it had royal blues and bone whites and hints of rose red. The wooden floors were the same smokey pattern of cool beige and deep gray-brown.

A draft caught the door, slamming it behind me, and flicked the rolling flames in the fireside. Embers tossed. I walked to the phantom wall. The ocean rolled out far below me. The world curved at the horizon, and the city sparkled. I felt dizzy knowing I was this far up and stepped back.

I plopped the box on the bed next to my duffle bag and spotted a door between the missing wall and the fireside. Thankfully it was a bathroom. I needed a splash of cold water to the face.

The large washroom was tiled in a dark gray-purple stone on the walls and floor. The ceiling of darkly rolling storm clouds had the same angry strikes of silent lightning; the light moving through it like a wave. A claw tub plated in moonstone sat against another phantom wall, and I took pause at the possibility of being seen. I decided to freshen up now and ask about privacy later.

I took one of many white, plush hand towels from the shelf and looked in the mirror. My face was gaunt. I had dark circles under my tired eyes and frizzy hair messed up from the flight. I usually dressed for convenience and comfort. My only concern for fashion was because I took pride in professionalism. Had I known I'd be in a palace, I would have packed for networking and not casualties. Pol was less than helpful in preparing me for the venue and itinerary.

With the possibility that I may run into someone important tonight, I started cleaning myself up. I brushed out my hair and twisted it in a simple low bun. I used a tinted moisturizer with a thin layer of cream blush and a tinted lip balm. With two quick coats of mascara and an oversized blazer over my modest black top, I was all but ready to roam the halls of a freaking palace on zero notice.

Pol guided me upstairs to the same floor we entered through. At the landing, we walked down the wide hall behind the staircase and to the dining room. He seated me at the end of a long, expandable table.

"It's late. The staff are resting. I'll heat up the plates they made for us. What would you like to drink?"

"Water is fine, thank you." I fanned out a cloth napkin over my lap, minded my posture, and appreciated the room. The whole palace had dark decor of rich purples, moody grays, and slick blacks. Occasionally there were pops of blossom reds, soft whites, and gold leaf accents. Dark, stained woods with ornate carvings were the common fashion on furniture, I noticed. The dining room had the same sort of fireplace with dark wooden mantel that our rooms had. This dining room was lit by a constant display of silent lightning that made the dim light shift and dance romantically around the space.

Pol came from a doorway and offered a plate of herb-roasted turkey and gravy, twice-baked potatoes, and candied carrots. I took the tall crystal glass of ice water first. The food smelled incredible, and I hummed happily. I smiled at him as he sat across from me.

"Thank you, Pol. This looks great," I said, nerves still showing in my voice. My eye caught a small two-inch gash in the table, and I wedged my nail into it, wondering what had happened. Stimming, my nail dug along it over and over, and I glanced up.

He stared at me blankly for a moment until a comfort to his face showed through. "You're welcome."

As we ate, I caught Pol staring from time to time. He seemed happy, but you'd never know it, the way he just sat there with his grumpy-looking mug. He stood and walked to a dry bar along the wall, grabbed a sweet rhubarb wine from a cold rack and poured it for us both.

"Welcome home, Daphne," he said softer than normal in a toast. *Home, huh?* I offered a small smile and raised my glass, not in the mood to argue the point. Neither of us were in the mood to talk anyway, but the silence felt peaceful. *It's always a good sign when you can hang out with someone and not have to fill every second with small talk,* I thought. *He's not so bad, I guess. And the food isn't poisoned, so there's that.*

"Walk with me," he said after the glasses were empty. He held out a hand and helped me out of my seat. The tour started with the other rooms on that floor. The ballroom was first, at the far end and to the left. It was grand with a romantic design and the same silent lightning bolt ceiling as the dining room that danced with a twinkle. It had rolling storm clouds of haunting gray and angelic white. A chandelier of ice-coated meteors hung in the center. The windows were tall glassless arches overlooking the endless ocean below, starting at the floor and ending just below the ceiling.

"This will be where the dinner is hosted tomorrow night," he said.

"How many people are coming to this *dinner*?" I asked, looking at the massive space. He was the only magical being I even knew.

"Just the court."

The kitchen was next, not noteworthy, as it wasn't meant to be a common space. But Pol insisted I was welcome to rummage for food after hours. *He must know from stalking me that I'm basically a raccoon after dark.*

Then, at the back of the hall and to the right, he showed me a small study that opened into a four-winged library with towering shelves. The library's ceilings reached many stories above us and had window arches that gave a stunning view of the Milky Way Galaxy.

The tall windows that reached from the floor to the ceiling separated the massive shelves of well-tended books. We stood at the top of a wide stairway that led down into it. I gasped.

"This is the library. It has four wings for each realm's works and histories and the center for our magic and studies," he explained at the top of the short stairway.

"Each realm?"

"Regna Oceanum," he said, remembering to point this time. His finger directed my attention to a scaly fishtail carved into the archway that led to the wing on the far left. "The realm of oceans and water."

He moved his finger to the next wing, which had a flaming mountain carved into the stone archway. "Regnum Magma, the realm of magma under the earth's crust," he continued.

He moved his finger toward the next wing, a cloud carved into its arch. "Regnum Caelorum, that's our realm. The realm of sky."

He pointed a final time to the last wing, a tree carved into the stone. "And Regnum Solo, the realm of soil, where I found you."

"There are people in all of these realms?" I asked curiously.

"Yes. There are many kingdoms—or other types of governed territories—in each realm. There are allies and enemies among those kingdoms and territories, just like you have in Regnum Solo. Each realm has beings with the potential to use their gifts if they hone them. Humans are by far the weakest; their vampires are in hiding, and some of their witches are undertrained or misguided. Others have been torn from their cultures by other kingdoms, and hindered their legacy of spiritualism; although, some still kept their culture close and strong."

I couldn't believe what I was hearing. Goosebumps covered my skin. I looked at him in wonder, and he indulged in my joy, slightly softening his usually flat expression. He pressed his free hand on the small of my back, nudging me forward as he gestured again to the arch of the Regnum Magma wing—*The Realm of Magma.*

"Magmans are a ruthless, war-hungry race that stay underground, training armies of the undead."

"Lava zombies?"

"Similar, but not quite. When a being dies, if their soul is strong or noble, a magman king may desire to breathe life into them and train them as a soldier or knight. Nobles of any realm can even make an offering of the dead and request for a knight resurrected in their care but at great cost. The rest of the dead live in peace there but are loyal to their rulers and will fight willingly."

"And the Realm of Oceans? Mermaids then? They're real?" I smiled, seeing Jesula's face in my memory.

Pol nodded warmly and pointed to the corresponding archway. "Regna Oceanum. There are many kinds of oceaman. Depending on the region, they can look quite different, from breathtaking half-human water spirits of the Atlantic, to the half-animal Ningyo near East Asia, to terrifying, slimy ice demons called Qallupilluit that steal children into the arctic waters. Some oceaman have scaly tails, some have webbed limbs, and some have tentacles."

I looked at him again, beaming. I hadn't been so hungry for knowledge since college. "And do all caeluman ride on clouds and have…" I'd never asked about his eyes. I didn't know if it was rude to ask, "…opals for irises?" I motioned shyly.

"Some can ride clouds if they train. Just like your witches and other magic or spiritual practitioners, if you don't practice, you can't develop the skill. And just like your schools, some have better programs than others, and the teachers you have can affect how powerful you become. Of course, nothing will replace your own work. Some of us have wings—the pixies mostly. They're mischievous. I'll warn you now. They're also some of our fiercest warriors." He looked at me with a rare expression of amusement. It faded from his face, my unanswered question hanging in our silence. I bit my lip awkwardly, worrying I may have pried too far. "All caeluman are born with irises much like humans. As they mature into adulthood, their eyes take on the stone that gives them something their soul desires or needs."

"What do opals give you?"

He paused, and a solemnness fell over him. "Mostly, the patience and moderation I need to wait for that which I honor." He turned and walked through the study and into the hall. "There's something I need to show you. Come with me."

I watched him walk for a moment before following. His cryptic words sat heavily in my chest.

The next floor up housed chambers for the servants and guards. The floor above that housed chambers for other members of the court, and the floor above that housed chambers for members of the small council and the royal suite.

"Why are you downstairs? Why isn't your room with the rest of the court?" I asked as we climbed the stairs. Passing each floor, the mood of the cloudy palace became lighter as we ascended. The higher the floors were the more they resembled the whimsical aesthetic of freshly fallen snow before dawn. Powdery and shimmering white clouds moved within the walls. The lightning was more of a constant bright, twinkling glow.

"I prefer my privacy.. and quiet. I don't like being around people." *No shit.* I laughed to myself. That made perfect sense. However, since he'd saved my parents, we had become more comfortable around each other. I started to develop a great sense of what his moods were behind his stony expressions. I liked our lower floor, and I liked being away from people too. It was also convenient that the floor just above us was for the royal guard.

"Speaking of privacy, is there a way to close off the bathroom wall? I'd rather not parade naked for all to see."

He shot a glance at me and cleared his throat. "The walls are enchanted, no one can see in. I can darken it for you if you prefer," he said as we reached the top level. This floor was the most airy and bright. The floor was a white sandblasted stone. The walls were blocks of crystalline clouds that shimmered like snow. Each door was white and seemed to be encased in ice with elaborate designs carved into them that I couldn't make out from the stairs.

"This floor is off limits unless you're escorted by a council member or a royal, and when you are escorted, you must remain within visual and audible range at all times," he said, motioning for the two guards to step aside. We started down a deep, wide hall much like the other floors. A blue glow cast over the space. Each door of the hall was guarded by two.

"Most of these rooms are offices for the council. Down here is the war room for council meetings and planning. The Queen's office is here, her Vice Majesty's is next."

As we passed the doors, I noticed their layers of thick, icy sheets were carved in three-dimensional portraits akin to classic playing cards. They were elaborate cameos of kings and queens and other nobles framed in a square.

We reached the back of the hall and turned to the left. This door was carved like a cameo playing card of a great warrior with a spike in one hand and a flaming ball hovering above the other hand. "These are the wings of reconnaissance, intel, and prophecy. We call them the RIP rooms." He motioned for the guards to step aside.

He guided me through the door and closed it behind us, an echo pulsing through the white-tiled room. The construction of the space was nearly a mirror of the library but with only three wings and a round center room to join them. The ceiling was low from our vantage point, but as the stairs into each wing went down into their own spaces, they became just as tall as the library.

Unlike the library, there were no windows here. The walls were plain, white, sandblasted stone, the ceiling the same, and the lighting a plain, cool white that got dimmer down the halls. There was not a cloud or decoration to be found. Rows of dark brown shelves lined the walls on either side of each wing, creating a pathway down their center, large enough for long tables to sit for study. Glass boxes and cases were placed neatly on the shelves and spaced out well, allowing you to see if any items in them had been moved or taken. The shelves illuminated their contents from underneath with a blue light, giving more transparency.

We walked to the far-right wing of the RIP rooms, where prophecies were stored.

"When Ouran's reign began, an oceaman oracle from an Atlantic kingdom foretold the story of his defeat. Oceaman rebels stole the prophecy, broke it into pieces, and only two remnants remain." He stopped by a case at the dim back of the wing. We stood near a stone carved with a language I had never seen.

"I can't read this…" I admitted.

He nodded and looked down. "A child of all realms conceived in ceremony, thus bonded by fate and destined to be anointed, will terminate the conquest actuated by Ouran, causing his dynasty to perish." His baritone voice echoed in the space, making the prophecy more haunting to hear.

"I don't understand, Pol. What does that mean?"

He seemed more stoic than usual. He raised his eyes. "You're that child, Daphne. Your ancestors are of sky, core, ocean, and soil. Your parents conceived a child through ceremony."

"What *ceremony?*" I whispered with a bite of disgust.

"The ceremony is a promise to join families. Two kingdoms seal their allyship through betrothal of their offspring. They mate on the altars below Venus with their allied kingdom, the ministers of ritual bear witness and perform the ceremony, and they conceive children bonded by fate, destined for love and to rule together. You and I are the products of that ceremony."

My chest tightened. I found it hard to catch my breath. For years I've wondered what happened to my parents. I wondered who they were or if they were alive. I sure as hell wasn't expecting Pol to know anything about them. *Shit, let alone dump a bombshell on me.* He closed the space between us.

"Ouran hunted your parents from the moment you were in the womb, so they hid you with a barren family in the Regnum Solo. We never knew who. There were rumors they'd moved you, but we never knew where." He cupped my face. "I didn't think I'd ever find you. But I knew it was you the first time we met. I could feel it like a magnet pulling me to you. But I could tell something was wrong; you weren't pulling to me." He came even closer, patient and possessive. His hand tightened on my cheek, his thumb pressing into my skin a bit as he stroked it.

I was stuck inside my head. I knew I felt a pull to him. It had been getting stronger since I stopped my medication. I thought it was just the trust he earned and our bonding. But it was more than that. I was forced to admit it to myself now. I could sense his emotions despite his muted expressions.

"But you can feel it now, can't you, Daphne?" His low voice vibrated between us. I trembled. My vision tunneled. I sucked in a deep breath. He leaned in, his lips closer. I could feel the heat of his breath. His voice rumbled in a low, haunting echo. "Can you feel it?" *Yes.* I nodded without thinking.

He pressed his lips on mine, running his thumb along my jaw. My mind and body felt separate. His lips were warm and soft. He pressed his tongue against mine, and heat welled in my core. I melted into it for only a second, but panic set in.

This isn't real. It's magical bullshit. Everything I was starting to feel... and he lied to me. I shoved him hard, and my palm made contact with his cheek. Pain shot through my hand. I made a tight fist and held it close to my chest, breathing through the pain. He stared at me, searching my face. I looked at him angrily.

"I need to get some rest," I muttered. Tears almost welled over. I wouldn't let him see. I backed away, turning for the exit. I pressed my fingers to my lips, still feeling them tingle from his kiss. He kept pace behind me until we reached the stairway down the hall.

I raced down the flights. The palace got darker and stormier the farther down I went—the last floor matching my mood: dark and angry, roiling with a storm inside. I reached my door and gave it my shoulder as I twisted the knob. I rolled inside against the door, shutting it with my back. I gave in to myself, taking a glass and throwing it at the mantle. I looked out of the phantom wall and realized how stuck here I was. Stuck with a man who withheld information I should have known before coming, withheld information about my birth parents that I had a right to know. A man I was forced to feel for more and more each day because of some orgy-born magical coercion. *Unless.* I pulled out the bottle of Zerpotine from my toiletry bag. I fumbled with a few pills in my palm and stalled. *Now is not the time to make rash decisions. You don't know who you can trust yet.* I let out a sob and returned the pills to my bag.

17

O'DOHERTY: MY ANGEL

"Will you stay the night?"

"Of course."

Fabian often stayed over, but not without an invitation. Tonight I made sure he knew he was wanted. Fabian's tenderness had taught me so much about myself and what I should expect from a partner. It made me realize how little I required of anyone, including my friendship with Daphne. I needed to be near him after the BBQ went sour.

We got settled in the house, Polpetta following at his heels wherever he went. But I had some work to do before I could relax. Fabian took Polpetta for a walk and played outside with her while the sun fell. I typed away at my computer in the dinette while the sounds of the most epic game of fetch crept through the window. He ducked behind a palm tree, faked left, and threw the ball three yards over. Occasionally their games would take my attention from work and I'd smile at the silliness.

Ping. An email notification popped up on my computer. It was from Demi Calusa, the daughter of Colee Calusa.

.   .   .

I HAD DONE SOME DIGGING AFTER HER ABRUPT DEATH AT THE hospital and had stopped by the wake to see if I could find out anything about the stones or why she was so upset. The gathering was well attended and rich with delicious foods, celebratory music, and colorful fabrics. I almost forgot how every culture handled death uniquely. I took care not to assume the vibrancy of the event meant the family wasn't grieving.

"I don't recognize you. Did you know my mother?" a young woman asked after some time. She had the same rounded cheekbones and dark eyes as Colee, but her black hair was free of any graying. I had not planned what I was going to say and had a moment of hesitation before I spoke.

"I did not know her well at all, if I'm honest. I went to her store the day it was destroyed," I said. I tried to keep the memory of my unprofessional approach with Colee distant.

"Oh," she replied, markedly confused. A haze of grief floated over her eyes.

"I went there to ask her about some work she was doing. It seemed like she had a lot to say, but we didn't get to have that conversation, unfortunately."

"What kind of work?"

"She supplied stones to a company. The company gave the stone to my grandmother," I said, feeling guilty for bending the truth. "Some of the people who got the stone, her included… They had some *episodes*. I was wondering if there was any way the stones were contaminated."

"My mother would *never* sell contaminated goods. She has sourced her products from the same vendors for many years, all of them close friends. There has *never* been an issue," she said with resoluteness.

"Of course. I didn't mean to imply she knew…" I said. She nodded stoically. I fished the stone from my pocket. "Do you know where she got these from?" She drew her face back with furrowed brows and then took the stone from my fingers to examine it more closely.

"This is not one of hers. I have never seen it before, at least. Actually I am not quite sure what this even is," she said, shaking her head. "It is probably lab made. She did not sell lab-made products in her shop."

"Well, the thing is…it *was* from her shop. Did she seem off before the storm? Was she—"

Demi sighed and dropped her eyes. I realized how much I was asking of her, and guilt wrapped around me.

"I'm so sorry. I'm just trying to find out what happened to my grandmother. I shouldn't have… Here, take my card. If anything comes to you…"

"She was stressed, quieter, and seemed nervous. But our father died a few months ago, so it was likely just grief. I am sorry. I do not know anything about this stone," she said before trading it for my card. I appreciated how helpful she was trying to be, considering I was intruding on her mother's wake to fish for information. I pushed my luck just once more.

"What about this pattern? Does this look familiar to you at all?" I produced the photo of the labyrinth from my phone and showed it to her. She looked even more puzzled.

"That is very strange. It looks familiar, but I cannot say I know what it is. If I think of anything, I will let you know."

"Thank you… so much. I'm so sorry for your loss."

Leaving, a feeling of defeat washed over me, and I knew a mineralogist was the only other option I had at that point. Walking to my car, I pulled out my phone and searched for local labs that could study the stone. Maybe they could tell me more about what it was and if it had any suspicious impurities. I came across the contact of a lab in the greater Orlando area and started to dial the number, but when I sat in my car, I stopped short. There was a slip of paper sitting on my dashboard.

I froze, took a sharp breath, and examined my surroundings. No one was in my back seat or lurking in the shadows. The car was locked when I was at the wake. But I was sure the note was not there when I had gotten out. My trembling fingers reached for the dash, retrieving the paper. It had the same wide purple ruling as the note from the day Daphne came home beat up. Inside I found the same perfect cursive from a fountain pen.

Stay away. Don't make me tell you again.

Chills ran down my spine. I looked around the parking lot again. In my side mirror, I caught movement. Someone dipped behind a van. I was certain I saw a sweep of white hair. I got out of my car, clutching the note in my fist and charging towards the shadows.

"Hey!" I yelled, hiding the fear that was alive and well inside me. But no one was behind the van. There was no one anywhere.

I lay on the pavement, pressing my cheek close to the ground. I could see no feet under the cars. Dirt and pebbles dropped from my clothes as I stood. When I finished brushing the rest off, I walked briskly back to my car. I stayed alert of my surroundings. The backseat was empty and I got in. As soon as the door was shut, I locked the car. I looked around the lot again. There was still no one, but the car smelled fresh of a fruity cologne.

Originally I thought the first note was left by Daphne's new boyfriend trying to isolate her—a man who I still wasn't convinced wasn't abusing her in some way. This new note gave me reason to feel different and the paper it was written on was vaguely familiar.

Could it be the white-haired man? Who is he? Why is he following me? And what is he so afraid of me finding out from Demi? Demi Calusa knew nothing of the stones and not much more about the labyrinth.

But perhaps that's about to change, I hoped as I stared at her email.

Dear Mrs. Sameal,

While going through my mother's belongings, I found where I had seen that symbol before. My mother had it sketched on a notepad when I first saw it, but she tucked it away into a book. I remember her scooping it up quickly and pocketing it when she noticed me looking at it, but she did not say much about it then. I am sorry to say that, after asking around, it means nothing to anyone in our family or community. No one knows anything about those stones either. As for the book, it is a beat-up edition of Ovid's Metamorphoses that came from a local library before it closed down. Attached is a photo. I hope this brings you the answers you are looking for.

—Demi Calusa.

I clicked on the attachment, holding my breath in hope. And there it was, a sketch of the exact pattern of the labyrinth. At first it didn't seem to tell me much at all. But then I noticed the stroke of a fountain pen that was scrolled out with expert calligraphy. It was a date, and not just any date. It was the date of *Mayflower's* destruction. The hairs on my arms stood up, and I stared frozen at the screen for a time.

Just then, a very breathless Fabian and a loudly panting Polpetta burst through the back door. I yelped, and Fabian laughed. He pulled his collar in and out to let in cold air and cool his chest. Polpetta loudly slurped water from a dish.

"Sorry about that, honey. It's starting to rain! I'm gonna go clean up," he said, pressing a sweaty kiss to my lips. He glanced at the photo on my laptop and hummed. "That's…"

"Yeah. Colee Calusa had it tucked in a book. Her daughter doesn't know anything about it. Any luck on your search?"

"No, but the photo I had of the labyrinth was pretty poor quality. I bet I could reverse image search *that* and find something though."

He looked at me and saw my worry lines creasing my forehead. "But not tonight. Why don't we relax, huh? You seem wound tight. I'm going to shower," he said, pulling off his shirt. I could eat him up. Before he walked away, he left a pink hibiscus flower on my laptop with an adorable wink.

Polpetta was absolutely exhausted as she trotted after him, trekking in trails of slobber. She gave up on her stalking by the time she reached the cozy living room. Finally, she found a bundle of blankets to nuzzle in on a recliner and decided to sleep off the day's excitement. She snored loudly for a little but eventually found a position that helped her breathe better.

"What will it be tonight, Love is Blind or Law & Order SVU?" a freshly showered Fabian said, plopping on the couch in nothing but plaid pajama pants. He smelled amazing. I kneeled on the floor between his legs and leaned forward for a kiss. His lips were always so smooth and warm. He threw the remote to the side animatedly and smiled into the kiss. "Or this. This is a good choice," he said happily before deepening into the kiss again.

I broke the kiss but stayed close, lowering my kisses to his stomach. His hardness pressed against my chest. I traced my tongue and lips down to his waistband. He took a deep breath. When I tugged down his pants from the sides, he had to pull the waistband out to set himself free, his cock springing out, stiff and girthy. I wrapped my hand around it and rubbed it gently for only a moment before I lowered my lips.

The moment my tongue met the tip, he groaned. I lowered my mouth farther down until I gagged just enough to make my mouth water. I let it escape from my mouth and drip down his shaft. My hand glided along the bottom of his shaft. I moved my head gently up and down over the top, occasionally taking it to my throat. His fingers combed through the sides of my hair, pulling it from my face so he could watch me.

"Sss. That's so good, baby. Just like that," he hissed. The praise drew heat from between my legs, and my heart pumped harder. His head leaned back as he groaned. I moved his cock into my throat again, relaxing the best I could. My tongue traced up his length to flick under the head of his cock. "Oh my God," he said in a gravely whisper, tightening his grips in my hair.

I continued moving up and down, giving a slightly stronger suck and rubbing now with a gentle twist in my wrist. "Look at me, baby," he asked. I looked up at him. He'd leaned back, both of his hands on either side of my head, guiding it down onto his cock. His chest rose high and fell deep. We locked eyes, and he bit his lip for a moment.

"I want to cum in your throat. Can you take it deep for me, baby?"

I moaned my enthusiasm over his length. My eyes roll back. I pushed him further down, stretching my throat, and came back up, sucking the tip. I moved my free hand to his balls, rubbing gently. My head moved down his entire length again. I gagged briefly before teasing him with more shallow sucks and soft massaging. I could tell by his groans of pleasure that I was bringing him closer. I kept the pace as I continued enjoying the taste of his cock. It felt so strong and incredibly hard in my grip. I kept steady strokes and slid my tongue along his cock. His balls started to tighten, and he pulled my hair tighter in his hands.

"Here it is, baby," he said. I took a deep breath. "Keep your eyes on me."

He pushed my head down, working his length into my throat, stretching it. I relaxed my throat, inviting him in. I looked at him eagerly.

"Oh fuck… ah," he groaned between open-mouthed panting. His cock began flexing in pulses as his hot cum pumped deep in my throat. His hands pulled my head harder, pushing himself as deep as he could. His jaw jutted out as his eyes burned into mine. "Ugh. Good girl. You like that, honey?" he said just before bucking his hips gently.

He eased his grip and gently pulled himself from my throat. He kept most of his girth in my mouth. I ran my tongue along it gently, tasting him as he softened in my mouth. He winced at the sensitive spot being licked. The last of his cum dripped onto my tongue. Finally, he pulled himself from my lips. His heavy cock softened and fell to the side. He wiped a run of drool from the corner of my mouth.

"You're fucking incredible," he said, leaning forward and kissing me. He scooped his arms under mine and pulled me to a stand. His arms scooped me up, and I wrapped my legs around him. He kissed me, walking us into the bedroom. "I want to try something with you," he said in a low voice. I nodded. He lowered me on the bed, thrusting his hips between my legs as he kissed me. He reached into my side table.

He broke this kiss and brought a blindfold and earplugs into sight. "I only want you to focus on what you can feel. Do you trust me?" I nodded. He smiled softly, looking down at me.

"Just lay still and let me do the rest."

Soon my sight was dark and I could hear nothing. He pulled my shirt up just over my head. Tucking the shirt behind my head, my arms were pinned up. He squeezed my wrists together above me, as if telling me to keep them there. His other hand reached under me and unfastened my bra with ease. My breasts felt a chill as he pulled the bra up past my peaks and left it laying loosely across my chest. He cupped my breasts and massaged them for a moment. I relaxed into the touch.

Then I felt the mattress spring flat. I lay untouched for a short time, anxious and uncertain. When it dipped again toward the weight that pressed into it, I could sense him returning to me. The weight pressed closer until his hands were on either side of me. Something warm, soft, and wet slid over my nipple. I felt it again. Then my nipple was pulled into that warmth. The sucking hardened them. The sensation moved from one nipple to the other, flicks causing me to gasp. A light touch danced down my belly and skated along my waistband. I started to grow anxious with anticipation, not knowing where or how he would touch me next.

An abrupt tug pulled my bottoms down to my mid-thighs, where they stayed. My legs were pushed up toward my body. They were held there by pressure laid across the backs of both thighs. His forearm, I guessed. I felt his fingers slide under the crotch of my lace panties. His knuckle dipped between my lips, up and down, and nudged at my clit. He tugged on the panties, pulling them to the side.

A brief moment of movement on the bed was followed by a wet, freezing cold sensation working up the underside of my clit. I drew in breath. The cold object figure skated around every inch of my pussy. Then it made its way to my entrance. Suddenly the cold was inside me. It was almost too much. Then, a sucking sensation pulled the ice from my center. My nipples tightened. The object was slowly pushed in and sucked out again and again. I could only hear the muffles of my moaning. He sucked it out again and dragged it lower. It teased the rim of my ass. I could feel it melting against my heat, a chilled bead of liquid running down my cleft. It almost pushed past the rim, but then it disappeared into whatever soft thing was now against my ass. A cold, soft, and wet sensation passed over my ass just once.

He stopped touching me. I grew restless with anticipation. A soft chill worked up the entirety of my center. After, he blew air against the skin, and a fresh tingle of mint lit up the surface. I felt the chilled wetness pass over and over again until my clit swelled with pleasure.

The mint tingled over me again. Something blunt nudged at my entrance. He pressed it into me, and the muscles in my pussy relaxed, eager to be touched. It twisted to the left and then right as he moved it in and out of me. It was thick and hard and filled me completely. My clit was pulsing.

Only my most vulnerable places were exposed as he left me haphazardly undressed. The thrusts were steady and firm. The chilled lapping on my clit was too much. As my orgasm crashed through me, my pussy clenched tightly. It pushed the object outward but met resistance. He worked it in and out of me hard as I came around it. My back arched from the pleasure. My muffled moans echoed in my head.

Then the laps on my clit and the thrusts of the cold object in my pussy slowed, along with my breath. The object slowly pulled away. I felt the unmistakable soft pressure of his kisses pushed against my clit, and then between my lips.

Pulling his kiss from me, my bottoms were tugged off completely. My legs fell open and relaxed. He kissed up my stomach and chest slowly, ending behind my ear. He pressed his hips between my legs, his hot, hard cock rubbing against it as if ready to make me take him deep. But my shirt was gently pulled over my chest. Then his lips met mine. Before the kiss was broken, the blindfold came off, and the earplugs were removed.

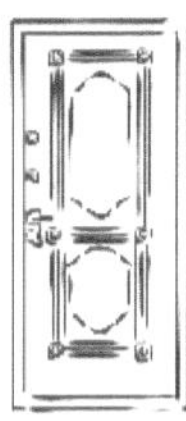

When I opened my eyes, the world rushed back to me, but he was the only thing in my view.

My angel.

18

DAPHNE: DEFINITELY TABOO

My eyelids felt like they were sewn shut. I could barely pry them apart, and when I did, the goose-down comforter and flannel sheets didn't make it very compelling to get up. And why should I? *So Pol can blindside me with more life changing information. Ass.* Anyway. I hadn't slept that hard in years. I was exhausted from lying awake with unanswered questions. Finally, I had cried myself to sleep.

Outside the phantom wall it looked like a late morning sky. I finally dragged myself from under the covers and washed up. Rummaging through my bags, all I could find were jeans and T-shirts. I threw them into the bag and sat on the floor by the phantom wall. *Bring a jacket? A jacket, Pol? To a damn palace? Ugh.*

I watched the waves roll up to the shores of Miami ten or more miles below. The phantom wall was actually starting to grow on me. The view was unlike anything I had ever seen. I smirked for a moment, knowing I wasn't stuck in that awful Miami traffic.

There was a knock at the door.

"Come in," I said, moving to stand. But when Pol came through the door, I settled and looked back at the traffic fondly.

"You missed breakfast," he said, putting a covered tray down beside me.

I looked between him and the tray. I didn't give him so much as a smirk. My body tensed as he towered over me. He sat down against the opposite wall, glancing out to the rolling waves for a moment, and then rubbed his face. "Last night…"

"Thank you," I said, uncovering the plate and snagging a piece of bacon next to the cloud puff eggs. "I don't have anything to wear— nothing appropriate. Is there somewhere I can go?"

"I can have Cynti's seamstress come. She'll have something for now and measure you up."

I looked at him curiously, still tense.

"Cynti is my sister," he offered, reading me wrong as usual. *Bonded by fate, huh?* For someone I was apparently destined to be partnered with, he wasn't very good at reading me at all.

"Am I confined to the palace?"

"No, but there's too much to do. A shopping trip isn't practical. And your arrival hasn't been announced yet." He motioned to stand. "Once it is-"

"What happened to my parents? Since you know *so much* about them all of a sudden."

He stalled, frozen in place, and then settled himself back on the floor across from me.

"Last night you said, 'allied kingdoms,' but they fled. What happened to their kingdom? Where are they?" I questioned. He was quiet for a moment.

"There were seven Caelum kingdoms over the European region. Your parents ruled one that is positioned over Italy—a kingdom called

Volare. You were to be the Princess of Volare. Our ritual conceptions were announced just months before the war broke out.

"Ouran had allied in ceremony with one of the seven, a kingdom called Spiers; his heir, Nahveel, and theirs would be mated. Ouran had already been mated through ceremony by his parents with a powerful kingdom over South Asia called Neela. He had allies with another of the seven, the kingdom of Luft, which was also very powerful. With those powers united, he planned to conquer the remaining four kingdoms.

"When he was told of the prophecy, he would wait no longer and tore through Volare first. This was the start of the war. Volare fell under the attack. Your parents fled, and it was rumored they birthed a child in the Regnum Solo. No one has seen them since. After that, two kingdoms were defeated without viable heirs and absorbed into Ouran's rule. The last one, Nuage, surrendered, merging their courts and taking a lesser position to serve Ouran. Nuagen citizens were outraged, and many rebellion groups organized. They'll be our allies in the war to come."

"Why wouldn't he just kill me if he knew where I was all this time?"

"There are a few possibilities." He looked away and pressed his lips together. "Prophecies can change, but not without difficulty. If you're killed in ritual, for example, your noble blood could offer him a second path, but he'd need a noble sacrifice of his own court in that ritual too. Like an heir to his throne."

"And if he killed me out of ritual?"

"You're an un-coronated noble. If he'd kill you any other way, a magman King would likely raise you from the dead. Those who are destined to be anointed but are cheated out of it by way of murder, they make the most powerful undead soldiers. They sit in the high courts of Regnum Magma. You would be a tremendous threat, gaining even more power potential. A chance at vengeance is almost guaranteed. But no one has been dumb enough to invoke the wrath of a Regnum Magma kingdom since the fall of 79."

"I don't remember reading about any lava zombie attacks in 1979."

"79 CE. Courtesy of *your* ancestors actually. A great Regnum Solo empire eventually fell. A treaty with the humans was put in place after and it stands today. These recent attacks are causing them to consider it breached." He paused for a moment and looked at me. "If he had killed you two moons before your birth, he would have no worry," he paused and then turned his eyes to mine. "And then there's the possibility that your life is being used as leverage."

"You think he has my parents?"

"I don't know what to think, Daphne." He made his way to his feet.

"You should have told me."

"It wasn't the right time."

"How do you figure? You had plenty of time. You should try communicating for once, instead of just staring me down."

He walked toward me, towering over me. My heart skipped a beat, my cheeks flushed, and I looked away.

"You have no idea the position I am in here." I didn't acknowledge his response. He walked to the door. "A lady of the court will be here soon to help you get ready. I'll send the seamstress first. Meet me in the library when you're done. We have work to do," he said. "You… should mind the profanity in the common areas."

I cocked my head to the side. As soon as the door closed, I threw the bacon down. "Ass."

A seamstress came shortly after, carrying a rack and tote. Tali was a seasoned woman with a tight bun and modest black pantsuit. She didn't speak much, but I noticed her labradorite eyes stop to note my jewelry while measuring me up. She allowed me to sift through the rack for clothes, but I left the choice to her. She left a sheer powder-white chiffon pullover and gunmetal pants on the bed, along with a peacock purple pair of low heels and matching earrings.

As Tali headed out, I slipped on a pair of purple low heels and nearly tipped over. A young blond woman caught me. Falece, a lady in waiting and apparently my handmaiden, had waves and braids elaborately woven through her hair, like anything I'd expect from a magic sky being. She was a tiny thing, only four feet tall yet fully grown. Her powdery ivory skin was smooth, reminding me of my naive days just a decade before. I noticed her greenish eyes hadn't turned to stones yet. As she turned, I saw wings like a dragonfly's. They glimmered purple and green when the light hit them. *She must be a Pixie...*

She did great work with my hair, gathering it and folding it into itself over and over again. She kept small pieces down and curled them into little wisps. Then she did my makeup in a mostly nude pallet, fluffing out my brows and oiling my lips. She didn't speak much at all, and I wondered why Pol insisted that pixies were mischievous.

Normally, I would engage with new people and learn something about them. But I was still in a sour mood that I couldn't shake.

"I'm finished, Your Highness. Will there be anything else?" she said sweetly. Her voice was like that of someone suffering from a cold, but in an endearing way, and she didn't seem sick at all.

I narrowed my brows hard. *Highness?* Everything about being called "Your Highness" made me cringe. *A worry for another day,* I told myself. "No. Thank you, Falece. This looks great."

I stopped in the doorway of the library, looking down the short stack of stairs, my back to the small study. Pol sat at a desk in the room that joined the four wings of the library. With him sat a dark haired, medium-brown skinned man with a frail frame and a face shortened with the absence of a jaw. I walked up, making a mental note that I needed to do better when meeting people. I forced a smile as both of them looked up at me coming down the short steps.

Pol stood from his seat, and I froze. His towering form, dressed in all black, made my face all hot. *Absolutely not,* I told myself and pushed forward my cold facade. I turned to his friend and reached out my hand.

"Hello, I'm Daphne," I offered to the smaller man. He stood and looked at my hand with confusion that turned to excitement. Then he took my hand and shook it roughly. He had no jawbone, causing his upper teeth to protrude over his bottom lip. I noticed a blue dome over his neck where a tracheostomy would be expected in any patient I had ever had with that type of condition. It was interesting to realize that these conditions affect caeluman just like they do humans. I started thinking about how the treatments for different conditions compared in a place with magic. I wondered what other conditions existed in this realm and the others.

When my eyes met his, I had a new thought that startled me a bit. What did ruby eyes give him? He signed with his hands, and I regretted not knowing what it meant.

Pol moved closer to me, and I tensed. That magnetic feeling he was talking about seemed stronger since he'd told me the truth. I didn't want this, this pull. He noticed my reaction and moved to stand near the man. "This is *Uripe*; he says, 'It's nice to meet you.' That is his study, in the entrance. Uripe manages the library and will be your tutor."

"My tutor? For what?" I asked as politely as I could. Uripe's hands signed in answer.

"I will begin with the basic concepts of magic, a brief history and geography, and other important things. As we continue to work, we will go into more depth," Pol translated.

"I'll be back in an hour to take you to training. You'll start earlier tomorrow and have more time. For now, you can get acquainted," he added as his own message. I wasn't fond of being told how my time would be spent here by someone who had freshly pissed me off. But I couldn't think of anything else to do and realized arguing would only serve my own pride. I'd let Pol figure out how my time should be spent for now and redirected myself. He came around the table, and I guarded my space, shifting my body away in a discrete recoil. I remembered the kiss. *It was nice.*

Absolutely not. Having my destiny chosen for me was not just a sour explanation for my… *semi*-growing attraction to Pol. *Whatever, he's hot; there is no denying that.* These feelings should have been my own choice, and I had no way of knowing if they were. So, despite how hard my instincts pulled toward him, I led with my brain and gave him no warmth. More so, I nearly cowered away from him, afraid the pull would take over if I gave in for a second.

And what do you know? He read me right for once and noticed. He watched me as he exited at a distance. I resented him more for making me want him to come back, even if it was just a tiny gnawing at my chest. *I can handle this magnet thing.*

Anyway. I realized I had no way to communicate with my tutor and turned to give Uripe a sorry look. "Uripe, I unfortunately don't know very much sign language."

The man waved a hand as if to say, "no matter," and retrieved a blue device from a drawer at his desk in the study. He attached it to the blue dome on his neck and moved the air around him to pass through it. His fingers worked as if playing a flute, and words sounded from the last chamber on the device in an airy voice.

"I have my voice box. I'll use it sparingly, as it requires magic to operate and expends too much energy," he said through the box.

"Holy crap! I've never seen anything like it," I exclaimed. I covered my mouth; I realized I let my excitement get the best of me. I didn't want to make him feel like a spectacle either. But he seemed perfectly pleased to have his assistive device admired. I smiled with more self-control. "Where should we start?"

Uripe gathered four books from the end of the table and arranged them in front of me. All were really gorgeous leather-bound books the size of a binder. They reminded me of antique photo albums. All were embossed with a decorative font, with silver foiled edges. They had the same cloud emblem on them that was carved into the Regnum Caelorum archway.

The first book was titled *Fundamentals of Magic*, and I could hardly contain my excitement. Also, I knew my independence and safety would rely on my ability to learn my own power. The second book was titled *Kingdoms of Regnum Caelorum*, and my heart ached at the chance to know more about my parents' kingdom. The ache reminded me of what was taken from me and what still threatened my adoptive parents back home in the "soil realm." The third book was titled *Loanan: The Basics of Politics*, and I felt fear for the dinner tonight, realizing I would likely be a small fish swimming with the sky sharks. It was likely the most important book should I want to have control over my options here in Loanan. If politics were at all similar to those back home, knowledge was my fiercest weapon. The fourth and final book was titled *Contracts & Treaties with Regnum Solo*. I furrowed my brows, realizing how much the government back home must know about the three other realms. I was furious and confused at their insistence on keeping their citizens in the dark.

I didn't know where to start and felt Uripe's ruby eyes on me, waiting.

"So, nothing on the Lava Zombies of Regnum Magma just yet?" I joked. Uripe's absent jaw did not dampen his humor-filled reaction. He arched his back and squinted, his chest jolting with silent giggles. Then he lifted a single finger to shake it. He tapped the table, drawing my attention back to the books in front of me. My brain urged me to choose Politics but my mind was making all sorts of excuses to rationalize why magic was the best pick. Conflicted, I decided to do something new and let someone else decide.

"Uripe, which topic do you think is most important for me right now?" I asked, hoping I wasn't putting too much trust in a stranger. He tapped a book, and a smile creased my cheeks on both sides. I was perfectly happy to start with magic and pulled the large book toward me. When I opened it, pages were tabbed with thin strips of colorful paper.

"Your reading assignment for today. Read the tabbed sections. Write questions here," he said, sliding a notepad and pen toward me. "Use this quil to underline what you want notes on, and they'll appear in this notebook. The ink will disappear from the book when you're done."

"Thank you," I said, examining the ordinary looking quil. He stacked the other books and put them to the side. I took my seat and began reading, underlining anything that seemed particularly important to know, and skimming over the rest.

 *Introduction To Magic:*
  Magic *is the ability to manipulate the world around*

us via channeling holistically. There are many types of magic and methods of wielding it, ranging from simple incantations to complex ceremonies. As with any other talent, the practitioner may be naturally skilled at one method of magic and find challenge with another. However, all beings are capable of magic, given the parameters of their realm-specific genetics. For instance, only caelumans can create and ride a cloud, but all beings can perform ceremonies. This book will focus on the broad spectrum of magic capable of any being and the magic exclusive to the Regnum Caelorum. For magic exclusive to other realms, source the respective Fundamentals of Magic texts for each realm of interest.

<u>An important note is that all magic requires energy and can exhaust the mind and body when pushed to its capacity.</u> Just as one burns calories when exercising, the body will burn calories while wielding magic. Just as regular exercising increases one's stamina, practicing magic daily will increase your capacity and stamina for wielding magic. There are many parallels between physical fitness and magical power with respect to nutrition, rest, and injury. The student must be prepared to care for themselves accordingly.

Section 1: Preparing to channel holistically.

*Prior to performing magic, one must learn holistic channeling. **Holistic Channeling** is serving as a medium for all interconnected parts of ourselves and the dimensions of our physical and spiritual world.*

Without competency in the skill of holistic channeling, manipulating the world around us would be both impossible and dangerous. Learning to channel holistically and being competent in it are not synonyms. <u>For this reason, no novice practitioner should proceed with manipulation without proper guidance and supervision from a sorcery master.</u>

*The most important step in preparing to channel holistically is being sufficient in the art of meditation. **Meditation** is the practice of focusing or clearing one's mind deeply for a period of time. The student should meditate daily and train their mind to focus on the task at hand. If a practitioner attempted to manipulate the world while distracted by other bothersome thoughts, they could channel incorrectly and do significant damage.*

*Meditation is a perfect time to learn the **<u>hasta mudras, or hand gestures necessary to help guide energy flow.</u>** Hasta Mudras are not only a valuable asset in successful meditation but are the foundation of the hand composition gestures used as a method of wielding in many types of magic. They're used by skilled practitioners, sometimes in place of a wand.*

The chapter continued explaining the history and process of meditation and mudras, and I underlined as I went to take notes. I planned to meditate twice a day and which meditations to use. I planned when and where, and for how long. The book suggested I start by focusing on the air around me and not be distracted by catching myself *being* distracted.

I soaked it all up like a sponge but took a mental break to drink water and stretch. Uripe was shelving books. I loved the quiet. When I sat back down to read, I finally reached the tab that told me that my reading for this section was done. I located the next tab and flipped the thick pages to see it.

Types of Magic & Methods of Welding It:

*Magic is a seemingly endless spectrum, but there are a few fundamental types and methods of wielding it. The **magic type** is a categorical reference dependent on the magic's characteristics. The **method of wielding** the magic is a procedural reference dependent on how one facilitates that type of magic. For example, a curse is a type of incantation, and one of many methods to wield the curse is the following procedure: Channel the dark spiritual dimension, utilize a traditional wand with specific compositions of gestures, or specific mudras (which require advanced skill), while speaking a specific series of words, manipulate the spiritual dimension to create the spell, and then pull it into our own dimension.*

More information on curses and other incantations will be covered in detail in Chapter 56. In the following sections, you will learn the fundamental types of magic and the possible methods of wielding them. More advanced types and methods are discussed at length in the subsequent texts, such as Advanced Magic *and* Applications of Broad Magic in Regnum Caelorum.

It is extremely common for practitioners to use multiple types of magic to achieve a desired outcome.

*This is called **compound magic**. <u>For example, a caeluman forming their riding clouds is a type of creation magic known as forming, but propelling the cloud to fly them requires a psychic type of magic called Moving.</u> Using compound magic is covered more in Chapter 106. Variations in riding cloud formations, such as the standard Cumulus vs the stormy Nimbus for example, are covered in more depth in* Advanced Magic.

Section 1: Incantations

    <u>Incantations</u> <u>are a series of words said as a magic spell. Some examples of incantations are charms, curses, and conjuring.</u> *Incantations rely on mental clarity and focus, memorization, proper pronunciation, and holistic channeling, usually with special focus on the spiritual dimensions. Other components to the method of wielding incantations include wands and hasta mudras, each specific to the incantation.*

    <u>Charms</u> <u>are a type of incantation that yields delightful and positive outcomes. There is no malice in charm casting. Therefore, the method of wielding it must include channeling the light spiritual dimension.</u> *As charms are an incantation, they also require explicit pronunciation and accuracy. Even charm spells can cause danger when care is not taken. Although charms may be easier to achieve when adding a wand to your method of welding it, the proficient practitioner will find it just as easy to yield the same results with fluid hasta mudras.*

> ***Curses*** *are a type of incantation that intend to inflict harm or cause negative outcomes. Although malice is the focal point, there are noble reasons for casting curses. Curses almost always require channeling the dark spiritual dimensions in its method of welding. Similar to Charms, the practitioner may find it just as easy to use wands or hasta mudras as part of the method of wielding, and proper pronunciation and memorization are imperative.*
>
> ***Conjuring*** *is a type of incantation intended to move an entire spiritual entity from one dimension or realm to your own and, in some cases, grant embodiment. Of note, only the anointed of the Regnum Magma can conjure the dead of our dimension for resurrection, but, in some cases, requires the supplemental magic of a caeluman to begin. Conjuring requires a specific series of incantations to be sung instead of spoken and cannot include wands in its method of wielding, as there should only be flesh and blood used for moving spiritual entities.*

I stopped to rub my eyes. This was a lot more than I expected to learn about magic and I was surprised at the similarities between my old textbooks and this. As I read, I kept thinking about the magic I saw Pol use before. I tried to make connections between what I was learning and what I had already seen. Anyways, somehow I expected magic to be more cryptic, but it was just like learning a magician's tricks.

 *Section 2 Creation:*

Creation *is the process of making a new tangible product by manipulating properties already in existence. Some examples of creation magic are forming, bridging, and shifting.* Creation *magic requires methods of welding unique to the kind that is being used. It is typical to channel with focus on our dimension and regard for the tools we have available in our surroundings. Another component to the method of welding is using specific hasta mudras.*

One example of creation type magic is ***forming***— *where elements are sourced from the world around you to be condensed into an entirely new thing. The most basic thing to form is a Riding Cloud, as only water is necessary and is plentiful in almost any environment. The method of wielding this kind of creation magic requires channeling our own dimension and the elements within it.*

***Other common things formed are gemstones, metals, plants, and pure oxygen. Gemstone creation for healing purposes requires compound magic, as the elements to create them are harvested from the eyes of dead caeluman. Because eye stones are sacred, channeling the spiritual realm for a blessing is required, and this is akin to conjuring except for the sung incantation. Gemstones are discussed in depth in Chapter 32.*

I stopped to reread the last few sentences. I underlined it thickly to copy notes about reviewing chapter thirty-two. It wasn't tabbed. I moved my hand to the "questions" paper. But I couldn't think of anything to write. The pen just sat there while question fragments flooded my brain. A blotch of black ink grew under the pen tip. The paper got soggy under the growing splotch. I didn't know what to ask or who to ask. *Is this topic taboo? This feels taboo.* The bracelet on my wrist caught my eye. *What the hell did Pol do for this jewelry? Was my comfort really worth disturbing the dead? Who's dead relative was I wearing? This is definitely taboo. Why would he let me walk around wearing dead people eyes? Why would he not tell me? What else had he not told me?* Then, all I could do was imagine punching him in the arm. No, the diaphragm. No! His eye! *But it was kinda sweet... No, it's sick...It's definitely sick.*

I realized how long I had been staring at the same spot, the ink now soaking through to the table. I was spiraling. I put the pen down, tucked my necklace in my shirt, adjusted myself uncomfortably in my seat, and tried to finish the reading. "How did you do?" Pol's booming voice cut through the silence, causing me to jump.

19

DAPHNE: CLOSE TO TOUCHING

Pol walked down the hall toward the grand opening and past the stairs. I followed out of the library, not closely behind him. I studied his slow stride. His silhouette against the lightning-lit ceiling was kind of cinematic. Or maybe it was how dizzy I felt from what I had learned. My vision must have been playing tricks on me, framing him at a tilt. The jewels hung heavier on my neck and wrist, knowing he had gifted me the eyes of dead caeluman. Again, I wondered whose eyes they were. *What kind of person would give them as a gift?* I refocused on my breathing.

Guards stood stiffer with his approach. He commanded respect wherever he went, yet he tolerated my rebellious ass calmly the vast majority of the time. He wasn't so calm with his mouth last night. *What the hell is wrong with me?*

I shook the intrusive thought from my mind as we turned down the hall to the right of the grand entrance, a hall not included in my late-night tour. The hall skirted the front of the palace and was lit by tall windows. At the hall's end was a room with glass walls. Outside of it was a paved courtyard. He swung the door open and held it for me.

"Today I'll get you acquainted with Chloe," he said, stepping into the paved courtyard. "They'll be here soon."

"I'm not dressed for this," I stated the obvious.

"You're not training today. We won't have time before the dinner party."

I walked past him cautiously, refusing to enjoy his scent. I needed to keep my guard up with him. I've never liked secrets.

Looking around at the large yard and endless sky, I noticed it was more of a deep violet-blue up here than the bright, pale blue I could see from Regnum Solo. I walked toward the edge to take in the view of Loanan's land. Surprisingly, there were fields of green, azolla-rich clouds rolling down the hill of the palace to the wall. Beyond the wall were other structures, all tall buildings of block that seemed to trap moving clouds of white or different shades of gray. The buildings had gardens of water lilies, lotuses, and hyacinths of all different colors.

There were decorative bushes of hornwort, yellow cattails, and parrots feather all nestled into the misty azolla ground. The clouds under them rolled up and skated over them like dry ice, giving the appearance of a never-ending fog you would expect in a spooky graveyard at night. But here in the bright light, it wasn't creepy at all, only magical.

No matter where I looked, there wasn't a sign of the world below.

"The windows in our rooms don't show any of this," I said.

"Our rooms are beneath Loanan. The barrier hugs it close. There's an entire world above it," Pol answered, now at my side but keeping his distance. The wind blew his scent to me, a wave of the smoky leather musk wafting under my nose, and I craved to be near him. I didn't show it for a second. "The rooms underground were built for the royal guard, to help us scout for trouble in the realms below us. It's how we've known where a rogue storm is."

I wondered if he took his rooms for other reasons. *I didn't think I'd ever find you,* he'd said last night. He'd said that he knew I was in the Regnum Solo but didn't know where. Did he look down at the world below and wonder if I was down there? Did I look up at the sky countless times, not realizing I was looking right at him? The magnetic pull to him was stronger than earlier, I noticed. It was taking more effort not to let my mind wander, or my desire for his comfort sway my decisions. I needed more answers than ever.

Pol leaned onto the wall, his forearms bearing the weight, and looked over his kingdom. "Chloe is the Master of Battles. They keep the forces on the premises trained and sharp. The forces all usually train in the morning. You'll be with Uripe then, so you'll train with Chloe and newer recruits later in the day."

"What exactly will I be trained on?"

"Fighting. Primarily defense. That's the most important thing right now. When Uripe starts magic practice with you, Chloe will help you with the defensive magic first."

"And you think I'll have these skills in under two weeks?" I asked, remembering the heavy content I covered today and how obvious it was that I had barely scratched the surface.

"I don't know how long it will take for the poison to be out of your system or when your power will show. But I hope after these next couple weeks you realize what's at stake, what you've been robbed of, and decide to stay. The goal is for you to make your own cloud and be able to come and go as you please and eventually protect yourself when I'm not around."

I followed him at a distance when he turned around and walked toward a rack of weapons, most of which I hadn't seen before. There were spheres of rock that looked charred with craters marring their surface, sword-like picks of smoking dry ice, golden ropes looped tight and fraying at their surfaces with blue, stiff, wiry strands, and closest to Pol were simple arrows. I wondered what some of these were made of.

"Pol," I said, still observing the strange weapons. "The gems in the jewelry you made me, they're sacred? Eyes of the dead?"

He gave me the briefest nod, running a finger along the sharp edge of an arrow.

"Is it okay that I'm wearing them? Is it normal to? Everyone seems pretty taken aback when they see them. Why did you do that? It… It's too much."

"Too much? I would gouge the eyes out of the living to spare you."

My jaw was slack as I shrunk into myself, both flattered and a little freaked out. I watched his finger still on the tip of the arrow.

"Pol, Your Majesty. It's great to see you back. I hear Princess Daphne is—" They stopped short when I turned to lock eyes with them. They were petite yet muscular, no older than forty, if I had to guess. Their skin was naturally warm but tanned a deeper gold, like the color of a harvest moon. This only made the dark amethyst irises in their heavily hooded, almond-shaped eyes more vibrant. I swallowed hard, wondering if they would take offense to the amethysts I wore. Pol's answer hadn't settled the worry at all.

"Welcome home, princess," they said with a bow that made their straight black hair fall forward. It was shaved on one side, but the rest framed their round face at the chin as they rose.

"Thank you. I'm Daphne," I said, reaching out a hand—the one *without* the bracelet on it—for a shake. They looked at it with confusion, and Pol lowered my hand with his. I pulled away from his touch.

"It's a human greeting called a handshake," Pol offered to Chloe.

"I see. I am Chloe, the Master of Battles," Chloe said, jetting out a hand awkwardly. I took their hand for a brisk shake and then pulled away, feeling awkward and out of place. "Pol has shown you some samples from our arsenal?" Chloe said and motioned to the rack behind us. "That rope. It's called a silt and can dampen powers. It's rare. The round one is an embercudgel, used for distance fighting. The longer one is a frospit, better for hand-to-hand combat. Both require magic to wield. Would you like to try?"

"She hasn't come into her power as of yet. Poison. No magic education either, apart from a first session with Uripe today," Pol said. I felt my cheeks turn hot at how weak I must look to Chloe, this insanely strong warrior. "She'll join you after her study sessions with Uripe to get the basics of combat for now. She needs to focus on self-defense."

Other caelumans piled into the space, young men and women of different heritage and builds, all with different stones for eyes. Some were smaller, with wings like dragonflies and sharp diamond-paved teeth.

"Today she'll observe," he added dismissively.

I watched as Chloe trained with the small group of new recruits. They moved in a fighting motion I hadn't seen before. Despite the cold climate up here, we were closer to the sun. Also, clouds didn't form naturally in the stratosphere above us, so we were left without shade this late in the day. When the sun got too harsh, the group formed a single thin cloud for cover.

Pol saw the flush on my skin. He formed a cloud above us for cover. I nodded at him, not ready to let up on the cold shoulder. Though being this close felt right. As they trained, Pol explained the moves. I kept my questions to myself, knowing I would have time to speak with Chloe another time. Still… hearing Pol's voice did something to me.

"THE DINNER PARTY WILL START WHEN THE SUN IS TWO HANDS FROM the horizon," said Pol in the stormy halls of our underground floor. "Falece will be here to help you get ready soon. The dress I gave you will match your jewelry." I pressed my thumb into the spikes of the geode and swallowed hard.

For a moment we just stared at each other from opposite sides of the hall, my back against my door and his back against his. The feeling of a magnetic pull was getting stronger by the hour, a result of the medication leaving my body and allowing me to feel what I couldn't before.

As it turned out, pulling apart a magnet was harder the closer you were. We had been side by side for hours by now. I couldn't take my eyes off him. I wondered how long he's had to feel this and how uncomfortable it must have been for him. Finally, I turned to walk into my room and measure the horizon with my hands.

Falece came to help me get ready. She saw the box Pol had given me on the bed and smiled big. Her smile was a row of sharp teeth that looked like they had a diamond-paved surface. The fangs poked out of candy-pink gums. They should have looked threatening, but they were gorgeous.

As she worked, I read the last of the sections I missed in the magic book. Uripe had lifted the words from the page and laid them on my notes. It was a short read.

> ***Grounding*** *is a compound type of forming used in making a Riding Cloud mountable that requires tandem use of the psychic type magic of emitting in which a barrier is formed by consolidating the emitted emotions of the practitioner.*
>
> *Another example of creation magic is **bridging**, which is often used to mend. When Bridging, elements similar to a broken or disjointed thing are drawn to the space between, merging it into one piece. This is common in broken bones and has similar methods of wielding to forming.*
>
> ***Shifting*** *is a unique and complex creation type of magic in that something whole and even multi-elemental is dismantled and transformed into singular elements and then reassembled to its original form. The most popular example is Misting, an advanced Shifting, specific to caeluman and reliant on compound magic of a psychic type called emitting. With misting, the caeluman create mist from their body, emit their entire existence to a different place, and reassemble. Shifting requires channeling our dimension, the spiritual dimensions, and more.*

I rolled my neck, ready to jump into Section 3 on psychic magics.

"I am finished. It's time to get dressed," Falece said. I caught a glimpse of myself in the mirror and slapped the notes down.

Falece had done my hair up insanely nice. She started a French braid at the nape of my neck, going up and ending just below the crown of my head. Her long, pointed fingernails had been scratching my scalp gently as she went. The next French braid started from my forehead, going to the back, meeting the first. She fanned out the braids, adding volume. The ends of the braids gathered at the crown and were arranged in a sleek, voluminous bun with a long, curled tail. Loose wisps of hair curled down from the bun and down my neck.

Falece prepped my face and color corrected my dark circles. She used a dewy, medium-coverage foundation, plum cream blush, a light contour stick, and a gold-tinted highlighter to dust my cheekbones, the corners of my eyes, and my cupid's bow. She kept my eyelids a clean neutral with purple undertones and lined them out with a deeper purple, finishing with a classic lash. Finally, she applied a black cherry lip stain heavily to the center of my lips and feathered out to the edges, topped with a matching plumping lip oil.

I couldn't believe the person in the mirror. I had never been so done up, and I looked…classy.

"Falece, this looks incredible. Thank you so much."

I opened the box Pol gave me and gasped sharply. Falece smiled knowingly.

"He had it made for you," she said with a tease in her voice. It was stunning. She giggled as she fanned out the curls on my neck, "He won't be able to keep his hands off of you."

Although the fabric was sheer and barely lined, it was heavy when I lifted it. The floor-length gown was weighed down by endless columns of Byzantium purple sequin. They left no material to be seen underneath it. It wrapped around me like a robe, tied off by a velvet belt. The large bishop sleeves hung loosely around my arms. It left my chest exposed by a deep V. The necklace Pol had made for me hung in the middle, the amethyst geode pendant with amber sun sparkling. Falece had taped my breasts to make them look round and perky. The pendant only drew more attention to my wide cleavage.

She helped me into the gold pointed toe heels of mesh with amber crystals sprawled upon them. I wobbled, and she caught me before I could fall. The heels somehow felt even higher when I stood again.

"One more touch," she said, dabbing an oil on my neck and the curves of my breasts, giggling the entire time. It smelt somehow familiar yet unlike anything I could recall—musky yet pleasant.

"Will Pol be walking me up?" I asked with no hint of interest in my tone. She rubbed another fruity and floral perfume oil on my neck as I smoothed the sequin downward on my hips.

"He's waiting next door. I'll get him for you," she said in a giddy way, baring her sparkling teeth. She skipped from the room and left my door open. Her wings buzzed and hummed, lifting her briefly with each skip. Her white chiffon column dress barely touched the floor. I heard her knock on Pol's door, then her murmur of my readiness, and then his unmistakable voice responding with thanks. Heavy feet thudded in the hall, and his door shut. I could feel him. I could feel him getting closer, and it made my heart race. I calmed myself. Before walking to the door, I happened to glance at the mantle to see the two oils, and I wondered what they were. *They're nice.* I thought while sniffing my wrist and reading the labels. One was clearly a perfume I'd never find in Regnum Solo, but the *other* was marked "Pheromones."

"Damnit, Falece…" I muttered, grumbling under my breath.

I heard her giggle again, followed by the buzzing of her dragonfly wings down the hall. Then Pol's heavy, slow footsteps came close. There was no time to wipe the oils clean. I walked to the door, trying not to fall in my heels. I made it to the doorway, ankles burning.

He was adjusting the cuffs of his all-black suit. His charcoal jacket was woven like carbon fiber; the high collar was unbuttoned. He looked up and breathed deeply through his nose when he saw me. A smile pulled at the corner of his mouth for only a moment.

"You look beautiful," he said, offering his arm. I pretended to be completely unaffected by his reaction. I closed the door behind me, leaving my hand on the handle for stability for one more moment. By the time I met him in the middle of the hall, I stumbled again, and he caught me. My chest fell into him, and the pheromone oil wafted all around us. His grip tightened, his fingertips sinking into my sides hard. I winced and stood up straight and then took his arm.

"Thank you. You look very nice too."

"I ordered those to be made with a low heel."

Damnit, Falece...

"They're perfect. Thank you. I just need to break them in." But he waved his hand, and before I knew it, the heel widened, and they lowered an inch or more. My ankles stopped burning, and I sighed in relief.

"Thank you."

It wasn't until we reached the doors to the ballroom that I felt my gut twist. Guards opened the doors and we were announced. Suddenly a sea of curious eyes were on us. The bend of my arm tightened on him, and he steadied me. "Please don't let me fall." As we made our way through the path of parting people I could see we were approaching a tall woman standing from her seat at the center of a great table. She had the same long midface and narrow eyes as Pol, with long, loose curls of silvery white spinning to her elbows.

She wore a cropped two-piece of midnight blue with silver filigree that looked more like gusts of wind than the leafy patterns I'd expect. The high-waisted, wide-legged pants moved like a skirt would, even boasting two half trains. The cropped top with high collar and fitted, full-length sleeves, however, hugged her tightly. Her crown of white gold was fashioned in tendrils and was adorned with diamond-crusted stars. It lay flat against her head, one star flush against her forehead just above her brow, the rest pressing her hair flat against her head.

By the time we reached her, I could see her eyes were pale, green-blue crystals of aquamarine. They darted to the geode resting in my cleavage, arched a single brow, and blinked once to move her eyes to Pol.

Pol bent forward, his arm pulling me at the elbow. The depth of the bow felt excessive and theatrical. I shot a look at Pol in question. *This is how he greets his own mother?*

"Mother, Queen Madgee," he addressed her formally.

"Rise." As he did, I did. She projected her voice so everyone could hear. "Princess Daphne, we are so pleased you have been found safe after so many years, and we welcome you to our court warmly. I pledge your safety in this kingdom."

Princess. The title was my new ick, but I figured I'd have to get used to it. "Your Majesty, thank you for your hospitality," I said, projecting my voice too. It wasn't unnatural for me either. It actually just reminded me of how I had to speak to some of my hearing-impaired patients.

"Join us at our table," she commanded, offering a hand to her right.

Pol pulled out a chair for me, and I sat stiffly. He took the open seat by my side, brushing elbows with a thin, raven-haired woman who appeared to be my age and looked strikingly like Pol. She had thinner lips, a stronger chin, and eyes the pale pink of rose quartz. Where Pol had a haunting, poetic beauty, she had a cold and confident beauty.

"Sister," Pol nodded to her. "This is Daphne. Daphne, this is my sister."

"Princess Cynti." Her hand shot out in front of Pol quickly, yet with elegance. "*Heir* to Loanan."

"Heir?" I questioned before remembering to mind my tone.

"The line of succession is typically carried through the women in many kingdoms here," Pol offered. I took a sip of water while I processed the social norms and wondered why the hell they insisted I come here. *If my throne was conquered and this seat is taken, what's the point?*

Pol piled food on our plates. Despite the freshly baked artisan loaf and delicious ham and apricot baked pastry, I could hardly stomach anything. I felt like a spectacle, and this wasn't exactly low pressure.

"It's very nice to meet you, Cynti." Before Cynti could speak, Queen Madgee interrupted from the seat next to her, effortlessly commandeering the conversation.

"And as Pol is your mate by ceremony, he will sit beside you when we avenge your kingdom. You will marry before then, of course." I nearly choked on a tiny bite of pastry.

"Mother," Pol interrupted firmly, pulling a cloth napkin down his chin. "That is still her choice to make."

"And yet here she sits, dripping in the jeweled eyes of your dead ancestors and fruitlessly fighting the strength of your bond. What choice does she really *need* to make? Fate has looked kindly on you, dear," she continued, looking at me.

"Your Majesty," I said without concern for her rank. "I didn't know the cost of these jewels when they were gifted, and I certainly didn't ask for them or any of this. I am here in good faith, but I'm not going to swear my future to anything without knowing what I'm getting myself into."

The queen gave the thin smile of a woman whose patience had been tested plenty through the years. "A cautious approach is often wise, princess. You are much like your mother, who I lay with in ceremony to forge your bond with Pol." *Did she just say...* I leaned back, recoiling from the statement. "Our ancestors would not have granted the creation of those jewels if they did not foresee that bond being sealed. Perhaps you fight the future for pride rather than reason. *That* is never wise."

I stayed busy chewing bread into sugar as she spoke to avoid speaking out of turn in unfamiliar company and to fill the ever-growing pit in my gut. As insistent and rude as she was, she never lost her grace. I considered her last insinuation and tried to push off any offense.

"With all due respect, mother, it's wise not to presume why the dead give us anything. She is of noble blood and has every right to wear the death jewels, just as any of us. The gifts were needed and not transactional," Pol said flatly as he spread a cloth napkin on his lap and buttered a roll. I cleared my throat, trying to cut through the tension.

"Were you bonded in ceremony too, Cynti?" I asked, hoping it would shift the conversation.

Cynti's face gave a reserved smile. "I am Pol's twin. Younger by minutes. I have no bond."

"Women can't bond with women?" I asked casually. Cynti's face flushed, and she sat up straighter. She gave a polite yet uncomfortable nod.

"It's not unheard of, but—"

"That's enough," the queen commanded and shifted in her chair quickly. "A dance then," she said as she stood. The room fell quiet beneath her gaze.

"You have an iron spine, I'll give you that," Pol said as we made our way to the room's center, arm in arm. I scoffed, too annoyed to pay attention to all of the gems staring at us.

"She was fine telling me how she fucked my mother, but the thought of her daughter bonded with a woman is *so* horrible?" I turned to him, staring straight ahead into his wide chest. He smelled so damn good. I placed one hand on his shoulder, and the other was lost in his giant mitt. His free hand pressed into my lower back. The music started, a slow tune played on a harp and complemented by the music of various instruments. I followed his lead, focusing more on not stepping on his toes or tripping than on winning the current spat.

"One is a duty; the other could end her dynasty," Pol offered. "Cynti will be given a husband and expected to wed him for an alliance. Whether she likes him or not, that is her duty. It's unkind to remind her of that—of being unbonded."

I ground my teeth for a moment before remembering our audience and lifting my chin to meet his eyes. My heart skipped a beat. My body felt glued to him. My chest warmed. I unclenched my jaw and relaxed my shoulders; even my tongue fell from the roof of my mouth. I let go of whatever was bothering me a moment ago, now infatuated with the way the twinkling lightning in the ceiling of clouds danced around Pol and occasionally caught a fleck of random color in his eyes. He held me close enough that if my knees gave out I wouldn't budge. The room seemed to slowly spin and shrink beneath us as we lost ourselves in one another. Silently we moved, woven together in an unearthly dance.

He lifted my arm and sent me in a twirl. It wasn't until I made the turn that I realized we were floating on a small stormy nimbus above the room of people, six meters or more in the air. My foot nearly slipped and I gasped. I pulled myself back into him tightly. Pheromones wafted up again, and his pupils dilated. I could sense his hunger. I could feel him stiff under his zipper. He gripped me tighter. Our lips were dangerously close to touching. *I need him.*

His smokey scent was intoxicating. The cloud rotated us. Purple light bounced off of my gown onto his jacket and face. My chest pushed against him, each breath deepening my cleavage. His breath matched mine.

The tantric dance swallowed us into ourselves. There was no concept of time or space or anyone around. It was only us dancing on a nimbus to a harp-lead quartet. He lowered his face. His lips were closer to my cheek than my mouth. I would only need to turn my head an inch to taste him. I struggled not to close the gap.

He leaned me back into a dip. My arm draped behind his neck. I closed my eyes to center myself. My control was hanging on by a thread. At the deepest point of the dip, my knee kept height with his hip. He pulled himself up my thigh, his hardness evident. I could feel my center prime for him. Our lips brushed. There was only one too-loud breath between us.

The music stopped. My eyes opened, and he lifted me to my feet. We were now planted on the marble floor. I hadn't known when the cloud appeared under me or when it disappeared. All I knew was Pol's possessive embrace and the way I could sense every atom between us.

Now grounded, I had to pull away and remember to maintain my control. I barely knew him, and he kept too many secrets. Magic wasn't going to rush me into anything. Pulling away was physically exhausting, but I showed none of it.

Pol clenched his jaw at the distance between us. Scorn was written in his eyes. I kept my chin high through a polite bow and turned back to the table under a cacophony of clapping and a less amorous song.

The queen held my eyes with an arrogant smile of validation yet clapped elegantly. "The bond is strong," she remarked as I passed her.

I took my seat and realized Pol hadn't followed me. Soon visitors broke their dance and came to greet us at the table. They were all well-wishers, and some of them had known my parents. Many held positions in court overseeing various aspects of social infrastructure. Uripe came, dressed in a very human formal fashion, although obviously struggled with how to tie a bowtie correctly. He greeted me with a handshake excitedly.

Chloe came too, dressed in a stunning caeluman-style suit that accentuated their supple cleavage without compromising their obvious fierceness. I didn't miss the way Cynti's eyes focused on Chloe when they kissed her hand. The tension was palpable, the queen's distaste for it even more so. I was relieved when the visits stopped and was bothered that Pol left me to do it all alone.

"Hah! Well, it won't be long now, will it? The stars only know how long he's held out, and he looked absolutely ill for you out there." Cynti jabbed with poise as she took Pol's seat.

"What's that?" I asked, giving up on my stagnant search for Pol. I looked at her with furrowed brows.

"You and my brother seem to be hitting it off, is all," she explained with a shrug. "Unless you've already *sealed* the bond?"

My eyebrows rose. "No," I replied softly. I guessed I deserved that after my line of questioning. I let boredom show over the topic of Pol and me. But just as I was looking for him again, I turned back to her. "*Held out?* For what exactly?"

A smile tugged at the corner of her mouth, and she made a show of sipping from her crystal wine glass before answering. "Well, you see. My brother has never cared to court a woman. Not that I've ever known of at least. He knew of the bond early. Perhaps that's why."

My face must have drained of color when I realized what she meant. Opals...*the patience and moderation I need to wait for that which I honor.* She let out a snort and leaned in.

"I can't be sure, of course." She paused. Her face dimmed, and she leaned in closer. "I love my brother very much. I don't care to see his heart toyed with. He's shown you every affection and respect. So while you sort what you are sorting, it would be kind of you not to lead him on a leash."

"I didn't choose this bond, nor do I expect you to understand how it feels since you *don't* have one. I won't apologize for sorting out what is my choice and what is magical coercion." I scanned the room, hot faced at her brazen remarks. This family had no sense of boundaries. I was starting to see where Pol got it from. "And your brother does *not* show affection, or any other emotion for that matter."

"That's just the way he is. That doesn't mean he doesn't *feel* them," she snapped back defensively. Her tone turned to disgust. "Hah. Forgive me; I was told you were a 'healer' in Regnum Solo. I figured you were keen on such divergence. Or perhaps that is the very reason you rejected him?"

...*Divergence?* I felt as though I swallowed a brick. It hadn't even occurred to me. I could hardly move air through the lump in my throat. *Damn it. Why am I such a bitch?*

I stared out into the ballroom, and my eyes easily found Pol standing at the back. I felt sick remembering every horrible way I interacted with him for simply not being able to express himself. My mouth hung open when I looked back at Cynti. "Not so keen, I guess...excuse me." I stood, determined to make my way to Pol. However, Pol had left and did not return. In fact, I didn't see him for the rest of the night.

20

O'DOHERTY: THE GHOST SHE SAW BESIDE ME

"Nana never liked the 'all black at a funeral' tradition," Fabian said as I helped him with his coral tie.

"Well, it's a good thing we aren't having a funeral."

"Yeah, this celebration of life thing should be nice." Tears were threatening to fall from his eyes, and his shaky voice cracked. "She would have loved that dress, honey. You look beautiful." He kissed my forehead, and we left for her celebration.

Everyone gathered in clothes of Nana's favorite color—coral—and ate her favorite food—chicken pesto—and played her favorite games—cribbage and charades. It was a fun time, although bittersweet.

Her health had been declining since the stroke she suffered the night of our first date. She decided to not only opt out of the medication trial but discontinue any treatments and call on hospice. They didn't think she qualified at the time, but soon enough, it was clear she had much less than six months left. She went peacefully in her sleep a few days after the BBQ.

I heard Fabian's room-lifting laugh for the first time in days as he won a game of cribbage without even knowing exactly what he had done to win it. Fabian often excelled at new things. He stood from the table, excusing himself from some of Nana's old friends, and walked over to his sister, Melly, and me. It was Melly who was there with her when she passed. Fabian wrapped his arms around my waist, kissed me through my hair, and gave his sister a simple, "How are you holding up?" Finally, Melly spoke more than I had ever heard her.

"You know, before Nana died, she kept telling me about her dreams. She said ever since the night of the storm she had a dream about the same thing. She said there was a man making tornadoes in the sky and that he was very handsome and never wore a shirt." She laughed as a salty tear fell from her cheek and into her lemonade. "She said he just floats there, 'looking like a sour puss and whipping up destruction.'"

We laughed about it then, but I wasn't laughing today. Today I was shaking. Nana was not the only patient who passed this week, nor the last one to share that they had experienced the same vivid dreams.

I went to the hospital early this morning to visit the few patients who were still hospitalized and in my trial. I had trouble finding a nurse at first, but my luck changed drastically when I spotted a group of them huddled in the supply room. I crept in, hearing the tail end of a conversation about unionizing that broke off when the door startled them.

"I'm a friendly, no worries." Some of them looked skeptical, but Jesula vouched for me. Much like many nurses here, she knew very well that Daphne and I were best friends. She pulled me into the room and helped the door to shut. "How's the, uh, organizing going?" I asked.

"It's going," one of them said dryly.

"I think someone leaked it. Management has been watching us closer," another complained, sucking her teeth.

"Let them watch! We have every right to organize, and they have no right to interfere. They get what they get, and they brought this on themselves!" Jesula asserted. The nurses murmured in agitated agreement. "What can we do for you, darling?"

"I have a patient, Mrs. Soto. Any changes?"

"Well, if hospice is a change, I'd say so," one of the nurses said. "The hospice nurse is in there with her now. Poor thing's hallucinating. It'll be soon."

I thanked the group and turned to open the door. There on the other side was Lyndie Pratt, hands on her hips and eyes narrowed in suspicion. Her stone-like form startled me, but I nodded with a smile and detoured around her.

"Ladies, there's been a lot of side meetings lately. Care to clue me in?" Lyndie asked the group as I walked toward Mrs. Soto's room. I was glad to get out of earshot of that predicament. Then again, Jesula's voice seemed perfectly calm and unwavering when she responded.

The hospice nurse was just outside of Mrs. Soto's room, charting at a pod desk on her computer. She was a tall, blond woman with a pink stripe of hair on the bottom layer that curled out through the side. I approached her carefully, not wanting to startle her the way Lyndie had startled me.

"Hi there. I'm O'doherty. Ms. Soto was on a medication trial that I'm coordinating. I hear she decided to stop taking it."

"Oh, hi!" The nurse responded, full of life and calm happiness. I thought it ironic, given her specialty. "I'm Penny, her hospice nurse. And yes, sweety, she signed on with hospice this morning. We're arranging to get her home and comfortable. I was told she started refusing all medications a few days ago though, if that helps."

"Yes. Thank you. It does." I took a note down. "And…her nurse told me she's hallucinating?"

"Well, it might seem that way, but no, not really. You see, many times when a patient is close to death, they experience a phenomenon called deathbed visions. It has many nicknames, but essentially dying people will often see a loved one who has long since passed away. They have conversations with them and everything. Mrs. Soto is currently visiting with her deceased sister, Mable."

"That sounds… terrifying," I said with wide eyes.

"No, on the contrary, the visits usually bring the patient a lot of comfort and joy and help them feel at peace with their death," she responded cheerfully. "Usually they'll tell them they're 'going on a trip soon,' and it's not long after that."

"And are there any coordinating factors in patients who experience this, clinically or otherwise?" I asked, strictly for documentation purposes.

"None. People from countless religions, ethnicities, cultural backgrounds, and ages have all experienced the same thing. No injuries, no weird lab results. It just happens."

"Do you mind if I see her? I have to enter an assessment."

"Oh sure, sweety! I'll be right here. You just let me know if you need anything!"

When I walked into the room, Mrs. Soto was indeed sitting up in bed, eyes wide and looking at an empty chair, laughing authentically and talking to no one. She had an energy you wouldn't expect from a dying patient. This was one phenomenon in hospice patients that I *did* know about. It causes the patient to have a "last kick" of energy right before they pass. A "rally," as they called it, often tricked family members into thinking their loved one was making a sudden recovery when, in actuality, it meant the exact opposite.

"Mrs. Soto, I'm sorry to interrupt."

"Oh, hi, dear. I was just talking to my sister. We haven't talked in years!"

I made my way to the seat and decided to pull up a new one so I didn't sit on her dead sister. I looked uncomfortably at the empty chair next to me but smiled at Mrs. Soto to feign acknowledgment of her invisible visitor.

"Mrs. Soto, I won't be long; I just have to ask you some questions, if that's okay."

"Sure, dear. Mable doesn't mind. She doesn't have anywhere to be. She's dead!" She laughed, but goosebumps pricked my skin.

"Oh. Okay… How are you sleeping? Any more sleepwalking?"

"No, no. I'm not sleepwalking. I'm sleeping fine. The dreams are pretty wacky, though!" she laughed.

"Dreams? Tell me more about that."

"Oh, there's a handsome man—a broody sort, though. He just floats in the sky, making storms," she said nonchalantly. The goosebumps came back. "Oh, Mable, that's not very nice."

"How long have you dreamt about him?" I asked, typing the familiar data into her chart.

"Since the night of the storm. You know the tornado that took the old folks' home?" I clacked at my computer keys as she spoke, entering in her exact quotes. "Mable! No, no. That will scare the poor girl."

I smiled a small wince at the ghost and continued my questions at Mrs. Soto. "Why didn't you tell me about these dreams before? I've seen you several times since then."

"Oh, the medications made me fuzzy. I couldn't remember much of anything, much less a dream. You know how they disappear as soon as you open your eyes. Well, not so much now… N-Now, Mable, you just wait… Now, where was I? Since I've stopped taking the medications, I don't forget my dreams at all! And I *know* I've had them before. I wouldn't forget a man like *that*! Haha. Shirtless too! Ah! Now, Mable, *please*!"

"Wh…what would Mable like to share?" I offered, trying to rid her of the distraction. I gave a sideways glance at the ghost she saw beside me.

"Ugh, honey, she says you're being followed by a man. He doesn't like you looking into those rocks and that if you don't stop, you might get hurt."

I felt the color drained from my face. Chills covered my body. I slapped my computer shut.

"See, Mable, the poor thing is spooked."

"Mrs. Soto, can you ask Mable what this man looked like?"

Mrs. Soto looked at the chair momentarily and then bucked her head in humor.

"Well, isn't that the darndest? That sounds an awful lot like the man in my dreams!"

"Mrs. Soto?"

"Yes, yes. He's a kind of light-brown skinned man like Dr. Kumar. But has dark lips and white hair. Ahhh… Young man, though—about your age. *Handsome*, very handsome!"

My heart stopped momentarily, and I could feel my hands shaking. She described the man who had been following me in exact detail. "Thank you so much. I'm afraid I have to go." I got up and started for the door.

"He's killed a lot of people, you know?" Her words made me freeze in place. "You should stop with the rocks, Mable says, or you'll be going on a trip like us soon!" Mrs. Soto turned back to the ghost and continued her conversation.

Penny popped out of her seat when I walked from the doorway. "Sweety, sit down. You look *ill!*" I couldn't hear her as she continued to fuss and fan me. My ears were ringing, my eyes were tunneling, and my breath went ragged.

The sound of my phone ringing finally pulled me from the state. I answered, waving off Penny and walking across the hall to lean my weight against the wall. "Hello, this is O'doherty Sameal." My voice shook.

"Hi, Ms. Sameal. This is Robert Dawson— the mineralogist. I'm calling about your rock sample," the man on the line replied with a deep southern drawl. I looked through the window to Mrs. Soto's room to find her looking at me knowingly, and then frowning.

"Ye...yes, hi. It's nice to finally hear from you." My voice couldn't stop shaking.

"I'm sorry for the delay, ma'am. Honest. We've had storms taking out our power since we got the sample," he explained.

"Heh. That's been a reoccurring thing lately, hasn't it," I offered, trying to sound casual.

"Yes, ma'am. Well, I don't know if the results will be helpful, but I've mailed them to you with the sample. It's a strange analysis."

"What's strange about it?"

"Well, it's *not* lab-made like you thought. At first glance, it would seem like a natural geode, but it's not that either."

"Okay, so what is it?"

"That's the thing. It's a combination of different crystals and minerals. Pure ones. Not a speck of imperfection throughout the whole sample, and we did chop. it. up. We ran it through. Very thorough."

"I don't understand. What does that mean?"

"It means there are pure crystals and minerals mixed into one stone that normally wouldn't be found together in nature this way, but with all tests, this is *not* lab made."

"So where would you find that?"

"You *wouldn't*, ma'am. That's what I'm saying. No lab could create this, and there's no known place on earth where you could mine it. It's….an anomaly; it's unnaturally natural… Or *supernatural,* you could say. The results are inconclusive as to its origins. I can definitively say that it contains the following in their purest forms: sodalite, sapphire, larimar, lapis lazuli, labradorite, moonstone, selenite, opal, and angel aura quartz. Only at the center is there obsidian. They're all arranged in irregular and inconsistent layers and with crystalline projections on the hollow inside."

"I don't understand… I'm… I'm not following." I mindlessly took notes of everything he said, not at all expecting it to mean anything. Mrs. Soto still stared at me, shaking her head. The goosebumps came back, and I rubbed my hand on the back of my neck to warm them. I saw movement out of the corner of my eye, but when I turned, no one was down the hall.

"I'm not sure I understand either. But if you find out where it came from, I have a lot of curious guys here who would love to hear about it. You should get your sample back with a full printout of the report in a few days."

"Thank you." I hung up my phone and shoved the paper in my pocket recklessly. The familiar sweet, fruity musk carried to me on a draft, and I spun around to see no one there. A feeling of dread and coldness fell over me. I felt eyes on me but didn't know where they were.

The next thing I knew, I was racing home in my car, texting

Fabian in a panic. He met me in my driveway and held me before I could fully leap from my car. I sobbed into him, and no matter how tightly he held me, he couldn't still the violent trembling of my body.

"So she had the same dreams as Nana, and her dead sister says the same man is following you?" Fabian recapped curiously. He poured hot water over a homemade bag of tea with mint, rose hips, and chamomile. The steam rising from the teacup let out a heavenly aroma under my nose, and I sunk my elbows into the table. I was finally calm and more clearheaded, but still very distraught.

"Yeah…"

"That *does* sound scary. Especially if a handsome man is so interested in my lady," he joked, pressing a kiss on my forehead before sitting down across from me. "Should I worry?"

"Fabian, I have been…followed by a man."

His face turned serious in an instant. "Jesus, honey, when were you going to tell me this?"

"Nothing's come of it…"

"How long has this been going on?"

"Since the day I went to the pharmaceutical place… And there's been notes left on… and *in* my car… telling me to stay away."

"*Dotey*," he said in a gravelly voice. I had never heard him so stern. He combed his hands through his curls. "Who is this guy? What does he look like? Has he hurt you? What…"

A tear fell from my eye, and my face scrunched in a sour pout that I knew was unflattering. "He's exactly how Mrs. Soto described him…" I said through a new wave of tears.

"I'm calling the police." Fabian stood up, but I stopped him.

"And tell them what? A ghost told her dying sister that he's following me? That I haven't seen him in weeks and he's never said a word to me? Never come near me?"

"That your tires got slashed? That threatening notes were left on your car? Why wait until he takes it any farther, honey?"

"He won't," I tried to assure him. "The mineralogist called. The results are inconclusive. They don't know where the rocks came from. It's all crystals and minerals. Nothing, no contaminants."

"What am I missing here? What does that have anything to do with some creep stalking you?"

"He only follows me when I'm looking into the rocks. They're neither natural nor man-made from what they can tell. He said *'supernatural,'* actually," I scoffed, throwing the crumpled list of information from my pocket on the table. "I'm at a dead end. And even according to *'Mable',* once I stop looking into the rocks he'll leave me alone."

"Sounds like Mable's on to something," he said in a bothered way, taking a seat and grinding his teeth.

I rolled my eyes. "Mable is a hallucination, babe." I sipped my tea. "Mrs. Soto must have seen him follow me at the hospital and stirred up a story in her brain."

"Okay, well. *I* think Mable is real. I think this *supernatural* rock thing is real. And I think you need to *stay away* from all of it," he said, straightening the wrinkles out of the paper and looking at it. "Please."

"Someone did something to those patients. *Nana* was one of them… Don't you want answers?"

Fabian folded the paper, held it between his first two fingers, and pointed at me with it. "I'll take this to the healer I see. She has almost all of these things in her shop. If she can't tell us what it means, we leave it alone."

"Your *healer*? Are you into all that now? Magical healing stones? Maybe you should pick one up for protection," I teased, sniffling up the last of my whimpers.

He came to his knees in front of me, put his elbows on my thighs, and took my hand in his to kiss it. "You're very clinical, but science failed you this time. *Yes*, I think there's something to that *stuff*. But not *enough* to it to protect you from a dangerous man. So tomorrow we're going to go over how to use my gun. You're gonna know it inside and out and take it with you everywhere."

"Fabian…" I soured my brows.

He kissed my hand again and looked at me pleadingly. I nodded at him in agreement, as if I could say no.

That night he slept by my side, him on the side of the bed closest to the door, in case of an intrusion. The gun was loaded in his nightstand. Polpetta nuzzled as close to him as she could. She adored Fabian, as did I. Fabian made me feel safe in so many ways, which is why I couldn't understand why I was rendered speechless and nervous by what he said next. Holding my cheek, he gave me a long, thoughtful kiss goodnight, stopping just once to say it. "I love you."

21

DAPHNE: RUSHINC TO MY DEATH

My first four days in Loanan sucked. I had no friends aside from the very quiet Uripe, whom I struggled to communicate with. Uripe was also a tutor, so as much as I enjoyed his company, confiding in him would be inappropriate. I wasn't on good terms with the royal family or council. The one person I craved to be near more than anything had kept his distance since the dinner.

That night, as soon as the party was over, I walked myself back to my room. I stopped at my doorway and turned to face Pols. My knuckles hovered inches above his door as I worked up the nerve to knock. I stood like that for a moment with intentions to start over but could feel my body betraying me. Even with the solid wood door between us, my thighs warmed at the thought of his smokey scent. I felt a scratch along my lower back, and I flinched at the mysterious pain. I dropped my fist, and the first step away from his door felt like pulling strong magnets apart again. Afraid he would feel it, I rushed to my room, where I began my meditation.

Meditation wasn't hard. It reminded me a lot of the relaxation sessions at Dr. Bailey's office. I meditated for an hour, focusing only on the air around me. When I would get distracted by a thought (and there was plenty on my mind), I'd let it slip through and refocus.

I had only briefly learned about the different mudras and decided to use Hakini Mudra for my first meditation. It would help with deepening respiration and concentration. Sitting on the floor on the edge of my phantom wall, I looked to the never-ending night sky.

I brought my hands into the mudra at the heart chakra. I shifted my awareness to the air around me, moving in and out of my lungs and all around my skin. Inhaling, I pressed my tongue to the roof of my mouth. Exhaling, I relaxed. I shifted my awareness to my third eye, and then pushed it as far out as I could, little by little for the entire hour. I pushed it into the clear night air in front of me, under the waning gibbous moon. I felt the air inside me and around me. The crystal-clear sky, from this impossibly high up, was cleansing. I slept well that night.

The next two days were similar. The princess sneered at me in passing. The queen was cold and reserved. Uripe was a gem but all business, and he kept my nose in the books. He answered my questions, and I continued learning about magic.

Section 3: Psychic Magic

<u>Psychic magic</u> <u>is the use of one's alt-consciousness to tap into and/or manipulate variables of their existence. Psychic magic is the most broad and complex of magics, and for that reason, it is exceedingly rare for one to master completely.</u> *Examples of psychic magic include but are not limited to, divination, moving, astral projection, emitting, empathing, dream projection, and* *optimized intuition. The method of welding psychic magic is specific to each type.*

*<u>**Moving** is the practice of setting objects into motion without physical force by way of connecting or bonding to the object.</u> To bond, one must feel the energy in and around themselves, between themselves and the object, and the object itself. This connection makes the object an extension of oneself and is set into motion by moving the flow of energy from the practitioner to the object. This often happens in a current like motion.*

The most common type of moving is that of a cloud. Once the cloud is formed, grounded, and mounted, the practitioner may move energy out of the body and into the object to direct its movement. <u>Moving an object grounded and/or in contact with you can usually be done without mudras. In some circumstances, and with novice practitioners of magic, hand mudras may need to be used.</u> Moving and basic riding clouds will be covered in more depth in Chapter 41.

This particular section was the most helpful then. I used psychic magic whenever I went to training after studies. Chloe was a great trainer, even though it was mostly yoga, pushups, and running laps at first. All of it was a great outlet for the pent-up rage I started to feel.

"You're irritable. That's expected. You're coming into your power. Mood swings come with the hormone changes. It's temporary. Keep meditating," Chloe told me. With the mood swings, I found almost everyone incredibly annoying. I wasn't in the mood to make friends.

Two of the new recruits in the class were obviously the favorites.

Mynt was a pixie with incredibly smooth, dark brown skin and shiny, purple wings. Her diamond-paved fangs seemed sharper and shinier than any other pixie I saw. She wore her raven hair naturally and picked out in an afro. Her hair looked like a magazine ad. It was shiny and bouncy, swaying with her movements. Between her perfect features and ridiculously golden-yellow citrine irises, she was easily the most gorgeous caeluman I had ever seen. I could see Chloe's pride whenever Mynt showed off a skill, magical or other, with perfection. "A natural," Chloe called her. I rolled my eyes.

Promise was the other student who excelled. Like Mynt, he was a pixie. He had deeply melanated skin, his raven locks were shoulder length, and he had eyes of onyx. His wings were vibrant pink. He was small—as pixies are—but strong and stacked with muscle. Like Mynt, he was clearly good at everything, cutting through each pose and using magic almost as well as she could.

Mynt and Promise would stare each other down intensely when they dueled. I was thankful for their rivalry because maybe people didn't notice how much I sucked at this. I tried not to compare myself to the pair of star students or anyone else. But everyone was excelling around me. I was the runt—the runt princess.

After group training Chloe would try to guide me one-on-one in forming a cloud or condensed air.

"I'll start with a cumulus cloud," I said.

"Great. For that, we'll use version-a of Varuna Mudra. It will help channel water," Chloe said, demonstrating. Let's start with meditation. Focus on the air and the water in it for a moment."

I closed my eyes and did as they said. Then, without prompting, I channeled our dimension. They must have realized it because they started again, picking up at the next step. "Now the mudra, eyes open." I fumbled with my fingers and finally got it. "Don't worry, you won't always have to use mudras. They help while you're training. Focus on the feeling they bring."

I couldn't manage much at first, but to my surprise, I held a ball of fog in my hand. I was overflowing with joy and disbelief before it disappeared. It strained me, but the excitement kept me pushing.

But then Pol would pass through the courtyard at a distance. I felt him before I saw him, the pull announcing his presence. He'd glare at me for a moment. Despite his stoic nature, I could feel his aggressive lust. I felt the scratch against my back again. I was overcome with vivid images of him holding me down and taking me. Images of water pouring down his face as he buried himself into me forcefully. Whenever I saw him, my face ran hot. My chest got heavy. Then my powers raged beyond what I could consciously wield. I could barely correct it.

The first time it happened I turned my clothes and hair into a sopping wet mop. It steamed off of me and evaporated the very next moment. Chloe sucked their teeth. I'd force myself to look away from him until he left.

The second time it happened was a couple of days later. I was soaked again. I shook from the exhaustion of using so much magic with such little control. By then Chloe caught on to the reason for the flair ups and recommended a new meditation for the night.

"I understand choosing to ignore the bond for now, but that *will* come with consequences. I don't envy you," they started. "Tonight, meditate with Abhaya Hridaya Mudra, or the fearless love mudra, at your heart chakra," Chloe explained the meditation.

After a hot shower, that's what I did. Seated on the floor facing the phantom wall again, I moved my hands to the fearless love mudra at my heart chakra, closed my eyes, and envisioned Pol. I envisioned a white light from his chest to mine. It felt amazing—unconditional love, pure and intense. I let go of any resistance to accepting the light and relaxed into it. Then I gave the same energy to him, white light releasing from my chest and into his freely. I meditated this way for an hour, envisioning Pol with me as we shared love without reservation. It was a safe place to allow myself to feel, receive, and reciprocate.

I expected to be tired after meditation like I usually was, but surprisingly I wasn't. I felt like a weight was lifted and I had clarity. I decided a midnight walk around the quiet palace would be helpful. *Maybe I'll stop at the gym and run*, I thought first. *Maybe I'll stop in the library and find a book on sign language to be able to communicate with Uripe better*, I thought next. That option won, and I jogged up the stairs.

It took me some time to find the book I was looking for. The library was dark. Only moonlight poured through the windows to illuminate the cases as I walked through the wing for Regnum Caelorum. *Sign Language for Beginners*, as it was titled, did not have any indication that it was different from North American sign language at all. I was hopeful that I could take the skill back with me to Regnum Solo. I tucked the hefty book under my arm and headed back.

Soon the soft patting of my feet was not the only noise to be heard through the main hall. As I crept to the dining room doorway, I could hear thuds and pained noises. Alarmed, I rushed toward the sounds, certain someone was being hurt. When I walked through the door, it was a very different situation.

Chloe, their chest bare with breasts jerking, had someone bent over the dark wood of the wine bar in the dining room. Soft, raven hair was tangled in Chloe's grip. Their other hand wrapped around her waist, dipping between her legs. Chloe's pants hung just low enough to reveal the leather belt of a strap-on. They

thrust viciously into her. I froze, hearing wet, slapping sounds. The raven-haired woman was spreading her ass apart. The hem of her nightdress was lifted from her ass, panties yanked down to mid-thigh. Her top was pulled down, her breasts spilling out.

"Does the queen know what a little whore you are?" Chloe taunted, working up a sweat. "Huh?" they added aggressively. They pulled the raven hair upward until a face came into view.

"No, she doesn't know I'm your little whore, baby," Cynti rasped through breaths and moans. She struggled to keep quiet. Her breasts shook with Chloe's forceful fucking. It was clear by the rising tone of her moans that she was approaching her climax.

I gasped, and the heavy book fell from under my arm with a thud. Startled, they jolted up. Chloe withdrew from Cynti, and I could see it was a very impressive double strap-on they were harnessed into.

I reached for the book to pick it up but knocked my shoulder into a tall vase, sending it to shatter loudly on the floor.

"Fuck," I breathed.

Cynti's face was stuck, frozen in fear and hatred. She pulled her clothes into place and scowled at me. Chloe looked as if they had seen a ghost. Both of them had a sheen of sweat. Sex hung in the air thickly.

"Okay, what do you want?" Cynti barked. "What will it be that buys your silence?"

"I'm sorry, what?" I asked, still stunned.

"No one can know about this. The Queen... My mother... would not respond well. What will it be?" her voice shook.

"I would never *out* you, Cynti. I wouldn't out anyone." I shook my head and offered a calming jester with my hand. "I didn't see anything."

Cynti's nostrils flared, obviously not trusting my word. "Chloe would be dishonorably discharged for this. Probably worse. You understand that, right? Mother already suspects." She urged with her brows raised. Adrenaline was coursing through Cynti's veins. It was like she would tear me to pieces to protect their secret.

"You have my word. I would never—" My attempt at comfort was interrupted. Heavy footsteps fell in the hall. "Someone's coming. You have to mist out of here. Go."

"You can't mist from inside the palace," Chloe said, struggling uselessly with the buckles of their strap-on. The footsteps came closer, and Cynti panicked. The smell of arousal and sweat in the air was undeniable. I charged to Cynti and grabbed her by the arm, hurrying her behind the wine bar and a large planter.

"Stay quiet." With that, I pulled my satin night top down past my breasts. I hit my knees in front of Chloe. Then I took the first dildo I could reach into my mouth, hoping it wasn't the anal one. Judging by the familiar taste of a woman, it wasn't. I wasn't exactly faking the enjoyment of kneeling at Chloe's feet. Tasting Cynti on the toy was hot. Even if she was a bitch. So, when the door swung open, it was very convincing to Vice Majesty Fenk that we were the ones making a loud mess.

"What is the meaning of this?" he shouted. Fenk was the queen's right-hand man. He was a bald man with a stick up his ass. Fenk had bird-like facial features, an unkempt beard of gray, and dull turquoise eyes. His shoulder blades extended out into bony wings and crossed each other like a short cape of feathers. While I faked my surprise masterfully, Chloe just looked confused. They looked between the two of us. I pulled my top back over my breasts, pretending to be modest, and I stood, covering myself. Chloe—forever chivalrous—offered me a strong hand in support.

"Vice Majesty," I said with a deep bow. I had to tug Chloe to remind them to bow. I won't lie, it was a funny sight with how the strap-on pointed at Fenk. I gave Chloe a wink before we rose. "I asked Chloe to accompany me for some wine, and I'm afraid I may have gotten a little too demanding of their services," I lied and acted frazzled. "Mood swings of new magic, you know?"

"Princess Daphne, not only are you bonded in ceremony to the prince, but you're also expected to have some damned couth! This is unacceptable behavior! *She* is not at your disposal for such things!"

"Forgive me. I'm finding the social norms here confusing. The way people keep bringing up how my parents had a public orgy to bond me against my will, I didn't think having a fling would be a problem," I said, trying to make a point. "I apologize, Chloe. I realize the power dynamic here wasn't in your favor. You must have felt very pressured into all this. It won't happen again." I was a shit liar, but I was pretty sure that did the trick.

Chloe bowed, tucked their artificial junk into their pants, and forced the zipper and button almost completely closed. "Thank you, Princess. It is an honor to... serve you," Chloe said before excusing themselves.

Fenk's eyes caught sight of the book at his feet, and he picked it up off the floor. I walked over to retrieve it, but he didn't let go. He tugged the book, pulling me forward with it. "Odd pairing, don't you think—midnight studies and creeping with a *transvestite*." His eyes were narrow as he spat the hateful words. It was becoming clear why Cynti was so afraid.

"I respectfully disagree. Books and sex are a very popular pairing where I'm from, Vice Majesty. Books *with* sex, actually…that's my jam." I smiled, unworried. I was trying to make him uncomfortable enough to leave.

"But now you are *here*. And while you are here, you will not disgrace our palace or disrespect your prince." He let go of the book and turned for the door. I sat the book on the bar and grabbed a glass from the rack to pour some wine. Before leaving, he stopped to look at the broken vase. "That was priceless, just so you know. The queen will be displeased to hear of its demise."

I didn't look at him as I sipped from my glass, let alone offer a bow. He left anyway. We both waited until Fenk's footsteps were gone for a long moment before letting out a breath. Cynti emerged from her hiding spot with a nervous face. I pulled another glass from the rack and poured her a drink. It took a moment for her eyes to lift from the glass, but when her rose quartz met my face, she spoke in a shaky voice.

"Thank you." We toasted silently before taking a sip.

"What do I do about the vase?" I asked.

She let out an exhausted laugh and waved me off. "I'll bridge it. Heh! Pol and I broke that vase at least three times when we were kids. It's a stupid place for a vase, right next to a door," she said, shaking her head and taking another sip.

She was hugging herself until she sat down her glass and walked to the shattered vase. Cynti contorted her hands into an unknown mudra, ring fingers pointed outward, and the pieces started to move back into place. Her fingers shifted so her pinky finger now pointed out, and the water evaporated. I picked up the lilies by hand and put them back into the vase.

"Fenk is shrewd. It's not wise to provoke him. He'll be watching your every move after this," she said with concern. She took a deep breath.

"I won't be here long. It's fine."

"You truly *detest* my brother?"

"No. Not in the least. I…"

"The bond doesn't just compel you to that person. It is from the moment of conception that everything about his body and soul is made to be right for you, and you him. I get your persistence with free will. I do. But if you gave him a chance, I know you would see. You fit together perfectly, Daphne. The bond is not taking your choice; it's giving you a shortcut."

"That's good to know, but…I don't know if I can leave my life behind. I don't want to lead him on. But the bond is pulling me, and it's… It is really hard."

"Sometimes you just have to take a leap of faith."

I smiled at Cynti, and she looked stunned for a moment.

"Your eyes. They were changing for a moment, I think. You'll have a stone soon."

We snuck off separately, and I crawled into bed. Exhausted, I fell asleep.

I woke early and meditated with the fearless love mudra again. I got dressed in the activewear dropped off by Tali and ran off to get breakfast so I could study with Uripe. To my surprise my magic book was replaced with *Loanan, The Basics of Politics*.

"I was told you are having trouble navigating social norms," Uripe spoke through his voice box. My skin felt hot. I respected Uripe and felt embarrassed that Fenk may have told him what happened last night. He wasn't acting strange, though, so I dove into the boring political book.

I didn't have many questions to write today. Their government was structured in a pretty standard way, with new names for positions I was already familiar with. Granted, there would be much more to go through, and I was certain to learn something new.

I stifled a yawn as I checked my watch, and then slammed the book shut. Uripe handed me my homework of questions and additional reading, and I gave him a handshake. He loved handshakes.

"Make sure you sign out books next time," he said, tapping a fountain pen on a paper log. I blushed again and nodded. So much for *that* surprise.

I was certain training with Chloe would be awkward, but they acted as though nothing happened through the first couple of hours. Mynt was now wielding frospits, and Promise was wielding ember-cudgels. They modeled their expert wielding for the class, and I couldn't help but roll my eyes. *I get it, you're awesome*, I thought to myself as they both smiled widely with shimmering fangs and bubblegum gums. I should have been happy for them. Deep down I was, but I felt angry most of the time, like the worst PMS to ever exist. And on top of that, my magic was being very stubborn. It sucked to… well…suck.

Mynt stood beside me when the demonstration was done and nudged my hip with her elbow. I looked down to find her smiling, her sharp teeth even more perfect than her power. She wore a golden lip liner only on the top and darkened the rest of her lips matte black. Her tear ducts were dusted with the same gold. *How are pixies always so well-groomed and put together?* I grumbled to myself, sweat making my frizzy hair stick to my skin.

"No one expects you to keep up yet. You're going to do great when your power comes," she said in a sweet, congested, helium-like voice. She was nice, damn it. I felt like a rat for being so jealous.

"Thank you," I offered. She giggled, nudging me again. Then Promise passed Mynt and her smile turned to a lip curling scowl. I laughed out loud. Mynt gave me a sarcastic side eye. *Maybe I'll make a friend after all.*

"Why do you two hate each other so much?"

"He's so smug."

"He's not too bad."

Mynt rolled her eyes. "I can stay after with you and Chloe if you want help."

When the other recruits were done and had left, Chloe started our one-on-one session, and Mynt sat on the sidelines, eating a snack. Chloe started to correct my mudra for cloud forming. They paused from shifting my fingers, let out a heavy breath, and held onto my hands for a moment.

"Thank you for what you did. That was pretty ballsy, and you didn't have—"

"It's fine. It's nothing," I cut them off. I let out a smile and huffed. Chloe returned the smile, bit their lip, and squeezed my fingers.

Then I felt it: jealousy, lust, aggressive sexual tension, and a strong pull. I drew a breath and knew Pol was near. I felt a sharper scrape against my back and saw white flashes in my vision. I pulled my hands from Chloe's grasp and brought my hands to Abhaya Hridaya Mudra behind my back, the same fearless love mudra that gave me peace. But when I looked at him, I couldn't center myself quickly enough. My heart raced, and I grimaced at the surge of power in my chest.

Chloe grabbed my arms and turned me from him. "Focus."

And I almost did. That is until Queen Madgee charged from the doorway over to me. A sting flushed my cheek, but it wasn't until seconds later that her hand even made contact. Then my cheek stung all over again, but worse. It was the most abrupt and confusing déjà vu I had ever had.

Pol was between us in an instant, palming his mother's shoulder to keep her from gaining more ground. Mynt stood but kept a respectful distance.

"You ungrateful, disgusting little whore!" Queen Madgee scowled over Pol's shoulder. "Let me make something perfectly clear. You are in *my* kingdom! In *my* home! We have given you *every* hospitality. Had you kept us waiting a day longer, I would have forced Pol's hand to drag you here, but he fought for you to come on your own. We gave you *that much*. You will respect my kingdom! You will respect my son. And if you give me one more reason to think you cannot conduct yourself with honorable decorum, you will be assigned a guard, and your liberties will *truly* be forfeit."

"Queen Madgee, this was all a misunderstanding." Chloe tried to intervene, but they were silenced by the wide-eyed rage of the monarch.

"Oh?" Her voice quivered, and she pointed at Chloe. "So, you didn't have our royal guest here, on her knees, choking down your sex toys in my dining room?" Thankfully, her voice was cautiously low. Chloe swallowed hard. They had nothing they could add. Queen Madgee turned back to me, her shoulder newly free of Pol's hand, which was now limp at his side. I could feel the pit growing in his stomach, the sour sting of nausea on the sides of his tongue, and the ache in his chest. But he just stared ahead at nothing, his back still turned away from me.

"You may have behaved like this in that realm of *dirt*, but you are held to a higher standard here. Whether you like it or not, you are prophesied to be our best chance at ending a war that is at our doorstep this very minute. No soldier will get behind someone who can't even show loyalty to the crown or respect the incredible gifts left at your feet. Get it together, princess. I will not allow your recklessness to endanger my people." She yielded space between us and stood taller. "And clean up that language of yours."

I stood with my chin raised, expressionless, as I took in her tongue lashing. I felt completely infantilized. Even if I hadn't done the thing she suspected, I had shunned Pol and an entire people relying on me. The promise to return home to my stressful yet simple life was a crutch.

Cynti's words the night before had stuck with me. I would never know if what I felt for Pol was purely magic or my soul responding to a truly perfect match. I wouldn't know if I didn't take a leap of faith. I needed to tell him what he did to me and how scared it made me.

"And, Chloe, if I hear so much as a whisper that you've had relations with a member of my court again, you will be gifted like a pig's dowry to the rankest kingdom there is. I trust you don't need to be told whose orders you obey from here on out?" Queen Madgee hissed out every word. It was at this moment that I understood where Pol's overly annunciated tone came from. "I'll take my leave now. *Bow*."

We all bowed, and no sooner did she charge off. Pol gave me an empty look, and then gave the same to Chloe.

"Pol..." Chloe tried reaching for him, but he turned and formed a nimbus and jumped on. I tried to get to him before he moved but failed. Tears fell from my face, unable to bear the feelings he carried. "We'll set this right, Daphne," Chloe promised.

But I couldn't wait for that. I focused everything I had on forming. An ugly nimbus was the product—gray and wet and rolling in front of me. It was unsteady and eerie.

"You're going too fast, and your mind isn't clear. You need to pull back," Chloe warned. I didn't listen. I tried to mount the deformed nimbus, determined to get to Pol. "Daphne, stop, that's not safe!" they yelled and grabbed my arm to pull me away. The nimbus flickered with lightning. Just as I was pulled from it, a loud crack of thunder vibrated through our chests. "Shit, Daphne! That was too close. You need to calm down. You're going to hurt yourself," Chloe scorned. Their voice then turned apologetic. "We'll set this right. Go to your room and meditate." They nodded at Mynt to escort me. Mynt stayed with me for a little until she knew I was calm and wouldn't do anything stupid. She didn't say much until she left.

"Good job on your first cloud, Daph," she said before leaving. The guards Fiore and Fern looked in on me before the door closed.

I meditated for hours, excusing Falece from her duties. She left some bath salts for me before fluttering her wings to the door and stepping out with a curtsey. First, I meditated in the moonstone tub and was able to relax enough to move the water. The bath salts eased my muscles, and it was then I noticed Falece had added CBD oils to the water. Of course I was relaxing.

Then, I meditated in my room, sitting on the floor by the phantom wall. I didn't even wait until I was dressed, just loosely wrapped in my bathrobe and sitting on the floor. I was able to tussle the night's wind through my hair to start drying it. It had just stormed in the Regnum Solo, and the night was clear but humid. The ocean below was still choppy and rolling. I was now moving the smoke from the fireplace to mix with the salty sea breeze that I drew up from many miles below. It smelt just like a bonfire on the beach at midnight. I could do these things as I envisioned Pol and moved my hands fluidly through the few mudras I knew.

I felt terrible wondering where he was or what he must think. I hadn't talked to him all week. It was just easier that way. But I was ready to try.

Anyway, I was still in nothing but my bathrobe, meditating and moving in front of the phantom wall. The room was dim, lit only by a dying fire and the large moon. Then, a hard knock pounded on my door. I opened my eyes, startled. My hair fell from the air as my hands abandoned their mudras. *The pull.*

When I opened my door, the frame was filled with Pol's towering presence. The guards were gone. He stalked in, inches from my chest. I could feel him, his anger, confusion, urgency, and a buried lust. My face burned fiercely as he kept stalking toward me. He backed me closer toward the phantom wall.

My mind came alive with flashing images of him pinning me down and thrusting himself inside me. The image was more vivid this time. I could feel the scraping against my entire back. My wrists and ankles felt bound.

The images were gone as soon as they came. I refocused on his approach. I was at the edge of the phantom wall.

"What are you doing?" I asked, with hot cheeks and a growing warmth between my legs.

"Helping you get home. I promised I'd make sure you were able to come and go as you please, and you obviously don't want to be here."

Before I could speak again, he shoved hard at my chest. I fell through the phantom wall and then through the barrier between worlds. I was rushing toward the ocean over ten miles below. The air ripped past my skin as I fell through the sky. For only a moment I panicked. My shrill cry of terror disappeared into the darkness.

I became deeply aware of my surroundings. I could feel the air and the water vapor in it better than I ever could before. I could taste the salt whisked up from the ocean. The air was markedly different from Loanan's, yet still crisp, and it washed over me as I fell. The ocean and stars and city lights could all be seen in their full beauty. Rushing to my death was the most beautiful bliss I had ever experienced. Calm washed over me. I had seen many deaths, none as peaceful as this.

This is a beautiful way to die. But I should try...

I moved my hands into the proper mudra. I could only form puffs of a cloud. I fell through it before it could fully form. I tried again and again. I couldn't form anything substantial enough to land on.

Finally, I landed on a perfect nimbus cloud. I drew in a deep breath and turned over on my back. I found the sky shimmering and black. There was no sign of Loanan to be seen. But in the darkness I could see something—something falling. It rushed toward me. When it landed on the nimbus, a puff of murky mist billowed up from it. Behind the mist, Pol stood over me. He dropped to his knees between my legs, and his fists dug into the nimbus on either side of my ribs. I noticed the misty aura around his skin had returned.

There was no hiding the strength of the pull between us. It had grown immensely since the last time we were this close. I flared my nostrils. I accidentally sent the surface of the cloud into steam. My heart beat against my ribcage at the sight of him practically mounting me. I felt the night breeze between my thighs and was reminded of the nakedness under the bathrobe. It would be so easy for him to take me. Where would I go?

"What the fuck, Pol!"

"Fear seems to be your best motivator. You won't get anywhere with Chloe's coddling. Let's try again." The nimbus dissipated. We plummeted again. I squealed, moved my hands, and again failed to make anything more than a fog puff to fall through.

I landed on another nimbus of his making. This time I landed on my back. He landed over me, his mouth close to mine, his opal eyes simmering with anger. My legs were open and uncovered, him between them. My skin prickled with heat, and the cloud steamed again.

"I don't understand you," he said with a rare sign of frustration twitching at his lip. "You're more terrified of me than you are of dying?"

"What the fuck are you talking about?" I said, trying to catch my breath.

He let out an exhausted huff. "Every day I watch you fail to make anything more than fog in your hand, until you see *me*. I see it on your face—the fear and hate. And then you're dripping in stormwater and boiling it into steam," he said. "But here you are, falling to your death in post-storm humidity, and you can't even form something to hold on to!" he yelled. "What exactly was it that I did to make you detest me so much?"

His closeness and prowling had me burning inside.

"I don't hate you. And I'm not afraid of you, Pol." I shoved at his shoulder hard in anger. He grabbed the offending wrist and pressed it down, squeezing it tight. It was taking everything in him not to force himself inside me.

There was a pregnant pause between us. Finally, I gave in. The pull was too strong. His body was too close. The guilt, too heavy. I crashed my lips to his.

Steam rolled up from the nimbus, rumbling a low thunder. It soaked our hair and skin. He kissed me hard, his tongue pressing into my mouth. The weight of his kiss pushed my head into the nimbus. I raked my fingers into his arms, pulling him in and latching on for fear of falling again.

Then, he pressed a hand at the base of my neck. He pushed himself away from the kiss. My heart ached. I wondered if I was too late to fix this. The vapor around us became as thick and hot as a steam room.

"What are you doing? Is this some kind of game to you? What do you want?" His deep rasp echoed in his chest.

"I don't know! I don't know if I want any of this. All I know is that I want you more than I can stand. I'm afraid it's not real. That…the feeling that's pulling me to you at every corner will slip away…and I'll realize it was all just some political game. Some *spell*."

He shook his head, refusing to believe me. "You and Chloe w—"

"You have to trust me; it's not what it sounds like. Please." I reached to cup his chin and pulled him back into a kiss. "I'm so sorry. This has all been a lot, and I just needed time. I *still* need time. But I… I can't stand pushing you away anymore." I kissed him again, swiping my tongue along his lip. Nothing had ever felt so right. I needed him. I deepened the kiss.

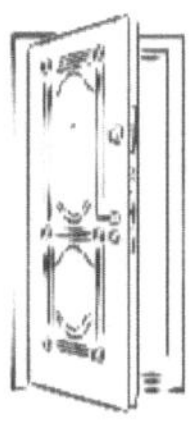

He let the kiss last, a slow and deep sliding of his warm tongue against mine. His mist seemed to flare and then pulse. Then he settled his hips between my legs. His hard cock jabbed into my leg. Steam enveloped us again, and he had to replenish the nimbus under us as we rolled our bodies against each other. His lips stayed against mine when he spoke next.

"You have to stop the steam." He cupped my breast. "Concentrate," he added while continuing to distract me. An eagerness grew between my legs, and I moaned, thrusting my hips to grind on him. I needed more. But he waited so long for this, for *me*. Fresh after a fight *wasn't* the right time.

My arms still around his neck, I moved my hands to the mudra of fearless love. I sent my light into him—the real him. He half-broke the kiss for only a moment to growl. His kiss returned with more passion. He pushed his hips between my legs hard. I melted.

The air around us cooled. Condensation beaded on our skin, dripping down. I shifted my fingers again, trying to reinforce our nimbus. Instead of a storm cloud, it changed into a bed of white-silver crystalline clouds like snow mounds. The cumulus shimmered with every bit of moonlight that touched it.

Pol's hands traveled from my breast to my hip, causing my robe to fall open as the tie fell loose. He pushed his fingers between my lips. They sunk deep into my hot, wet center.

"Oh fuck," he groaned. I grabbed at his wrist, trying to pull it away. I tried to speak. He wouldn't let me do either. He only pushed them deeper.

"Wait," I pressed with his tongue still massaging my mouth. But he didn't. He pushed his fingers into me again, calling my bluff.

"I'm done with your games. Open your legs." The massaging of his strong fingers inside me made me melt. I moaned. My legs fell open. "Sss. Good girl." I sucked in what air I could. I felt a warm puddle forming under my back. The cloud was a nimbus again. Now dark gray, it leaked rain and shrunk.

"Focus," he demanded, pushing deeper inside of me. He massaged my clit with his thumb. A weak moan slipped from my mouth. He wasn't replenishing the cloud. I knew that if I didn't, we would eventually fall again. But what was worse? I was moments away from ripping open his pants and begging for him to fuck me. There was still too much unsaid.

I tried to reinforce the nimbus. All I could do was think of his giant dick rubbing against my leg. He groaned deeply in my ear with the sound of pleasure. He was growing wet in his pants, but his cock was still hard, and he picked up the intensity of his passion.

As he took my nipple in his mouth, I looked down. I saw the cloud I formed escaping through the fabric of his pants. He pulled his hand out of me. The emptiness left me eager. I let out a breathy cry in protest.

The sound of his buckle coming undone made me ravenous. The sound of his zipper made my nipples harden under his tongue. I bucked my hips, closed my eyes, and turned my face. I knew if I saw it, I'd lose all control. *Not yet.* This nimbus wouldn't hold us for long.

Before I could think, he plunged his fingers back into me. He lowered his mouth to my pussy, licking between my lips. His hot tongue moved over my clit, and I whined as I surrendered to him.

I gave into my power. I formed warm water around his cock. I glided the wave up and down his length. He groaned and sank his mouth deeper into the cushioned lips of my pussy.

He thrust his fingers into me again and again. The nimbus under us thundered with my moan. Phantom lightning flickered, lighting our nakedness in strobing flashes. It had shrunk to half its size and poured water to the earth. I couldn't care at that moment. He was licking me so well. I had to bite my lip hard to stop myself from begging him to fuck me. I brought my hand to a new mudra. With that, I moved the water into a twisting cyclone around his throbbing cock.

"Ah, fuck!" he growled, muffled by my heavy lips. I moved the warm water spout up and down his cock, stroking him. He dug his grip into my hip and forced another finger inside of me with the other hand. He was grunting and grinding. His hips thrust to fuck the funnel hard as he sucked my clit into his mouth.

Finally, his jaw went slack. He let out a long, loud growl into my pussy. His face stayed buried deep between my lips while he worked through the waves of his orgasm. He breathed out muffled sounds of intense relief. Each thrust of his fingers was in sync with his panting and grinding.

Still breathless, he looked at me as though he was hellbent on making me scream. The lapping of his tongue against my sensitive clit made my head fall to the side, and that's when I noticed our nimbus was nearly gone. My heart skipped.

"Pol, the nimbus," I urged him through a subconscious moan. I was unable to manage much else. Between everything that happened, my magic was nearly spent. I was on the verge of cumming. "Pol!" I yelled, grabbing at his hair. He licked and sucked my pussy. Then he formed ice over my nipples. The nimbus shrunk under my shoulders as my body rocked from the hard thrusts of his fingers. I was helplessly caving and nearing climax. I arched my back into the last few moments before finishing on his face. I didn't care if I fell to my death with his tongue in my pussy.

The moan of my release came out breathy and harsh. The rush of tickling warmth was so intense it was the only thing I was aware of. The moment it ripped through me, the nimbus gave out.

The adrenaline of falling filled my heart as I came, hands still tangled in his hair. Pol wrapped his free arm around my waist to hold me to his mouth. I wrapped my legs around his head. He kept his face buried between my lips, determined to make me ride out the orgasm while we free-fell toward the earth.

Between moans, I called for him into the shallowing sky. Ecstasy consumed me. The updraft turned us and flipped us. I was riding his face in the wind, icy nipples hard against the challenging gusts, when the last of my release poured into his mouth.

As I released his hair and relaxed into the fall, our bodies finally came apart. The glittering earth below me

rose fast. I welcomed death in this blissful afterglow. But the view became foggy as gray clouds formed to catch us.

The moment we landed in a puff of nimbus, I noticed the neon glow coming from beneath it. I realized we had drifted over Miami's city proper at some point. I wondered to myself if his cum rained down from the cloud, and I laughed out loud at the hope that his jizz landed on Lyndie Pratt's stupid, bitchy face. Pol looked down at me, chest heaving, and tucked his satisfied length into his pants.

"That was creative. I went my entire life without using a water-spout to jerk off," Pol said, falling in a puff at my side. I let out a hearty laugh. He pulled me to him and nipped at my neck for a moment. "When did you start covering advanced psychic magic?"

"What do you mean?" I asked.

"Moving the water like that. Moving is psychic magic. I haven't seen you guys practice it yet."

"We haven't. I just connected with the water and willed it to do its thing. Tried a new mudra." I shrugged. He stared blankly, but I could feel his shock. I remembered that new magic can be dangerously unpredictable. I was sure that fucking like human lovebugs counted as supervised practice, but Pol didn't seem to share that sentiment.

"I'm impressed, but next time you try a new magic for the first time, maybe don't use it to put my dick in a miniature tornado."

"Waterspout, and you didn't seem to mind," I responded with a laugh. I turned to him and kissed him softly. We stayed like that for a moment, kissing each other. I reinforced the nimbus and turned it into a firm cumulus of ice crystals, the different color neon lights from below shimmering through. His aura mist sparkled in the moonlight and glowed colorfully too. I waved my hands through it and watched it kick up into the air and return to him.

"What is this?" I asked.

"It's an emanation. We call it an aura. It helps acclimate us to the Regnum Solo. At this rate, you'll probably be making them without even thinking about it."

I had read about eminations but didn't realize what they were. It wasn't until then that I noticed how hot and abrasive the air was this close to the ground. It scratched against my skin like hot, wet sandpaper, and I felt the pins and needles of heat rash stinging my face and back. I grimaced, feeling the pollen, pollution, dirt, and whatever else embedded into my skin. The only comfort I could find was nuzzling into his aura or burrowing into the cold, plush cumulus. I played with his emanation for another moment, but a wave of exhaustion weighed on me, and I needed the soft, cool air of Loanan.

"We should get back," I suggested.

We couldn't be separated that night. I lay in his bed exhausted and watched as he plucked the strings of his lyre in front of the fire. He hummed a tune in his deep, haunting voice that echoed in an unearthly way. His scent surrounded me, and the tune tugged me to sleep like a lullaby. I felt safer than I had for as long as I could remember. When the last of consciousness had nearly slipped away, I felt him come to bed and wrap his long arm around me, holding me to him posessively.

22

O'DOHERTY: WHAT YOU'RE AFRAID OF

"And then he said he loved me, and I froze and didn't know what to do! I've just felt distant from him ever since, like cut off in a way. I don't know why. He is the most amazing person I have ever met. The thought of being without him makes me sick to my stomach. Ugh. This should not bother me," I ranted to Dr. Bailey.

"What is the worst thing that would happen if you were in love with him too?" he challenged.

"I guess it would just feel real. There is no going back. This would be it."

"And what would you be missing if that was *it*?"

"Someone that has been putting me on the back burner for years, I suppose…"

"Oh? I don't recall anyone like that. Tell me more."

"It is nothing really. Nothing that I should be holding out on Fabian for. He is in my life right now. Even Polpetta can see that."

"O'doherty, I'm concerned that you seem more excitable over this topic than the man following you. Why haven't you gone to the police?"

"Nothing is coming of it. Not really."

"Hmm. So, Fabian's healer friend didn't think anything of the rocks?"

"Oh no, she had plenty to say about the rocks!" I corrected theatrically.

"Oh? What did she say?"

I laughed. Dr. Bailey was usually one to steer me away from such nonsense and focus on the bigger issues. But it was humorous, so why not?

"Ohhh. That they are rocks from the sky, formed by other beings, out of the eyes of a rebellion army!" I said as if telling a scary tale. He looked uncomfortable at my enthusiasm, and I humbled my excitement. "It is silly. Fabian seems to think it is something, though. He said he could see the fear in her eyes. She is convinced that we are all in danger. He brought home a bunch of stones for protection yesterday and has been smudging the house daily."

"Do you feel like you're in danger?"

"No."

"And when was the last time you saw the man following you?"

"I haven't, but...I feel like I am being watched sometimes," I admit. "And the paper the notes were written on, the notes from a few weeks ago..." He waited for me to finish, and I realized there was no backing out now. "I found an old diary in my other nightstand. Some blank pages were torn from it. The tear patterns and purple ruling match the notes."

Dr. Bailey's brows lifted, and his eyes went wide. "That's extremely concerning. Does Fabian know about this?"

"No. He would freak out. He has already got me carrying his gun."

"It's my advice that you should file a report with the police immediately," he said sternly. There was no way I was going to turn *that* diary into the police as evidence.

"The notes were a while ago now, and there is no sign that he has been back. Besides, now we have Polpetta as our little guard dog."

"Polpetta? She's staying with you?"

"For about a week now. Daphne has been on a work trip. Fabian dotes over Polly, you know. He is always walking her, snuggling her, and feeding her gourmet food. She is getting quite fat and spoiled. I don't think Daphne will be able to keep her happy once she comes back."

"Have you heard from Daphne since she left? She hasn't picked up her refill, and when I spoke to the pharmacist, she was concerned about her last pick up. Said she seemed a little off. I've tried phoning her, and it goes to voicemail," he asked. I was taken back by this. He was walking a fine line with patient confidentiality. I offered a harmless response.

"She has not responded to my texts or calls either. Maybe she finally found the bottle she was missing and didn't need it this month? And last time she did these classes, she was swamped. Honestly, they are really intense courses. I am not surprised."

"Hmm." He seemed put off by my response. Something told me he was worried. Suddenly, I felt validated that things with her and Pol were *not* just in my head.

"You know, she was caught in a storm last month. She had a head injury and didn't get care and…I looked at her search history one day when she didn't come home. There were things about 'riding nimbuses.' And she met a man who saved her. He gave her jewelry. Then she got mugged after that, and he was there again. Another piece of jewelry. His name is 'Pol,' and I *never* get to meet him." Dr. Bailey shifted in his seat and cleared his throat.

"What do you make of that?"

"I don't know, it is just strange. Every time she sees him she's all beat up and then given something nice. She goes on this trip out of nowhere and doesn't answer. And she's just been *withdrawn* lately."

"Withdrawn from your relationship or withdrawn in general?"

I clammed up. I was in no way trying to give Dr. Bailey a reason to learn about our *relationship*. Had Daphne told him…

"In general. You know, I'll be stopping at the hospital after this. I can see if the nurses have heard from her. You know how she is with work. It would be very concerning if she were not following up with them every other day at minimum."

Dr. Bailey's small mouth was swallowed by hearty cheeks when he smiled. Our time was up. He gave me my prescription, made me promise to call the police, and asked me to think about what we talked about—what it is I'm afraid of. But I knew the answer.

THE NURSES SEEMED TENSE TODAY. RELUCTANTLY, I APPROACHED THE nursing station to greet one of them and see if I could locate my patient's nurse. Dean, one of the medical surgical nurses who Daphne was working with, lifted his head and offered a smile.

"Hey. What's going on around here? Every floor I go to, the nurses look angry."

"Captive audience meetings. Seems management is wise to our unionizing plan. They're starting in two weeks. Mandatory. Bringing in some professionals they probably pay thousands of dollars to lie about how bad unions are," he complained.

"I am sure Daphne has a plan for that. She has dealt with it a million times. By the way, have any of you guys heard from her?" I asked casually.

"Jesula says she and her boyfriend aren't back from their trip yet. She should be back next week if they get everything taken care of. She left Jesula with all the resources, though. We should be fine," he said while typing up a nurse's note.

"Trip with…her boyfriend?" I asked.

"Yeah…" he paused and looked at me over his rectangular framed glasses. "Jesula knows details. By the way, if you are here to see Mr. Ginger, he passed away. He went on hospice and didn't make it too long after that." My skin crawled. I didn't have many patients left who were still alive, and Daphne was lying to…*someone.*

"Any significant changes in Mr. Ginger before passing?"

"Just bad reactions to Ambien. He was having bad dreams about a guy with white hair making tornadoes." He laughed. "He went peacefully though, thank God. Do you want me to pull up his chart for you?"

"No, I think I'll stop by the ICU and look at it there. It's quieter there, and I want to say hi to Jesula anyway. But thanks."

I took a computer at the empty ICU nurses' station to start researching Mr. Ginger while I waited for Jesula. For as quiet as ICU typically was, the nurses were always busy, either in the patient's room fighting the grim reaper or right outside of the room charting on a pod computer. However, Jesula was a seasoned nurse and preferred to sit by the monitors when she charted, so that's where I made camp.

Sure enough, Mr. Ginger's chart was suspicious. The dreams were well documented in the chart as recurring and of a young man with medium brown skin and white hair making tornadoes. Mr. Ginger was apparently convinced the man had been in the hospital and was afraid another storm was going to come with him soon.

"Well, hey there, Ms. O'doherty," Jesula greeted me in a tired voice.

"Hi! Jesula, I heard about the captive audience meetings. Is everything okay?"

"Ugh!" she exasperatedly waved. "It's rough. They haven't even started yet, and people are getting skittish. Some of the original crew are planning a get-together so we can go over what to expect. It's messy."

"Hard to believe Daphne isn't all over that. Have you heard from her yet?"

"No. Not yet. But you know she prepared us for all this."

"I wonder what's taking them so long," I fished.

"She wouldn't have gone with him if she didn't trust him. Whatever it was that he needed to show her, it sounded important. Just give them time." I stared, blinking twice.

"Yeah, I just wish she would answer her texts, is all. How hard is it to use her phone?"

Jesula laughed and looked at me sideways. "I don't think they have phones where they went, child." Then Jesula paused for a long moment and studied me. "Daphne didn't tell you where she was going, did she?"

Shit. My mouth stayed slack a moment longer. "She did…" I half lied. "She left out a few details, is all. I'm worried."

"Listen to me. I don't need to be dragged between you two, Okay."

"I know, I'm just—"

"*Do* you know? Because you are sneaking around trying to *trick* me. I don't appreciate the position you've put me in. She's your best friend. If you suspect she kept something from you, you take it up with her."

I sat back in my chair and stared at my screen. "I think Pol is dangerous. If you know how to get ahold of her—"

"I *don't*. And if Pol wanted to hurt her, he would have done it months ago. He's done nothing but cater to her stubborn self every day. I think he likes her even."

The pit in my gut only grew. She had clearly confided in Jesula more than me, and I did not understand why. Sure, Jesula was down to earth and seemed to know things, but we were best friends. I couldn't go further with my prying. Jesula made her boundaries clear.

"Good luck with the captive audience meetings. I hope you guys can keep your support," I said, getting up and pushing my chair in.

"Give her the benefit of the doubt. She's probably just trying to protect you."

JESULAS WORDS STUCK TO THE FRONT OF MY BRAIN LIKE A POST-IT note the whole drive home. I shut my door and walked to the mailbox, dragging my exhausted feet.

Protection from what?

I pulled out a small box from the mailbox and quickly determined it had been more than tampered with. The small box was torn open. The cardboard was creased and bent from being forcefully shoved into the mailbox. I could still make out the return address from the lab where the mineralogist worked. It was undoubtedly my rock sample and the reports. Unfortunately, it was empty inside, save a slip of paper. Chills ran down my arms as I slipped the paper from the box and recognized it as a piece torn from the same diary as before. Unfolding it, I snarled at the perfectly scrolled letters.

Don't make me tell you again. I won't be nice about it.

I shoved the note in the empty box. I ran to the car and grabbed Fabian's gun from the center console. With shaking hands, I held the gun in front of me in the house. I cleared each room as if I were in some police movie. I found no one and nothing inside. I sat on the side of my bed and rested the gun on the nightstand. The room smelled of the same fruity musk. He had been in here again and recently.

My fingers still shook as I opened the drawer to find my diary. The tear pattern on the note matched that on the newly missing page. And then I noticed the ribbon bookmark was moved from the last time I looked at it. I opened it to the marked page. It was an entry from years before, detailing yet another unsatisfying sexual encounter and how I had to pleasure myself quietly once he fell asleep. It described in detail what I thought about and how hard it was to get off with him snoring next to me. *Oh god...* He read how I fantasized about being watched. My face flushed. I threw it back in the drawer and slammed it shut.

I took a hot shower and cried under the cover of the water, the tears blending in perfectly with the stream of water. I wanted answers, but he was playing the game well. There's no way I would turn in a diary full of my sexual history and weird fantasies as evidence, and he knew it. But if he was still doing all this, I must not have been at a dead end after all. There was something I was missing.

I got out of the shower refreshed and with a new sense of fury. I pulled out the diary and a pen and left a message for the creep.

I'm going to find out what you are afraid of.

I marked the brazen new entry with the ribbon, threw it in the drawer, and slammed it shut.

I turned for my dresser to get dressed. It was clear that I was leaning on Fabian to do the laundry a little too much.

Shit. Where are all my panties disappearing to?

I checked my hamper to see if they were all buried in an unwashed pile that I could wash quickly. My skin crawled when I realized the t-shirt I had thrown in there just before work was gone, the same clothes under it left untouched. Not a single pair of panties were left in my house.

Fabian opened the front door. He called for me and I came from the room, attempting to act normal.

"Hey, I got a hit on the labyrinth photo!"

I perked up. "And?" I urged him.

"Well, first," he paused, taking a few Almond Joys out of a grocery bag, "I got you some chocolate for shark week."

I took the chocolate and smiled at him. Then I wondered how I would wear pads without underwear. "Thank you. But what did you *find*?"

"The same thing happened at other nursing homes across the east coast. The ones that got hit by tornadoes, remember? They had a labyrinth too."

"Does anyone there know what it means?"

"No," he said, and then hesitated with a smile. I raised my brows impatiently. Shark week was wreaking havoc on my patience. "But I *did* finally find something similar on the dark web. It says the labyrinth is called a Prexa. There are stories of ancient *beings* using them to break spells. Like *wizards* or something!"

My excitement dwindled, and I chewed the candy slower. I tried to feign excitement for him. He was clearly impressed with his magical knowledge.

"Oh, come on, Dotey!" he begged enthusiastically. "Listen, according to my sources, it's part of a bond-breaking ritual. It has the power to un-shield us from mother nature itself, but humans have to do it. Humans have to do the ritual. What about the storms lately? I mean, how many coincidences do you need?"

I nodded slowly and bared my teeth in a fake smile. He looked at me, waiting. "I do not know what to do with that, Fabian. I'm sorry. It sounds like a lot of superstitious stuff, and I really need facts." I shrugged apologetically.

"Okay. Well, my *superstitious stuff* has turned up more answers than your *science stuff*. Fabian: Two, Dotey: *Zero!*" he said, laughing before scooping Polpetta in his arms and walking her to the back door. "Come on, Polly. We'll keep an eye out for the rock wizards ourselves."

I laughed at the show he put on, but I was truly disappointed that all we could find was nonsense. *Something* I was doing was irritating powerful people. What was it?

23

DAPHNE: CATCH A SHOOTING STAR?

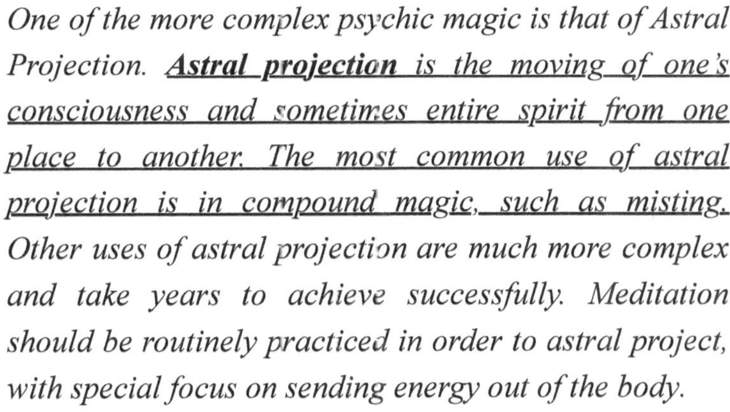

> *One of the more complex psychic magic is that of Astral Projection. **Astral projection is the moving of one's consciousness and sometimes entire spirit from one place to another. The most common use of astral projection is in compound magic, such as misting.** Other uses of astral projection are much more complex and take years to achieve successfully. Meditation should be routinely practiced in order to astral project, with special focus on sending energy out of the body.*
>
> *When spiritually astral projecting, it is essential to channel the spiritual dimensions and our own, separate soul from body, and guide it through energy currents to its destination. Nausea and vomiting are extremely common for beginners, and it is recommended to carry a healing sapphire or lapis lazuli when training begins. Of note, some uses of astral projection are outlawed*

within most kingdoms of the Regnum Caelorum. Astral projection will be covered more in Chapter 42.

"THAT LOOKS LIKE A PERFECT CUMULUS, DAPHNE!" CHLOE CHEERED. "Let's see if it's mountable this time."

I climbed on the cloud, my feet sinking into it and then eventually falling through until I wore the cloud like a tutu. I walked out of it and huffed. I was so close. I could form a small cloud without any help from Pol. I could move it about five feet from me before it stalled out. I could even mold the clouds into nearly perfect shapes, once playfully forming a cumulus into a hand flipping off Mynt.

Mynt usually stayed behind to "hang out and stretch" now while I did my one-on-one sessions with Chloe. She got caught helping me once, and Chloe gave her a stern warning. She promised not to intervene again but never held back her cheers of support when I succeeded. Sometimes she even gave me tips for how to improve.

Lately she had been helping me speak a little more…royally. I wouldn't say she had a magical swear jar, but her soil curse was close. Every time I used profanity I'd taste dirt for an hour. If I ignored it and kept swearing, I'd eventually end up spitting out actual mud. Anyway, all of it helped. But I couldn't yet form a *mountable* cloud.

I batted away puffs of cloud from my hips.

"That's okay. Let's try again. Focus just below the surface and form a sheet."

"A sheet of *what?"*

Chloe let out a sigh. "Dense clouds. Just focus. Remember your readings on psychic magic. Imagine something that grounds you."

I grounded myself in brief meditation, somehow finding comfort in the routine of work back home. Then I focused that grounding on the cloud, much like sending the white light to Pol in meditation, and watched as it became more opaque near the surface.

"That's good," Chloe said cautiously. "Whatever you're feeling, you will eventually work up to associating it with your cloud. Take a moment to steady the grounding."

"I'm ready," I said before walking up to the cloud eagerly. Chloe crossed their arms and watched. Mynt let her diamond-like smile shimmer wide in the low sun, her bubblegum pink gums exposed. To Chloe's disapproval, she encouraged my hardheadedness.

I stepped onto the cloud, my feet only sinking a few inches before meeting the familiar sensation of stepping off an escalator. The grounding worked. I smiled wide at Chloe and laughed in a cheer. Mynt hollered in excitement, clapping only once. I could hear the buzzing of her wings as they flickered in excitement.

"Well done!" Chloe said.

I bonded to the cloud, a psychic technique I learned in the advanced psychic magic text that Pol asked Uripe to start me on last week. Bonding would help me connect with an object to move it with me, like an extension of myself. I already knew how to bond, according to Pol, but the book gave me a better understanding of what I was doing and how to move more efficiently and safely. I tried my luck, sending the cumulus to glide forward just a bit too swiftly.

"Bend your knees and lean into it!" Chloe hurried to say, clearly taken by surprise at my improvised moving. But it was too late. I fell backward, arms windmilling before my back slammed into the stone of the courtyard.

"Fuuuuck," I groaned. Chloe's form came into view above me, shadowed by the sun at their back and dark bluish-violet sky around them. Though their face was dim, I could see a tight, sarcastic smile as they shook their head and extended a hand. "You need to learn how to pace yourself." I came to my feet and brushed off invisible dirt out of habit. Mynt hadn't recovered from her child-like laughter at my expense. I poked my tongue out at her briefly. Suddenly the taste of soil coated my mouth. I cringed, and she laughed harder.

"Mynt, please keep your cackles to a minimum volume," Chloe called over.

"I'm close," I replied and brought the cumulus to me.

"Not close enough to ride to and from your realm safely. You need to pace yourself. You've only been at this for less than two weeks. Now, should you find yourself in an *emergency*, let's say forming a cloud mid-flight, remember to move it downward with your fall as you form it and then stop it *after* you land. Otherwise, the impact will hurt, or worse." Chloe often gave me these tidbits of information when the sessions were ending, but I wasn't ready to throw in the towel for the day.

"One more time," I said, barely mounting the cloud successfully. Chloe palmed their face tiredly. Mynt rested her chin on her knuckles, ready to watch me eat sky dirt. I crouched and leaned forward, bonded, and drove the cumulus cloud slower this time.

By all accounts, it should have gone well, but my back foot sank, and the forward motion of the cloud sent me tumbling backward again. This time I landed in Pol's arms. He caught me under the armpits and leaned forward to hover over my face. I looked up at his silhouette above me. It was a pleasant surprise to see him so early.

"You're tired. Your magic is spent for the day. If you do much more, you'll be feeling it for days," he said before lifting me to a full stand. He didn't quite let go, though, and spun me to face him, pulling me close. "It's time to eat, princess."

I felt it then. My body was heavy with exhaustion, and every step would feel like I was trudging through mud. A short kiss from Pol gave me the small spurt of energy I needed. He recoiled though.

"You've been swearing again," he said, spitting dirt flavored saliva on the ground. I waved to Chloe and Mynt. We headed for the palace door hand-in-hand. As I looked over my shoulder, I saw Mynt throw a blast of icy air at Chloe, who barely blocked it. With a high-pitch helium laugh from the warrior pixie, the two started an advanced sparring session behind me. If I didn't know any better, I'd think that Mynt, with her endless reserve of energy, never slept. Pol followed my eyes and admired Mynt's strength too.

"She's going to be lethal on the battlefield one day," he said, nudging my lower back and ushering me into the palace and then the dining area.

Similar to Astral Projection is ***emitting****, or the projection of energy, light, feelings or other internal variables other than consciousness and spirit. Emitting is practiced frequently in meditations and is one of the easiest psychic magics to master, yet another characteristic setting it apart from astral projecting. The most common use for emitting is to create groundings and barriers such as those that supplement protective enchantments. Emanations, or auras, are largely crafted by emitting as you push your energy field only inches from your body's surface and allow formed water vapor and pure oxygen to suspend in the energy field. Emitting is covered in depth in Chapter 43.*

"Will you be reading the entire meal?" I looked up to see Pol sulking over his dinner plate. "You've read that section four times."

I kept my smile hidden and cocked my head. Of course, I wouldn't ignore him another moment, but he didn't need to know he had me wrapped around his finger. A wind picked up the front cover and slapped the book shut. I bit my lip at his silent demands. He grabbed a forkful of salad and nodded at me to start eating. I really did need my energy, so I stabbed a piece of meat and ate.

"I have to go home soon, Pol. I just want to be able to come and go. It will already be two weeks tomorrow."

"You're always able to come and go, but you realize this kingdom needs you here? *Here.* Eventually, Daphne, you will need to let go."

I knew he was right, and it wasn't that I hated the idea. I loved it here, which made me even more passionate about doing my part in the war to come. Prince Nahveel was leading attacks on the Regnum Solo, pissing off the human government. The storms were spacing out farther apart and didn't always make sense to the intel forces.

One location was hit several times, always affecting the power grid for the same buildings that housed factories or geology and mineral labs. Finally, Pol ordered people to stake out the area, and they were able to spot one of Nahveel's men brewing a storm. They chased him and fought. Eventually, our guys killed the Cumbren before obtaining any information. We still didn't know where they were hiding and why they hadn't attacked Loanan directly yet.

All week Pol had gone out with his men fighting storms and tracking Nahveel's company. While his army traveled much farther, Pol wouldn't go too far from me, never traveling beyond Orlando. I couldn't help but wonder if Disney actually closed their park for these storms. That's how humans *knew* it was serious, and it was the only time that the section of highway with Mickey Mouse shaped power lines—which I'd nicknamed *The Mouse Trap*—would be free of gridlock.

He'd return home grimy from the crusty, humid air of the Regnum Solo getting into his aura when it weakened after a fight. Then he'd take a long hot shower. I would be done with my meditation and just starting to read by the fire when he came out of the bathroom, still glistening wet in nothing but a towel. He'd close the book, pull me to my feet, and make a ceremony of kissing me, holding me, and swaying me in a rhythmless dance.

"How are you feeling?" he would ask, knowing I had started my period the day after he pushed me from the window. My cramps had been exceptionally painful, and my period was lasting longer than normal. I had plenty of practice with magic as a means to manage the blood and stay fresh. I'd never bother with tampons and pads again. Though finally, today it seemed to be light spotting, and I knew it was only a matter of time before I jumped on Pol and climbed him like a tree.

Anyways. *Today*, Pol got in much earlier than usual, and seeing him in training was a nice surprise. It was rare that we got to eat together so I decided to pull myself out of my head, and books, and live in the moment.

"How are you feeling?" he asked from across the table this time.

"I'm doing okay. Small cramps. *Very* hungry. How about you? You're back early. How was your day?"

"I stopped by to check on your parents. They're doing well."

I smiled at the thoughtfulness. But I could sense something else in Pol that he wasn't saying. The nonchalant hovering of the two guards, Fiore and Fern, gave me more reason to worry. I had become familiar with the two men during my stay. But their station was usually reserved for the hall where our rooms were. *Unless Pol wants to throw me out of a window, of course.* So why were they now following us from training to dining?

"I appreciate that. But what has you feeling so uneasy, then?"

Pol studied me for a moment as if trying to figure something out.

"What makes you say I'm feeling uneasy?"

"Pol, stop avoiding the question. What is it?"

There was a long pause and a glare from Fiore's bloodstone irises to Pol. He was clearly urging him to tell me something.

"Nahveel may know you're here," he said. "They haven't attacked in a couple of days, but the air isn't quite right around Loanan's barriers."

"That doesn't sound like enough to think they know about us finding each other."

Pol only nodded, got up from his chair, and took my hand to bring me to my feet so we could walk to bed. He hugged me from behind, smelled my hair, and whispered into my ear, "I'm increasing security. You won't be out of my sight. I'll kill anyone who tries to touch you."

Fern and Fiore followed in toe and stationed themselves directly outside of our door.

__Divination__, also known to some as prophesying, is a type of psychic magic where one may project their consciousness through space and time and seek out probabilities. It can take years to make even a few successful attempts. Although rare, some beings have a natural proclivity for it. Oceaman and their hybrid descendants are the strongest practitioners. There are many different methods of divination, some more reliable than others. While tea leaves, tarot cards, and crystal balls are a popular method in Regnum Solo, they are seldom practiced in Regnum Caelorum or Regnum Oceanum. While Current Visioning and Trench

Pon-Seance's are a popular method in Regnum Oceanum—and result in the most vivid and boundless prophecies—they are unheard of in the other realms. Because the methods vary by realm, the experience of practitioners also varies.

One method popular in Regnum Caelorum is this procedure: Channel the physical dimension, connect with the immediate surroundings, and project consciousness through the barrier of time. <u>When done correctly, one will perceive sounds, images, and/or physical sensations associated with future events, and these experiences can be quite vivid. Some practitioners report seeing, hearing, and/or feeling a sensation anywhere from seconds to months before the causative event or factor occurs. When the event does occur, the practitioner will likely feel a sense of déjà vu.</u> Divination, and in-depth discussions of the methods of welding it relevant to the Regnum Caelorum, will be discussed in more depth in Advanced Magic.

The book slammed shut under a gust of wind, and I looked up at Pol, freshly showered. Judging by the heat of his wet skin, I left him enough hot water.

"Could you at least give me a bookmark before you do that?"

He kissed me, and I melted into him. I smacked him on the arm to let him know that a kiss didn't make me forget. "We have to get to bed early. We have a big day ahead," he offered.

"Oh, why's that?"

"Did Chloe not tell you? There's a meteor shower. Chloe, Cynti, and I will be taking you up."

I nodded, but I had no idea what he was talking about. I was just thankful that Cynti finally explained what happened with Chloe and me. The awkwardness was gone between the three of us.

Pol hadn't responded how she hoped. He was relieved I wasn't having a fling with one of his oldest friends. But he tried to lecture Cynti on how bad her sexuality was for the kingdom, as if this wasn't the source of her angst from the moment of her sexual awakening. I was glad to find a reason to leave before it started. The fight was brutal from what I heard—not at all the dream "coming out" discussion. Pol understood how wrong he was after, and they had since made amends.

Cynthi was not naive to the fact that she would marry a man of another kingdom for an alliance and likely conceive in ceremony for another alliance. Regardless, it wouldn't change who she loved, and he understood why she could never be faithful to whatever poor son of a bi—...man...whatever *man* she was betrothed to. When she asked that he imagined his soulmate was a man, he pitied her. "We can't help who we are attracted to, Pol. But I fully intend on doing my duty," she said to him before he gave her a long hug and promised her that he would speak no more of it.

Tonight, though, that was the farthest thing from my mind. I grabbed my book while darting daring glances at Pol, and then climbed into bed. "I'm going to finish *this* page."

***Empathing* is one of the most difficult psychic magics, and few have ever mastered it. Defined as the apprehension of the mental or emotional state of another individual, empathing is a rare and dangerous skill. So rare, in fact, that it is one of the least studied or understood**

types of magic. While empathy itself may be a strong characteristic of the practitioner, having a strong sense of empathy does not guarantee that they will excel at the skill of empathing. Successful empathing has been described as experiencing emotions, either vaguely or intensely, that have no correlation to their own experiences, and are unintentionally projected or otherwise unknowingly unrestrained from/by the source.

It is imperative to note that empathing for use in healing and medicine is explicitly forbidden in all realms. This is due to the difficulty almost all practitioners have in accurately performing empathing, or inaccuracies in distinguishing their own projected experience from the subject they're apprehending the information from. This can lead to mismanagement of symptoms, thus resulting in injury, suffering, or death.

Empathing is considered a skill that wins wars, so anyone excelling in this practice at an above average pace should keep their practice modest and hidden, save at the instruction of a Master Sorcerer within the Royal court of their kingdom. Because of the unlikely need for instruction on empathing, it is not covered in depth in this text but can be studied further in Advanced Psychic Magic, Volume Four.

Dream proje—

Slap. Whoosh. The text was closed on the nightstand in a matter of seconds.

"I guess I could thank you for marking the page this time," I said, as Pol took the space where the textbook was moments ago. He laid over me and kissed my chest.

THE NEXT MORNING, I READ THROUGH MY TEXTBOOKS WITH URIPE. He insisted it was time to deep dive into *Kingdoms of Regnum Caelorum*—"Know thy enemy" and all that. Apparently, the council had cause for concern that war would break out in this realm soon and would not be contained to random attacks in the Regnum Solo for much longer.

I was growing curious about these meetings. I wondered how to bring it up to Pol that perhaps I should be included in them. After all, they want to take *my* kingdom back. Shouldn't I be a part of the plans? Not to mention that I was starting to feel like I was being left out of the loop when it came to certain things. The query distracted me from the reading and Uripe to notice.

"Pop quiz," his voice box hummed out. "What Regnum Solo country is Prince Nahveel's Caelum Kingdom closest to?"

"Spain," I uttered without pause.

"What is it called?"

"Cumbre."

"What kingdoms has Cumbre conquered?"

"Nuage, near France, and Volare, near Italy."

"And…"

I sat looking at him from under my brows, eyes ready to flick toward the page and search. It was no use. By the length of this silent stare, he would know that I *didn't* know. I signed, "I don't know."

A wind pulled the cover up and over, shutting the book with a thump. He did it much more gently than Pol.

"You'll be relying on rebels, still loyal to their true kingdom, to fight against Ouran with you. It is wise to know what they're fighting for." His eyes met with Fiore's in the hall. Fiore didn't talk much, but I could feel his strong hope for me to do well at everything. I brushed it off.

"Of course, I know, Uripe. I'm feeling kinda overwhelmed. I have to leave soon, and there is still so much to know. Can I take this textbook with me? I think I just need some fresh air and a change of scenery."

Uripe signed something with his frail brown hands that I pieced together enough to recognize as "Yes," and "It stays in this realm." I signed "Thank you" as I got up from my seat and pulled the large book from the table.

I tucked it under my arm, but before I could turn to walk away, Uripe motioned with his short face at the sign out log. I walked toward it but was stopped by a fountain pen floating in front of me. When I reached for it, it bounced through the air just out of my reach, and my hand grabbed at emptiness. I shot a tired smile at Uripe. Then I put my hands into a mudra and moved the pen to the sign-out sheet. Much like signing a digital signature, my name was sloppy and angled oddly. *That kinda says my name, sure.*

I climbed the short stack of stairs to see Fiore and Fern flanking Pol. As promised, he hadn't left me out of his sight, and when he had to go to meetings or take care of personal needs, he had a third guard to replace him. We stopped in the kitchen and grabbed some left-over steak and Caesar salad, rich with iron. I hoped it would replenish my energy after one of the worst periods of my life. I ate in his room, perched on the floor near the phantom wall. It was one of my favorite places to sit now. So much so that he moved the armchair from my room to his, just near the edge. The clouds below looked like brilliant, white, cotton candy icebergs floating in the dark royal blue ocean miles below them. Miami was insignificantly small from here, a speck on Florida's East Coast. But I could feel a strong pull to it. Something didn't feel right, and guilt sat in my gut like a heavy brick.

I put down my plate and curled up in the chair by the fire, cracking open the book. The chair swallowed me, and I sank into it until my eyes shut, the unread book propped open in my lap.

WHEN I WOKE, IT WAS DARKER, THE SUN LESS THAN A FINGER FROM the horizon. I sat up in a panic, sure I was late for or missed *something*. The book was on a shelf, marked where I'd left off, or more accurately, where I never started. Pol was leaning against the bookshelf, looking out of the phantom wall.

"How long have I been asleep?"

Pol turned, looked at me, and said, "You snored 2,880 times. I'd say about five or six hours."

I pulled myself from the lounger and wiped some drool from the corner of my lip. "I missed lessons with Chloe. Why didn't you wake me up?"

"You'll have a lesson tonight. I was just about to wake you. You'll want to dress in something warm and easy to move in. Tali put some options out for you. Mynt came by and chose for you though."

I made my way to his arms by the time he finished his sentence and caught the last of the sun reflecting off of his opal irises before the sky went dark. I rocked to my toes and reached my lips up to his. In my periphery something caught my eye in the sky. It was like a shred of light zipping by to the far northeast. I looked out to the darkening sky with furrowed brows. "Did you see that?"

"Yes. That's the first of the meteor shower. It's time to go." He gave me another kiss before nodding toward the outfit Mynt chose for me.

By the time I was dressed in thick, fleece-lined joggers, chunky black sneakers, and a fitted, fleece-lined pullover, there was a knock at the door.

"Come in," Pol said, adjusting the leather gloves on his hand.

"They're here. Do you need another set of eyes, Your Highness? I am more than willing to come," Fiore offered from the door in an Italian accent.

"No, Fiore. That's alright. Chloe is the equivalent of ten men," Pol said, half joking.

"Hmph."

"Are you ready to go?" Chloe asked me, walking past Fiore's stocky body. The door closed.

"I guess so. I'm not really sure what to expect."

"We'll be at the top of the mesosphere first. The meteors start to burn there. We should catch them well before they enter the stratosphere and get too charred."

"Catch…them?" I asked, looking for more clarification. "Catch a shooting star?"

"You'll be using magic; your aura should be about 80% water tonight, and you have to keep it from freezing by micro-moving the water particles to warm them so they stay liquid. You'll slow the meteor with moving so it doesn't hit you at full speed, and your aura will cool it. You'll be cold and the air is extremely thin, so we'll need to use magic to form pure oxygen and use micro-moving to make heat. Pol will help with the cloud and supplemental oxygen only. Clouds never naturally form there, so it will take a lot of his energy to do just that. Cynti will provide some baseline warmth to conserve energy. She'll also stand guard in case something goes wrong. This takes a lot of energy, so we go in a group, stick to our designated tasks. We'll take care of business before enjoying the show at the base of the mesosphere. Got it?"

"Oh…kay?" I said, glancing at Pol, whose face hid his humor well. I didn't absorb half of what they said, still wondering why the hell I was catching a shooting star.

"We'll walk you through it as we go. Come here," he said with a hand outstretched. I walked toward him, near the phantom wall. He formed a cloud just outside and helped me onto it. "Conserve your energy. You'll need it."

The cumulus was large enough to accommodate the four of us comfortably. We all crouched down, Cynti tucked into Chloe's arm and me tucked into Pol's. "Hold on," his low voice rumbled into my ear.

The cumulus cloud zipped us up into the sky, and icy air stung my face. The sun was now well hidden behind the earth, not even a glow of it left, and as we went up into the pitch-black sky, I could see the curve of the darkened planet. Below us was the shape of Florida taking form. The state had veins and patches of gold light that shimmered over the large cities. I could see clouds far below and off to the north, with lightning illuminating them in pulsing zaps. I realized now where Loanan drew inspiration for the palace lights embedded in the ceiling of clouds.

When we stopped, I took in the sight around us. The Big Dipper was a massive display from up here. Dwarfing all of us, I felt like a tiny speck in its presence. It was the most recognizable constellation, but other stars were just as brilliant against the onyx sky. Then my eyes adjusted well enough to see the dusty star-speckled belt of the Milky Way faintly visible around us. It cast a sparkling dusty line of blue and purple, studded with stars across the endless black of space.

The moon, with all of its craters, hung clearer than ever, and I gawked at it all.

"This is incredible," I breathed out as enthusiastically as a whisper could be. My breath frosted, and I shivered violently, reminding me to heat myself. Cynti and my jewels could only do so much, and my hair was already laden with ice.

A sizzling sound whizzed by with a flash of bright light, and I crouched low.

"*Shit,*" I said, my mouth instantly filling with the taste of dirt.

"It's alright. I won't let one hit us," Pol said, pulling me up. "After you catch one, it'll be a good time to practice forming oxygen." He sucked from his palms as if blowing on them in cold weather. He offered me his palms, and I sucked in the oxygen from them. Another sizzling hiss sounded closer, and now a rush of shifting air pressure and heat grazed my cheek. It was a welcome heat, although brief, and smelled strange. I only gasped this time, not wanting to spit mud. Ice crystals were stiffening our lashes now.

"We can't stay this high for too long. It's too cold and will pull too much of our energy," Chloe said while Cynti used her magic to heat the air around us a little more. "I'll go first, then you'll go after."

Chloe pulled their own tiny cloud from ours, looking toward the cold darkness. "You won't see them easily at first. You will see a faint brownish ball, if you're lucky, then a spark, then flames. We'll move toward the spark. Cup your hands like so," Chloe motioned as though holding a balloon. "Focus your aura—a *wet* aura—on your chest, arms, and hands." Chloe's aura thickened and sparkled around them. They were coated in a clear puddle at the front. The way they swayed on their cloud, knees bent, and hands out, reminded me of a soccer goalie waiting for the ball. "You'll use moving to slow the spark by gently applying opposing forces. If it doesn't slow, move fast. There!"

Chloe zipped their cloud to the left below a new spark that grew into a ball of bright flames.

The meteor slowed, and the fire around it became more fluid in movement. Chloe's aura shimmered, and when the meteor made contact with it, the flames hushed, and steam swallowed it. The aura protected their face from the rush of steam. It slowed before it could touch Chloe, enough to gather ice on its lightly charred surface. Chloe grabbed it and carried the rock to our cloud. When it fell from their hands, it landed on the cloud with an oddly pleasant puff of sulfur-like stench. My mouth hung wide.

"Ready?" Chloe asked.

"Not at all," I said, shocked. "You want me to just c-c-catch a shooting st-st-star?" I stuttered through chattering teeth.

"It's easier than it looks. Go on. We can't be here for long," Pol nudged, giving me a turn with his hands cupped full of oxygen. I walked to Chloe, who stood behind me, hands on my waist, and lifted us onto another cloud segment.

"Get your hands and aura ready first," said Chloe, and I held out my hands, holding an invisible balloon, my aura watery. "Look up. Tell me where."

"You're c-c-crazy. It'll kill us b-b-both."

"Focus. Everything we are doing, you've done a hundred times by now."

I looked out into the sky. I saw something brown and then sparks, but none close enough to catch before they burned up. Then, a star ahead flickered dark a few seconds longer than usual, and a brown form came into view.

"Ahhhh!" I squealed. It sparked and ignited. The meteor was barreling toward us. I cowered and squealed louder, but Chloe moved us with ease. "Fucking shit fuck!" My mouth filled with dirt. I spit it to earth, where it burnt up as it fell. Chloe moved the cloud back and laughed.

"Good job spotting. Next time, instead of squealing and cussing, move it with opposing force until it slows. I won't let it hit you."

Chloe moved the cloud again like a goalie guarding a net. I spat a few more times to clear the remaining dirt and wiped my lips clean. Then I centered myself and saw another darkly flickering star followed by a tumbling brown mass. "There!" I screamed loudly. Chloe moved quickly to it. It was like they already saw it. It was heading right for us. I moved the meteor, applying an opposing force. To my surprise, it responded with ease. It slowed quickly and practically glided into my wet aura. Chloe moved the cloud backward as it approached, narrating the movement for me.

"We go backward with its direction and slowly stop. There we go. It's just like forming a cloud mid-flight. Move with it, and then slow down," they said calmly. Catching it was like a dance. The weak flames sizzled and steamed, sending up a foul stench of sulfur and then…wet hay?

"The skies and everything in it are the root of your magic," Chloe said. I watched the steam sparkle into crystalized ice against its dark, charred surface and finally held the meteor. "Shooting stars were once thought to be what our bones are made of. We connect with them in a way no other being can connect to them." As Chloe spoke, they lowered the cloud, and I admired the gorgeous ball. "This is your first meteor. It will be your prize weapon: an embercudgel. It'll need a few weeks of work before you can use it. Careful crafting by the smiths and mages of Loanan."

Our cloud was now merged with Pols. Cynti's warmth was noticeable, and Pol refueled us with oxygen. Stars fell around us, but none was more stunning than the one I held in my arms. A little over a foot wide, black char was polished and shimmering with ice over the rock. Pol cupped my cheek and pushed my face up.

"You did very well. I'm so proud of you," he said with a rare physical smile. "Now, make a wish." I smiled and went to speak, but his thumb pressed against my lips to stop them. "Not out loud. No one can hear it. Your star will know, though."

I wished in silence—a wish no living person would ever know.

The cloud lowered slowly. In the corner of my eye, I saw Cynti press a kiss on Chloe's lips. When we got to the lowest point of the mesosphere, Chloe cleared the area. With Cynti in tow, they borrowed a chunk of our cloud and set out for some privacy to watch the rest of the shower alone. I could see why. This was one of the most romantic sights I had ever seen. The shooting stars skidded across the sky like matches striking a strip every few seconds or so.

"This is why we come early. Later in the night, when the shower is at its peak, they're harder to avoid getting hit by," Pol said. He was right about needing to conserve energy. Between heating and oxygen and having a functioning cloud this far up, it was exhausting our magic. I was already weakened from bleeding heavily and was glad to start recouping my energy.

We lay on the cumulus, watching the shower of fireballs, most of which burned to ashes or pebble-sized meteorites before reaching us. I practiced creating oxygen and heat. I was nuzzled into Pol's side, offering cupped hands of air for him to test.

Looking at him, I knew this would be the perfect night to make it his first—once we got back to the palace and didn't have to rely on our magic, of course. I looked at the silhouette of his face for a long moment, his strong nose like a mountain that the shooting stars dove behind.

Pol caught me admiring him and grabbed my wrist. He held the bracelet in his fingers and formed a new charm. It was round, black, and dented, encrusted with tiny diamond chips on the ridges like ice. It had a flamelike tail of rose gold encrusted with amber flecks. The charm was the shape of a shooting star, and warmth and strength nudged at my bones a little stronger.

"The center is from your meteor. The smiths and mages will work on your embercudgel, but this will always be part of it and respond just the same, so be mindful when wielding. You'll always have a piece of it with you now."

"It's perfect. I love it. Thank you."

He kissed me, sliding his tongue past my lips. He stopped and recoiled, covered my mouth with his hand, and rinsed the taste of soil with water flavored with mint and lemongrass. "You could counter Mynt's dirt curse all this time, and you didn't tell me?"

"You didn't ask."

I shoved at his shoulder, biting back the word' *ass*,' and kissed him.

He slid his tongue into my mouth again, pulling himself onto me. I kissed him back gently, guiding his hips between my legs. His fingers combed through my icy hair, reaching the back of my head. He gripped the frozen hair tightly and thrust his hips up between my legs. My hair crunched with glittering ice. I groaned happily and lifted my chin. His lips traced down my jaw to my neck. The wet kisses froze into lip-shaped ice crystals on my skin. My fingers kneaded into his shoulder blades. I arched my head back, my crown buried into the cloud. I opened my eyes to watch the shimmering sky as he kissed me lower. It was then that I swore I saw the form of a man just out of my periphery.

I gasped. Pol took this for excitement. He pushed his hips up again—this time, his hard length rubbed against my pelvic bone.

Enthusiasm nearly fogged my better judgment. But I looked around again. I couldn't see the man now.

"Pol," I said, tapping his shoulder. "Let's pick this up at home…"

He kissed me again, and the cloud sank fast enough to lift us from its surface for a moment. The speed sent our hair whipping through the wind. Through the chaotic tussling locks, I saw it again. What I thought was a cloud, and a person was now somewhere high above us. I broke the kiss.

"Pol, someone is watching us." But when he turned, all that we could see was the diamond-littered sky of black and the periwinkle pixie dust band of the Milky Way.

"Many caeluman come to harvest meteors during showers. Whoever they are, they're gone now," he said. But he didn't kiss me again. Instead, he pressed two fingers to his temple. Seconds later, Chloe and Cynti were misting at our side. As we sank back to Loanan, we all stayed on alert until we reached the palace. Chloe took off to the war room. As they commanded, Cynti returned to her own room.

Once past the barrier and in his room, Pol muttered an incantation. He scouted the sky beyond the phantom wall for a long moment. Then he turned from me and cracked open the door to murmur something to Fiore and Fern. When he shut it, he turned to me, stalking toward me knowingly.

Our magnetic pull was stronger than ever, eased only by being near each other. But when the tension was tight between us, it was nearly impossible to resist. He pulled off his shirt. He cupped my chin possessively, and his mouth melted into mine. I heard his belt come undone, and my knees nearly buckled, a tickle fluttering through my core. My fingers clawed into his chest. He grabbed my wrists and slammed them over my head and into the wall. I moaned, but the sound could hardly pass through the lock of our lips.

With magic, he yanked my pants down fast. He tore my panties on one side. I was ready for all of it.

But as my eyes slid open, I was overcome with feelings of deception, dread, and futility—feelings not of my own. It pulled me from the moment. I broke the kiss and gave him a wild look as I evaluated him.

"What is it?" he asked. These feelings weren't coming from him. He was full of an almost violent passion and lust. He was radiating with need, pheromones seeping from his pores. He was straining to pause and stifle his impatience. These *other* feelings, though, were coming from another source... No. From sources. Some sources far, and some near.

"Something's wrong." I pulled my wrists from his grip and gently nudged him a step back. The pull to him felt impossible to avoid, but I followed my feelings. My eyes peered out the phantom wall and into the glittering city. "I have to go back. Something's not right." I tried to pull up my pants as I spoke, but his hand stopped me.

"What?" Pol said, shocked. "Are you so afraid of losing control for one minute?"

"This isn't about control, Pol. Something is happening. Odie... The nurses... Something else that I can't put my finger on. Something bad is happening."

"Right now? How would you even know that?" He grabbed my face with both hands, and his words came out almost pleading. "You're killing me. Pulling me in and pushing me away. What will it take to let your guard down? For you to see, I'd never take your choice."

"Pol, this isn't about that!" I shouted, pushing him from me. The moment was tangibly sour now. *Great.* "Listen to me!'

"You want to run away from this! From me! You can't even let me touch you!" Pol yelled. He was still radiating the same aggressive passion, but now frustration and fear coursed through him. The same scrape stung my back again, burning hotter this time. I wanted to wrap myself around him, but needed him to listen. "If I take you back there now, how do I know I'll ever see you again? You go back to your easy life where you move every piece in its place…"

"How could you say that? What do I have to do to show you, Pol?" I yelled and pushed against his chest. He grabbed my wrist tightly and stuck out his chin. Anger still coursed through him but didn't dampen his lust. He felt a primal urge to take me but was showing nothing except unrivaled restraint. It just made me hotter for him. I could focus on nothing else. I shoved him again to provoke him. He growled low and flexed his jaw. He couldn't possibly think I didn't want him. But he did, and if proving him wrong would make him listen to me…

I hit my knees and unfastened his pants. I pulled them until his large cock sprang free. I needed to taste him. I'd let him unleash every primal urge he had and give up all control. He gripped my hair in his fist, keeping my lips at bay.

"What are you doing?" he demanded.

I put my wrists behind my back and created a rope to bind myself. "Fuck my face." The taste of dirt laced my tongue.

He tightened his grip in my hair, and his cock flexed. I could feel it; he loved this. He was fighting hard to hide it. "Daph…" he said, still angry.

I looked up at him from my knees. The violent eagerness I felt in him was making me rabid. My chest rose and fell with quick breaths. He ground his teeth. After a few labored breaths, he gave in. His grip tightened, pulling my hair at the root and shoving me toward his cock.

"Ask nicely... Beg for it.' My face ran hot. He tightened his grip in my hair again, and his breathing picked up pace as he nudged the tip just out of my tongue's reach. Cum beaded at the tip. "Beg for it."

"Please... Please fuck my face," I asked. He let out a heavy breath. Again, an image flashed in my mind, now of him holding me down by the neck, my nails clawing at his arm, and water rolling down his face as he buried himself inside me. The violent image should have given me pause. It only made me crave him more. I tried for his cock, but he restrained me with a hair tug. I begged harder. "Please, Pol. Fuck my mouth. Please make me swallow your cum. Choke me with it." My mouth was turning gritty with dirt.

"Fuck," he said. He was throbbing. He pulled my face to him. "Open wide."

Thumb in my mouth, he pulled my jaw down, my lip tugging down with it. He clicked his tongue. "Dirty, dirty girl," he said, looking at the thin layer of dirt on my tongue. "Swallow it." I obeyed without hesitation. Pleasure ran through him at my obedience, and he rinsed my mouth again. "That's enough of that for now." He lifted the dirt curse.

His thumb pulled my jaw wide again, and without warning, he filled every inch of space in my mouth with his girthy cock. Both of his hands gripped my hair tightly now. He pulled my face down his length. His cock stretched my throat, and I gagged. He sighed in pleasure. The gagging made my mouth water, easing his strokes. He pushed his cock in deep again and again. My eyes watered.

He tightened the binding on my wrist. Then a small, cold chill grew my ass.

"Beg me to fill your ass," he said, looking down at me. He pulled himself from my mouth just far enough to rest his cock on my lips. I gasped for air.

"Please, fill my ass, Pol," was all I could get out before his cock was working down my throat again. An icy hardness grew inside me. It was a large plug of ice twirling just past the hole. I squealed and moaned and looked up at him with watery, pleading eyes. He fucked my face over and over again. He watched me as if daring me to surrender. "You're not going anywhere."

Ice shackled me at the knees. A bar grew between them. It lengthened quickly, forcing my legs wide apart as the icy shackles slid across the floor. A cyclone of warm water swirled around my clit, and my eyes rolled back. My throat relaxed, and he fucked my mouth deeper. The ice growing in my ass reshaped and was now half the size of his cock, stretching my ass wide and plunging in and out of me. I was nearing climax quickly.

Tears rolled down my cheeks, and my moans pushed past his hard cock. He was so happy with me, and I dripped cum.

"You like choking on my cock? You want my cum, baby?" he asked, his voice breaking. He slowed his hips, still fucking me deep. The icy toy in my ass thickened to the size of his cock and stretched my ass painfully. I flinched, but the restraints squeezed tighter around my wrists and knees like a snake squeezing its prey. He made sure I took all of it from both ends, the icy thrusts now harder, making my ass sore with every pump. I gagged as he forced himself into my throat. The water swirling around my clit warmed. "You're going to come for me now."

But I was breaking before his sentence was through. Harsh moans and cries of pleasure vibrated past his length. He pushed himself deep into my mouth. His cock jerked with the squirting of hot cum down my throat. "Sss. Fuck," he hissed between grunts.

The tip of the icy dildo in my ass started to turn to warm liquid. It filled me in rushes like hot cum squirting into my ass. It still pumped in and out of me, though it grew smaller as it melted. My ass could hardly contain the massive load. The large plug at the end forced me to bear every drop, even through my gagging and guttural moans. My pussy spasmed in orgasmic waves, dripping out wetness. It ached to be fucked too.

I pushed my face against him, submitting to him, inviting him to stay deep in my throat. I couldn't breathe. My vision darkened. I didn't care. I stuck my tongue out and rubbed it on his balls. He groaned.

"Fuck yes," he said, giving my throat a few last deep jerking thrusts before withdrawing in a loud sigh. I gasped for air, and the rope around my wrists came undone. I threw my arms forward, catching myself on the floor by my fingertips. His steady grip in my hair kept my face raised to look up at him. I was in a pose of worship at his feet. The pulling of my hair kept my palms from touching the floor. I went to come up to ease the pull.

"Stay."

I obeyed him. He was looking down at me with trembling lips, rubbing his softening wet cock on my cheek as I gasped and bowed to him. A small puddle of my own cum had collected on the floor below my pussy. I knew I would go mad without him inside me soon. The thought caused me to dig my nails into the hardwood as I panted.

The flood of warm water filling in my ass solidified into a strand of beads that got larger as it exited my body, my ass stretching and releasing around each subsequent orb on the strand. His magic pulled it out slowly, and he bit his lip, knowing how large he was making the next one.

"Good girl," he whispered slowly, never breaking eye contact. The beads grew as wide as kiwis. I let out tiny, raspy moans from my aching throat as he pulled each anal bead from me. "That's my good girl." When the strand of ice beads ended and clambered on the floor, I finally eased my breath. I panted deep and steady. The ice shackles and bar forcing my legs apart melted and evaporated.

Then, finally, he let go of my hair. He reached for my arm, pulling me to my feet and then pushed me backward. I propped my tired body against the wall. He closed all of the space around me. My chin was wet with saliva, my chest still heaving slowly. His thumb traced my plumped lips to my sore jaw. "Give me one more night in my bed. I'll take you home as soon as the sun is up."

"I'll give you anything…everything," I said to him, and I meant it.

WE LAY IN HIS BED THAT NIGHT. POL HELD ME CLOSE AND FELL asleep fast. But now that the pull to him was satiated, I could feel the same troubling emotions from before. No sleep would take me. Something was happening back home. Something was coming. Something was already there.

24

O'DOHERTY: SHHH, MI CIELO

FABIAN AND POLPETTA WERE INSEPARABLE, AS ALWAYS. I STARTED TO worry that both of them would be devastated when Daphne came home. I giggled to myself at the thought of them having an E.T. and Eliot reaction, both dying from some magical bond that connected them despite being apart.

It had been two weeks since Daphne left, and even Jesula was starting to worry. She wouldn't admit it, but I could see it in her eyes. The captive audience meetings started and were led by what Daphne would have called a "professional bullshit artist" named Judia Shank. He was a union buster. The hospital paid Shank thousands to scare the nurses with his lies. It was growing even more difficult to keep everyone on track with the union plans.

The managers of the units would come around with snack carts, and quiz the nurses on Shank's anti-union propaganda, and reward them with cookies when they recited the fabricated rhetoric. I couldn't imagine why management thought patronizing the nurses would be strategic. All it was doing was irritating them.

Jesula and I traded numbers after Lyndie Pratt reminded me that the last of my patients were discharged or deceased. She suggested I complete reviewing their chart for the last time, to free up computers for staff. It was no secret that I was friends with Daphne, and she probably didn't want me helping the union efforts.

I was taking my time, though. I didn't want to miss anything in the patients' charts as I searched for this missing piece. I combed through the chart of every patient in the trial who had ever been admitted. I needed proof of what Fabian and I had found the night before.

Last night he came over and finally asked if I was okay. Between him announcing his love for me and the secret panty thief threatening me, no, I wasn't. I shared only half of that with him.

"I can't explain it. I'm just scared. I am still completely smitten by you, and you have done nothing wrong. I've just never been in such a normal relationship before, and I think I'm panicking that this is too good to be true?"

"Sounds like you're explaining it fine," he said with a smile. "I'll wait forever for you, honey." And he meant it. It wasn't that he hadn't tried to be intimate, but when I brushed him off, he was very respectful and offered a caring touch. He had never tried to make me feel bad for not wanting intimacy, but the change was noticeable. I could tell he was concerned about *me*, not just our sex life. He also loosened up about the man who followed me. Although, he still scouted the area frequently and kept the place locked up tight.

"What about work? Did anything happen?"

How could I lie to him? He deserves the world. Ugh.

"I think there's something big—a missing piece that I can't find. I've been retracing everything from day one all week, and I am hyper-focused on it. It's just nagging at me. I need to know."

"How can I help?"

"I mean…short of hacking into my company's system and seeing what they have?" I said jokingly. But Fabian just leaned back with a smile. "Fabian, that was a joke. If we got caught…"

"Honey, this is my expertise. I got it."

"Fabian, we could get in a lot of trouble."

"Yeah? How do you like dating a *bad boy*?" he asked while wiggling his fingers to warm them up and cracking open his laptop. I couldn't help the smirk that split my face. Fabian was *not* a bad boy. Yet here he was, breaking a big rule, and so I entertained his self-proclaimed criminality, leaning in and biting my lip.

I admired him even as the harsh reflection of the computer screen on his glasses blocked his toasted honey eyes. His head jerked back slowly.

"Hey, did you know *Heartly* was involved in evaluating the patients for eligibility?"

"What?"

"Yeah. It looks like before you were assigned to the trial, a doctor from *Heartly Mental Health* came out to *Mayflower* to evaluate them."

"What doctor? Does it say?"

"Yeah. It's Dr. Benton Bailey."

"That's strange. He never mentioned that. Does it say anything about the patient interactions?" I asked. After a moment, Fabian looked at me with furrowed brows, and a coldness washed over me. "What is it?"

"They were given free 'relaxation and auto-suggestion sessions' by Dr. Bailey prior to and several times during the treatment trials." He didn't take his eyes off of me. "Dotey, I think he was hypnotizing these patients." He swore he never signed off on that for Nana.

He hacked into my director's emails next and found that the stones delivered to the patients by the pharmaceutical reps were used as focal points during the sessions. In other words, they were visual hypnosis aids.

"Okay, that's enough. Exit out of there before we get caught," I said, biting my nails.

I lay awake all night, determined to scour every chart. I had to find evidence of hypnosis and unconsented treatment from *Heartly*.

And now, staring at the fortieth chart of the day, I came across one clue.

> Patient states, "That fat man who makes me look at rocks, he makes me uncomfortable and smells like Pepto Bismol. I don't want him here again." No record of any visitors that fit this description. Will follow up with the facility.

I printed the paper, and as I made my way to the printer, I felt eyes on me again. I looked around to see no one but the nurses running around and dodging the anti-union snack cart. I continued through more charts, printing off any mention of "the fat man," "rocks," "dreams," or "therapy sessions." I made sure I had contact information for family members to ask if they consented to any treatment through *Heartly*. By the time I was done, the sun had just gone down.

The drive home was dull. My phone rang. It was Fabian.

"I'm stuck in traffic, honey. There was a bad storm at work, and it nearly took out my car!"

"Oh my gosh, are you okay?"

"Oh, I'm fine, honey. I'll just be home late. There's a meteor shower tonight, though. I'd like to watch it with you if I make it home in time."

"Oh, that would be so fun. I'll try to get my work wrapped up by then. I found something in a patient's chart! You'll never gue—"

"Honey? Are yo— …ere?" His phone cut in and out.

"Can you hear me?"

"You're cutting in — —ut a bit. —ere- a storm ahead. I'll —e you — I get ho–"

"Be careful. Take your time, babe. And drive safely."

"You too, hon— I love you. See —ou —on." My chest tickled at the words. He had said them a few times casually since that first time, but I never said them back. They felt nice to hear, though, and I hoped he wasn't hurt that I was not ready to say it.

I pulled into my driveway and could tell by the darkness of my street that the power was out *again*. I grabbed my laptop and papers and headed into my dark home. I headed back to the dinette table and opened the laptop to start entering the data into the patient's chart. I'd make a paper trail no one could ignore. After getting it set up, I decided to change into something more comfortable first. I headed into my room, careful to navigate in the dark.

I hadn't had time to get more panties, so when I pushed my scrub pants down and had nothing on underneath, I was reminded of the thief. Grumbling to myself, I swapped my scrub top for a t-shirt and turned for my bed to grab the shorts I had worn the night before. That's when I noticed my nightstand drawer was open, the diary missing, and a strong fragrance.

I gasped and turned, but a large hand grabbed me by the neck. He slammed me against the wall. His grip wasn't even that hard, but somehow, I couldn't scream. I clawed at his sweaty wrist. I kicked my bare legs at him. It was dark, but I could see he was the same white-haired stalker following me for weeks. His large irises were like pure black stones, lifeless and demonic. He was shirtless, and his skin seemed to glisten in the dark.

"Three times now, I have asked you nicely to stop this," he said in a thick Spanish accent. "You're making my life very difficult, O'doherty. I don't have time to keep watching you." He came closer, easing his grip. The faint smell of his fruity musk wafted up, along with something strange. I could only gasp anxiously as he pressed his groin against my naked hips.

"It's not that I don't *enjoy* watching you," he said, grazing his lips against my cheek.

I screamed and tried to push him away. He sunk his fingers into my neck again. I could feel his hard length through his pants, rubbing against my navel, and he hummed. I writhed in revulsion.

"Shhh, mi cielo. I could never hurt you. No, no. It will be someone else. I can appreciate how well he takes care of you, so I don't *want* to hurt him." My eyes went wide. This time, when he released my throat, I was utterly still and silent. His fingers squeezed my chin, pulling my lips near his.

"Yes. There we go. You see, I could have taken out his car today. I could kill him in his sleep tonight."

"No... I'll stop. Please just leave him alone."

He smiled and moved his thumb over my lips. "And why should I take your word for it? You are a sneaky delinquent." A tear rolled down my cheek and wet his hand as my breath shook. He continued in a breathy tone. "Hey, hey, hey. You don't have to be afraid of me. I am a reasonable man."

"Please, don't hurt him..." I whimpered. "I'll do what you want. I won't look into it anymore. I promise. Please."

"I'll tell you what," he said. "I'm going to take your papers, and you are not going to document a *thing* about any of this…Fabian won't get hurt." I nodded in agreement as he spoke. Then he smirked in a devious way, obviously humored. His top-heavy lips came close to mine, brushing them. "And in exchange for my leniency…you will never wear panties again. Sound like a deal?"

I let out a disgusted breath, and another tear fell. I hoped my reaction and the dim light hid the flush of my skin. Heat prickled all over me. Even my legs felt hot. My body betrayed me. *Creep.* I squirmed to be rid of his touch before he noticed it.

"Shh, shh, shh, sh, mi cielo. That's enough. Stop that. You do what I ask, no one gets hurt and I stop visiting you. Huh? How about it?" he said while cupping my chin with rough affection, his thumb stroking my bottom lip. My breath quickened, and my face stung as I looked at his face. His length flexed against me, and I jumped.

I forced myself to nod. "Okay…" I whispered. He breathed a sigh of relief through his nose. After placing a long, slow kiss on my forehead, he spoke onto my skin.

"I'm so sorry I scared you. I hate that it has to be this way. I do," he said, lowering his free hand from the wall and slowly stroking my body as it made its way to my bare hip. He squeezed my hip. His thumb rubbed just inside my hip bone as he studied my face from inches away. My breath hitched with a sob.

As he backed up, his hand still cupped my chin. When he released it, he pulled my diary from the back of his waistband. "Oh! I forgot this." He kissed the book and handed it to me. It was damp when I received it and smelled of his fruity scent and, again, something strange.

Headlights wandered over the walls of the room, lighting his face enough for me to see how endlessly black his eyes were, with no beginning or end from pupil to iris. My heart raced in fear. Fabian had pulled in. The man pressed his finger to his lips, gesturing to be quiet.

"Not a word of this to him, mi cielo." He walked out of my room. I stood frozen for a moment. Then I realized Fabian was walking straight to him. I threw my diary on the bed, grabbed my shorts, and ran into the living room. But no one was there. Wherever I looked, there was no sign of him. I ran to the dinette, where my laptop still glowed on the table. My papers were gone.

Fabian opened the door. My body shook as I threw my shorts on in the dark.

"Hey, you know Polpetta got outside?" he called from the door, and I could hear the tiny metal clinks of Polly's collar as she trotted in with him. I ran through the kitchen and threw my arms around his neck, still shaking. I sobbed uncontrollably.

"Hey! What's wrong? What happened? Are you okay?" I was crying too hard to answer. "Dotey! Talk to me, honey! What happened? Did someone hurt you?"

My phone rang, startling me. Slowly, I let go of him to answer it.

"Hello?" I whispered cautiously, afraid to hear the man's voice again.

"O'doherty, hey, it's Tonya," the voice said.

"Who is it?" Fabian demanded.

"It's my manager," I whispered, covering the receiver. I took a deep breath and wiped my nose, sniffling. "Hey, Tonya. What can I do for you?" I tried to sound as normal as possible. Fabian moved closer, brushing off Polpetta's short hops and cries for attention.

"Hey, we're pulling the Meriflec trial. We need you to put in all your notes by tomorrow. No more visits effective immediately."

"W…What?" I could hardly manage to get it out.

"Yeah. I know it's short notice, but it just came down the pipeline. Probably the mortality rate."

"Can't I at least let the patients know? I only have a handful left and they're safe at home or placed."

"No. They want to pull all involvement in that trial. The patients will get a notification from a doctor."

"*What* doctor?" I pressed before realizing she had no context for the accusation in my tone.

"O'doherty… I don't know. This is coming from the top though. They didn't seem happy about it. I'd tread carefully and…just do what they say, okay?"

"And what am I supposed to do after that?"

"Well, they don't have another trial lined up, so I guess cash in your PTO. There will be an inquiry about outliers in data though. You'll be paid for that time."

"My PTO? An *inquiry?* Am I getting fired, Tonya?"

"No. You're definitely not getting fired. Not that I can foresee. Let's…call it a sabbatical. I'll call you tomorrow when I hear more. Get some rest."

I slapped my phone on the counter and looked at Fabian.

"Honey?" he asked.

"We fucked up, baby. We fucked up big."

We went to bed early. Fabian stayed up, holding me and telling me everything would be fine, but eventually dozed off with Polpetta under his other arm. I hadn't told him about the intruder, just that I felt watched, and the darkness scared me. I rolled over softly so as to not wake him and grabbed my diary that I hid in the drawer before he could see it. He would lose his mind if he knew I was pen-pals with a dangerous man who threatened us both. I opened it to the marked page. It was the same page I had written to the man on. He had written back.

Promises. xo

"Fucking *creep*," I sneered and threw the book into the drawer. Fabian stirred, and I turned back to him. I touched his cheek and gazed at him as he slept. His perfect angelic face coaxed a kiss from me. I couldn't imagine being without him. Nothing was more important than his safety and happiness, and I'd never give that creepy, white-haired sicko a chance to hurt him. I nuzzled into him, and a tear fell from my eyes.

25

DAPHNE: BLOOD-SOAKED FANGS

THUMP, THUMP. FOR HOURS, I LAID MY HEAD ON POL'S CHEST AND listened to his perfect heartbeat. *Normal sinus rhythm*, I guessed. It had not missed a beat and had a steady rhythm, telling me his electrical faculties were without abnormality. *Electrics working*. The perfect thump-thumping told me he had strong, perfectly structured heart valves, clear of vegetation. *Plumbing's good too*. I listened to the air move in and out of his lungs without any adventitious sounds. I traced my fingertip over the greenish vein that ran along the skin of his upper arm like a fat cord poking through—spongy and sturdy and perfect for an eighteen gauge IV. I pressed my first two fingers over his brachial artery to feel the strong pulsation from the deep vessel nestled safely beside a bone.

Thump, thump. I would lay awake like this every night if it meant I was listening when the first abnormality came. When the first abnormal beat of his heart or crackle in his lungs happened, I'd catch it and take him to a doctor. I'd definitely be their worst nightmare, demanding every test. *Helicopter wife* they'd call me; not that I'd care. His health was more important than what any stranger in scrubs thought of me. How old would we be then, when his heart started to get tired? His smooth arms would be wrinkled with our beautiful memories by that point. That perfect vein would roll away from the IV then. I could get it though; his vein wouldn't be able to roll away from me. I wouldn't let anyone bruise up his perfect, wrinkled arm. I wouldn't let anything happen to him.

Thump, thump. Thump, thump. I realized how morbid my thoughts were and knew why. While Pol slept off his immense satisfaction— which I took great pride in—I was haunted by some intuitive force. I was empathing and didn't know how to control it or how to tell my own feelings from others. I hadn't told Uripe, or Pol, or anyone. *Empathing is considered a skill that wins wars,* the book read. As my growing sense of approaching destruction intensified, I debated waking Pol and telling him, but Uripe didn't know yet. The book said I was supposed to tell him first. But I trusted Pol. *What if it's dangerous for him to know?* His heart pounded louder in my ear.

Thump, thump. Thump, thump. Thump, thump. There was a feeling surrounding us, growing closer. I didn't know if it was my own paranoia or an extremely rare gift. I was now sweating from the nerves. His heart thumped in my ear again, louder now. I decided I wouldn't risk never hearing it again.

"Pol," I said gently at first, sweat beading on my forehead. When he didn't wake, I said it much louder. "Pol. Wake up."

With a deep breath, he stirred awake and looked around the room. There were only the stars of pre-dawn shining brightly outside the phantom wall. Then he turned his tired eyes to me.

"What's wrong?" he asked with a dry throat. I didn't exactly know what to say.

"Something's not right."

He propped himself on his elbows and scouted the room again. By all sights, it was a perfectly peaceful pre-dawn night, serene even. He turned his face back to me, searching for an answer, then pulled me to him and rubbed my back slowly.

"Pol, please. I'm telling you something isn't right. I can't sleep."

He ran a large hand through my hair and sighed.

"Everything's going to be alright. I won't let anything happen to you. Everything is fine." He kissed my forehead.

"It's *not*. Something is—"

Yelling came from outside. The room shook. A loud boom sounded with it. Pol was out of bed before I could register his movement. His hand stretched forward. He muttered words of some protective enchantment too low for me to hear. A silky black barrier covered the phantom wall. Then it covered every phantom wall of the palace. A wind threw the armoire doors open. His frospit sword flew into one hand, bow and arrows into the other. There was another palace-shaking boom followed by yelling.

"Daphne, get behind me."

I did, pressing my forehead against his bare back and taking one last moment to enjoy his smoky scent before all hell broke loose.

"Pol, what's happening?"

"I was hoping you could tell me. Come with me."

Fiore and Fern were already on alert and opened the door before we could reach it. Fiore's eyes fell on me first.

"We're under attack," Fern said, pulling fingers down from his temple. Pol pushed my lower back forward.

"Come. Stay close." I followed behind Pol as we marched down the hall. Fiore and Fern flanked me on either side. The dim, lightning-lit ceiling stirred and flickered off Pol's broad, pale shoulders. I took a chance at creating armor to cover him. It was a vest of golden-colored

Kevlar with sharp shoulders and sapphire buttons to protect him. He stopped at the base of the stairs to look at it. Then he turned to me. I was looking over my satin nightshirt and shorts. I had just started to turn them into armor, but Pol grabbed my wrist to stop me.

"Fern is going to take you to the RIP room. There's a bunker. It's the safest place to be," Pol said. Fern reached out a hand. Fiore gave me a sorry look.

"The fuck he is. I'm not going anywhere but—"

"I'm sorry. I can't lose you," he said and nodded at Fern. Before I could say another word, he and Fiore were jogging up the stairs. Fern grabbed my arm and tugged me up the stairs. It was pointless tugging. I was charging up them quickly.

"Pol!" I screamed. *Did this man really just order me to be locked in a tower?* What was the point of the training if he wouldn't let me fight?

Near the front entrance, Pol was nowhere to be seen. "Pol!" I yelled for him, no one paying me any mind. Lines of guards and warriors ran to their stations. I could hear Queen Madgee calling orders. Finally, she came into view, hurrying down the stairs. Her eyes met mine.

"Queen! Your Majesty!" I tugged my arm from Fern's grip and ran up the stairs to her. "Let me fight. Pol is out there. Let me—"

"You'll go with Fern," she said in a brisk trot past me. She kept hurrying down the stairs, ignoring my slack mouth. Clearly, this was pre-decided in a meeting *I* wasn't invited to. Fern grabbed me around the waist this time. Another boom rocked the palace, lighting a fire under his ass.

"Stop…kicking," Fern demanded as he hauled me up the stairs to the RIP floor.

"Let me go. I can fight!"

Fern planted my feet on the ground, pinning my arms at my side. He looked into my eyes. He was a brawny, older man with salt and pepper stubble on his tanned face, cool undertones, and eyes of purple labradorite.

"Yeah? You can fight, can you? After just two weeks, you're a seasoned warrior?" he interrogated like an angry father. He shook me as he yelled, and I cried. "You can protect your prince from death itself, huh? Did you stop to think that your sacrifice in a *battle* could cost us a *war*? You have much to learn, and Pol is in more danger trying to protect you now than he would be when you're ready." He hauled me on his shoulders and carried me like a useless sack of potatoes down the hall. "Hate him for it now. This is bigger than you, princess."

From his shoulders, I could see through the tall front windows that the predawn sky was now orange. But it wasn't the sun glowing yet. It was the wielding of embercudgels as fiery as the day they were caught. Light snaked across the windows left to right and then right to left.

We made it to the ice-covered doors of the RIP rooms. Before Fern could open them, a small embercudgel busted through the front wall, shattering a window. It flung across the space and into his side. The weapon knocked the wind from him. I was thrown from his shoulders. Several soldiers posted in the hall drew frospits. Fern made his way to his feet, gasping for air. His dented armor was charred and smoldering where he was hit. The broken wall was a misty mess, clouds escaping and smoke swimming up.

"Get in the room, Daphne! There's a trap door under the main desk. I'll be there soon," he gasped. Blood dripped from his lip, sweat from his brow. He drew a frospit and yelled at me angrily, "Now!" I scrambled to my feet, tears filling my eyes again. I pulled on the door. It was locked.

"I can't open it!" I tried to yell. The words were muffled by the sound of more walls breaking. Enemy soldiers soared toward us on clouds. The battle broke out in the RIP hall. Beyond the broken walls, the battle raged. It looked like a gruesome night-time version of Michelangelo's *The Last Judgment* come to life.

Pixies on both sides flew with incredible agility and ripped their fangs into the necks of their enemies. What were once stunning diamond-like paved teeth were now blood-soaked fangs. I could hardly pull my eyes away.

But Fern's frospit clattered in battle and rang like tuning forks. I snapped out of it and pulled the door hard again. I used what magic I could to try and unlock it. No luck. Blood spatter dripped down the face of the icy white cameo carved on the door. It was like the face was crying blood— *A bad omen.* War cries and blood and the smell of sweat all carried through the air.

I screamed with another loud boom. It shook the ground from under me, and my knees buckled. Fern turned and saw me struggling with the door. He reached his hand forward. With his magic, the door flew open. Tugging when it finally gave way, I fell on my still-sore ass. The soreness only reminded me of Pol. Panic clawed at my belly with worry. I made my way to my knees to crawl into the RIP rooms reluctantly.

Before I could close the door, I saw the enemy soldier. He kicked Fern's feet from under him, sending him flat on his back. He raised a frospit for a stab. I gasped and motioned for him, but Fern rolled swiftly. The bloody blade pierced the white floor instead.

Three of our soldiers in the hall were down. Fern was outnumbered. He sliced his sword through a man's neck. Arterial blood squirted in pulses. Partially severed ligaments struggled to keep the man's head from completely falling off. The man's knees hit the floor. His severed trachea bubbled as air escaped. Then, all at once, the blood turned to ice, the color like a rose petal in a snowstorm.

Fern turned quickly. The man's blood could only spray his shoulder before freezing. Fern's frospit cut through the air. Spinning, he pierced the gut of another. The blade found the man's abdominal aorta. Bright red blood sprayed out. Then, the man's eyes turned to lifeless stones. The blood spraying from the wound froze in crimson spikes, jutting out from his core. The blood in his veins froze too, causing his body to freeze in his death pose. Fern cut another through their heart, killing them before the freezing blood could. Four more enemies flew in on their clouds or with their wings. I knew if I shut that door, Fern would die.

I swung the door open. I heated the embercudgel that had struck him until it burned molten-hot, Then I moved it like a torpedo toward his attackers. In one strike, I hit three heads. It decapitated them and crushed their skulls into bone and meat. The heat of the weapon cauterized the smaller vessels in what was left of their necks. The smell of burning flesh and fresh sulfur turned my stomach. All that remained of the men's necks when their bodies hit the floor were mangled cervical bones, frayed ligaments and tendons, limp slabs of shredded muscle, and holes where their trachea and esophagus once functioned to sustain their lives.

I pulled the embercudgel back. It broke a new enemy's leg. He fell at least nine feet from his cloud, landing on his head. His neck snapped with a loud crunch. Fern and the other soldiers had finished off the rest of their attackers in the hall by the time my opponent's boot hit the floor. Like a scorpion, his back folded, the boot landed near his head. Through it all, I felt nothing.

Fern turned to me. Anger almost masked how impressed he truly was. "Get in the rooms," he repeated, calmer than before and now ready to accompany me. And I had every intention of listening to Fern, until I saw Pol over his shoulder through the smoke of the broken wall. He was getting slammed in the chest with an embercudgel. I mounted the cloud of a dead enemy and took off toward him expertly.

"Daphne! No!" Fern yelled furiously. He limped and climbed a cloud to chase me, but I was already outside. I watched the slaughter in awe. Even in the ebbing darkness, the scope of the battle looked like swarms of angry hornets around Loanan. In the distance, I saw Chloe leading a blood bath with a blood-curdling battle cry. Cynti was nowhere in sight. I scanned the area where I saw Pol get thrown. I found his unmistakable form lying limp.

"Pol!" I yelled, moving the nimbus at breakneck speed. My shorts and top provided no warmth. I shivered when I approached him. Pol lay obtunded in a bed of water hyacinths, propped on the palace wall, his chest steaming. The sound of stridor scratched through his throat.

"Daphne!" Fern yelled again, moving to my side.

"Fern! Please help him! Please!" I shrieked.

Fern hurried to Pol's side. He placed a hand over his heart and created tiny amethysts in the shape of his handprint. The amethyst handprint on his golden vest was for function only. The brute was not the intricate jeweler that Pol was.

I cupped pure oxygen into Pol's mouth, forcing it into his lungs. His eyes, dazed and glassy, looked up at me. They widened in fear as they focused. He roused rapidly. He grabbed my arms and threw me down, hauling his body on top of me. His breath screeched and hitched as he panted. An embercudgel crashed into the wall where he was moments before. Chunks of the wall pelted the side of our faces.

"Goddamn it, Daphne," Pol said in a wheezing voice, gripping my hair. He rolled over to find Fern.

Standing over us, in hand-to-hand battle, Fern was squeezing his attacker's neck. His fingers snapped tendons and cartilage in audible popping. The man's eyes were bulged and bloodshot around blue topez irises.

Pol grabbed his frospit and pierced it through the gut of an enemy coming up behind Fern. I grabbed Fern's fallen frospit and sliced it through the torso of another. His top half slid off his bottom like carved salami. As his bottom half hit the ground, yards of tangled intestines spilled out. Some were sliced through, releasing the stench of feces. Through it all… I felt nothing.

I threw the frospit handle first to Fern and gave him a look of no regrets. Pol picked up his bow and arrow for himself and handed me his own frospit.

"Please. Get to the RIP rooms!" he pleaded, shaking his head slowly. His chest still smoldered, his breathing still hoarse.

I mounted a cloud, turning it into the icy cumulus I preferred. I barely waited for Fern before taking off for the *fucking* RIP rooms. I was happy to fight on the way and was clearly able. Chloe would be proud. As I ascended high on my silver cloud, the sun began to peak over the horizon. It glinted off my borrowed sword as I held it in a defensive stance.

But an aura chilled my back and wrapped around my waist. No, not an aura. It was a mist, and then arms around me. I was immobilized in someone's arms, a short sickle of a frospit wedged at my throat. It drew blood that froze as it traveled down my neck, not cutting deep enough to freeze my body.

"Ah, Princess. It's so nice to see you again. Now, drop your weapon, please," the man said in a buttery Spanish accent. His fruity scent was overpowering. I dropped the sword. Fern stopped, frozen in front of us. Chloe, painted in crimson blood and amethyst eyes glimmering in a glare, arrived next to him. They gripped a frospit in each hand tight enough to whiten their blood-soaked knuckles.

"Nahveel, let her go!" Chloe commanded.

"I don't think so. She'll be of much use to us," he responded with a laugh. Mynt and Promise flanked him. Mynt wiped the blood from her mouth. One of her wings was punctured through and smoldering. It didn't stop the strength of her flight. She smiled, unleashing her fangs, ready to tear Nahveel to shreds.

Nahveel laughed. I felt his skin turn to mist, and I knew he was taking me. My skin chilled and began to dissolve, too. My sight was a fizzy haze of Fern and Chloe. But before he could mist another cell away, an arrow shot through his chest. It nearly pinned my arm to him. He stumbled back. His arms loosened just enough for me to mist on my own without carrying him.

I had never tried misting before. It was a complicated maneuver that I had only read about. Even so, I was able to do it. The problem was I hadn't chosen a destination until the last minute.

26

DAPHNE: TOUCH ME OUT OF ANGER

IMAGINE THE MOST PEACEFUL PLACE YOU CAN THINK OF, I REMEMBERED Dr. Bailey telling me during sessions. And so I did. I went to a cloud in the sky. Not just anywhere in the sky but the place Pol had hushed me at sunset the night I first came to Loanan. When my body came back together, I was falling through a cold rain cloud in the Regnum Solo and tumbling toward the ocean. The clouds barely rinsed me, dampening my hair to a matted frizz and moistening the grime on my cheek. The rising sun painted warm amber on my skin and on the ocean that I fell toward.

I formed a cloud and fell through it. I formed another farther down and landed hard. It knocked the wind out of me. I realized the error in making it stationary. I screamed in pain. Cupping my shoulder, certain it was dislocated, I rolled over. I gasped, struggling to regain my breath.

I was cut up. The cloud soaked up my blood like a red snow cone. I didn't know how to get back to Loanan. I lay there for a short time, panting and exhausted and groaning in pain. With my pathetic cirrus cloud shrinking, I knew I'd be in the ocean soon. I debated if I should lower myself, risk drowning, and swim a quarter mile to shore, or push myself to find the portal to Loanan before the cloud gave out and I fell to my death. I couldn't even think about leaving Pol behind. I had already been gone for too long now.

I looked toward a quick motion in the distance. It was gone before I could focus my sight. In the next breath, someone had misted behind me again. I yelped. I spun around, fear coursing through me that I was in Nahveel's clutches again.

"Daphne! Are you okay?" Pol asked, pulling me into his arms. I winced and whimpered as his embrace squeezed my injured shoulder.

"I had a hard fall," I said, hardly able to keep my cirrus cloud whole. He replenished the cloud with what little magic he had left in him. Now, on a tiny cumulus, he moved us to the portal of Loanan. His breathing was still strained. I cupped air over his mouth.

"Save your energy; I'm fine," he said before opening the portal. As soon as we stood on Loanan land, I gave up on the cloud, and we landed on the misty ground.

I nearly fell to my knees, but Pol caught me. He wheezed as he carried me under his arm like a limp doll toward the gates of the palace, or what was left of them. My feet dragged on the ground all the way to the iron gate.

The bars were mangled and bent. Beyond the gates, the palace steamed white where the cloudy cinder blocks were smashed. Around the palace the city bustled in chaos. Caelumans of all kinds hurried around. Some homes were left unscathed; some were destroyed. Inside the mangled iron gates a new kind of chaos ensued. The enemies were gone and our forces were regrouping frantically.

"What happened?" I asked.

"Cumbre attacked… It looks like you were…their main target… I shot Nahveel. I doubt he'll…survive it. They retreated…not long after that," Pol said through wheezes.

"Pol!" I heard Fern yell. He and his new companion "Doc"—a fitting name for a healing warrior—ran to us. Pol propped me in Fern's arms. Doc supported Pol as we limped toward the palace's doorstep. When we finally made it there, Fiore rose to his feet with urgency and stole me from Fern's arms. His bloodstone eyes looked at me with sorrow again, and he handled me gently. His tanned olive skin and peppery goatee were drenched with sweat. Pol and I were guided to a seat on the doorstep, and the three tended to us.

"Where's Uripe?" I asked, panicking. I needed to tell him immediately.

"He held the library just fine. I wouldn't worry about him. He's a tough old shit," Doc said while unbuttoning Pol's vest to examine his injuries. "He took out a pack of those Cumbre shits with hardly a scrape to him."

"And Mynt?

She's getting her wing tended to. Tough cookie too, that Mynt. She'll be fine," Doc said.

"And Cynti? Where is she?" Pol asked, scanning the ground for his twin. No one answered, but troubled looks were exchanged.

"Prince Pol. We'll be meeting in twenty minutes in the war room. Your mother is expecting you," Fenk interrupted from behind us. Queen Madgee followed behind him, both of them sporting scratches and torn clothing.

"Where is Cynti, mother?" Pol demanded of the Queen, batting Doc's hands away from his wounds.

"We're looking—"

Just then, a shriek clawed through the air by the west wall. We all looked. Cynti had Misted in. Chloe caught her in their arms as she fell, bloody and beaten. Her eyes were swollen shut, and her lip was split deep. Her night clothes were torn. Her knuckles looked like raw meat beaten with the pointy end of a tenderizing mallet. A fingernail was dangling from the flesh, and blood dripped from it like a leaky faucet as a broken frospit slid from her grip.

Chloe grabbed at her face and rubbed her temples with their thumbs as they held Cynti up. They crooned to her with reassurance. Tears left clean tracks down Chloe's bloody face as they yelled ferociously for the healers to tend to her. There was no mistaking the emotion Chloe was showing, even for those who couldn't do empathing at all. This was the display of fear and grieving for a lover. "Why didn't you stay in your room like I told you," Chloe could be heard saying. They yelled again for the healers to come.

The queen's lip curled at their commotion, and she cut her way through the crowd.

"We'll take it from here, Chloe. Be in the war room in twenty," Queen Madgee commanded coldly. When the healers carried Cynti off, her hand clutched Chloe's until the last finger slipped from reach, blood sliding their hands easily away. The dangling fingernail finally fell to the ground. The Queen ignored the sentiment and followed the healers. Chloe, knees buried in trampled hyacinths, stared helplessly at Cynti's limp body as she dripped a trail of blood on its way to the infirmary.

Pol, horrified by his sister's state, lunged forward with a wheeze to go to her. Doc and Fiore held him back by his bruised chest with great effort and kept him seated for care. He wrestled out of their hold and settled, panting angrily. Chloe's eyes turned to him, and they rose, walking to us.

But before Chloe could speak, Fenk stepped down the stairway. He blocked Chloe's path to us and opened the path for them to go inside the palace instead. His face boasted a familiar disgust as he nodded for them to continue into the palace. Pol's hands clenched.

"Fuck…" he muttered under his breath. Chloe walked past Fenk and into the palace. Fenk turned to me.

"The way you bridged that vase so seamlessly, without *any* training at all, did seem very unlikely. It sure didn't fool me," he said before turning his bird-like face to the palace entrance and walking away. His long eagle wing shoulder blades dragged on the floor.

"Yeah…" I said to Pol.

Mynt fluttered to me and waited for Fiore to be done doing what minimal healing magic his sausage-like fingers could manage.

"You fight like your father. He would be proud," Fiore said before leaving me in my room in Falece and Mynt's care. He left to secure the area. I didn't quite have the energy to ask what he knew about my father.

Falece drew a bath of epsom salt and rosemary while Pol attended the debrief. Mynt joined me in the large tub. We sat in silence for a bit.

"Do you think Cynti will be alright?" I asked her, splashing water on my face.

"She…" Mynt hesitated. "It was three on one until Promise got there. She killed them all, but…"

"They can heal her, can't they?"

"I'm not a healer, Daphne. I know they will try their best." She spun her hands and moved the water into a slow whirlpool. It felt nice, and I sank into the water, my mind dwelling on Cynti.

"What happened to your wing?"

"I saved Promise from an embercudgel. It broke apart, and a piece hit me," she said, turning and fluttering her purple dragonfly wings. I touched the patched wing with my finger gently. It was healing already.

"Saved him, huh?" I laughed. With a swift flap of her wings, Mynt sent water splashing into my face and laughed, too. "Don't even start."

We stayed in the room, Mynt, Falece, and me. When we were done with a bath, we curled up by the fire. Pol pleaded with me to stay in the room, guarded, and after almost being kidnapped by the enemy prince, I listened. Not that I had the energy to do anything else on no sleep and no food.

Six new guards were stationed around the room, Fern not among them this time. Guilt pulled at me as I wondered if I got him in trouble. Fiore was still guarding me though, watching me through a crack in the door. I asked him to send for Uripe as soon as he was available.

"Fiore was a young soldier of low ranks in Volare during the first of Ouran's conquests, you know? When the kingdom fell, he was ordered by your father to bring word to Loanan," Falece told me as she brushed my hair. "Here, he pledged loyalty to Queen Madgee in hopes of avenging Volare one day. I heard that your father and Fiore were like brothers. They grew up together." Now it made sense how protective he always was of me when his priority should have been Pol.

A knock rapped at the door. Fiore let Uripe in.

"Guys, I need a moment alone with Uripe," I said. Mynt nodded, swaying her sparkling afro. Falece followed her out. Uripe was in perfect health, aside from a few bumps and bruises. I embraced him with a one-armed hug, my other arm in a sling that Falece and Mynt helped me throw together. I sobbed.

"I'm so glad you're okay." I didn't realize how relieved I would be to see him safe. He patted my back with his frail brown hands and pulled away to motion for the seats by the fire.

"I'm happy to see you're okay too. What is it that's so urgent?"

I looked at the cracked door, Fiore indiscreetly watching us, and decided to use my best signing to avoid anyone hearing. It wasn't perfect, but Uripe understood. I walked to the phantom wall, now free of the silky black barrier, and pointed to where each feeling was coming from and signed them.

"I felt the attack before it happened," I told him in a whisper. My voice picked up in pitch as I continued, "I woke Pol. I was certain."

Uripe pressed a finger to his lips to tell me to keep my voice low. *When did this start?* he signed.

"I can feel Pol. He doesn't show a lot of emotion or use a lot of body language but…before I came to Loanan…I thought it was just instinct. Then I thought it was just…" I signed whatever I knew how to sign as I spoke and kept my voice low. *The bond.* "But he doesn't seem to read me the same way I can him."

"Intuition is something almost all living beings have. Some stronger than others. This sounds like more than that. You need to train immediately. This can have detrimental psychological effects on you as it gets stronger," he said quietly while signing. "Tell no one. I'll handle the proper notifications when you're able to use this in a way that protects you."

The door opened, and Pol walked through, still dirty from the fight. He closed the door on Fiore's watchful eye.

"Well?" I asked.

"They're gone. Pulled back for now. They're probably crossing through Atlantica with help from rebel oceaman, revising the plan and building back up their forces. It's not over. The war has started. We think there will be an attack on the east coast in a matter of weeks, and they will be determined to take you. We need all hands on deck to patrol. We are contacting our allies. We'll have more instructions from Chloe when they're…better."

"And Cynti?"

"I don't know."

"I have to warn Odie. I have to get my parents and Polpette. They need to evacuate. Who knows what Ouran is planning. And I need to talk to the nurses."

Uripe looked at me with urgency and disapproval. Pol just looked at me like he was waiting for the punchline.

"I'll be gone for less than 24 hours. They're gone, and even if I'm not back in time, they have no reason to think I'd be in the Regnum Solo. I'm safe, and I've *more* than proven I can fight for myself."

"You're not going anywhere," Pol stated.

"Pol, I'm going, and so help me, if you ever try to lock me away again, I will *never* forgive you," I spat with venom, leaning in to meet his eyes.

Pol's eyes ignited with challenge. Silence hung in the air, tension sizzling between us. Uripe excused himself, giving me a pleading look before stepping out. The door clicked shut, and breaths passed before either of us spoke.

"Did I ever actually have a choice, or was that all for show?" I asked. Pol just stared at me for a long moment.

"I *won't* lose you, Daphne. You belong with me."

"You promised me."

"That was before Prince Nahveel tried to kidnap you and slaughter half our kingdom! I can't leave here right now, and I can't leave you alone down there!"

"I'm leaving. You said you'd never take my choice. Keep your promise, and I will keep mine."

"My mother, *the Queen*, will kill us both for it."

"Your mother is too busy struggling with her homophobia and mangled heir to even notice. It's *one* day! They're gone, Pol. This is the only chance I have to protect my family, my best friend. It's my only chance to salvage whatever the fuck is happening with those nurses," I whisper-shouted at him.

Pol turned, and his fist crashed into the bookcase, splintering the wood. "They'll notice me being gone! You can't leave!"

"Are you going to lock me up, Pol?"

He scrubbed his face, and then his jaw ticked. He spit venom in his words as he closed the space between us. "I *should,* shouldn't I? I should lock you up. I should chain you to the floor until you come to your senses." He leaned in, only an inch from my face. The phantom wall to my back, I had nowhere to retreat to. "I should keep you by my side where you belong. I should save you from yourself, from your own *stupidity*."

I raised my hand to shove at his chest, but he grabbed my wrists tight in one large hand, gripping my hair with the other and pulling until my face lifted to his. "But I'll take you myself." He forced a kiss on my angry lips. "And I'll come back when the sun is just under the horizon, and you will be there on time, or I will rip apart Miami looking for you and drag you back." He kissed me again with anger. I exhaled my relief. "Then you will come home with me, and I will never let you out of my sight again… you hardheaded…"—another kiss—"stubborn…"—another—"stupid little angel."

"I'll never leave you."

He shook his head. "If you *ever* leave me, I'll make sure it's the last time you do," he said. "You belong to me now." He released my hair, pushed my wrist from his fist, and formed a small stratus outside the phantom wall. My tears cooled my face in the breeze as I mounted it with him.

On the way down, we stopped above the ocean to watch the sunrise. It was oblivious to the carnage. "You fought well," he said as he surrounded me in warmth. "Let's go."

When we landed by the laurel tree, I coughed at the dust and dirt that kicked up. My power was too depleted to bother with an aura. I also had to reserve power in case I needed to fight. I decided I'd acclimate to the itchy air the old-fashioned way—by desensitizing myself to it. Yet, as the seconds passed, the urge to bathe scratched at my skin.

Pol placed a hand on my good shoulder. "Wait here," he said. I did. When he was done clearing every room, he helped me off of the stratus with more care than necessary. "Don't use your powers unless you're fighting."

"I know. Believe me, I don't have much left to waste."

"Comforting to know," he quipped. "Tonight. Be here," Pol said, inching closer. He brushed my hair from my face and grabbed the back of my neck tightly. He leaned down for a kiss. His tongue swept over mine, and I pulled at his bottom lip with my teeth before letting it go and smiling up at him.

"Don't let Fiore find out."

"I'll tell him you had bad fowl and are ill."

I laughed and kissed him again. "I'll count the minutes until I see you again, my dear. Trust me."

"Don't make me regret this," he said, tightening his grip on the back of my neck. "You come back to me tonight. That's not a request." He turned his opals to the sky, knowing he was expected back in the war room after a wash and breakfast. He held my hand as he mounted the stratus tiredly and kissed it before floating up. He looked down at me as he rose slowly. My heart skipped a beat.

MY PHONE CHIMED ENDLESSLY AS I POWERED IT ON IN MY CAR.

"Shhh…" I said, avoiding profanity even though the dirt curse was broken. I sighed heavily when I saw texts from Jesula and several nurses.

> Can you guys meet for lunch?

I texted Jesula.

> You're back late! Yes, we need to talk NOW. When and where?

She replied.

> 1:30 pm at Mac's Rooftop. You know the place?

I was hoping to get one last meal there before I left Miami forever.

I ran some errands and headed to my parents' next. They've never given me reason to think they knew about all of this. Perhaps my birth parents kept their true nature a secret like I had with Odie. I knew they wouldn't evacuate if I tried to make them, so I did the only logical thing I could think of—tapped into my savings account and bought them a month-long stay at an all-expense-paid resort in the Maldives. According to the textbook I barely finished, there were old allies in the Regna Oceanum in the North-Indian Ocean. It was the safest place I could think of.

"Happy early anniversary!"

"This is too much-ahh!" my dad said.

"It's perfect! When do we leave?" my mother said, covering Dad's mouth with her polished nails. I laughed.

"Tomorrow. I've arranged transport to the airport. They'll be here at 8 am. It was the only time slot left for the promotion they had going on. Is that okay?"

"Of course! Yes!" my mother cheered, her hands in the air. She turned to my dad. "See this? We raised a daughter well, and now she is able to send us to the Maldives!" Then she headed to her room to start packing, singing a butchered version of the pina colada song.

"I'm very proud of you. You've done well for yourself," my dad said, smiling and patting my shoulder with a rolled-up crossword puzzle from the day's paper. "I hope you're not spending it all on us now. You have to do something for yourself."

"Well, actually..." I hesitated, "I'm moving. More space...just a bit...north-ish."

"Oh, that's great!" my mom shouted from the other room as she packed her bags excitedly and hummed the rest of the song. My dad gave me an attentive look, waiting to hear more.

"I met someone. His name is Pol. He's very good to me. We'll be closer this way. I may not be around as much though."

Now my mother poked her head out of the room, curious humor scribbled across her face. My father had no such humor.

"Am I finally getting a nonno? Oh! Daphne, are you having a little bambino?" my mom squealed in a thick Italian accent.

"No! Mother, I am *not* having a bambino *any* time soon."

"You better not. I want to meet this one...this ...Paulo," my father fussed. I had never introduced them to a boyfriend before, so my father worked through new feelings for a moment.

"*Pol*. He'd love to meet you. When you get back, we'll visit sometime. But I have to go. I have to see Odie and head to work. Have fun!"

I kissed them both and hugged them tight. As my father walked me out, I checked the time. It was 11:30, and I was running out of time. How could I uproot my life in under twelve hours? Settle my duplex, my car, my utilities… My job?

One thing at a time.

"This Paulo…" my dad said with a waddle behind me to my car.

"*Pol*, Dad," I corrected with a laugh.

"Pol. Is-ah Pol responsible for this?" He moved his finger up and down, pointing at all of my injuries. "You show up, ah-sending us off, looking-ah like that. Your car seems fine. What was it?"

"Pol would *never* touch me out of anger, Dad," I said in a very serious tone. "I'm clumsy. You know that very well."

He raised his brows and nodded in agreement. Still, he looked less than happy with the answer.

"I had a few too many drinks with some friends at Harvard to celebrate the end of the course. Please don't tell Mom." I winced in fake embarrassment. His groan told me it worked. He playfully smacked the back of my head and threw his arms up for a hug. "Have fun, Dad. I love you guys so much."

"I love you too. And-ah you tell Paulo if he touches you-ah, I will cut off his fucking balls with ah rusty machete-yah."

27

O'DOHERTY: CRYING AT HER FEET?

"Good morning, beautiful," Fabian said in my ear before tracing my jaw with kisses. My eyes could hardly open. I didn't sleep well, worried about the creep who broke in and threatened us, worried about losing my job, worried about Daphne disappearing off the face of the earth with some stranger. But as I wrapped my arms around his neck, those worries were worlds away. I pulled him on top of me, settling him between my legs. He was unable to move his morning wood out of the way.

"I love you," I said, my eyes still closed. He stopped kissing my jaw and moved to my lips instead.

"Yeah?"

"Yes."

"Say it again; I like it."

"I love you." Then I leaned my lips toward his ears and smiled. "And I *want* you so bad."

Fabian wasted no time reaching down and pulling my shorts down my thighs. I lifted my legs to pull them off,

but he didn't mind them at the ankle. He ducked under them and caught the bend of my knees in the crook of his elbows as he leaned down again. He kissed me deeply. His cock was already pulled from his gray sweatpants by the time our lips touched.

"Let me grab some condoms," he said, not wanting to stop kissing me. He nudged his thick head at my entrance.

"I don't want anything between us. Is that okay?"

Fabian seemed to shrink into himself with excitement. He reached down to rub his cock along the entrance and wet it. He groaned at how soaked I was.

"Are you sure, honey?"

I kissed him deeper and tucked my hips to answer. He kissed me softly and pressed the tip in, stretching me. He moaned, and his breath quickened, pulling back just to push in a little deeper. He groaned again, burying his face in my neck as he slowly worked through the tight resistance of my pussy.

"All of it," I whimpered.

"I don't want to hurt you, honey," he said with a significant length of his girthy cock still waiting to work itself into me.

"It's okay, I like it," I breathed before kissing him deeply. I reached past my legs, still pinned up under his arms. Digging my fingertips into his hips, I pulled him closer. He hesitated for a moment, and I pulled harder. "Please."

With a long breath, he forced his entire length inside me. He settled his weight between my legs. I gasped and moaned as he filled me completely, pulling my lips apart.

"Oh fuck," he said. He kissed me so hard that the pillow bowed over my ears. "Are you okay?"

"Again. Please."

"It's going to hurt, honey."

"Please."

He withdrew halfway, and when he pushed back in, he tucked his hips up and rubbed himself against my clit. I moaned, wincing.

"Oh fuck. You like that baby?"

"ah huh," I said gasping. I clawed at his hips, pulling him forward for more. He fucked me slow and hard. My lips were pried apart by his fat cock, and he grinded against my clit harder. He pulled up my top and sucked my nipples. They stayed anchored in his mouth as my breasts jerked with his thrusts. I moaned for him. "More, baby. Don't stop. Please, don't stop." I could hear my soaked pussy getting worked into. He groaned with each thrust. I could feel my clit tingling, ready to send spasms through my core.

"Say my name," Fabian demanded.

"Fabian."

"Say it," he growled, with more force in his thrust. I yelped, and he groaned in pleasure.

"Fabian!"

"Again," he demanded until my head dipped back and the orgasm crashed through me. All I could do was moan his name over and over again. Fabian pounded into me even as my sore pussy convulsed, nearly pushing him out. His cock rode the wave of my walls, demanding to stay deep. I came on him until his balls dripped white.

He dropped my knees, my feet padding into the bed. Then he pushed my knees open wide, laying his weight on top of me. "Keep your legs open wide for me, honey." Fabian spent a long time fucking me slow and hard. He paused, still inside me, for a moment at a time to draw out his pleasure. It was clear he had waited long enough for this and was taking his time. "Tell me if you need a break," he said. Then he sucked my nipples harder as he took his pleasure from me.

Soon, my legs grew sore from spreading them, but I kept them wide, feeling another orgasm start. I came again, calling his name weakly. He buried his face in my neck and had to stop for a moment so my tightening pussy didn't make him cum. "Good girl, honey. Cum on my cock for me," he said as his hips stilled. He hissed through my orgasm, trying not to let the spasms of my pussy finish him. As my climax slowed and he worked his cock into me gently, I tried to nudge my knees together to ease the pain growing in my thighs, but he pushed them open in response. His hands tightly gripped my inner thighs and pressed them into the bed, groaning. I winced, and he eased himself out of his frenzy.

"You sore from opening your legs for me, honey?"

I nodded, still moaning. He groaned and picked up his pace, slamming into me harder and harder.

"Is your pussy sore from this cock?"

"Yes." My legs shook, and I whimpered at the pain.

"Let me cum in your pussy, and you can close them when I'm done."

"Okay, baby."

"Say it."

"Cum inside me."

Fabian pounded me hard again, moaning his pleasure with my words. "Say it again," he growled. "Come on, baby, you know what I want to hear."

"Cum in my pussy, Fabian. Fill me with your cum. Please"

"You like opening your legs for me, honey?"

"Yes, baby," I moaned louder.

He slowed and lengthened his strokes while his face was buried in my neck. Finally, he released my thighs from his hold.

"Keep your legs open." He scooped his hands under my shoulders and pulled me down onto him hard, pushing himself as deep as he could go. "Oh fuck! Take it." His large cock flexed hard. I called out for him loudly as he came inside me. He flooded me with warmth, thrusting his hips in satisfied jerks that shook my thighs. I felt the warmth leak past him and run down my ass. The sweat between us made his body slide against mine with each movement.

"Good girl… *Good* girl," he panted as he fucked himself into me on the last of his strokes. He pounded his cum into me deep. "God, I love you." He paused to catch his breath and sucked on my earlobe. "You took that so good." Still, inside me, he moved his hands softly to my outer thighs, pushed them up and together, and worked the last of his hardness into me slowly. He wrapped his arms around my legs so my calves hugged his neck. He closed his eyes as he gently worked his softening cock in and out and calmed his breathing. "Oh God, you took that so good. Ssss. Fuck, I love you." My face ran hot from the praise.

Now, even his calm, panting breaths caused his sweaty body to slide over the back of my thighs. He groaned tiredly, his cheek against my leg. I felt him soften completely inside me, and the hot cum leaked with my short giggle at the tickle of his breath on the back of my knee.

"Are you okay?" he asked, kissing my calf. Sweat pressed his curls to his forehead, and he wiped it away.

"I'm doing great."

"Did I hurt you?"

"You're fine. I promise," I laughed. He

pulled out of me, watching himself slide out with a half-smile. His thumbs kneaded at the back of my thighs to soothe them for a moment, and then he looked up at me with a lazy smile.

"How about some squash and eggs? I'm starving."

I laughed. "You're always so hungry after coming," I said. "I'd like that but maybe a few more minutes of cuddling? I need to recover." He dropped on the bed next to me and pulled me to him. I rested my head on his chest and pulled the covers over us for warmth.

Polpetta woke from her nap and trotted in. She chased the bumps in the sheets from our feet as we kicked them around playfully. "Oh no, it's the blanket monster, Polly!" Fabian joked. "Save us." We laughed at her playfulness. She had gotten quite chubby and needed the exercise. A loud knock at the door caused her to fly off the bed and sprint toward the noise.

"I'll get it," I said. I groaned at my sore legs as I pulled my shorts past my bottom. Fabian smiled with exaggerated pride, his hands tucked under his head. The shorts were too loose to stop his seed from dripping down my leg, so I grabbed a t-shirt from the ground and wiped it away as I hobbled out of the room toward the second round of loud knocking.

"I'm coming!" I called.

"Again?" Fabian asked jokingly.

I laughed and hurried to the door, but when I opened it my morning glow dulled. Standing there—gaunt, exhausted, and battered—Daphne looked back at me. She hurried in and hugged me. Her hair was tangled, face bruised with cuts and scrapes, and her arm was in a makeshift sling. She had dark circles under her eyes and looked like she had dropped ten pounds and had been forced into bloodletting.

"We have to talk," she said, passing me in the foyer and rushing into the kitchen. Polpetta barked and hopped at her heels, but Daphne only patted her on the head in passing. Rummaging through my cabinets, she finally found my medication, popped the lid off and headed for the garbage disposal. She poured my pills into the sink and flipped the water on.

"Hey! What are you doing?" I said, grabbing the bottle from her. As I reached over her, I knocked a wine glass into the sink, and it shattered. That didn't stop Daphne from trying to grab the tablets before I could get them. Scooping them up frantically, she cut herself on the glass. She didn't even seem to notice. I got the bottle and put the few tablets she hadn't gotten back in it. "What is your problem?"

She tried for the bottle again, her cut finger staining the inner rim before I pulled it from her reach. She gripped the pills from the sink too tightly for me to get them from her. Her blood had ruined them anyway.

"You can't take these, Odie! They're poison or placebos at best."

"What the hell are you talking about?"

"Odie, listen to me. Something bad is going to happen soon. You have to get out of town for a while. The west coast maybe. Just not the east coast and definitely not Europe. And *don't* trust Dr. Bailey."

"Daph…" I said softly, grabbing her arm and leaning to meet her eyes. "How long have you been off of your medication?"

"Almost three weeks, and I feel better than I ever have," she said with such strong conviction.

"Did Pol tell you to do that? It seems like since you've met him you've been having trouble taking them."

"Pol didn't *make* me do anything. He only wants what's best for me, and by the way, he was right about them being poisonous. Odie, you have to trust me. You can't take those. If it was having that effect on me, who knows what they're doing to you."

"Wow… um," I rubbed my temples to try and process what I was hearing. "And, what exactly was it…*doing* to you?"

"I can't…" She paused and shook her head. "You wouldn't believe me if I told you."

"We've been best friends since childhood. I'd like to think I can trust you."

Daphne rubbed her hand over her face and inhaled deeply before speaking. "Odie, Pol isn't human. His eyes even, you'll see them. He has opals for irises. *Real opals.* And he can ride on a nimbus cloud! Like fly to and from our realm to his. That's how he took me!"

"What…?"

"And *I* can, too. I can make a cloud now that I'm not taking the medication. It was stifling my power. But I'm stronger now. Not as strong as I'll be in maybe a few more weeks, but…it takes time to get out of your system, but I can ride on a cloud *too*."

"Daphne, you're not making any sense, and you are scaring me."

"I know how this sounds, I do. But there is a war coming, and I have to go back with Pol tonight to help. Take Fabian and—"

"What will Pol do if you don't?"

"What?"

"Will he hurt you? If you don't…*go* with him?" I gave her an obvious once over.

"No! This is… This is nothing," she assured.

"Daphne, he convinced you that your medication is poison, and every time you are with him you are all beat up. And you lied to me about being with him the last two weeks? This isn't you!"

"Jesus, Daphne!" Fabian exclaimed, having finally pulled on his sweatpants and come out to see what the commotion was. He hurried between us and held Daphne by the arms to evaluate her closer. I could see his heart beating out of his chest with anger.

"Who did this to you? Did Pol do this? Is he hitting you?" he said, clearly irate.

"No!" Daphne said, pulling from his grip. "We were attacked. And they are coming back and who knows what they have in store for Miami. You have to *leave!*"

Polpetta was now crying at her feet. "How did you hurt your shoulder?" I pressed. She sighed, pressing her fingers to the bridge of her nose.

"I fell…from the sky and…landed on a cloud too hard," she said exasperated. Then she laughed. Fabian's brows nearly hit the ceiling. He reached for her again to comfort her.

"Okay… Let's all calm down." He started rubbing the side of her arm.

"You think I'm crazy."

"No, Daph," Fabian whispered. He shook his head but wouldn't make eye contact.

"Show me. You said you have power now. Show me," I offered calmly, trying to help her see her own flawed reality. Fabian looked at me concerned, and then looked back at Daphne, dropping his arms to give her space.

She raised her hands and moved her fingers into odd positions. Nothing happened. Then her eyes focused on the deep gash from the broken glass. It was coated and laced with residue powder from the pills and bottle.

"Fffu— urg," she said, hurrying to rinse her hands, milking the cut to push out the powder. "I'm weak from the fight, and I haven't slept or eaten, and the medication is in my system now. It's not going to work. But you *have* to believe me."

Fabian and I stared at her for a long moment. Tears started welling in my eyes. Daphne pushed past Fabian and grabbed me by the shoulders. "*Tonight*. Meet me at my place. I have to leave with Pol, and we have to go on his nimbus; you'll see it. You'll see his eyes. They're *real* opals. *Trust* me," she insisted. "Then, once you see, you have to promise me you guys will get out of here. Please. Take Polly and Selene and get as far west as you can go."

I nodded my head as a tear fell from my eyes.

"Don't take your meds, Odie, and *don't* tell Dr. Bailey *anything*."

"Daph… I can't—"

"Doesn't it strike you as odd that you can get endless refills practically on demand? Odie, I think he's been messing with my mind. He did a relaxation session and I heard him saying something about clouds. He did something. I don't trust him." Fabian and I straightened. *Relaxation sessions?*

This was the only thing she said that actually sounded remotely coherent—not very, but still. I did have my doubts about Dr. Bailey, given what I found out just yesterday, and something tugged at me to actually trust this nonsense. I couldn't be sure.

"Okay, why don't you take a nap here and…I'll take you home tonight and…I'll meet…Pol," I said, stuttering.

"Yeah, I'd like to meet Pol too," Fabian said, jaw ticking. He leaned against the counter, cracking his knuckles, and then crossed his arms over his bare chest. Daphne hesitated to answer.

"I'll meet you guys there. I have to take care of a few things," she said before scratching Polly and running toward the door. I couldn't let her drive like this. We followed her to the foyer.

"Daphne, you look exhausted and beat up. Just rest a little. Fabian was just going to make breakf—"

"I have to take care of work. I'll get food there," she said, turning away. She ran for her car.

"Daphne!" Fabian tried, following behind me as we jogged to the driveway.

"Trust me, Odie!" she hollered, climbing into her M3. It was parked haphazardly on the curb. We chased her down the driveway to stop her, but I was too late. It all happened so fast. She peeled out and was down the street in no time. Fabian kept his sprint strong just a short way down the street before throwing his hands up and grabbing at his curls. His back flexed, the muscles dancing under the large scars on his back. Polpetta cried as she lay by my feet. We watched the street go vacant.

Fabian jogged barefoot back to me, blowing a breath out slowly.

"What do we do?" I asked.

"Honey, I…I don't have the first idea. What do you think?"

I was left to process what she said and hold on to nothing but hope until tonight. I turned for the door. Fabian wrapped an arm around my shoulder and kissed my forehead as we walked back inside. I replayed her words in my mind. *Relaxation techniques?*

28

DAPHNE: MY BROKEN WINDOW

"I'M SO SORRY I COULDN'T COME BACK FASTER; I HAD AN ACCIDENT toward the end of my trip. So, I spoke to my contacts at the union. He can see the spreadsheet. You guys have done wonderfully and should be good to launch authorization cards," I started, pulling out my laptop. I wouldn't start with the obvious elephant in the room. I let them bring it up, which they did quickly. The captive audience meetings, they said, scared many of the staff before they even started. I wasn't surprised or worried at all because, truthfully, it was a pretty standard reaction.

"I heard. Honestly, I've been waiting for that. So, let's prepare for what to expect!" We went over the common union-busting tactics, and they planned to prepare the staff. Eventually, the food came. This time, I tried their Extra Stout Irish Chili and was surprised that it was the most delicious thing I had eaten there. The nurses seemed calmer as they ate and joked and discussed the plans for battling futility amongst the staff.

My eyes wandered over the view of Miami in the distance and the patches of battered communities around it. I had never been there during the day and regretted not spending more time there. It was nearly 16:00 by the time everyone was done eating, and business talk was over. I ordered a round of prosecco to celebrate the progression, and Carla offered a toast.

"To Jesula, who has been our rock," she announced, and the entire table thrummed in agreement. Jesula, ever humble, just smiled and lifted her glass. A flock of birds flew over as our glasses clinked. I knew I would miss this, but I didn't know how much. For just a moment, I felt my nose sting with the threat of a cry, but I swallowed it back. I knew I'd have to come back and check on them.

After about an hour and one more round of drinks, people started to say their goodbyes. As usual, Jesula stayed behind to talk. I ordered a harder drink for us, locally sourced spice rum and tonic.

"You look like you had fun," she quipped.

I laughed tiredly. "Jesula, I have to go back. There's a war coming. It's bad."

"Should I be worried?"

"Yes and no. I don't know what will happen, but *Amett Health* seems to be in with the enemy. None of their facilities or their affiliates have been hit.'

"Now that you mention it, not many employees have been affected either."

I furrowed my brows and had a realization. It wasn't just a protection of their partner's assets and workforce. Nahveel and his men must have been hiding in one of the facilities for *Amett, Heartly,* or *Parsons & Dodds*. It would be somewhere with low traffic, where lower-level workers and clients didn't necessarily *need* to be. I could do nothing with this information now, but I'd make sure to tell Pol immediately so their intelligence could scout out for any troops or plans left behind.

"Hey, are you okay?"

"Yeah." I tried to say it convincingly.

"So where does this leave us with the union?"

"I'm going to call my mentor. I'll make sure you guys are covered and stop in when I can."

"And what am I to tell the others?"

"That I'm injured. It's not a lie."

I had her stay while I called my mentor over video chat. I formally introduced them. They got along well; I knew they would.

"Well, I'm really calling because I need to take medical leave. As you can see, I'm pretty beat up, and I'll need surgery on my shoulder."

"This is terrible timing. Can you work from home?"

"I'll be as involved as I can, but we need a primary organizer to step in," I offered. I planned on resigning, but I couldn't bring myself to do it yet. "I'll have more information on my condition in a few weeks.

"Okay. I'll get Adrian down there immediately. You can debrief her in the morning."

Relief washed over me when I heard the name.

"Adrian is the best choice. She is bold and fierce and has been organizing since the '80s. She taught me a lot as a 'baby organizer,'" I assured Jesula. "If anyone in the union could square up to a fickle priss like Lyndie Pratt—and have the press list turned to premium—it will be Adrian."

I turned my attention back to my mentor. "Tonight would be better, though," I pressed. "As soon as possible."

"I can fill her in better than anyone, child," Jesula chimed in. I smiled. She was born for this. And she was right. She was the embodiment of *The Workers Are the Union.* We wrapped up the meeting, and when done, Jesula and I sat for a long moment. Then I looked at the time.

"Shhhoot. It's already half past five. I have to head home," I said, seeing the sky dim.

"Stay safe. I'll see you soon," Jesula replied with a hug.

Before I let her out of the embrace, I whispered, "I learned about mermaids, by the way."

"I know! I was there when I told you about them in the first place," she quipped. I laughed and headed down to drive home.

WITH FOOD IN MY STOMACH, I WAS FEELING A LITTLE STRONGER. Against Pol's orders, I used some power on the way home. It was the last of what I could do on no sleep, but the atmosphere made my skin crawl, and I had been scratching myself raw without an aura. I could only manage the emanation for a half hour, but it was better than ripping off my bra after a long day. When the aura sputtered out, I sighed.

I got to my place and was surprised to see that Odie's car was already there. I was going to miss her, but I was thrilled for her to finally meet Pol. Hopefully, she brought Polpetta with her. I was juggling the idea of bringing Polly with me. I smiled at the thought of her chasing cloud animals I would form for her and shitting in Fenk's slippers.

Once I was in the garage, I got out and admired my M3, knowing I'd have to give her up too. I wondered for a moment how much magic it would take to airlift her to Loanan on a cumulus. I knew it would be more than the sparse amount I had left. I tried my luck with a cloud under the wheels and tried to move it up. I couldn't manage anything more than a faint fog that danced around the tires for a few seconds before disappearing. I tried again, but nothing happened, and I felt dizzy. *It was worth a shot.* I turned for the door and walked in to see Odie and Fabian at the kitchen table. She got up, looking wary.

"So…where is he?" she asked. "This sky man…"

"He'll be here soon enough," I smiled.

"And where exactly is he taking you?"

"Loanan. It's not far. Just off the coast of Miami, right before the stratosphere. There's a portal, so you can't see it," I explained calmly, knowing she would believe me soon.

"And you get there, how?"

"His nimbus cloud. Or my own cumulus," I answered.

"So, you hurt your arm and face falling from Loanan onto a *nimbus*?" She pressed her fingers to the bridge of her nose.

"Cirrus cloud… It's a long story, Odie. And I can't tell you everything."

"Just that all of Miami is in danger and possibly Europe too?"

Fabian looked as though he wanted to console her, and she looked as though she wanted to cry.

"Odie, I already told you this. Why are you asking me all these questions?" I pushed.

"We're just worried about you," Fabian answered when Odie couldn't manage to speak through her tight lips.

"I'm fine," I reassured.

"We called Dr. Bailey," Fabian said. Odie covered her mouth and started to cry.

"I'm so sorry, Daphne," she whined, pouting behind tears.

Then, two police officers and a medic walked from behind the foyer wall and through the kitchen entrance. My heart sank, and I backed toward the garage entry. One of the men reached out a hand, motioning for me to stay still.

"Hi, Daphne, I'm Officer Carter. We just want to talk and help you out, okay?"

"Odie, what did you do…?" I whispered with a shaky voice. She couldn't even look at me.

"Daphne, this is Christina; she's a paramedic. Can she take a look at you? You seem a bit beat up," the officer asked, one hand on his holster, the other making calm introductory motions to the medic.

"No. You don't have my permission to treat or touch me," I said robotically.

"Can you tell us, for *our* safety, where is the person who did that to you?"

"No one did this to me. I fell. I'm fine. I decline treatment. Please leave my property."

"Well, it looks like you're having some trouble making safe decisions, so I'd like to—"

I ran through the garage entry, slamming the door shut behind me. My palm pounded the garage door opener. I made my way to the car door, knowing the beast of a car could outrun any police officer. I swung it open, lunged in, and slammed the door shut. It was locked just in time for the officers to reach the door. The engine roared to life. Before the garage door could finish opening, I threw my car in reverse. With a bang, I folded the bottom of the garage door as I pulled out. It dropped from its tracks on one side, nearly taking out an officer.

The officers gave chase in their cruisers. I zipped through the streets, shifting through gears like I had done when Pol was in my car. My heart raced. I didn't know where to go. Where would Pol find me? I turned to the onramp. My tires skidded in an intersection on the way.

The police were already far behind. Determined to lose them, I downshifted and floored it again. I used the shoulder to pass other drivers. I upshifted and floored it once more, weaving aimlessly. Finally, I decided where I'd go—where I'd at least hide until I had the strength to use magic. I headed for *Northern Miami Hospital* and hurried toward the place where I had first met Pol.

I could see the small overpass for the irrigation canal. Smiling, I knew I was close. I was focused on the wooded area around the approaching canal. I didn't see the intersection or the truck coming at me. The truck slammed into my rear fender, sending my car rolling toward the canal. My car slammed on its roof, then its side, then its tires. It bounced and crunched and rolled until it was on its roof again and sliding toward the edge of the canal. Hanging upside down, my vision went red with blood. I slipped in and out of consciousness. I could see nothing but my hood rocking forward and back toward the dingy water at the bottom of the canal.

Then someone was reaching through my broken window. They held my shoulders as they reached for my seatbelt. It came undone, my body slamming down. The stranger pulled me from the window headfirst. I let out a cry of pain. The cry was muffled by the ringing in my ears. They dragged me through shards of broken glass and onto the hot, stiff, pricker-filled grass. I could see police lights racing toward us. Rallying the last of my strength to stand up, I ran toward the woods.

"Hey, wait!" my rescuer called after me. "Ma'am, hey! You need a medic!"

I need Pol. I need to get out of this grimy realm and get home. Pol trusted me. I wouldn't let him down. I ran from the sounds of police commands behind me. I was too dazed to hear their words, my ears still ringing. Then, all I could feel was excruciating pain, shooting through me and shaking my brain. It took my feet out from under me. I could barely speak. My chest and face thudded onto the itchy earth; my body frozen in an artificial seize.

I couldn't process the mess of all of their words, radio chatter, and sirens. All I knew was relief when the taser let up. I felt a pinch in my arm and got drowsy. The sounds of more radio chatter lulled me into darkness. For only a moment longer, I knew the feeling of stiff dead grass on my cheek and the nauseating feeling of being lifted from the ground. My vision went black.

29

DAPHNE: TOO LATE

THE FIRST THING I REMEMBER WAS MY STERNUM BEING RUBBED HARD with knuckles until my eyes flew open. I was blinded by light that strobed between ceiling tiles as I passed under them. Then I heard the words, "Responsive to noxious stimuli," being yelled over me in a matter-of-fact way. That memory was a fleeting few seconds.

The next thing I remembered was being stripped naked and bathed, half asleep, and then dressed in paper scrubs. My limbs were too heavy, and I groaned as they were flung about carelessly. Had I peed myself? This was also a fleeting few seconds, but it was just as humiliating as ever.

The last thing I could remember was the loud banging of the MRI machine as I was jammed into the tight hole while in four-point restraints. That was a longer and louder few seconds.

When I woke for the final time, I was in an emergency department room with cords, bags, and sharp objects stripped from the area. My eyes focused on a young girl in scrubs, sitting in a chair by the doorway, playing on her phone. She glanced up at my movement.

"Oh shit," she mumbled under her breath and turned to the hallway to call for someone. "Your patient is awake… yeah, *awake, awake.*"

A familiar face poked into the room. Dawn walked toward me and sat on the bed, looking solemn. The horrifying realization hit me; I was a Baker Act patient at the hospital I was organizing. Everything was going to fall apart. "Hey, girl. How are you feeling?"

"Dawn, what happened? Why am I here?" I asked with a dry throat.

"Well, you're on a seventy-two-hour psych hold and awaiting medical clearance."

"For *what*?" I asked, clearly upset.

"Apparently, you were off your medications and had a bad reaction. You've been in a state of psychosis and got yourself busted up pretty bad."

I couldn't debate this with Dawn. She was one of the leaders of the union efforts from ED, and I needed her to know I was coherent. "This is a misunderstanding. Have I had any visitors?"

"Your name is unlisted for safety. We were given reason to think you might be in danger. Without a passcode, we won't talk to anyone else about your care," she explained, wrapping a blood pressure cuff around my arm.

"Anyone *else*?"

"Your friend… O'doherty Sameal was listed as an emergency contact. Your parents are out of town and couldn't be reached," she said, pressing the start button on the monitor.

"My parents are out of town?" I asked, confused. The cuff inflated and squeezed my arm to a pinch. I cringed at the squeezing. She nodded. "Dawn, how long have I been out?"

"Almost twenty-four hours. You were brought in last night around

18:30 after a motor vehicle accident. I'm sorry to tell you… Your car is totaled. I know how much you lo—"

"No… Dawn, I need to get out of here now. I'm late."

Dawn sighed. "I'm sorry, Daphne. I really wish I could help with this one, but I can't."

She stood up and walked toward the door slowly, sorrow in every step. "The doctor will be in soon. It's shift change. I have to give report to the night shift."

I wanted to argue, but I knew exactly what position she was in and decided not to make this situation any worse.

There was nothing to do in that room but watch the time tick by, anxiously reminding myself that Pol had no idea where I was or how to get to me. I was told I was on bed rest and was ready to jump out of my skin with boredom. I was thankful that at least the curtain was drawn across the large glass sliders that made up the front wall of the room facing the nursing station so no one else could see me. Finally, Jesula and Dawn walked in the room together to do a formal bedside report.

Jesula, for the first time ever, looked defeated.

"Unlisted name… Daphne…is a thirty-year-old female with a history of depression and anxiety. No known allergies, full code, standard precautions, on day one of a seventy-two-hour psych hold, on one-on-one observation, unrestrained. Unlisted name in the system due to a patient safety concern." Dawn began her bedside report regretfully. "We are advised to alert security and the police immediately if a man that goes by 'Pol' shows up. If anyone calls, they must offer the code 0512 to get any information. She was admitted yesterday evening after a motor vehicle crash. According to her best friend, she had gone on a trip with unknown whereabouts for two weeks, presumably with the man named Pol, and returned injured and having severe hallucinations. She told her friend that she stopped taking her depression medication three weeks ago and that since then she…" Dawn looked at me and gave an apologetic nod. "She's been hallucinating about a man who rides a nimbus cloud. Pol allegedly convinced her that her meds are poison, and she no longer trusts her psychiatrist, Doctor Bailey. Dr. Bailey has been made aware and will be rounding tonight."

"No. I don't want to see him. Someone else, please," I requested.

"*Heartly* is the only group with privileges here," Dawn answered.

"I'll have my daughter see her," Jesula said. Her daughter was an ARNP here. Finally, I felt comfort and nodded at them.

"She had an x-ray of the head, neck, and chest showing a hairline fracture of her left clavicle and dislocation of her left shoulder joint. The MRI of the head and brain is consistent with both old head trauma and a new concussion. The patient's friend states this is consistent with her getting caught in a storm a few weeks ago. She states she had a head injury and never got treatment for it. Dr. Bailey's notes state this could have been the causative event that started the decline. Her serum levels for her medication were subtherapeutic. She has a twenty gauge in the right A/C. No fluids ordered. Now alert and oriented. She woke up knowing where she was but not the day."

Dawn went through the rest of my assessment and then moved on to the plan of care. "She's on hourly neuro checks until tomorrow morning. She has Dilaudid ordered for pain; available any time. We have standing orders for…" Another sorry look. "For Haldol, if she becomes combative or dangerous. And she is on an IV version of her home medication, Zerpotine…"

"No. I need that changed. I don't want that medication anymore. It's what got me here in the first place."

"We'll talk to the doctor about that," Jesula promised.

When they were done with the report, Jesula promised to come back around for an assessment and to go over the plan of care. I felt lucky that she, of all people, was floated. That was until she came back and explained during her assessment *why* she was my nurse.

"Lyndie knows you're here, and word is she's floating the leaders to the ED and making the charge assign them to you."

"She's doing this on purpose!" I growled.

"I know. We all know. She wants us to see you at your worst and lose trust in you," she said before sitting on the bed. What could refusing them as providers do but make me look like a non-compliant patient? I was stuck. "Daphne, I am so very sorry."

"What on earth for?"

"I shouldn't have played into this. I have my beliefs, and it got in the way of a real medical condition. I should have done more to help you. I made it worse. I even encouraged it."

"Jesula, no. You didn't. This is real. That's why I have to get out of here and find Pol."

"I know this is real to you, but this is a textbook noncompliance with your medication. I didn't know you were on it. Daphne, I don't think Pol is real, and if he is, he's a real jerk."

"*Don't* talk about him like that. That's *not* true."

"Hey." She leaned forward and grabbed me by the shoulders. She took a deep breath that cleansed us both. "We *need* you, dear. We have all risked a lot to get as far as we have, and we can't drive this home if everyone thinks we were led into it by a mad woman. I need you to snap out of this, Daphne. This is no joke. Please."

I trusted Jesula more than I trusted most people. I respected her more than I respected most people. The words hurt, but I'd at least play along. I'd at least work compliantly with the doctor and put on a show until the hold was up. Pol *was* real. The way I felt for him was real. I sat with her words in the dim room, scratching my itchy skin raw as if it were proof she was wrong.

After a short while, a woman with a thick fluff of golden, spiraling curls floating just above the shoulder, walked in wearing a white lab coat. Her skin was light brown with some loss of pigment in patches, likely from a skin condition called vitiligo. It reminded me of the Tonna Oleria shells I'd find on the beach as a girl. She moved fluidly as she came into the room and sat beside the bed. As she got closer, I saw the similarities to Jesula in her burlwood eyes and full lips.

"Hi, Daphne, I'm Sadie, the nurse practitioner tonight," she said in a melodic voice.

"You're Jesula's daughter?" I asked.

"I am! Yes."

"It's so nice to finally meet you. I don't think we ever got to work together," I said formally. For a moment, I forgot that I probably looked like a crazy woman.

"Do you mind if we have a talk?"

"Sure." I sat up and adjusted myself in bed, ready to play the best game.

"Can you tell me a little about what happened to you the last few weeks?"

"I wouldn't mind if it wasn't going in the chart. I work with these nurses, you know? It doesn't feel private at all when I have to continue a relationship with them."

"Okay, what if I agree not to put the details in the chart until you're discharged? They won't have access to your chart then."

"Unless I wind up back here. Then they have full access to my history."

"Okay. I'll meet you halfway. I'll vaguely describe only as needed."

I sighed. I wasn't going to tell anyone the whole truth anyway. But she left me with little excuse not to give her *something*. For the sake of getting out sooner, I did what I could. First, I glanced at the sitter. Sadie excused her and shut the door.

I sighed again. "A couple months ago I got caught in a storm. The tornado next door, remember? I ran into the woods to get to the irrigation canal and get low. When I was there, I met a man."

"Tell me about him."

"He was tall, light eyes that sparkled."

"Sparkled? You described them to your friend as opals. Is that right?"

"They often look like opals. Just the same as yours look like burlwood. There's a lot of dimension," I shrugged.

"And was this the man you saw on a cloud?"

"I'm not sure anymore. It's all a bit hazy."

Sadie tilted her head the other way, her eyes swimming with curiosity. "Did you hit your head that night?"

"Yes. The back of my head got hit by, ah… a branch or something. Knocked me down the canal. I took a tumble."

"And why didn't you get medical attention for that? This hospital is right across the street."

"They were slammed, and I was feeling better. I didn't want to waste resources."

"Where you were that night, is that near the old jewelry store?"

"Yes, just behind it."

"Did you walk by it on your way to your car?"

Memories of walking through the streets where the jewelry store was once intact skipped through my mind. Pieces of images, my shoes crunching glass into pavement, tripping over a rock, were all I saw. It was hard to remember clearly. "I can't really tell you much about how I got to my car. I remember walking through the woods and somehow making it to the intersection."

"I understand Pol gave you some unique pieces of jewelry. Any chance it came from *that* store?"

My eyes narrowed. "I don't know."

We recounted events that happened after that, including that my medication went missing and the loss of time when I got home. I told her *some* of what I overheard Lyndie Pratt say and how Pol was in her office.

"Is it true he left bruises on your neck?"

"He wasn't trying to hurt me; he was trying to hide me."

"Was anyone else there besides you and Lyndie and Pol?"

"The security guard that let me in. I don't remember seeing him when I left, though."

"The security guard that let you in. Odie says you used to be flirtatious with one of them. Is that him?"

I laughed and nodded.

"Could *he* have hurt your neck? Or... assaulted you? Perhaps taken your advances too seriously?"

I only stared at her. She went on to ask about meeting Fabian and how it made me feel for my close friend to be moving on.

"I'm happy for her, of course."

"Were you jealous of Fabian at all?"

"What?" I laughed. I met her eyes and realized what she was getting at. "Odie told you about us?"

"She did," Sadie said, nodding. I had enough of the leading questions.

"With all due respect, can you tell me what it is you're trying to get at here?"

Sadie cleared her throat, "Well, Daphne, you had a head injury, a near-death experience, a high-stress work project, and then faced the loss of a lover with whom you're very close. Mix that with stopping *that* medication cold turkey, and you have quite the recipe for a severe psychotic event. Given the paranoid displays, the soda can alarm system I believe O'doherty mentioned, it sounds very much like that." She folded her hands. "Sometimes our mind creates scenarios so we can cope with things out of our control. A man leaving you romantic gifts, a fictional person for whom you'll surrender control for, an escape from an impossible—"

"Are you telling me missing a couple pills gave me auditory, visual, and physical hallucinations? Do you realize how hard that is to believe? How far-fetched that is?"

Saide smacked her lips gently and took a calm breath. "Zerpotine inhibits dopamine production. Being on *that* dose for as long as you have been means you've built a dependency on it. Once you're off of it, your body will hyper-produce dopamine, *unchecked*. As your neuroreceptors and synapsis become flooded with it, it triggers neurons to fire inappropriately down different pathways, and the result is hearing, seeing, or even *feeling* stimuli that don't actually have a source, and it *can* be *very* vivid. It's similar to the theoretical pathophysiology of a patient with schizophrenia. For you, it's not just one area of the brain; it's all of it. So, yes. It's very likely that you had a full body experience that didn't—"

"Stop." I couldn't listen to it anymore. It sounded painfully true, and I felt panic rising in my chest. "You can't imagine how confusing it is for someone to tell me that the most amazing person I've ever met is a lie."

"I don't know if Pol is a lie. But I know that according to Dr. Bailey's notes when you do your sessions with him, and he tells you to imagine the most amazing place on earth, you imagine—"

"Myself in the clouds."

"I understand this was real *to you*. It was as real as the clipboard in my hand is to *me*. But I think we can both agree that a man riding a nimbus cloud sounds…"

"Far-fetched."

"There are a lot of parallels to this Pol man…and your life. I'd like to follow up with you in the office and talk more about that."

"Are you clearing me to go?"

"Ah!" Sadie laughed playfully. "No, ma'am! No. Ma'am! You aren't even medically cleared, nor are you therapeutic on your medication yet. We must ensure your symptoms are resolved and you are medically stable."

"I want to change medications," I insisted. She gave me a questioning glare. "I don't ever want to go through this again. Can you think of one reason why I should take this medication over a more standard one?"

"I'll tell you what. I'll look into it, and we'll make a plan tomorrow. Why don't you get some rest. Tomorrow you can tell me more about the last two weeks and what you think it means. "

As soon as Sadie left, I burst into tears. The sitter, now a young girl fresh out of CNA school, hurried to my side. "Are you okay? Do you want a tissue?" she said attentively.

"I just want to be alone." I lay down and turned my back to her. Sweetly, she left a cup of cold water and a box of tissues on my bedside table. She sat in the door frame, busying herself with a book.

My heart twisted in my chest as I came to grips with what Sadie had just suggested. I had to admit, the more I thought about it the more it made sense. I felt like I would be sick. I replayed every interaction and could see parallels to my life in almost all of them. Chloe and Cynti and the queen's homophobia. Were they real or reimaginings of Odie and me hiding our relationship from Selene and my parents? Did the security guard I teased all contract hurt me? Was Pol real at all, or was the only person I could ever submit to fake?

A new wave of sobs twisted my face like I had eaten an entire bag of Sour Patch Kids. The one-ply tissue tore at the skin under my nose, and my head throbbed. *Not Pol. He has to be real. Please, not Pol.*

As a figurative brick weighed down my stomach and stole my appetite, I heard a familiar noise. I stopped sobbing for a moment and propped my body on my elbows, turning my eyes to the door. The sound got closer, and my heart raced. My teeth clenched. Closer now, the clacking of Lyndie Pratt's heels came to my door, and I watched them approach through the glass that was exposed under the drawn curtain. And then there she was, stopped in the door frame in scrubs, heels, and a lab coat.

"Inessa, would you like to use the restroom and get a drink? I'll watch her for a moment," she offered to the sitter in a cheerful and sweet voice.

"Oh, thanks!" said the young tech, springing to her feet. Lyndie sat primly in the chair and looked at me with cold humor.

"What are you doing?" I asked.

"I'm a team player. I came in to help my work family! I'm a resource nurse until 12 AM. I'll be here for Inessa's lunch break too," Lyndie said in the most sickening customer service voice I had ever heard. "Do you need more tissues?"

"You can empty the commode," I quipped. "You can pretend to be part of the team all you want, Lyndie. It's too little too late. It won't stop anything from happening."

"No, you'll do that for me. Do you need some medication? You seem restless."

Later that night, Lyndie gave the sitter a lunch break, too, and never took her eyes off of me. Technically, this was what a sitter was supposed to do, but I saw *this* for what it was—intimidation and provocation. I wouldn't sleep well. Even after Lyndie left, my heart was crushed. The union efforts would fail; I totaled my prize possession; I blew $15,000 in savings, sending my parents on an insane panic vacation; my best friend had me locked away; and worst of all, Pol wasn't…

30

O'DOHERTY: OH. MY. GOD.

I felt horrible. I felt guilty. I felt ashamed. Even though I knew I did the right thing, things would never be the same between Daphne and me. Regardless, I had to face this head-on. I walked through the doors of the ED and gave them the privacy code for Daphne. A security guard walked me to the nursing station to check in with the nurse. Mayra, one of the leaders Daphne was working with, was floated from PCU to care for her under Lyndie's orders.

"Is it okay if I go see Daphne? Is she okay?"

"Ummm. If she'll have visitors, sure. She's been okay, just…sad. Not her normal self."

I nodded and headed into the room. Daphne was lying on her side in the dark, back to the door. The sitter was watching TikToks and laughing to herself.

"Knock, knock," I said coyly. I could see Daphne's back stiffen. She didn't turn to me. I looked at the sitter long enough to get her attention from her phone. "Privacy? I'm a nurse." The sitter shrugged and dragged her chair loudly against the floor until it was in the hall-

383

way. When I heard a viral TikTok audio coming from her phone, I decided she was distracted enough, and I could talk freely.

I sat next to Daphne's bed. "Daph, can we talk."

Daphne scratched her eyes with her fingertips and sat up, turning to me. I gasped at her condition. In addition to her sling, she now had bruises and gashes from head to toe. Tears welled in my eyes.

"I'm so sorry."

"You mentioned that," Daphne said flatly.

"Please. You have to understand."

"You sold me out. You got me locked up. And here, no less. *Here,* Odie, where I'm trying to do important work."

"I didn't have a say in where they took you. And if you recall, *you* drove straight here. Where else were they going to take you?"

"How could you call Dr. Bailey? I told you I *don't* trust him. He fucked with my head during sessions. I fucking *caught* him. If there's anything I know for a fact, it's that Dr. Bailey *can't* be trusted."

"Who else was I supposed to call?" I cried.

"No one! You could have just talked to me. Talked me down! Waited for Pol to show and confronted me with whatever came or didn't."

"Oh, yes. Let me wait for some violent man to show up. Daphne, do you not remember how you were?" I raised my voice now in defense. "Because I remember vividly. You were impossible to talk down. You were rambling on about nonsense. You were rambling about...about...opals and a nimbus!" I threw my hands up.

"I have lost everything because of you!" Venom laced her voice. I matched it.

"I did not send you here. I did not crash your car. You went missing for two weeks!"

"I wasn't missing! I just didn't tell you where I was going because

I knew you'd freak out! I should have lied to you again! I can't believe you did this to me, Odie!"

"Yeah, I would have freaked out if you told me you were going to some fantasy sky kingdom with an imaginary man! We were just trying to help."

"*We*? Who, you and *Fabian*? Where is he? It isn't often you're not up his ass."

"Oh fuck you, Daphne!" I screamed. Fury throttled through my veins, and I forgot myself in anger. "You're just mad because I'm not available for you to fuck anymore! All I ever wanted was you. I *loved* you! But I was nothing but a piece of ass for you, wasn't I? All you wanted was a good fuck, right? So excuse me if I find someone who treats me like I'm worth a damn! Find someone else's fucking face to sit on."

Daphne's mouth gaped open, and she was speechless, tears falling from her eyes. I can't say I didn't care, but it felt too good to get it off my chest. It had been knotted there for so long. I stood and started for the door but stopped in the doorway and turned to her once more. "And stop calling me Odie! You know I hate that! I'm not a *fucking* dog!"

When I walked out of the room, the Emergency Department was strangely quiet. An abnormally large group of nurses, respiratory therapists, and techs had congregated by the nursing station. They were focusing extra hard on the charts in their hands or EKG strips they were measuring. One nurse sipped water from a straw loudly with eyebrows raised high, and her chin pushed back low. The sitter, the least inconspicuous of them all, just stared straight ahead at nothing with her eyes wide and her mouth awkwardly tight.

"Show's over," I said, walking toward the exit. *Goddamn, do nurses love drama.* Daphne and I would be the unit gossip for weeks to follow.

I CRIED THE WHOLE WAY HOME. WHEN I GOT THERE, I CRIED EVEN more. I ate half a yam and pecan pie that Fabian made a few nights prior and binged *Love is Blind Sweden.* My phone pinged and an email popped up from Tonya.

> *O'doherty,*
>
> *I hope this email finds you well. As we discussed, the Merflec trial has been suspended, and an inquiry is being opened to discuss some of the outliers in the data collected. Please be in the office on Wednesday for a formal inquiry about the trial. Business attire is recommended. The meeting will be recorded for reference. Bring all notes relevant to the trial. In the event of severe weather, please take shelter and contact us when you are safe to reschedule.*
>
> *-Tonya Calilung*

Before I was done reading it, a text from Tonya popped up.

> I just sent an email. I know it sounds formal and scary, but don't worry. You're one of our best and I have your back. 😉

Tonya was always the cool boss with her colorful hair and fun glasses. I knew she meant what she wrote, but it didn't help the knot in my stomach. I dug a fork into the pecan pie and shoveled it into my face. Polpetta had the nerve to let out a sigh as if her life was so hard. I scratched her pudgy back, and she looked up at me.

"Your mommy's pretty pissed at me," I said through the congestion from crying. "I'm pretty pissed at her too." Polpetta tilted her head as if invested in the tea. "But just know that whatever happens between us, we both love *you* very much!" I poked her nose with "you." Polpetta let out a whimper and a small bark, stood up, and repositioned herself on my stomach.

I wrapped my arms around her warm, fat body and closed my eyes. She was the perfect snuggler, and my eyes were tired from hours of crying. Then keys rustled the lock of the front door, and before I knew it, Polpetta was springboarding off of me, jabbing my full stomach with her paws to jump. She flew through the air, landing a surprising distance away, before racing to the front door in a choir of happy barking.

"Hi, Polly Poll, baby *girl!*" Fabian said, crouching down to scoop her up. Polpetta looked like a stuffed animal in his hands and stared at me as if to say, "I'm his favorite." I laughed and pulled myself off the couch, sending an avalanche of pie crumbs tumbling from my lap to the floor. Fabian noticed my glassy, pink eyes, and his shoulders slumped, Polpette dropping with them. "Oh dear. I guess it didn't go too well with Daphne?"

My forehead wrinkled as a new wave of tears poured out. I shook my head 'no' and he promptly plopped Polpetta on the floor and wrapped his arms around me, swaying me and combing my hair back with his fingers to kiss my temple. Polpetta groaned her annoyance but then dulled her disappointment by eating the large crumbs and loose pecans on the floor.

"It's going to be alright, honey. You just have to try again. Give her some time. She's been through a lot," he crooned, wiping tears from my cheek.

"Daphne hates me. I'm going to get fired. Selene's out of town, so as per the norm, she won't even answer the phone when I need her, and…and…" I gasped three times in rapid succession as the cry overwhelmed me.

"You're *not* going to get fired. And if you do, then I'll take care of you and Polly," Fabian said. I wasn't sure if he was joking, but I couldn't imagine leaving work. I burrowed my face in his chest, and he rubbed circles on my back. "Why don't I heat you up some pie, huh?" he whispered playfully. I *uncovered* my face and looked at him with guilty eyes. It took only a moment for him to spot a piece of candied pecan stuck in my curls. He picked it out and looked over my shoulder at the nearly devoured pan that Polpetta was now snout deep in. *"Okay.* Well, why don't I make you some hot ginger tea?" he tried again with the same loving smile.

"Can we order pizza?" I asked, sucking in three breaths again as the tears dried. Fabian picked me up and carried me to the couch. He wrapped his arms around me. I lay my head on his chest, listening to his perfect heartbeat. His laugh sounded so much deeper when my ear was pressed against his chest. I forgot all of my sorrows as I listened to him through his chest wall, ordering the pizza and baby-talking Polly.

He treated her like a whole child, and I couldn't help but think he really meant it, that he would take care of us. *He would be a good father,* I thought silently.

"You're going to be an amazing dad one day," I thought out loud. Fabian paused and looked at me with raised brows. He kissed me on the forehead and smiled softly, then squeezed me a little in his arms.

•　•　•

"ARE YOU FEELING ANY BETTER," FABIAN asked after I scarfed down half of a pineapple and ham pizza. I nodded and sighed, with a hand on my distended gut.

"I'll be much better when Daphne forgives me, but I am better, thank you."

"What did she say exactly?"

"It's more of what I said..." I blurted out before I realized what can of worms I just opened. I backtracked. "But essentially, calling Dr. Bailey when she explicitly said she didn't trust him was a huge betrayal. Also that she's lost everything and it's all my fault."

"Okay. Well, that's a bit harsh," he commented, tucking hair behind my ear. "Although, I think we can all agree Dr. Bailey is sus. That whole patient trial, hypnosis thing. I mean, you can't mess with people's heads like that without their permission."

I stared forward, remembering Daphne saying she caught Dr. Bailey "messing with her head." *Could he have...* I stopped chewing.

"Uh oh. I know that look. What is it?"

"What look?" I said, chewing the rest of the pizza, knowing I'd regret it the next time I stepped on the scale.

"The 'I have a sneaking suspicion, and I'm going to stop at nothing to get to the bottom of it' look. I don't know how it doesn't get you in more trouble."

If you only knew. I sat up and turned to him.

"Well, Daphne said that... She said she caught Dr. Bailey 'fucking with her head,' and now I'm just wondering, what did he do?" Fabian smiled deviously back at me.

"Uh oh! Now *I* know *that* look!" I said theatrically.

"Whaaaat?" Fabian said in a high pitch. "What look?"

"The 'I'm going to hack someone's computer because I'm impervious to consequences' look. *Really, I don't know how it doesn't get you in more trouble,"* I teased.

"Let's just take a peek."

"No!"

"Why?"

"Because digging through confidential information is not only a huge breach of trust but it's illegal. I could lose my license, Fabian."

"*You* aren't doing it. I am. Come on. If they knew that I hacked the other system, they would have come for me by now. No one's gonna know."

"Would you really take care of me if I lose my license?"

"Oh, *forever*, honey."

Eep. I smiled. "Okay, but not *her* file. Find something else."

Fabian made a show of warming up his wrists and fingers and cracking his neck before going to work on his laptop. He hopped IP addresses a few times, then tapped into Dr. Bailey's emails first. He had a bad habit of never deleting anything, so there were quite a few emails to dig through. I sipped my ginger tea while Fabian scanned for anything suspicious. I glanced over his shoulder and stopped him.

"Wait, wait. Go back!" Slowly, he scrolled back up until an email came into view from Darling Rituals. "That's the store that got destroyed a town over. The shop owner… Remember she died after I questioned her?" Chills ran down my spine. I remembered Ms. Soto's words. *"He's killed a lot of people…"* she had said. But this was what I was chasing this whole time. How would that creep know? I looked out the window and back at the computer.

"Open it."

Dr. Bailey,
Your business partner dropped off the stones this evening. As he

asked, we will be charging them under the new moon. We will ship them to the pharmaceutical company where your partner will check on the product quality. I am sorry, but I cannot continue our partnership after this delivery. Please tell your business partner where to drop off the next batch if you need more charged and delivered. I don't wish to see him again.

—*Colee Calusa*

"That's the patient! When was this sent?" I asked excitedly.

"It was about a month before the trials started. Sounds like Dr. Bailey's business partner is a scary dude."

Chills pricked the back of my neck, and I became increasingly aware of my lack of panties. "Exit out of there," I urged, reaching over his shoulder to hit the back key.

"It's fine; we won't get caught," he assured, blocking my arm.

"It's not that. Just exit... *now* please....The trials are over. Let's focus on Daphne. Try his personal email."

Fabian shrugged and then pounded on the keyboard until he accessed Dr. Bailey's other email. He had to dig through another over-stuffed inbox but...

"Wait..." Something caught my eye again. "Why the *hell* did Lyndie Pratt email Doctor Bailey at his personal address?"

"Who's Lyndie Pratt?" Fabian inquired while opening the email.

"*Daphne's arch nemesis*," I half-joked. "The Director of Nursing at *Northern Miami Hospital*. Why would she be emailing a doctor who works for *Heartly*?"

"Holy shit..." Fabian froze. I froze. Neither of us could believe what we were looking at.

Dr. Bailey,

With regards to your patient Daphne, she's becoming increas-
ingly problematic, and I suspect she is trying to talk the staff into
unionizing. There's no denying it now, doctor. She's taking
photos of lists. I kept my part of the bargain, and she's gotten
dosed with the drug in her water every shift that she's actually
compliant with leaving her cup in the breakroom. It's time for you
to keep your end up. Whatever hypnosis you're working on her
isn't aggressive enough. If she is not in a full psychotic meltdown
by the next full moon, our business partner will hear about it, and
we both know we don't want to make him angry. I don't have
time for that nonsense when we are trying to satisfy his requests
for the entire east coast. Get her under control. No excuses!
—Lyndie Pratt, RN, MSN, MBA.
DON Amett Health Northern Miami Hospital

"Holy *shit*. They were drugging her!" I yelled.

"They were doing more than that. It's the same as the patients in your trial. The good news is this dum-dum sent it from her business email."

"What's good about that?" I asked as Fabian worked the keys. Soon the screen reflected a new desktop. There was a photo of a beach and a miniature poodle held by… Lyndie. "What are you doing?"

"Remote accessing her desktop."

"*Why?*"

"Watch and learn," he said in his sexy nerd voice.

Fabian opened Lyndie's email and accessed her sent folder. It wasn't there. He checked the trash folder, which was littered with emails. He scrolled down to the same date Dr. Bailey had sent it. I noted it was around the same time Colee Calusa sent her email. I watched in confusion as Fabian accessed the same email to dr. Bailey.

"Babe, we already read this."

"Hold on," he said in a high-pitched voice.

Then I realized what he was doing. I gasped as I watched him hit 'forward' and access the entire hospital's address book. Before I could have a say in it, Fabain hit send. He forwarded her email to everyone who worked in the hospital, from the laboratory technicians to the CEO. My mouth fell open in shock. I laughed at his callous behavior.

"Ohhh, ho ho ho. Oh. My. God. You just did that." My scalp tingled as goosebumps worked through my hair.

Fabian smiled and closed out of the programs quickly, then stood up with a satisfied grin and kissed me. With a crinkle in his nose, he declared, "I think Daphne can find it in her heart to forgive you now."

I laughed and kissed him again, then skipped away to my phone on the counter. Quickly, I sent a text to Jesula, who was on shift tonight.

> Check your work email ASAP! Tell everyone to.

31

DAPHNE: IF ONLY IT COULD LAST

I WOKE UP ON THE HARD MATTRESS OF THE STRETCHER, CURSING THE ED Gods for holding. I just wanted a normal hospital bed with a mattress that was thicker than two inches. But that's not what woke me. The curtains blocking off the large sliding glass doors were pulled back. The sliders extended the entire length and height of the wall. They kind of made the room a display case. I was exposed to the entire nursing staff like a circus attraction. The light from the hall blazed through the window and stung the back of my eyes. The time was 00:01, and the last face I wanted to see on earth was staring back at me; Lyndie's smug face with her vicious smile. She took a deep breath and let it out indulgently.

"Hello again, Daphne. It's officially day two of your psych hold in *Amett Health Northern Miami*'s Emergency Department!" she notified me cheerfully. "I thought you may need to be reoriented to self, time, and …place. You know your *place,* I trust?"

This twat was enjoying this way too much. "I need water. I'm thirsty," I said, showing no reaction. I sat up and adjusted my seat on the uncomfortable bed.

"Once the sitter gets back from lunch, I'll be happy to get you some water myself."

"You're a real *cunt*. You know that?" I said, unbothered. For a moment, I waited for the taste of dirt, but it never came. I was reminded that the dirt curse wasn't real. I never thought I'd be so sad about it.

Her eyes widened, and her brows raised. "You're getting aggressive. I think we should call security to restrain you. I'll tie the knots myself." She poked her head out of the room and smiled. Looking back at me, she cheerfully filled me in on the obvious—security was by the nursing station just outside my room. Her smile widened at the convenience. "Security, I'm being verbally threatened. This patient needs to be restrained immediately."

The guards looked at each other and then glanced to a group of nurses by the nursing station. One was on the phone. Something was off about all of their expressions. *Something* seemed very strange about this whole interaction.

"Right over there, officer," I heard Jesula's voice call from down the hall. Then Jesula's curvy body came into frame, flanked by two police officers. And if it wasn't Officer Carter and his partner walking toward the entrance, I was definitely hallucinating now. I panicked, waiting to be charged with resisting arrest or reckless driving. I felt the tears threatening to rise as my chest pumped heavily. *Just what I need.*

As they walked up to Lyndie with her bitchy-ass smile, I wanted to die. But the way they addressed *her*...

"Lyndie Marie Pratt?"

"Yes," she replied, still smiling yet confused. She lifted her wrist to direct their attention to me, but it was met with the cold metal of handcuffs. They spun her around and slammed her against the glass door. Her face smushed against the glass like a cartoon. Her shrill squeal of privileged rage echoed down the hall. The nurses lined the front of the nursing station, watching the new circus act.

"What is the meaning of this?" she hollered, her makeup smudged on the glass in a distorted face print.

"Lyndie Marie Pratt, you're under arrest on first-degree felony charges of infliction of bodily harm—"

"What are you talking about!" she screamed. As they continued the list of charges, they swung her to face the hall, and she rolled her heel in her stilettos. The officers were not gentle in stopping her fall. "I didn't drug anyone!" She screeched in a panic as she was nudged down the hall like cattle being jabbed with a poker. Officer Carter stopped, looked through the glass, and gave a friendly smile and nod. Then he walked after his partner and a still-screaming Lyndie.

When he was gone, all that was left on the other side of the glass was a row of nurses smiling and high-fiving. The tech who sat for me on day shift was still here with her phone in hand, apparently working a double. I was psyched to see she had her phone recording the whole thing. She cackled about how they could, "Fire me now because that bitch is going viral *tonight!*" and zoomed into the imprint of Lyndie's face on the glass, taking care to leave me out of frame. I heard her scroll through viral sounds on the clock app to add to it. Everyone burst out laughing when the phone sang, "Oh no, oh no, oh no, no, no."

Jesula and the other nurses smiled at me through the glass, and I knew at that moment the movement wasn't lost. This would make the rounds and reignite whatever was damaged. In fits of laughter, I recounted the events with the nurse as she took my vitals and did an assessment. "Officer Carter will be back soon to take a police report."

"A police report on Lyndie?" I asked, smiling yet confused.

Her face dropped slowly, and I felt the mood shift. "The doctor will be in soon. I'm going to draw some labs, and we'll need a urine sample when you can provide it," she said sweetly as she left a specimen cup on the bedside table.

Even though I knew something was wrong, I was too tired to question it. I needed this win, so I clung to this feeling. Knowing the nurses could organize, that the techs would organize next, that I wasn't getting arrested, and that Lyndie got what was coming to her— it all made me feel happier than I had been in days.

Still, I wasn't as happy as I had been with Pol. When I laid down to go back to sleep, I stared at a ceiling tile and imagined the most peaceful place on earth. I imagined I was on a cloud, curled up to an imaginary man of the sky who ate pussy like a demon and made me feel safe. Pol didn't smile, but I could see it pulling at the side of his mouth. *I miss you…*

THE NEXT MORNING I WOKE UP TO SADIE SENDING THE SITTER ON A bathroom break and pulling up a chair next to the bed. She seemed troubled but still walked like she was gliding on the water. My nurse for the day (notably not a union leader) and a hospital administrator came in behind her, closing the door.

I sat up and yawned way too loud. "Sorry, it's early."

"That's quite alright. Good morning, Daphne. Did you sleep well?"

"Yup. Like a baby," I said cheerfully, trying not to be petty and bring up the events last night. But then suddenly I worried it was a dream. "Hey, was I hallucinating, or did Lyndie Pratt get dragged off by the police like common scum last night?"

When no one laughed, I figured it had to do with the suit behind Sadie, Daniel Strong, CEO of *Northern Miami Hospital.*

"No… you weren't dreaming. That is what I want to talk to you about," Sadie said with an excessively professional tone. "Daphne, it is my unfortunate obligation to inform you that Lyndie Pratt, probably by accident during a disoriented state… from being on night shift, I'd guess…" She drew out what she wanted to say, but the suit behind her cleared his throat to compel her to finish. "She sent out an email, forwarded it actually, to the entire hospital staff. In this email, she admits to drugging your water whenever you left it in the breakroom over the course of your contract here. We are unaware of what substance was used, how many times it happened, or what the effects of this drug are."

I sat up straighter and stiffened.

"We are still waiting for the lab results to tell us what it could be, but so far, your blood work indicates all normal parameters, and your vitals are perfectly normal. Your neurological exams have also shown no abnormalities since you woke up yesterday."

"Stop, stop, stop," I said, throwing my hand up. "What… *Why* would she do that?"

Daniel Strong stepped forward and spoke. "In the email Lyndie states she thought you were trying to talk the nurses into organizing a union. I assure you this was not anything the board or any administrator was aware of or condones. She has been terminated, and we are launching a full investigation."

"Are you telling me that she *drugged* me as a *union-busting tactic?* She wanted to kill me?"

"We don't have any reason to think murder was her intention," Daniel corrected.

"Daphne, this email she forwarded was originally addressed to Dr. Bailey. It appears they were working together in some way. Part of her role was to drug you, while his role was to use hypnosis. Their actions may have contributed to your severe psychosis," Sadie informed me, resting her hand on my lap in comfort. Her eyes moved annoyingly to the side when Daniel chimed in again.

"And Dr. Bailey has not only been arrested and charged, but he has lost all privileges at any *Amett* facility. They'll both be investigated by the board. The Board and the police have our full cooperat—"

"Please shut up and get out of my room. I'm not in the mood to hear your panic-driven damage control, you *fucking* donut," I demanded angrily. Daniel looked like he was going to add something to the conversation but bowed his head and left swiftly, taking a seat at the nursing station. I turned my eyes back to Sadie.

"This whole thing was to get me to stop you guys from unionizing? What was the point of keeping me here? Why didn't she just fire me?"

"I don't know, Daphne. Apparently, part of their bargain was that she would drug you, and there was mention of a business partner. I can't say much more," Sadie said. She looked at the bedside table and then at the nurse. "Could you get Daphne more ice water?" she asked her.

"Sure. Our ice is small and melts fast, though. Should I get the ice from med surg? They have the good ice."

"Yes, that would be a good idea," Sadie said, smiling at her. The nurse left with a wink.

"That should give us a little time. Daphne, The hospital is

panicking because everyone has this email. They think you're going to sue and go to the news. They want me to release you immediately, and I have to tell you I don't think that's the safest option."

"Well, I probably am going to sue their asses. They owe me a new M3. I think my parents are going to expect more extravagant anniversary gifts, too. I'll need to finance it. And donate to the nurses strike fund, of course."

Sadie smiled but returned to the topic that I was dodging. "Daphne, I can't let you go today. I'd like to hold you for one more day and start weaning you off of the medications. After that, you'll require supervision as we decrease the doses to watch out for these episodes. I recommend a facility."

"No. I'm not going to a facility. Are you joking?"

"Daphne, you *cannot* be alone. After what's happened… Unless you have a licensed provider with you, monitoring you 24-7, for at least a week, it's not safe to transition you to another medication."

"She can stay with me," a voice said from the door. I turned, and my eyes welled with tears when they saw O'doherty. "I'm on leave from work for a few weeks. I won't let her out of my sight."

"Odi—…O'doherty…" I swallowed hard, and she came to my side. I embraced her hard and wept on her shoulder. "I'm so sorry," I whispered through tears.

"No. I'm sorry. I said horrible things," she said, muffled by my shoulder. She let go and turned to Sadie. "I'm a registered nurse, here is my license. I'll be a temporary legal guardian if I have to. She can come to my house. I have a spare room."

Sadie studied O'doherty's Florica-issued, blue paper license and sighed. "Okay. I need you to visit my office outpatient two times a week."

I gasped like my mother just approved a sleepover. "And I need you to visit this psychiatrist within three days of discharge." She handed me a paper with a name scrolled over it.

"Vitoria Penochi," I read out loud. "Okay, I can do that. When can I go home?"

"Tomorrow, if your vitals, labs, and neuro status are normal, I'll clear and discharge you. If you don't keep these appointments, though…"

"I'll keep them!" I beamed. O'doherty was beaming, too. It had been so long since I had seen her beautiful smile.

"Anyone for a honey bun?" Fabian said, coming into the room with an armful of vending machine food.

"I could mess up a honey bun right now," I said, finally having a bit of an appetite.

"No, but I'll take the—"

"Gummy bears? Knew it," he said, handing the bag to O'doherty. She wiggled her shoulders in a dance as she tore open the package. I was so happy for her. She found a man who treated her how she truly deserved to be treated. Fabian was an excessively great guy. She deserved him.

"If you have no further questions, I'll see you tomorrow. Get some rest," Sadie said, noting the change in my demeanor as I looked at O'doherty. At the door, she met the nurse carrying ice water and motioned for her to turn around. "And I'm discontinuing the one-on-one observation."

"O'doherty, I'm so sorry. This wasn't your fault, and I… I'm just really sorry," I said. Surprisingly, she accepted the apology instead of waving it off like it was nothing.

"Thank you," she said simply. "And I am very sorry for not listening to you about Dr. Bailey. I hope the show last night made up for it," she smiled deviously.

Made up for it? I tilted my head in question. "Was that you? How?"

"It was Fabian." Fabian, biting into the last of his honey bun, did an animated bow. "Between you and me, he's pretty good at hacking," she whispered.

For a bit longer, we laughed, and I told her about Lyndie's arrest. She pulled up the clock app, and we found the viral video of her arrest, which had over a million views since just after midnight. We watched it way too many times. Fabian's face was red with laughter, which only made us laugh harder. Finally, things felt normal again. If only it could last...

32

DAPHNE: THAT ROCK!

It had been a little over a week since I was discharged from the hospital. I kept all my appointments and really liked this new psychiatrist. We had to review years of therapy to get her caught up and get to know each other. She was very easy to talk to. Now, in our second session, I felt like I could tell her anything. And I did.

I told Vicky about how I met Pol, and how he'd convinced me to come to the Regnum Caelorum. I told her about the textbooks and Uripe's medical device. I told her how I caught a shooting star and rode on different magical riding clouds. I told her how sad I was that Mynt wasn't real. I told her maybe one day, if I was brave enough, I'd write a spicy fantasy book about it and self-publish under some pretentious, single-word pen name. We laughed. I even told her about the explicit intimacy that Pol and I had. I talked about Pol a lot.

"You're still very attached to this man," she noticed. "Why do you think that is? What was it specifically about this Pol that you were most taken with?"

"He didn't fake anything. He was more real than anyone I've ever met," I started. "And he made me feel safe, like I could surrender and not be hurt. I trusted him."

"Is there anyone in your life that you feel that way about?"

"No. I mean, of course, I trust O'doherty, but it's different. We're just friends."

"Well, I think it is a good idea to get closure. I'd like you to write Pol a goodbye letter. Then destroy it."

"Sure. Sounds easy enough."

"And I think it's safe for you to head home sometime soon. You seem to be doing fine. I'd still like to see you once a week for the next month and reevaluate."

"Oh, thank God. I don't know how much more I can stand of the Fabian and O'doherty love fest," I said, rolling my eyes.

"How is it seeing O'doherty with Fabian?"

"I'm a little jealous, actually. I miss when it was just us, but Fabian is good people. It's hard seeing them and missing Pol. I'm not sure I'll ever find a real Pol or a Fabian, for that matter."

"Well, would you take time from work to pursue that if you did meet him?"

"No. Leaving my dream job for a man was a one-time thing. Besides, the nurses have been collecting cards for a week, and they're at eighty-seven percent in support of a union. In a *week*. That's unheard of. This is happening! Anyways, I can't stop now. Something bad will happen and set it all back."

"Now, why do you think that?"

"It's just been a rough few months. We nearly lost it all. I can't help this feeling, like this strong intuition that something is coming. Something bad is going to happen."

"Like before the attack broke out at Loanan Palace?"

"Yes, but not as intense."

"Have you ever had these feelings before? The sense of dread or impending doom?"

"I guess so, just not this strong."

"Well, it could be that we are weaning your meds and lowering the dose. By Monday, I want you to start cutting your new dose in half. We'll see how you feel on Wednesday when you come in."

"Okay. Thanks. You know O'doherty is talking to her doctor about switching too. I think she got a little freaked out."

"Well, she should be. That medication shouldn't have made it out of trial, in my opinion. There was no reason not to have you on a traditional medication," she said, adjusting her frames. "Our time is up! Ah. You look great, kiddo. Call me if there are any changes, and I'll see you next week. And don't forget your homework!"

"Write to Pol. Got it."

WHEN WE CAME THROUGH THE DOOR, POLPETTA STOOD ON FABIAN'S stomach and remained glued to him as she barked for me. Even though I was back, orders were to take it easy, so Polly was still happily in Fabian's care. She had gotten pretty fat, and I shook my head when I saw her eating Cheetos off of his chest. *Her vet is gonna kill me.*

"Hey, Jesula was going to come by and hang out tonight. Do you think I could take my lady out for a nice dinner?" Fabian asked.

"Oh, sure! And by the way, my doctor says I can go home this weekend. Are the security cameras up yet?

"They should be done by tomorrow morning. I'll have them set for motion sensors, and the feed can be streamed, but they won't record. One is going on your roof, facing the tree in the back. Another on the front porch and another on the garage."

"Thank you," I said. I felt silly asking for them. I've come to terms with the fact that none of it was real, but during the whole episode, when I *felt*, I *really felt*. I couldn't help but wonder if someone did come mess with me while I was hallucinating and hurt me, or worse. It wouldn't be the first time a mentally ill person was assaulted in crises. I wondered where I was when my mind was in Loanan. When my head was in the clouds, did I fall from a tree?

THE SMELL OF JESULA'S PULLED PORK, AND FRESHLY-BAKED COCONUT croissants filled the house by dusk. I finished spinning freshly rinsed arugula in a salad spinner and sliced some fresh cotton candy mangos from O'doherty's tree. I hoped my modest side salad was enough as I wrapped it and set it in the fridge.

Jesula sat on the couch to work on her computer, updating the progress on the authorization cards for the union. Victory was basically a given. Jesula and the other organizer, Adrian, were spearheading the rest of the campaign. I was already starting to work with the techs and the many others who would organize in the same bargaining unit.

The loveseat groaned as I sank into it and set pen to paper. I started writing Pol. I poured out my heart as I said my last goodbyes, and I hoped Jesula couldn't see the tears slowly dripping down my cheeks. I wrote him a love letter—a true goodbye. I held back nothing. If I were to give myself closure, I would make a ceremony of it.

Polpetta trotted at my heel as I got up. We headed to the back door by the kitchenette.

"I'm gonna let Polly out before the storm gets too bad," I called to Jesula.

"Okay. When you get back, I need you to show me how to do

conditional formatting on this spreadsheet. I want to color code those *malfrendeng, trèt* in red!" she answered. I gathered she was still upset that old friends were working against her in the union campaign and smiled, figuring that term was some type of Haitian profanity.

Polpetta ran out into the drizzling rain as soon as the door opened. Not really caring if I got wet, I stepped out, too. It was getting dark, and the warm, humid wind tossed my hair. There hadn't been a tornado in a few weeks, but there were still gloomy clouds hovering over the city almost every evening, and it rained every day. There was never a chance to watch the sunset when the sky was full of rolling dark grays and dusty dark blues.

But this evening I walked into the rain and didn't mind as long as it wasn't lightning. The rain seemed to call for me. I closed my eyes and lifted my face to the sky. I took a deep breath and felt the small drops of rain on my face. It felt pretty nice. I stayed a moment, getting lost in meditation as I listened to the rain hit the grass and leaves faster and faster. I started to sway in the wind and reminded myself that I need to open my eyes soon and finish my final goodbye by destroying the letter to Pol. *It's now or never, I guess.*

I opened my eyes with a breath and unfolded the letter as the rain grew heavier. Reading the letter out loud made my voice crack the smallest bit.

Dear Pol,

I miss you. Knowing you're not real and that I'll never see you again makes me feel like my heart is in a damn vice. I don't know how my mind made you. I have never known someone as perfect as you. I can feel myself pulling to you again. It hurts to know there's no one on the other side pulling back. Whenever I feel like giving up on

life, I'll look at the sky and feel your spirit, real or not, and you'll keep me grounded. I'll watch the sunset every night that I can. I'll think about you by my side, wrapping your arms around me and smelling smokey and warm. I mourn the loss of you. But mostly, I mourn for those who will never know you for themselves. Goodbye.
Always,
—Daphne.

By the time I was done reading the letter, the rain made the ink bleed and pulled the words apart. I cried into the downpour, the tears blending in perfectly with the drops. In my hands, the paper got soggy and tore apart, his memorial slipping through my fingers. The charm bracelet on my wrist shimmered. I wedged my thumbnail between the magnetic clasp, released it, and pocketed it. Just the same, I removed the necklace and pocketed it.

"Hey, get in here, you crazy girl! It's pouring!" Jesula said. Polpetta took cover when she opened the door to yell for me. She shook her damp fur out, and Jesula sucked her teeth as she got splattered by wet dog. Apparently, she wasn't too fond of dogs. I laughed and headed in, sopping wet. "Go change into some dry clothes before you catch a cold."

"You know just as well as I do that's a myth," I said. I motioned as though I was going to wrap my arms around her, and she backed away in a hurry, waving her hands and yelling at me to, "Get away." I laughed and tracked water through the kitchen, making my way into the guest room.

You would never guess that anyone was staying in the guest room, by the looks of it. I only had a few outfits that stayed hidden in the nightstand or in a bag in the closet. Some undergarments I stuffed in the back of a large dresser and I repacked my toiletries after every use. I made the bed and cleaned up after myself scrupulously, trying not to overstay my welcome. It was already uncomfortable knowing Fabian and O'doherty were trying their hardest to keep their sex quiet in their own home (many times failing). They would go at it for hours.

My wet clothes hugged my skin as I pulled them from my body. They sagged and dripped when I draped them over the shower rod. I squeezed my hair with a towel, patted my body dry, and rehung it as if it were decorative. Shivering, I headed for the dresser, setting the jewelry on top. I pulled out a comfortable loose t-shirt and sweats, skipping the bra, because *why not*. Then I pulled open the underwear drawer. It was empty. My brows furrowed, and I looked in the other drawers to find no panties. I dug through the few clothes in the small hamper and looked under the bed and could find nothing. I slipped my sweats and t-shirt on and made a note to ask O'doherty if she knew anything about it.

I headed for the living room to see Jesula eating a fruit cup and looking in annoyance at a begging Polpetta.

"This dog is fat and greedy," she said. Polpetta gruffed and laid down at Jesula's feet. "This is what happens when you spoil a dog."

The front door swung open, and the happy couple walked in. Polpetta sprinted for her favorite man in the world. Fabian scooped her up, and Polpetta was a proud pup as she looked down at us peasants who were not in Fabian's arms. I couldn't help but laugh.

"Did you guys have fun?" I asked. O'doherty only smiled and looked secretive. I squinted and looked at Fabian, who was equally mute and giddy. "Well?"

O'doherty held out her left hand to present a gorgeous gold ring with a yellow cushion-cut diamond surrounded by elaborate curls and tendrils. The sides were encrusted with blue sapphire. She bounced on her heels and giggled. "I said yes! We're engaged."

"Ah!" I screamed. In no time, O'doherty and I were jumping and screaming like schoolgirls. "Oh, my God! It's freaking gorgeous! Did you know?"

"No, I didn't have a clue!"

I turned to Fabian and wrapped him in a tight hug. It felt like I was gaining a brother. "Congratulations!"

"Let me see that rock!" Jesula said, pushing through. "Oh wow! Yes. That is something special!" she said enthusiastically.

The night was filled with laughter and celebration. Dotey told us the story while Jesula and I ate dinner. To my surprise, Jesula warmed up to Polpetta a little bit, offering her a piece of mango.

"Okay, now shoo! Don't beg so much," she said to Polly, waving her hand. Seeing O'doherty wrapped in Fabian's arms looked like something from a Hallmark movie. They were starting a new chapter together. At that moment, it couldn't feel more right for me to go home.

33

O'DOHERTY: TELL ME YOU UNDERSTAND

THE STORMS HAD PASSED. I FELT SUN ON MY CHEEKS. I WANTED TO try and convince Daphne to detour and take us to the beach. She used to love the beach. Now, she said the sand and salty air was too coarse and bothered her skin. "Okay, I'm all set!" Daphne said, swinging a key ring around her finger. "It's no M3, but it'll work until I get the insurance payout." Daphne frowned at the gold Toyota Corolla parked in the rental car lot.

"At least it's got a sunroof." I offered with a shrug. Daphne nodded and inched toward me to give me a long hug. "Fabian says the cameras and alarms are all set, by the way."

"Fabian better take care of you," she said. "I'm going to miss you."

"He'll never come between us. No man will ever come between us."

"Not even imaginary ones?" Daphne joked.

"Wow."

"Too soon?"

"A little bit," I said and kissed her goodbye on the cheek. "Not even imaginary ones."

I released her, and she tossed her keys up and caught them. Then she whistled for Polpetta to come with her. Polpetta waddled alongside her and happily got in the car, ready for the wind to blow her jowls around. Daphne pulled out and drove off the lot. A pang of worry interrupted my peace.

Our friendship would never be the same, and we had a lot of trust to rebuild, but I would worry for her all the same.

On the drive home, I kept my left hand propped on the steering wheel so I could see my engagement ring shine in the sunlight.

Last night, Fabian took me to the restaurant where we had our first date, and we got a table outside under the bistro lights. It was a bit tattered this time. Storms had torn through the area, barely sparing the restaurant, and they hadn't finished repairs yet. He ordered prosecco and clinked our glasses with a toast to us.

Behind our laughter, I heard *Lover* by Taylor Swift start to play and lit up, reminding him for the millionth time that—as an avid Swifty—it was my favorite song. I started to sway my shoulders and sing along, but I stopped when he stood, offered a hand, and asked me to dance. There wasn't a dance floor, but the staff didn't seem to be bothered, and neither did the patrons.

The wine had relaxed me, and him too, I guessed. He didn't particularly love dancing but did it for me. I smiled as he sent me for a twirl, only bumping into an empty table once. Then he kissed me softly and slowly, and I melted into the moment. My arms rested on his shoulders, his arms around my waist. I took in every single part of him, trying to remember this perfect moment forever. My angel. My love. Nose to nose, he smiled at me subtly and looked as though his lips were shivering.

He sent me for a twirl again, and I obliged with a giggle, only to twirl back to a very nervous Fabian who was dropping to one knee. I stopped, frozen in my own shock. Tears stung my eyes, and I gasped. I knew I was holding my breath but couldn't find a way to let it out.

"O'doherty Sameal, you're the most amazing person I've ever met. You've healed my body and filled my heart. You've been there for me through some of the hardest times. You complete me, and I never want to be without you. I want to grow old with you and give you my children, and I know you'll be an amazing mother. I want to take care of you forever," he said with a shaky voice, reaching into his pocket and pulling out a blue box with shaky hands. He cracked it open, and the stunning yellow diamond shimmered in the bistro lighting. "Will you marry me?" he asked with a breaking voice. Finally, I let out the breath and sucked in a fresh gulp of air as tears rolled down my cheek.

"Of course, I will," I said. He let out a laugh of relief and pushed the ring onto my finger. Before I knew it, he had stood and scooped me off my feet in a hug. I pressed my lips to his, tasting salty tears, but I was unable to determine whose they were. It was only then that I could hear the clapping of onlookers. Before that moment, he was all I could see and hear. It was the happiest moment of my life.

Now, racing home, I played Lover on repeat for the whole drive, singing and swaying in the car. I couldn't wait to see him. I called for local Chinese food, sat in a slump at the kitchenette, and pulled out my phone as I waited for the food and my fiancé. *"Fiancé,"* I said with a smile as I pulled up Tonya's number.

Any word from management?

I texted her.

It had been over a week now since the inquiry, and they informed me that I'd be on leave. Meanwhile, they did a formal investigation. My phone pinged, and Tonya's text illuminated the screen.

Nothing yet, girlfriend. Don't let the timeline fool you. They're just investigating. It is purely bureaucratic.

I dropped my phone to the table, letting it clatter as I rubbed my hands over my eyes. I sat like that, listening to the downpour of rain against the glass. Keys rattled the front lock, and it felt so strange not to hear Polpetta's body scrambling for purchase as she lunged to meet Fabian. He came through the door, still giving his thanks to the delivery driver and balancing a wet bag of Chinese food in his hand. As his keys jingled and clinked on the counter, he looked at me and said, "Is it not weird without Polly?"

"It *is!*" I said and pulled him into a hug.

It was almost dark out, and a storm was rolling in. The chow mein nearly made it into my mouth before my phone buzzed, vibrating against the granite counter. I lost my appetite, thinking it may be a text from Tonya or an e-mail from the company. Returning the noodles back to the box, I wiped my hands on the side of my pants and picked up my phone. It was an ambiguous text from Daphne.

Hey,

The dots pulsed below the message, indicating she was still writing, and then they disappeared.

Hey, you okay?

I replied.

The dots pulsed again and then disappeared without a message. I stared at my phone blankly until Fabian grabbed my attention.

"Everything okay?"

"It's Daphne. She just said 'Hey' and hasn't texted back," I answered, looking back at my phone to see the dots pulsing once more.

Yeah, I'm fine. Just making sure you got home safe.

Love you.

The message read when it finally appeared.

Oh, yeah I got home earlier. Eating dinner now. You got home safely too?

I texted back.

She responded quickly this time.

Yeah. I'm heading to bed early. Meds taken. Night.

I looked at my phone for a moment, feeling uneasy.

Love you, Night.

I wrote back. I waited for the message to be marked as "read" but it never came.

"That was weird," I said to Fabian.

"What was weird about it?"

"Nothing, really. I'm just overthinking. I'm gonna go to the bathroom."

When I walked away, Fabian was opening his laptop while shoving a forkful of beef and sprouts into his mouth. I heard the quick clinking of those strong fingers against the keypad and smiled at the memory of them working quickly inside me.

As I washed my hands, a flash of lightning and a loud crash of thunder surrounded the home, and our lights flickered. I jumped, clutching my chest. Not a second after I dried my hands on the towel did I hear Fabian shouting as if the house was on fire.

"Oh fuck! O'doherty. Fuck!" He hollered. I was startled and frantic. Fabian never used profanity unless he was severely hurt or cumming very hard. "O'doherty, we need to go now!"

I ran from the bathroom. Fabian was loading his pockets with something from the cabinet. He swiped up his half-open computer with security feed on the screen.

"What's wrong? What's happening?" I shouted.

"There's some *fucking* guy at Daphne's," he said, his voice hoarse with urgency. He grabbed his gun and wedged it in his back waistband. "It looks like they're fighting. Come on."

I nearly destroyed my mailbox, backing out. Fabian's laptop was still half open on his lap. He pulled out his phone and dialed 911.

"911, what's your emergency?" I heard a voice say on the other line.

"Hello? Our friend is being attacked; she needs help now!" Fabian shouted.

"He..o.h..lo?" The voice on the line crackled. Then, three dull beeps toned. The call was disconnected.

"Fuck!" he shouted.

"What's wrong?"

"There's no service!" he said. He opened his computer to check the feed. Another threatening lightning strike stabbed into the earth. It lit up the sky and rattled my bones with thunder. From the corner of my eye, I could see the screen glowing with movement. Fabian let out a horrified breath.

"Oh… God…"

I looked over to see what was so horrific, but the screen pixelated and went dark. "Fabian, what's—"

Our phones blared an alert for severe weather in the area, capable of producing tornadoes. Fabain's hands shook as he pressed them into his face.

"O'doherty, when we get there, I want you to stay in the car. Don't come out unless there's a tornado and you need to get to cover. Keep trying the police until you get a hold of someone. Do *not* come after me, no matter how long it takes. Do you understand?"

"Fabian, is Daphne okay?" I asked, my voice cracking as tears welled. He didn't answer fast enough. "Fabian! You're scaring me." He paused and pressed his lips together, clearly shaken.

"Everything's going to be okay; just get us there."

When I pulled into Daphne's driveway, heavy sheets of rain blocked our view. The street was pitch black, and Daphne was parked outside.

"The power must have been out when she got home. Maybe the front door is unlocked." I offered, reaching for the door handle. Fabian reached over to my arm and grabbed it.

"*Stay* in the car. Lock the doors. Keep calling the police until someone answers. *Tell me* you understand," he said in a stern tone.

I nodded. He pressed a kiss to my lips and opened his door. "I love you." He got out hastily. Then he reached for the gun wedged in the back of his waistband and cocked it. Tears fell from my eyes. He slammed the car door and ran for Daphne's front porch, walking inside. My hands shook so violently that I nearly dropped my phone as I dialed the police.

Again, no service.

34

DAPHNE: SOAKED WITH BLOOD

Home sweet home. I pulled into the driveway with a few fingers of sun left. I realized I no longer had my garage door opener and grunted. I opened the car door and felt sprinkles fall on my skin. Polpetta jumped from the car, squatted in the yard, and then hurried to the front porch so she wouldn't get wet. When I got inside, I piled my belongings in my arms and kicked the front door shut with my foot.

"Ugh. It's muggy in here," I groaned. I dropped my stuff on the counter. Making my way to the thermostat, I pulled off my shirt, finally free to walk around naked again. The thermostat screen was blank, and I realized there was no power—home *sweet home.* I thought even less enthusiastically.

I pulled out the leftover pulled pork that I brought home and ate it cold in the dark silence. Sitting at my high-top two-seater, I was ready to take a sledgehammer to the walls. I never realized how closed off and dark the room was.

I could see the living room and the sliding door if I got that wall knocked down. I thought to myself as I ate. *I could see if anyone came. If...*

Polpetta, for once, wasn't begging. She sat alone on the kitchen floor, staring at a wall, looking bored as ever. I dropped my fork. My appetite was not much better than hers.

After a short shower, I pulled out a nice cotton nightgown that looked more like a very long, white, oversized button-up shirt that hit mid-thigh. The wide collar caused the shoulder to fall away on one side. When I pulled open my top drawer and saw the stacks of panties, I remembered the ones missing at O'doherty's. I almost texted her but decided against it. There would be time for that. She and Fabian were enjoying their first night alone as an engaged couple, so I pulled on a lacy pair of boy shorts instead of bothering them.

I rubbed at my bare neck, then my bare wrist. I felt naked without the jewelry now. I grabbed the jewelry from the dresser and plopped on the bed. Turning my back from the window, I laid down and raised up each charm in what little light came through it.

The charm of an obsidian cloud that had dulled my pain on my first flight was still as shiny as ever. The sun charm made of an amber bead with white gold rays of fire sparkled as I propped it up to the waning light coming through the window. The sun must have just set. The last of its light could barely shine through the storm clouds rolling in.

Finally, I admired the shooting star charm: a dented black rock encrusted with diamonds, rose gold, and an amber-flecked tail. This one was my favorite by far. Then I held the necklace's charm and admired the sun-shaped amber embedded in the amethyst. As I turned it around, I noticed a shooting star was etched into the back and encrusted with diamonds and amber chips so small you could hardly notice them until they sparkled in the dim light. How had I not seen it before? It was increasingly hard to see with the sun now under the horizon.

Rain fell louder, and a single tear pulled from my eye. Through the pattering of rain, I heard a sound that haunted me. I froze, clutching the jewels tightly. The spikes of the geode dug into my skin. I held my breath. Listening closer, I tried to decide if it was real. I sat up on my bed, breathing heavily. Adrenaline coursed through my veins. Polpetta stood at attention at the back door. The hair follicles on my scalp tightened. Her low growls told me I wasn't imagining the sound.

I carefully took two steps toward my dresser, afraid to face the window. I grabbed my phone quietly and hid the light from the screen.

Hey.

I messaged O'doherty. It was all I could manage to send. I didn't know what to say. I started to type again but deleted it and held the phone to my chest. Slowly, I turned my head to the window. My breath shook. My eyes watered. I was unsure of what I would see through the cracked blinds.

I closed my eyes for a moment. I could hear the sound of Pol's lyre. The deep drone of his voice sang a sad song on a pentatonic scale. I opened my eyes and let out a long, shaky breath. It felt like a punch to the gut, and I bent over. Tears fell, and I blinked them away frantically. I didn't want to blur my view of Pol on his nimbus, taking partial cover from the rain under a low branch of the tree. My phone buzzed, and I turned away, panting.

Hey, you okay?

My fingers shook as I typed. I hid my screen light from the window.

> O'doherty, I think there's someone outside…

I deleted it and looked at the dresser. The bottle of medication sat in the middle of the jewelry. I hadn't taken it yet. I set the phone screen down on the dresser and grabbed the bottle. I unscrewed the cap and sprinkled a tablet in my shaking hands. Throwing the tablet in my mouth, I swallowed it with saliva. Seconds felt like hours. I waited for the singing and strumming to stop. It didn't. I grabbed my phone again.

As my fingers moved to type, I paused again to look at him. I did what I was supposed to do—I took my meds. They'd kick in soon, and he'd be gone. What was the harm in challenging the illusion? Just to see him one more time? I can do this.

> Yeah, I'm fine. Just making sure you got home safe.
>
> Love you.

The message read when I finally sent the lie. She responded quickly.

> Oh, yeah, I got home earlier. Eating dinner now. You got home safely too?

I sent one last text as quickly as I could, afraid that Pol would disappear before I had time to see him.

> Yeah. I'm heading to bed early. Meds taken. Night.

I placed the phone on the dresser and grabbed the jewelry. Tangling it in my fingers, I nearly crushed them in my grip. I walked from my bedroom doorway. Polpetta's whines in the other room got louder. She stood up and looked at me, begging to be let out. I looked up, peeking around the curtain to see him again. His song was sad. It sounded like he was stirring up the storm.

I should watch from here and should hide in the dark. I told myself. The drops of rain on the sliding glass patched my face with tiny shadows. I needed to look closer. I pressed my hands against the door, fogging the glass with my breath. The coldness of the glass reached my lips. I would have given anything for his lips to warm them.

I would try my hardest not to lose it, but I needed to see what it felt like to touch him. I smiled and stepped away. Finding a pen on the coffee table, I wrote a note on a small notepad. Just in case I never recovered from this, I wrote a goodbye to whomever. I ripped the paper off the pad and weighed it down with the pen.

Stepping into the rain, Polpetta followed behind me and ran into the darkness. The strumming stopped. The singing stopped. Pol sat on his nimbus, a few feet off the ground. It flickered with phantom lightning. His eyes fixed on me in disbelief. Rain rolled down his face. I could see his chest tremble with breath. I was frozen too.

It's so real, I thought to myself. Tilting my head to the side, I squinted through the rain. I walked forward. *It's so real.* I got closer, feeling no sense of danger. I reached out a hand to touch its face. My mouth hung open. I pulled my hand back, but he grabbed my wrist tightly. I startled, pulling away from him, but he wouldn't release me. Panic flooded my veins. I pulled and tugged. His grip was too strong. He barely even moved with my fighting.

Lightning cracked overhead. The world lit up in flickers. Rain poured from the sky, and deafening thunder came with it.

"Daphne, where have you been?" he asked. "I've been looking everywhere for you. I couldn't find your car anywhere." My eyes were wide in disbelief. I had spent weeks being convinced this man was a dream. I wasn't about to go back to the hospital or be locked up inpatient. I had to get away, or I'd never let go of this. *It's not real, just fight it.* I punched at his arm with the fist that still clenched the gems and tried to pull away. "Daphne, what's wrong with you?" he shouted now.

My nightshirt was soaked and clung to me. My breast peeked through the white cloth. I punched at him again. He grabbed my other wrist and pulled my body forward. He wedged me between his knees. My face was so close to his. I sobbed at my weakness. *Fuck he's beautiful.*

"Where have you been? Why are you…" He stopped yelling. His face turned flat, but he flared his nose in anger. "Poison? You're joking."

"You're not real," I said. "I'm hallucinating. You're not real. I need to get my phone and call for help."

"What?"

I cried. My knees buckled from the tightness in my chest. He tightened his grip and yanked me to my feet. I tightened my eyes shut. *Get it together, Daphne.*

"Please let me go," I cried. I leaned in too close. I wanted to lay my head on his chest. I needed to snap out of it. *I'm not going through this again.*

"You're not real," I whispered. "You're not real," I yelled. I thrashed in his grip again. Then I sobbed harder. I gave up, realizing my fight was useless. I looked up at his expressionless face. Rage burned behind it.

I miss this, even if it is all in my head.

His cloud disappeared, and he came to his feet. His bow and arrow fell to the wet earth. The strings of his lyre hummed in vibration as it fell, water shaking off of them. His warm, solid body pressed against mine. *How?* I rested my head on his warm chest and closed my eyes, waiting for him to disappear. I heard his perfectly beating heart.

He let go of my wrists and wrapped one arm around my waist. He pulled my face up by my chin to kiss me. *Oh, I missed this.* I melted.

"Am I real yet?"

I didn't answer, refusing to open my eyes. *Snap out of it, Daph.* I stepped back. He followed me, never letting our lips fall apart.

He kissed me again. It was warm compared to the rain dripping down our faces.

"Am I real now?" he asked firmly. I stepped back again. He quickly took the space, pressing another kiss to my mouth, this time with less patience. He gnawed at my lips and messaged my tongue with his. My center heated, and my heart fluttered.

Hang in there. It will be gone soon. You have to try.

"Did that feel real enough to you?" he asked, frustrated.

"It's not real," I repeated, stepping back. My heel hit a root this time, sending me windmilling back into the tree trunk. My body rested in its twisted bend. Pol looked down at me as he walked forward.

He pressed his body against mine and kissed me deeply again. He tore my gown from collar to breast. The rain hit my nipples as he grabbed at them. I loved the feeling of his warm hands cupping my breast, and I sighed.

"Does it feel real yet, Daphne?" He didn't wait for me to answer. He tore the other side of my collar down. His tongue claimed my mouth. My skin ran hot, and I moaned again. I didn't want to wake up from this.

Wait... Hang in a little longer.

Pinning me to the tree by the neck, Pol kicked my legs open, reached between them, and tore the crotch from my panties clean off. "Am I real?" he asked as he slowly freed his buckle.

I didn't answer, only shook my head. His jaw ticked. He freed his cock from his pants. Scooping his arms under my knees, he pulled my legs to my chest and pinned me. The tree bark dug into my back, scraping it, and I gasped.

"Wrong answer," he said. Before I could say a word, he guided himself to my entrance and forced his entire length inside me. My pussy ached from the stretch as he filled me. He spared no time to start thrusting into me hard. He growled and hissed as my pussy clamped tightly around him for the first time.

His kiss muffled my shrieks of pained pleasure. He locked his lips on mine, sliding his tongue in my mouth. He fucked himself into me again and again. A groan of pleasure rumbled from his chest as he felt my wet heat around him. The bark dug deeper into my skin with each brutal thrust. I arched my back in pain. A high-pitched whimper escaped from my throat. He hurt. I wanted him to hurt me more.

But then the bark seemed to soften. My body sank into it slowly, like quicksand.

"You will never leave me again, do you understand?" he growled in my ear angrily as he took his pleasure from me over and over again. I only cried out, my clit swollen with pleasure. He fucked me deeper into the tree as the bark melted around me. I squeezed my eyes shut and turned my face from him.

"Am I real?" he asked again, gripping my hair tightly. He pulled at my hair until he turned my face to his. I tried to look away even as my sore pussy pulsed with need. He yelled now, anger apparent in the force of his thrusts. "Look at me when I'm fucking you!"

I did, and when I saw him, I panted louder, inching closer to climax. The rain poured down his face as he held me still. Lightning split the sky again. Its roaring thunder muffled my cries.

I was deeper into the tree now. It held my body still for him as he worked himself inside me, forcing my legs wide. With it holding me in place, he freed his arm from my leg and reached into the tree to grab my throat. He fucked me with long, deep, grinding strokes as he pressed the heel of his palm against my neck. My breaths were strained. I grabbed at his arm, but he was too strong.

Water splattered warm on our faces with every thrust. In the distance, I could hear an alarm chiming on my phone. He pulled my hair harder into his grip and glided himself over my clit with each thrust.

"Say it," he demanded before biting my lip hard and pulling it down. He squeezed the sides of my neck, and my vision began to tunnel, euphoria consuming me. My pussy clenched around him; I was ready to come undone. The bark had nearly reached my ears.

"Who's fucking you?" he demanded in a pained voice, pressing harder on my throat. I could hardly breathe. But I couldn't hold back any longer. The tree pried my legs apart wider, and the pleasure between them exploded into an orgasm.

"Pol," I called out in a choked rasp, hot cum squirting from me. "Pol!"

"That's it. I'm here, baby," he said, working himself into me faster as my pussy spasmed around him. He squeezed my neck harder. It gave my orgasm a second wave before it was through. I squirted hard again.

"Pol!" I called again, my voice strained and practically breathless. He panted and pressed long kisses on my lips as I struggled to moan through his tight hold on me. "Pol… Pol… Pol…" I whispered with each thrust as my orgasm fluttered to a finish, my sight nearly black. Then his thrusts picked up pace. I was weak with relief and practically limp, teetering on the edge of losing consciousness.

"I'm here, baby," he whispered as I fought my darkening vision. The bark passed my ears nearly to my eyes. I sank faster as he fucked his cock into my sore, wet pussy. I could still hear his muffled groans of pleasure as he worked up to his own climax. Finally, he eased his grip on my neck just enough to keep me awake and make me watch him cum inside me.

"You're mine. You will *never* leave me again," he said with the last few brutal thrusts before his pleasure took him. His voice broke. He pushed himself deep inside me. His hot cum flooded my center. His cock flexed hard with each squirt.

"Ahh. Fuck," he growled, letting go of my throat and hair and reaching into the tree to force my ass closer. I gasped for fresh air. "You're mine. You cum when I make you. You breathe when I let you." He pressed his hips against me hard, emptying himself into me as deep as he could. He dropped his warm lips to my cheek so I could hear him through the bark.

"Sss. You're mine. Do you fucking hear me?" he growled, stirring his warmth inside me with a circular grinding of his hips. I nodded, breathing heavily between moans, limp and satisfied.

Few parts of my body hadn't entirely sunk into the tree—my knees, my center, my nipples, and my face

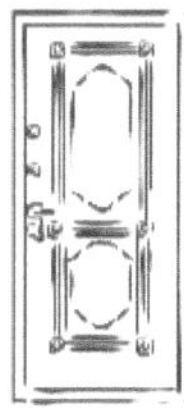

were the only unrestrained parts. He laid against me and the tree, catching his breath as his length softened inside me.

Finally, he pulled away just far enough to meet my gaze. His hands held my face. Worry was written in his eyes. I could see and feel that his power was almost exhausted from whatever he had done to the tree to restrain me. His mist was nearly gone. But that didn't explain the look of regret on his face.

"Pol?" I tried to reach for him, but my arms couldn't pull from the bark. I couldn't move any part of me that was inside the tree. I wrestled a little more to no avail. He looked at me for a few more breaths before pressing his hand into the tree to rest a palm on the center of my chest, caressing it. "Pol? What is it?" I whispered, panting. He leaned back down and kissed me slowly; I crossed my tongue over his top lip.

"Please forgive me..." he said, with his forehead pressed against mine, rain dripping down our faces.

Before my face could shift deeper into confusion, his hand pushed against my chest, submerging me into the tree completely. As I sank back, I felt his cock pull free from me. I drew in my last breath before the bark closed over my eyes, and I was weightlessly suspended in darkness.

I floated in a waterless womb. My body was now free to move. I touched his hand, still flat against my chest. I held it over my heart, hoping he could feel me and know I wouldn't have left. But his hand pulled from my chest, and no matter how tightly I tried to hold on to it, it slipped away and out of the tree.

There was no gravity in this space, only the purest air and endless darkness. I swam toward where his hand disappeared, my hair dancing around me like it was moving through water. I was met with only dark, bark-like walls. I clawed at it, but it was no use.

"Pol!" I screamed. My voice echoed back at me. As I swam down, I sensed the jewels lying over the dirt at my roots. I swam deeper, my body morphing to fit in the small roots. I felt his feet above me, walking away slowly. "Pol!" I screamed in a panic again, banging my palms on the top of the roots as I followed his steps. I reached the end of the longest root when his footsteps disappeared. I cried loudly, scared and alone. My voice shook as I tried one last time, only able to manage a whisper. "Pol..."

I swam back to the more spacious trunk and floated in the void. His seed dripped down my thigh as my center ached from him. I pulled my nightgown back over my shoulders and hugged myself in disbelief as I wept.

Then, a sound vibrated through the tree. I swam to the bark walls and pressed my ear against them to hear better, but I couldn't make it out.

After some commotion, the walls of my prison shook. Pain stabbed at my heart like a hot knife. Again and again, the prison shook, the stabbing pain with it. I screamed with every quake. Finally, the searing sensation shot from my neck to my belly. My vision went blurry from the pain. I floated down to a bed of roots that opened into tunnels. With the last of my strength, I guarded my core, curling into a ball and giving in to my exhaustion. Meanwhile, the soil around my roots was soaked with blood. Everything shook one last time.

35

O'DOHERTY: ON A DAY HE DID NOT EXIST

I COULD SCARCELY MAKE OUT FABIAN'S FORM AS HE RAN THROUGH the rain and entered Daphne's home. Panic overwhelmed me. My relentless attempts to call for help were fruitless.

"Come on!" I screamed at my phone. I shook it as if reception was a loose part that could be wiggled back into place. The thunder boomed overhead. The wind whipped around the car, shaking it. The sheets of rain made it impossible to see anyone coming or going. Seconds felt like hours. *What if Fabian gets hurt? I'd never forgive myself.*

My spiraling thoughts consumed me. They fueled me into action. I pushed myself out of the car and sprinted to the door. Fabian could forgive me later.

Inside, everything was dark. From the front door I could see the back slider open. I made out two figures arguing in the rain. I slowly crept through the dark home, walking straight to the backdoor. The wind whipped rain through the threshold.

The curtains twisted and flapped as wind blew through the home.

As I got closer, a pen rolled on the floor, crossing my path. Papers fluttered around the dark room. Fabian's voice carried through them, yelling in rage. I stood shrouded in the darkness. The other man came into view.

Fabian, gun drawn and pointed at the man, was standing by the tree. Daphne was nowhere in sight. The man was a thin, gaunt giant. He looked like he was about to fall to his knees in exhaustion. He glared at Fabian in anger. I was relieved to see who had the upper hand. I stayed hidden until he needed help. I tried the police again. Still no service.

"I said, where is she?" Fabian yelled hoarsely. The man didn't move, nor did he speak. He only lowered his brow in a scowl. "I saw you. I saw you on your cloud. I saw what you did to her!" Fabian yelled. He pointed the gun at the security camera and then back at the man. I lowered the phone from my ear to listen closer. Surely, he didn't say… The man's nostrils flared. His chin lifted in anger. He did not speak.

"Where is she?" Fabian yelled again, moving his feet to the side. His foot crunched on something hard. He looked down. Under his foot, he saw the jewelry Daphne had worn since she met Pol. He crouched down to pick it up. While examining it, Pol gave a motion. Fabian quickly stiffened his aim, drawing Pol to a halt. Fabian tried to rest the jewelry on a bend in the twisting trunk. The tree seemed to repel the jewels. They slid… no… *flew* off of and away from the tree. He turned his eyes to Pol again.

"I saw what you were doing to her. Is she here? Did you put her in the tree, you creepy wizard *fuck*?"

What? I forgot to press redial this time. I looked at Fabian like he had two heads.

Pol stepped forward. Fabian retrained the barrel of his gun, and he froze, breathing heavily. Fabian reached into his pocket. He pulled out a medium crystal wand from the healer's shop. He gripped it in his hand. The sharp, pointed end faced behind him. He squared his face to Pol and met his eyes. He pulled his hand forward and, with one mighty swing, flung his arm backward to stab into the tree behind him. Thunder cracked overhead, and the tree seemed to tremble.

"Stop!" Pol finally said. "Don't..." he said calmer. His voice was terrifying, and my chest tightened.

"Is she in the fucking tree, asshole?" Fabian said. Again, stabbing the tree, the spiked wand caused shatter-lined craters in the bark. The tree trembled again, and Pol tried to gain ground. Fabian fired a warning shot, grazing Pol's shoulder. Blood sprayed into the rain and then oozed from his skin. "She's in the fucking tree, isn't she, you wizard fuck? You raped her and put her in a fucking tree." Fabian yelled again, stabbing the tree over and over again. "Get her out! Now!"

"I can't!" Pol yelled, falling to his knees in exhaustion and screaming now. "Stop! You'll kill her!"

I walked forward, watching the strange interaction unfold. I was confused and shaking. *What the hell did Fabian see on those cameras?* My body shook. Fabian slammed the crystal's pointy tip into the tree again.

"Daphne?" he yelled, turning toward the cracks. "Can you hear me, Daph? I'm coming for you!" With one more blow, the tree split. It extended from the top of its trunk to a root. The split was only an inch wide and not very deep. Fabian let out a laugh of relief. Smiling wide, he drew his hand back again, ready to open the tree wider.

I stood in shock. It was impossible, yet happening right in front of my eyes. Fabian was cracking through the tree with nothing but a small crystal wand.

"Daph—" His words were cut off by the gurgling sound of blood filling his throat. I was so focused on the splitting tree that I hadn't seen Pol taking aim. I screamed as I realized an arrow had pierced Fabian's neck. He fell to his knees, gasping wetly.

"No!" I screamed. I ran into the rain and fell at his feet. A shriek poured from my lips. "Fabian! No, no, no, no. No!" He fell back into my arms, blood shooting from his lips like a fountain as he coughed. I tried to turn him on his side. He stopped me, his bloody hand cupping my face. His lips, slick with red blood, mouthed the last words he would ever speak.

"I love you."

"I love you too, baby. Everything is going to be okay," I promised, my cries cracking my voice. I tried to stop the bleeding, but it was no use. Tears poured from my eyes as I watched the spark of his beautiful spirit leave him.

Rain washed the blood from his mouth. As his pulse ceased, the fountain of blood died with it. The wind flew from my lungs as if I had been punched in the gut. I gaped in disbelief. Finally, I screamed in agony.

"No! Fuck! No! No!" I rocked back and forth, holding his lifeless body in my arms as I wept.

The sound of crunching on the ground nearby startled me. I lifted my eyes. My mouth trembled as I stared at Pol with rage. I scrambled for Fabian's gun and pointed it at him. My shaking finger was light on the trigger.

"What did you do?" I yelled. He fell to his knees and leaned his chest against the barrel, making eye contact. I looked into his eyes and saw them. His irises shone with shimmering pastels in an array of colors. His irises were... *opals.*

"What *are* you?" I shivered.

"Put down the gun," he stated flatly, slowly enunciating every syllable. I shook my head, realizing everything Daphne said was true.

"You have magic. Daphne told me." My voice shook. "Do something. Do something!" I yelled, shoving him with the barrel and pulling Fabian closer. "Do something!"

I cried and pleaded, Fabian still limp and lifeless in my lap.

"Put down the gun."

Reluctantly, I lowered it from his chest.

"Get back," he ordered. I placed my hand on Fabian's chest and leaned down to kiss his pale, lifeless lips. I rose slowly. Shaking, I moved backward on my hands and knees. My heart was too weak to stand. I crawled desperately to clear some space for him to do… anything.

I sat on the ground a few feet away. Pol's tired form placed a hand over Fabain's chest. A rumbling song came from Pol's throat, and his face was pained. The earth shuttered under us. The tree shed wet leaves as it shook. They landed in his hair, crowning him. His breath was strained. I sensed he was sputtering out. My teeth clenched hard, willing my strength into him so he wouldn't give up.

The earth glowed amber through a tight cleft forming under Fabian. Heat kissed my cheeks. The remaining blood fell from Fabian's face and neck. His skin seemed to glow through cracks like embers inside a charred log. Pol let out a long shout and winced. Fabain's skin was suddenly normal. It was soft and smooth and vibrant with color. Pol fell to the ground, all but lifeless.

I scrambled to my hands and knees. I crawled frantically to Fabian's side.

"Baby?" I asked softly. As my hand caressed his face, it crumbled into ash. His body fell away. The trickling rain soaked him into the hot ground within moments. I sat frozen as his ashes were washed from my fingers by the tiny droplets falling from the sky. His body soaked into the earth. All that was left was a hot, ember-lit crack in the ground that filled with soil in an instant before going dark. Then it was over. It was as if Fabian's body had never been there, and the earth had never split.

I scraped my hands against the earth, dirt caking under my nails. I dug through the wet dirt as deep as my cold, numb fingers could go. I cried, shaking my head.

When I finally realized there was no use, I grabbed the gun again and aimed it at Pol's unconscious body. I scowled at the rising of his chest and gritted my teeth. My lip curled and twitched as I let out shivering breaths, ready to take my vengeance. I had no doubt in my mind that I would end him. My trembling finger squeezed the trigger without a moment of hesitation. I squeezed with all my might to fire the kill shot into his chest. As the bullet ignited, I was satisfied with his death before it even came. But before the bullet could spring free, the gun was thrown from my hand. The bullet scraped the bark, which bled with crimson sap.

"Get away from him," a dry, husky voice said calmly. I looked toward the voice and saw a gorgeous warrior with warm, naturally tanned skin. They had raven black hair, cropped close on the side and hanging down in a pin-straight sheen. They were floating on a cloud, if my eyes were not betraying me.

The warrior jumped from the cloud, crunching boots to earth as they stalked slowly toward Pol, never taking their eyes off me— their...*amethyst* eyes... They pocketed the jewelry, then pulled Pol's body from the ground. He stirred and groaned. Pol's massive form was lopped over the warrior's shoulder with much effort and carried to the cloud. They dropped his body onto it like a cart collecting the dead after war. They picked up his weapons and a crescent-shaped lyre and stacked them on top of the cloud near him.

"He killed my fiancé. He was supposed to bring him back, not turn him to ash!" I screamed, hoping this strong visitor could offer some help. "Please. He took my best friend, and he killed my fiancé, you have to help! He said he would help!"

"Pol doesn't have the power to raise the dead, dear girl. None of us, not in your realm or mine, can do *that*," they said, collecting the last of his arrows and Daphne's jewelry. But knowing him, I'm sure he tried. If he said he would help, I know he did his best. But his power was clearly spent."

The warrior mounted the cloud and looked down at me in earnest pity.

"I'm so sorry for your loss. I know what it means to lose the one you love."

"No, you can't just..." But they were gone. The cloud flew up into the sky, stars now shining through naked patches in the clouds as if the storm had given out with his power.

Daphne was missing, Pol had flown away, Polpetta was nowhere to be seen, and Fabian was *dead*. I lay on the earth where Fabian's body disappeared. The ground was still slightly warm. Laying by his crystal wand, I wept. The roots around the tree cradled me as I closed my eyes. I wished to sink into the warm soil and die with him.

A cold gust kicked up air in the house, and a paper flew from the sliding doors. It tumbled across the yard and pasted itself to my wet back. I reached for it and read it silently. It was a note from Daphne.

To whoever,
If I go crazy tonight, I'll live happily that way.

Lock me away somewhere so I can live with my head in the clouds.
        —Daphne

I told her she was crazy... I thought. I tucked it in my bra lazily, and I lay there until my consciousness gave out. And there I slept, hoping never to wake on a day he did not exist.

36

O'DOHERTY: ASH IN MY HANDS

It was a little over a month since Pol killed Fabian, and did God only knew what with Daphne. Polpetta was missing, too. I was alone, and I was *not* grieving well. I didn't shower for weeks at a time. I kept my long curls tied in a tight bun so they wouldn't tangle from lack of care. I couldn't eat much; nothing tasted quite the same, and when I did eat, my nerves usually wouldn't let me keep it down. I cried myself to sleep most nights and had vivid nightmares, reliving what was undoubtedly the worst day of my life.

The police found me on the ground early the morning after Fabian's death, sleeping in the dirt under the tree. Responding to reports of multiple gunshots, they came in with their own firearms drawn and cleared the property before rousing me. I was mute for days, unable to verbalize anything.

No one will believe me. Where would I even begin?

So, when I did speak, I told them I couldn't remember anything. I said that Fabian and I arrived at the house because he saw someone attacking Daphne. I tried to call for help, but when I couldn't get service, I went in after him. The rest was a blur. They found his gun and collected it as evidence, along with the crystal wands and stray bullets. They swabbed my hands for gunpowder. They questioned me relentlessly about where Fabian and Daphne were, even asking if they might have been having an affair that I found out about. I scowled at the accusation and shut down again.

"I don't know where they are. I don't know what happened," was all I could say. The rain…and I suppose magic had wiped away any biological evidence, so they had nobody to declare either of them dead. And they never would. I wish I could give Melly closure. Fabian would be hurt to know his sister was left with no family *and* no answers as to why.

For days after that, I lay in my bed, only getting up to use the restroom or get water. Finally, Tonya called. Regretfully, she informed me that they were now downsizing and had to initiate layoffs. "Convenient timing," I retorted without emotion. Tonya seemed more upset about it than I was, apologizing through tears and vowing to see it righted.

They offered me a generous severance package, and I never heard what they found in their investigation. I didn't quite care. I knew it was that creepy white-haired panty thief running off their investigators, just like he had run me off.

I hadn't seen him again either. I didn't have the energy to shop for groceries or clothes, so I stayed panty-less and lived off vitamin water and saltines for the first week. I didn't care. I felt nothing but an unbearable loneliness and guilt. I had no one.

It took Selene a good week to even come home when she learned what happened. She left me warm meals on my counter and cleaned my laundry while I slept, not bothering to wake me up or say hello. When she finally did face me—yet another week later—

and saw the state I was in, she shook her head and simply said, "Oh dear…"

I had been staying at her house since, occasionally staying out way too late on the deck to overlook Biscayne Bay. Every day I woke up was a struggle just to exist. She cooked all my meals and put more effort than she ever had into my hair, which isn't saying much. She hadn't cut it off for her own convenience this time; I would give her that much. Instead, she combed out the curls and tried to plait it into a fluffy braid, sucking her teeth when stray strands flung loose. I rolled my eyes and batted her hands away.

"I have a business trip overseas. You're coming with me," she told me.

"I'm fine here."

"I'm not asking… And no, you are most certainly not."

So, as exhausted as my body constantly was, I packed. We were flying out that night, and truth be told, I didn't even ask where we were going. All I knew was that I needed my passport and a fully charged set of headphones. My script for Xanax would stay in my purse. I didn't do well on planes. It didn't help the fact that after Fabian died in my arms, I was already experiencing debilitating panic attacks. This was *not* going to be a great flight.

The plane would depart at 19:00 from *Miami International Airport*, which left me some time to visit Jesula at the rally. The nurses had collected ninety-one percent of the cards necessary to file for an election and were now meeting regularly to stay connected.

Today, the gathering was to ensure everyone had a solid vote plan for the coming union election. This was a much larger event than most. As I arrived, there was a crowd of scrubs swarming the grounds. It was warm outside, but the palm trees swayed in a nice breeze. Upbeat reggaeton music played, and people gathered to dance.

Some nurses ate around the food truck, talking with old friends and laughing. The food would have smelled good any other time.

I weaved through the crowd. The leaders Daphne had gathered were scrupulous. They were set up at tables, conversing with high energy. They confirmed and reconfirmed that everyone qualified to vote had a game plan. "This is where you go to vote. Who is driving you, and when will you be there?" Dawn asked another nurse. As the nurse answered, Dawn put emergency numbers in her hand. "Good. If they can't take you, call this number immediately. We have people signing up to be transporters." She pointed to a table to her right. They had designated drivers signing up to pick up those who either didn't have the means to take themselves or whose transportation would spontaneously fail.

"I get it's your family reunion. We will fly you from New York to Miami and back to get you here and vote. Every vote matters," Adrian, their new organizer, said. Then she lifted her megaphone to her mouth and yelled into it, "When working families are under attack, what do we do?"

"Stand Up. Fight Back!" the crowd chanted with their fists raised. They chanted over and over again.

It was crowded and loud. I was getting over-stimulated. I worked my way through the large group of chanting nurses, pumping their fists into the air. Finally, I found my way to a small podium with a portable speaker system set up.

"We will not be held down any longer! We have come too far and fought too hard! Will you stand with your coworkers and *vote yes* for our union?" Jesula yelled into the microphone. The crowd cheered loudly. Their response thrummed at my eardrums. Jesula threw her arms up and pumped her fist, smiling as she ran off the stage.

Adrian, with her short, cropped hair and endless vigor, came to the stage with her megaphone at her side. Her voice was hoarse from starting chants all day, but it didn't stop her. As Adrian started speaking, Jesula's eyes found mine. She headed straight for me.

Before I knew it, I was embraced in a tight hug. I could smell her sweet perfume and lingered in her comforting hold. I was on the brink of tears with even the slightest recognition of why she held me so close. I swallowed and pushed the thought away.

"How are you doing, my dear?" she asked, holding my shoulders.

"Better every day," I lied, my weak smile winning me no conviction.

"Come and sit. Let's get a bite to eat. You look thin."

I pulled a mini calzone to my mouth and nibbled. It's not that my stomach wasn't hungry; it was the thought of food entering my mouth that made me turn away. I had no appetite. Besides, losing more weight would shut Selene up.

"You need to eat, my dear. You want me to come over and make you a dish?"

I put the miniature calzone down and chewed, waving her off.

"How is it going?" I asked, twirling my finger around at the gathering.

"Oh, we are doing great. Management has not a leg to stand on. We're passing out stickers that say, 'vote yes,' and wearing them to work every day. The people who don't wear them look like fools," She laughed. "And fools they *are*."

"Daphne would be elated," I managed to get out without my voice cracking. I pulled my top lip between my teeth, smiling with my tired eyes. Jesula nodded.

"Still no word from her?"

"No…" I said, marking the start of a long pause. I looked around us to see that no one was listening. "Jesula, the day she went missing,

Fabian hacked her security camera. She texted me something that was just off."

"I heard."

"Yeah…" I paused, nervous to continue. But Daphne had confided in her before, and she seemed to believe her then. What if she could help? And if she couldn't, I'd be out of the country before she could get anyone to put *me* on a seventy-two-hour psych hold. "He was really shaken by what he saw. He wanted me to stay in the car."

"Baby girl, it's not your fault, okay? Whatever happened, it's not—"

"It's not that," I said. I *did* blame myself every second of every day, but that wasn't the point I was trying to make. Jesula's eyes fixed on me with concern. "Jesula, I went into the house and saw Fabian fighting with a man. I think it was Pol."

Jesula's eyebrows raised, and she leaned back. "Did you tell the police?"

"No. They wouldn't understand. Fabian was yelling things. He said he saw him on a cloud and kept asking if he put Daphne in the *tree*."

"Is there a chance he was seeing things?"

"That's what I thought. But then…" Tears welled in my eyes, and I tried my hardest to keep my voice low as I sobbed the rest. "Jesula, he shot Fabian with a bow and arrow through the neck. I tried to get to him, but it was too late. And then he came over to me, and… I saw his eyes, and they were just like Daphne had said! They were *opals*. And then I *knew* she was telling the truth. I begged him to do something to help Fabian, and he just made him glow and then Fabian turned to ash in my hands!"

"Shhh, shh, shh," Jesula hushed. "What do you mean he made him glow?"

"His skin, it looked like a fire log, and the ground below him had cracked and was amber, and then all of a sudden, he looked normal and healthy. But then when I touched his face, it just…" A sob took my breath, and I covered my face with both hands, breaking into a crying fit and shaking.

Jesula looked like she had seen a ghost. "He turned to *ash,* you say?"

I nodded and pulled my hands away from my face, sniffling hard. "Then a warrior or something came and took Pol away. He was unconscious after he did that to Fabian, and this…person just scooped him up and put him on a c-cloud. I'm *not* going crazy, Jesula, I prom-ise. You *see* why I can't tell anyone?" I squealed into a crying fit.

She hugged me and shushed me a few times, rubbing my back and rocking me. "Have you seen anyone like that again?" she whispered.

"No," I sobbed into her chest.

"O'doherty, who have you told this to?"

"No one."

"Good. Tell *no one.*"

"You think I'm crazy, you—"

"No, child, I don't think you're crazy at all. But other people will."

"What do I do?"

"About what?"

"Daphne! She's still missing. What if she's…"

"I'll look into the tree business. Not a word of this to *anyone.*"

I wiped away my tears and felt a weight lifted. I was so glad I trusted her. After all, Daphne trusted *her* more than she trusted me in the end. If there was a chance Jesula could help me get Daphne back, then she could use the powers she said she had. She could find Pol and *kill* him for what he did to Fabian and to her. She could find some way to bring Fabian back. She said she had magic. I should have listened.

Jesula walked me to the bathroom before I left, holding my arm like I was an injured doe as she texted a number that was definitely out of the country. "I'm going to look into this. Give me time," she said. I nodded and headed to the bathroom to freshen up. I sat on the toilet longer than needed as I sobbed against the dirty wall of the stall. I wasn't sure if my stomach would let me hold down the food, but luckily it had. Finally, I collected myself, hoarded several loops of toilet tissue into my pocket, and went to wash up.

Selene texted me that she was here waiting to pick me up, our bags in her trunk, and ready for our trip. I didn't tell Jesula I was going anywhere on the off chance she tried to have me committed after all. Judging by her reaction, I gathered she was more stunned and reflecting rather than giving me false reassurance before turning me in. Still, I wouldn't take the chance.

I met her outside the bathrooms, and she walked me to the corner where Selene was parked. I hugged her goodbye and felt her pocket vibrate as it chimed. "Take care of yourself, my dear," she said, waving goodbye and retrieving her phone from her scrub pocket. I assumed it was probably a call about one of the thousand tasks that come with organizing. But as I settled into the car, I turned to look at her one last time. I saw a look on Jesula's face that told a story of her heart in her throat. The phone pressed to her ear, she looked frozen. I kept my eyes trained on her as she tried to steady herself. Selene pulled away, and I decided it was better not to take on someone else's grief in my state. I would check on her in a few days.

37

O'DOHERTY: RIPPLES SHIMMERED IN THE SKY

MIAMI INTERNATIONAL AIRPORT WAS A MAZE OF LUXURY GIFT SHOPS, terminals, and not-so-great restaurants. Not that it mattered; I had no one to buy gifts for, and I'd rather let my stomach eat itself before I ate another bite of *not*-Fabian's food. But my body was exhausted, and I decided to try my luck with a chocolate protein shake from a vending machine. I tolerated it well and grabbed a few more for the flight.

The flight was ten hours in business class. Selene would never stand for being packed into the tiny seats in the back. She paid top dollar for her comfort. She was paying top dollar for a lot of things lately, probably trying to buy me out of depression. Two glasses of sparkling wine arrived at our seats. I was curled up, leaning my face against the glass of the window, when she offered it to me.

"A toast!" Selene said cheerfully.

"To what?" I asked grumpily. "What could I possibly have to celebrate?"

"To us! To us taking a long overdue trip! To us finally getting the time together we should have! To us—"

I had already chugged the drink with a Xanax and was leaning past Selene to ask the stewardess for another glass. This was going to be a long flight, and I intended to sleep through it.

"May our flight be quiet and full of flatus-free passengers," I said sarcastically, raising the newly filled glass. Selene clutched invisible pearls, aghast at my crassness.

"What has gotten into—" She stopped herself and sighed. "O'doherty, this trip is *important*. I understand how difficult it is to try, but I do hope you make the best of it. This is a new chapter," she said cheerfully, tipping her glass to her mouth. I went to sip mine. "Careful with that. It's not calorie-free, you know."

I smiled and put my headphones on, listening to Lover and imagining what our first dance would have been like at the wedding.

I watched the clouds waiting to see that pasty fucker, Pol. I daydreamed about breaking into the cockpit, locking it, and punching the pilots out cold so I could take the wheel and run Pol through the engine until his body was carved into dog food.

No such opportunity arrived as we flew into the dark sky high above the clouds, not a sky kingdom in sight. The stewards took my uneaten dinner, along with everyone else's, and shut the lights. After three glasses of wine, I was thoroughly relaxed... well, inebriated, really. I twisted my engagement ring on my finger and looked out of the window at the clear sky. The Big Dipper filled the window, bigger than I had ever seen. *It always kind of looked like a stethoscope to me,* I thought as I stared at it peacefully until my eyes pulled shut.

♫ Can I go where you go? Forever and ever and—♫

MY SORE EARS FELT A TUG, AND SELENE'S VOICE WOKE ME FULLY.

"We're landing. Get your belt on," she said, the earpiece of my headphone still in her hand. She was holding an Irish Coffee in the other hand. The smell turned my stomach.

I batted her hand away and moved the headphones onto my neck. Bright light shone through the window. I squinted my eyes and contorted my face. The wine and medication had knocked me out, but my head was spinning now. With a very turbulent landing, I couldn't hold it back much longer and vomited buckets of protein shake and alcohol scented stomach contents all over the floor.

"Oh dear God!" Selene shrieked, lifting her knee away and patting my back gingerly. I looked up at her in misery.

"I need to go to the bathroom."

After relieving myself, I rinsed my mouth in the sink and splashed cold water on my face a few times. After a black coffee, analgesic, and protein shake, I was feeling much better. Even with the hangover passing, I kept my sunglasses over my glassy, swollen eyes.

"They'll have our bags at the hotel. We have an appointment!"

"We?" I grunted.

"You," she corrected. "I have shopping to do. *You* have an appointment."

I didn't bother to ask where the appointment was. I wasn't even sure what country we were in. I kept my earbuds and sunglasses on like a moody 16-year-old as we walked into the hair salon. I saw Selene embrace a woman like she was an old friend and then motion her arm to me. I must have looked horrid because she grabbed my arm and pulled me forward laughing, an embarrassed laugh I knew too well from years of her demanding nothing but perfection from me.

She pulled up a few pictures of me to show the stylist and ran her hand along my long, puffy braid as she showed her its state. She gave me an instructive nod, and her hands motioned for me to let my hair down. I pulled out the band, unfurled the thick braid, and then fluffed it out in all of its majesty. The stylist smiled in delight and examined my hair, waving Selene off and guiding me to a chair.

It had been five hours before she was finished, and I hadn't taken my earbuds out once. A man with bleached hair and a fantastic tan applied makeup to my face as the hair stylist worked. I sat there like a sad clown, getting ready to take the stage.

I'll cry it off by dinner. Why bother?

But then she turned the chair, and I saw a shell of myself that I hadn't seen in over a month—the vibrant, energetic me who had things together and never gave up. But…inside, I *had* given up. This was the face of the woman Fabian fell in love with but the soul of a woman who failed to thrive without him. Tears fell from my eyes. The pair rushed to me with tissues and pulled out my earbuds. One bounced my long, silky black curls in their hand.

"Do you not like it? We were going off of the photos! We can fix it!" the woman said in a Spanish accent.

"No, it's beautiful, thank you," I said. Like clockwork, Selene walked through the door with bags slung into the crease of her elbows and squealed at the sight of me.

"Now there is *my* O'doherty! How do you feel?"

"It looks very nice," I said, smiling. It was a weak smile but a genuine one.

"Well, stop crying then and go change!" she said, pushing a bag into my arms. "We have a very important dinner party to attend for work."

As I walked to the bathroom to change, I could hear Selene instructing them to bag whatever products I needed and charge them to her account. I took my time in the restroom. When I was done changing, I looked in the mirror for a long while.

The delicate white dress with gathered, lavender organza was fitted to the knee, hugging my body all over. The wide v-neck floated away to cuffed, off-the-shoulder sleeves. Canary yellow pumps with purple rhinestones gave me a couple inches of lift while the dangling gold earrings and charmless necklace tied the look together.

My hair hung down my back, nearly to my butt. It was cut in a V, layered, and had perfect raven black spirals shining and bouncing with the slightest movement. They had parted it to the side, and a false bang hovered over my eye.

Fabian would want me to take care of myself, I told myself. It was all I could do not to fall on the ground and cry. I made my way out of the bathroom to comply with Selene's plans for a dinner party. She gathered the purple organza of my dress, covering the only visible dimple of cellulite under the white cloth. We walked outside, where she had a driver pick us up at the door.

"O'doherty, we haven't had a chance to talk about—"

I stuffed earbuds in my ears.

♫*Have I known you twenty seconds or twenty years?*♫

THE DINNER PARTY WAS A GORGEOUS DISPLAY OF PEOPLE I HAD NEVER seen before nor cared to know. The fancy clubhouse at the base of a volcanic mountain was cluttered with white cloths over round tables. It had a vineyard-like aesthetic. I huffed to myself, realizing that

Selene had brought me to a work party strictly to chaperone me, no doubt.

I wished I had brought my earbuds as I picked at the olives in a Greek salad she insisted I eat. I finally dared to try some chicken. It soured in my mouth, but I swallowed it anyway, knowing Selene would be horrified if I spit out food in front of her colleagues. She would faint if I so much as slouched or rested my elbows on the table in public. The chicken settled fine, and I was thankful.

I pulled out my phone, trying to busy myself. To my surprise, Tonya had sent a message.

I had a feeling I knew exactly who that someone was and couldn't be happier to be separated from it, but I didn't want her to get hurt.

I scrolled to the thread I had with Jesula and was disappointed to see she hadn't reached out. I extended a message.

I texted Jesula.

The message immediately went to 'read,' but no response came through. I looked at the screen for a long while, waiting for anything at all as I slowly chewed a salty olive to a paste.

"I don't think they are going to text you back," a familiar voice said, startling me to a stand. I spun to see black eyes sparkling back at me. They were like giant pupils blown out so wide that no color was left around them. "You look beautiful tonight, mi cielo."

"Shhh-it!" I whispered. I backed away on shaky legs and nearly tripped over a chair. "You…"

He nodded and thankfully did not reclaim the space between us. Still, I knew I had to get away. I turned and jogged briskly. Weaving through groups of people at a time, I searched for Selene. We had to get to safety. There was no sign of her in the crowd. My heart skipped a beat, wondering if he did something to her. Then I turned a corner and jogged into a hall of rooms that I knew I had no invitation to enter. I stopped and turned on my heels only to come careening into his hard chest.

"Ah!" I yelped, backing away. This time, he reclaimed the space. My breath shook. "I didn't tell anyone. I lost my job for this. I lost *everything* for this. Please," I pleaded, backing away. He followed me.

"I told you I wasn't going to hurt you; now calm down," he said in his buttery voice and thick Spanish accent.

"He's gone. You can't hurt him either," I said with venom. The words only made my eyes well with tears. It burned not to blink them away. I flared my nostrils and pinched my lips together to brace myself. He came closer. My legs stayed planted in terror and grief. He rubbed his thumb along my jaw softly. I froze as he stroked it.

"I know. And I am truly sorry for your loss. He was a much better man than me." I searched his seamlessly black eyes for answers. That actually sounded genuine. "Take a walk with me," he said, holding out his arm with nauseating temerity.

"No. I need to go. There are people waiting for me. They're expecting me any—"

"Your godmother is upstairs on the patio," he corrected. Seeing the worry on my face, he elaborated. "She is safe. Come with me now, mi cielo. I want to show you something."

I didn't have a choice, I decided, and I took his arm. It was hard and bulky. As we walked through groups of people, I searched for just one set of eyes to connect with—just one person to communicate my danger to. They were all too wrapped up in their conversation to even notice me being walked off to my death. I imagined myself on a TV program like First 48. None of these people would see the last person I was with. I would only be the girl who picked at olives on her plate with her elbows on the dinner table. They'd never find me.

Maybe he will kill me, and I'll see Fabian again, I thought. It brought a concerning comfort to me. I knew I shouldn't entertain the thought, but it made walking with him less frightening as we approached the exit. He walked me out, away from anyone who could help. There was no turning back. I won't lie. I just didn't care if I survived him. Losing Fabian was the worst thing that could happen in my life. *My life is over anyway. Let him kill me. Let him do his worst.*

"I am in a predicament, O'doherty," he began. We walked under the moon. "I have an enemy who I *would like* to kill, but he has something I need very desperately, and no one seems to know where he hid it." I listened in horror as he spoke so casually about murder. "You see, I had it in my grasp, and he shot me! Do you believe it?"

"Something tells me you deserved it."

He frowned and nodded his head to the side. "Yes, well, I guess to *him*, he would think so."

We had gone far away from the crowd. I realized that under the music, no one would hear me scream. I didn't even shudder.

"What do you want from me?" I asked, stopping and turning to him. He leaned in toward my ear.

"There are too many things to count," he said in a devious whisper, his mauve, top-heavy lips smiling at the clear absence of panty lines under my dress. I pulled at the organza, covering the dimple of cellulite. He moved his body closer, tipping my chin up with a finger. "But in *this* case, we share a common enemy. I can help you bring him to justice."

I had only one true enemy—only one person on the planet I would be comfortable with, no... *happy* to discuss murdering.

"Pol?" I spat, my eye twitching at his name.

"Pol," he confirmed softly with a smirk.

"And if I don't agree to help you?" I said, shivering from the chill of the breeze as the wind picked up. He paused for a moment, and I realized I had been staring into his eyes for too long. I wouldn't break now; it would be a sign of weakness.

"I suppose it will make for awkward living arrangements, but I will respect your choice."

"Ha! Living arrangements? Are you moving into my house now?"

"No, mi cielo. Of course not," he said, confused at my question. "You are moving in with me."

He raised his hand and pointed a finger. I broke eye contact to see what he was pointing to in the sky and saw nothing. With a quick look around, I yelped and clung to him.

"Let me down!" I said, grabbing onto his jacket for fear of falling. He wrapped a strong arm around me, held me tightly against him, and grinned. If I wasn't floating on a cloud high above the building, I might have tried to break his fingers.

"What are you doing? Get me down!" I yelled, shoving uselessly at his chest as he held me tight. The cloud rose faster. My curls spun in the air.

"No. I will not let you down. Unlike you, I do actually have people expecting me," he replied. I shivered as the air grew cold and thin. He removed his jacket and hung it over my shoulders, never leaving a hand off me. He pulled me in tighter, the warmth regretfully welcome. But the anxiety attack consumed me. I started breathing too fast, hungry for air, and freezing. My sight swayed, and I tried again to convince him, tugging on his shirt.

"I can't help you. I don't know where Pol is. I don't know where he hid…*whatever* he hid."

"Not whatever. *Whoever*."

"Daphne? What on earth… could you possibly want with… Daphne?" I said in slurred words. I panted faster, my eyesight going dark. My knees buckled, but his grip kept me barely standing, my face pressed into his hard abs. I couldn't catch my breath.

"Ad caelum, mi domus," he said. Ripples shimmered in the sky.

I slipped in and out of consciousness. In the first brief moment of lucidity, I was cradled in his arms, face against his chest, my arms limply bouncing as he walked. The next moment, I was laid on a soft surface as he spoke to three women about healing me. Finally, my eyes opened again. I was lying on a tall bed. It was dark, but voices by a strange fireplace chattered in hushed arguments. Familiar voices. The man and…

"You could have waited until I had time to explain."

"You've had nearly thirty years. Please tell me more about the time *you* didn't have."

"She is *my* goddaughter, Nahveel."

"No! She was your *ward*! And you will address me as 'Your Highness.' She is mine to—"

I sat up, and my eyes focused to see Selene fighting with the man.

"Selene, get away from him, he's dange—" I stopped at the signal of her hand telling me to relax. He cleared his throat and looked at her.

"You are out of time. If you want the privilege, you should take the opportunity now, Selene," my abductor said. "Rápida. I am not a patient man."

Selene approached me, and as she got closer, her eyes lit up in a nearby flame. Her irises were pink with veins of black.

"Selene, what happened to your eyes?" I asked in horror as irises like rhodonite stared back at me. They offered a cold comfort as she placed her perfectly polished hand on my knee.

"There'll be enough time for that. O'doherty, this is Prince Nahveel of Cumbre. There's so much to explain, but he is…" she stalled. "Daphne, she told you about her friend, Pol?"

I nodded. "Well, Nahveel is like Pol, and you are, in a way…"

"What?" I whispered, groggy and confused. Nahveel smacked his lips and stood.

"We are bonded by fate," he said, walking past Selene, who sucked her teeth and shook her head. "Pol is to Daphne as I am to you. You are *mine*."

"What the *fuck* is that supposed to mean?"

"Watch your mouth, young lady!" Selene scorned.

"Fuck you, Selene! I got kidnapped by a sky demon who thinks he owns me, and you're just sitting here drinking black wine and trying to play mommy? Are you fucking crazy?"

"I am not a sky demon," Nahveel corrected calmly, with mild offense.

"He broke into my goddamn house! He threatened Fabian, he —"

"Enough!" Selene shouted. "I did *not* raise you to speak like a common low life. You will watch your mouth. You will tell Nahveel what you know about Daphne's whereabouts, and we will settle this tomorrow."

"Even if I knew where Daphne was, why would I sell her out to a murderer? She's my best friend. She's—"

"Going to run back to Pol the second she gets a chance, if she hasn't already. Fabian's murderer or *not*. She's the enemy, O'doherty; she always has been. Your friendship was part of a mission, and that mission ended the day the enemy found her and brought her to Loanan. Now, our success in this war is dependent on getting *her* back in Cumbre possession before Pol can turn her into a lethal weapon."

"Well, I don't know where she is, so I guess you're pretty screwed. Now get the *hell* away from me," I hissed. Rage like I had never felt before coursed through my veins.

Her palm struck my face and stung my cheek. Nahveel grabbed her by the offending wrist and threw her across the room. She hit the strange, orange-glowing stone wall, cracking it. It seemed to leak a slow steam.

"If you ever touch her again, I will cut off your hand and sear your limb in the fireside. Do you understand?" He snarled at her. She nodded. "Good. Your time as her guardian is over. You are now in *my* service, and it is *long* overdue. Now, leave as she has requested," Nahveel said matter-of-factly.

Selene kept her cold glare fixed on me as she opened the door. Godmother or not, I was furious at her betrayal. At her lies! She tried to snap at me, "Remember who raised y—"

"That will be all," Nahveel interrupted, holding up a hand. With two fingers, he motioned for her to close the door behind her. He pulled up my chin and examined my face, clicking his tongue thrice at the pink flush across my tawny skin. "That's okay, I think," he said, rubbing his finger over the mark. I pulled away from him.

He walked to a table with a pitcher of some black wine and poured it into a crystal glass.

"You can do this the hard way or the easy way. I personally think the easy way is faster and a better experience for both of us," he said, turning to me and walking over. He swirled the drink and smelled it. Finally, he rested his hips between my knees.

"This has an antidote for your medication. It will clear you out in under 24 hours, giving you full access to your magic. But you may struggle to restrain that magic safely, and… you will also feel things that you may not be ready to feel." He came closer, tilting his head. "And I will *not* turn you away," he whispered with a smirk.

"*Or?*"

"*Or*, you can let the medication pass naturally. It may take about a month or so. Your magic will appear gradually. Either way, you will start training as soon as you are well."

He set the glass down on the nightstand and walked to the door. "There is a bathroom over there, and I had some clothes laid out for you on the bed. If you need anything, I will be just down the hall. You should knock before coming in. I am often naked."

He opened the door and stepped into the hall. Before he closed the door, he turned to me and offered one last sentiment. "You are safe, mi cielo. If anyone harms you, I will give them a slow death."

As the door shut, I let out a breath. A body chain of gold was draped between my cleavage, adorned with seven large stones of polished amber arranged vertically between my breasts, each a few inches apart from the next. I was wearing a woven dress robe of richly colored threads, and I pulled the sides together over the exposed parts of my chest.

Getting up from the bed, I now felt a matching leg chain jingle down my thigh and calf. My bare feet padded on the stone floor as I walked in the dark to a nearby window overlooking the water and a mountain range thousands of feet below. A volcano was far below us. I swirled the black elixir in my glass.

It was at that moment that I knew I didn't need Daphne's help or to let her get in my way. I would kill Pol and get Fabian back myself.

TO BE CONTINUED...

AFTERWORD

In this book, you read about the struggles that a psychiatric patient may experience when dealing with hallucinations. Although the science used in this book is drawn from supported research, this book does not accurately depict their everyday life, symptoms, or reality. Unfortunately, most patients with schizophrenia and other disorders do not typically get to thrive and coexist in society normally. Partly, this is because of the stigma that Hollywood has perpetuated, painting them as dangerous or unappealing in media. Nothing could be further from the truth, as this population accounts for a minuscule amount of violent crimes. I encourage you to learn more about schizophrenia, bipolar disorder, and other mental disorders and how it affects patients. Please consider donating to the Schizophrenia International Research Society.

https://schizophreniaresearchsociety.org/

ALSO BY NANDER

Opals and A Nimbus (book 1)

8 Full-Color Illustrations in Hard Cover

Oceans and A Nimbus (book 2) - TBA

Unillustrated PB and full-color Illustrated Hard Cover

Obsidian and a Nimbus - TBA

Chain Mail (book 1)

black and white PB edition

Full color special PB edition

- A dark paranormal romance about a sleep paralysis demon obsessing over a human girl in 1998.

Nine Lives of Love (a stand-alone novella) - TBA

-A romantic comedy. Love Is Blind parody featuring Puss 'n Boots in the Shrek Universe.

ACKNOWLEDGMENTS

First and foremost, I want to thank my husband, David. Working full-time and being an amazing father is hard enough. But he has supported me with my many passions through good times and bad. I love you so very much. Thank you to my mom for always supporting my dreams. Thank you to my little sister Kristi for helping with our son, walking me through the whoas of the circuit, and being my Beta Eater. Thank you to my older sister Samantha, who has always hyped my stories since we were young and now has her book club ready to read this book. Thank you to the many people who inspired characters or were consulted to make the story as accurate as possible. Also, I want to acknowledge the amazing BookTok & AuthorTok community. Without them, I would never have learned how to publish a book.

About the Author

Born and raised in Florida, NANDER has worked as an ICU nurse, activist, social media influencer, and union organizer. In early 2023, she reconnected with her passion for reading and writing as a means to cope, finding a new favorite genre of spicy romance. Wanting to spread her imaginative wings and share her passions for teaching, empowering, and storytelling, NANDER put her knowledge and creativity to paper. Now a mother, wife, and proud indie author, NANDER brings her genre-hopping, rule-bending preferences to the table in original written works.

www.NANDER.co

www.ingramcontent.com/pod-product-compliance
Lightning Source LLC
Chambersburg PA
CBHW022254310726
48973CB00001B/59